Turned into Girls!

A steamy collection of feminisation erotica

Rebecca Sterne

Contents

Turned into a Girl at the Office

An Explicit Tale of Male Feminization

Rebecca Sterne

Chapter 1

It was Julian's first day in a new job and he was nervous. He'd not been living in the city for long and it'd been a daunting change from his small home town some three hours drive away. There was little to tempt him back now that his adoptive parents had moved away. With little work available there'd seemed no choice but to relocate elsewhere in search of a job. It suited him fine, he'd never really fitted in there, and at twenty-one years old he was ready to try making it on his own.

He watched the daily news being played out on the T.V. as he ate a modest breakfast, trying to distract himself from the inevitable moment he would have to take the subway to his new office. He'd been surprised at how quickly he'd found work. The woman at the agency had seemed quite excited at the sight of him, and when he'd confessed he'd no experience of working in an office she'd shown no hesitation in recommending one law firm in particular. They specialised in business law of one kind or another and apparently her main contact was in need of a new member on her team.

There'd been no interview as such. His prospective

employer had simply asked for a photo to be emailed to her along with a description. The reply had been surprisingly swift and they'd asked him to attend for a trial period starting the very next day. He'd been excited at first, but then the idea that it'd all seemed a little too easy began to play on his mind. Still, he couldn't complain and although the agency woman had been vague on the details she assured him that if he got on well they'd make sure he was well taken care of - as they always had with her previous clients apparently.

The subway was busy with the morning rush and he was forced to stand in the cramped confines of the carriage. He spent his time idly looking around at the other people, all intent on their daily commute to work. Looking down at himself he realised how he must stand out, with his somewhat tasteless tie and his cheaply made suit that was slightly too big on him. That would be one of the first things he'd buy when he got paid, a nice new suit.

Before he knew it he was following the crowd off the train and back up to street level. He took a breath as he was orientating himself, trying to remember the directions he'd been given. Heading along the main street as instructed he spotted a side road that he was told to look out for and turned off the main thoroughfare. About halfway down this smaller street he turned into another even smaller road before finally locating his destination. The company was called "Executive Business Services" and their discreet entrance still managed to look suitably impressive to a young man attending his first job in the city.

He tried the door before realising he'd have to use the intercom to gain admission. Clearing his throat he tried to put his innate shyness to one side before pressing the button. It was an anxious wait as he watched the speaker, straining to hear whoever would be speaking from within.

'Good morning, Executive Business Services, how can I help you?'

The friendly female voice that answered seemed to put him at ease and he leaned in to reply.

'Oh...G-Good morning, m-my name's...um...Julian and I'm supposed to be starting work today.' He mentally kicked himself at the less than impressive introduction. 'S-Starting work *here*...that is.' He added as if this were not already clear.

'Of course you are.' The female voice responded, a note

7

of amusement in her voice. 'Please come in Julian.'

The door buzzed and he immediately pushed it open. The sign pointed to the second floor and he took the elevator as he tried to compose himself. As the doors opened he was greeted with the sight of a reception area, with a woman in her mid to late twenties who was gazing at him from behind the desk with an amused look in her eye.

'You must be Julian?' She said as he stepped out. 'Please take a seat and someone will be with you soon.' She said, smiling.

Julian looked around and headed for the chairs on the other side of the reception room. He had the uncomfortable feeling that the receptionist was purposefully eyeing him up. He glanced back in her direction and caught her eye. She seemed quite content to hold his gaze until he looked away again, feeling even more self-conscious than before.

'Ah, Julian. My name's Marlie James. You can call me Miss James. I'm the senior P.A. to MS Rush whom you'll be working for.'

Julian jumped at the sudden entrance of this woman who gave every indication of being in charge. She held out her hand to him, waiting for him to shake it in greeting.

'Hmm, quite a light touch I see.' She nodded approvingly at his less than confident handshake. 'And soft hands too, good. Follow me.' She ordered and promptly led him away.

He felt like a lost puppy running after this woman who clearly saw herself as being very much in charge of him already. It was reassuring in one way, a little intimidating in another.

'You'll be working under me. Lynsey'll be your co-worker.' She nodded at a young girl about the same age as Julian as they entered another office. 'This is your desk. Your first task will be to file these papers in the filing room behind you, okay?'

'Um...yeah, I think so.' He said, a little thrown at the brief introduction to his new job.

'As I said, you'll address me as Miss James.' She looked at him steadily, waiting for a response.

'Yes, Miss James.' He said.

'Good. You'll meet Ms Rush later, but in the meantime I'm sure Lynsey will show you around.' Miss James turned to Lynsey. 'You *will* make sure our new junior understands the rules, won't you?'

'Yes, Miss James.' Said Lynsey with a slight grin.

With a final look toward Julian the woman turned and left the room. Julian was feeling an odd sense of foreboding at the way she'd referred to "the rules". He looked at Lynsey questioningly, waiting for an explanation.

'Well, I suppose the main rule to remember is to do what you're told.' The girl began, looking thoughtful. 'Ms Rush can be a bit...stern, especially with the new gir...er...boys.' She eyed him up and down as if to establish that he was indeed a boy. 'In fact, they don't normally last that long and the ones that do are normally found work with our clients.'

'So they get on alright then?' He asked.

'You could say that.' She smiled broadly. 'Now, if I were you I'd get on with that filing. It's fairly self-explanatory. Just file everything in order, okay?'

Julian nodded nervously as he peered down at the pile of papers on his new desk. He'd never done anything like this before but it didn't sound like a difficult task exactly. He assumed all of this was quite normal for someone starting an office job and decided he'd better just get on with it.

He'd been busily trying to work out the filing system for nearly an hour before he heard someone enter the room behind him. A quick glance over his shoulder revealed a woman in her mid thirties with short dark hair and a steely expression. He wondered whether it was the boss, Ms Rush, and stopped to look up at her. She looked him over appraisingly.

'You must be Julian?' She said, raising her eyebrow.

'Y-Yes.' He wasn't sure whether to shake her hand, call her by name or simply bow. In the end his body did what could only be described as a half curtsy as he absently waved his hand in her direction and dipped his head. He realised how silly this must've looked and stood to attention, looking at the floor.

'How cute.' She said, a sly smile spreading across her face. 'But I insist that you refer to me as Ms Rush. Let me have a look at what you've done so far.'

She stepped further into the room as her eyes searched for signs that he'd accomplished his task. She tutted her disapproval as she withdrew a folder from an open drawer and refiled it.

'I see that filing is not your forte, maybe we should try you with something a little less...taxing.' She said, an air of superiority

9

emanating from the woman. I'd like some coffee brought to my office in ten minutes. Lynsey will show you where everything is.' With a final impatient look she exited the room, leaving Julian to stare after her feeling somewhat intimidated.

He quickly tidied up what was left of the filing and scurried back into the main office to find his co-worker.

'L-Lynsey, I need to make some coffee for Ms Rush. I don't think she liked my filing!' He blurted out as he saw the girl sitting at her desk typing.

She grinned over at him. 'Oh dear, you haven't displeased her already have you? There's something I should've mentioned about the office rules. There may be certain...punishments that she'll make you suffer if you do things wrong, but don't worry, you'll get used to them I'm sure.'

'Punishments?' Julian's anxiety leapt into his mouth as he imagined himself being disciplined on his first day. He needed the job enough that he'd been desperate to make a good impression. He wondered how likely it was that the agency woman would put him forward for any more positions if he failed at his first attempt.

'Like I said, don't worry. I'm sure you'll be fine. Now, let's show you the kitchen.'

She led him down the hallway and into a small kitchen area where she proceeded to explain how Ms Rush liked to be served coffee in her office. He desperately tried to remember every detail so as to avoid annoying her any further. By the time the ten minutes were up he was shakily positioning everything on a tray in a bid to not be late into her office.

He hurried back along the corridor and managed to balance the tray and its contents with one hand as he knocked on her door. He listened intently for a response. Hearing a faint acknowledgement he carefully pushed the door open before entering.

'H-Here's you coffee Ms Rush...Oh!' As he looked up to find the woman sitting behind her desk the coffee pot wobbled and as if in slow motion it began to topple. He tried to grab hold of it but in the process knocked the milk jug over, causing it to spill down his front. Some of the coffee slopped over the side and added to his misfortune. 'I...I'm s-sorry...I...' He floundered as he tried to decide how to proceed, aware that he was now standing there soaked in milk and coffee.

'Oh really!' Huffed Ms Rush, frowning. 'Put that tray down before you drop it everywhere.'

Spying a nearby table he managed to shakily lay the tray down but not before his garish tie found its way onto it to soak up some of the coffee. He was feeling quite distraught by the time he straightened up and looked down at his bedraggled appearance. He could smell the coffee on his trousers and the milk was already soaking through into his underpants.

'Lynsey, come in here please.' Ms Rush spoke into her intercom before sitting back and staring at her new office junior.

'Yes, Ms Rush. Oh!' Exclaimed the girl as she entered behind Julian, staring at the mess he'd made.

Chapter 2

'Our junior has had himself a little accident.' Said Ms Rush. 'Boys are so clumsy aren't they? Please help him take off his wet clothes.'

Julian looked at Lynsey in surprise, 'I...I could go back to my apartment and change if you'd like, Ms Rush?' He offered. 'I've nothing else to wear.'

'Don't be silly, Julian. I'll not have you leaving the office so soon in the day. Now, take off your wet clothes.'

Julian whimpered, feeling embarrassed and annoyed at himself. He turned toward the door.

'I'll take them off in the bathroom.' He said.

'Stop being a silly little boy and take them off now!' Ordered Ms Rush.

Julian looked from one to another, feeling unsure of himself. This seemed quite inappropriate to him, but never having experienced an environment such as this he wondered if it simply wasn't the norm. Reluctantly he slipped his jacket off and removed his tie. Lynsey took them from him as Ms Rush continued to observe his discomfort. His shirt was next. He stood awkwardly for a moment, wondering how he could possibly leave himself in

12

just his underwear in front of these two women.

'Come on, Julian. Hurry up.' The woman prompted impatiently.

Slipping his shoes and socks off he was left to unbuckle his belt. He glanced about himself as if looking for an escape before finally stripping down to his underpants. He saw Lynsey giggle as he handed his clothes to her before placing his hands in front of him.

'You can't leave them on, they're wet.' Said Lynsey.

'I can't take them off, I'll be naked!' He pointed out in a shrill voice as his anxiety levels rose to near panic.

'YOU WILL TAKE THEM OFF RIGHT NOW!' Said MS Rush in a firm voice as she got to her feet and marched around the desk. 'I will not have an office junior talk back to me like that. Maybe it's time you learnt a little discipline.'

Before Julian knew what was happening she'd taken him by the arm and pulled him towards a nearby chair. He resolutely kept his hands in front of his crotch, desperately trying to preserve some dignity. This was not how he was hoping his first day in a new job would be going. As he glanced behind him, looking to Lynsey for help he was jerked downward and found himself falling across the woman's lap. It was only now that he realised what was about to happen.

'N-No!' He cried, just as she locked him in place with one arm across his back. Her other hand grasped his underpants and tugged them down, baring his bottom.

He'd been forced to put his hands out as he'd fallen across her lap and there was nothing he could do to stop her from taking his last remaining shred of dignity. He began to struggle, but then a firm blow to his bottom stunned him into inaction.

SMACK!

He cried out, as much from shock at what was happening to him as from pain.

SMACK!

'You will learn to do exactly as you are told in future, is that clear?' Asked Ms Rush.

His hesitation in answering as he tried to process the situation was clearly seen as a further rebellion as she landed two more stinging blows in quick succession.

SMACK! SMACK!

'IS THAT CLEAR!' She repeated.

'Y-Yes.'

'Yes what?'

'Yes...Ms Rush?' He hoped this was a satisfactory response.

He could feel his cheeks stinging as they quickly reddened under this womans hand. His face was hot with embarrassment as he imagined how he looked to the girl standing behind him, barely older than he was.

SMACK! SMACK!

'I don't expect to have to tell you to do something twice again, is that understood?'

'Y-Yes, Ms Rush.' He responded immediately, wanting this ordeal to be over with.

He felt her pulling his underpants all of the way down his legs before tugging them off completely. He was suddenly aware of how his naked penis was pressed against this woman's stockinged leg. Closing his eyes he hoped that he could avoid any unwanted arousal, although having little experience of women, even this was starting to feel like an erotic experience now that he was aware of it.

'Stand up.' Ms Rush ordered.

He squirmed his way off her lap, inadvertently rubbing against her and causing his little cock to stiffen. He tried to cover himself as much as possible with his hands but he wasn't quick enough to stop the woman from spying his arousal. He felt vulnerable and humiliated.

'I do believe our little junior is getting turned on by being spanked.' The woman commented, reaching out to grasp his wrists and pull them apart.

'Argghhh!' He cried out from embarrassment as both women looked straight at his erection.

He'd never had a very impressive manhood but now more than ever he wished he'd looked a little more like a man than a boy.

'It's not that big is it?' Commented Lynsey, 'Quite cute though.'

'No, it looks more like a girl's clitty to me.' Agreed Ms Rush.

Much to his amazement rather than his arousal dissipating at this added humiliation, Julian realised he was just as aroused if not more so by having these women both eyeing him up in such an

14

intimate fashion. He whimpered some more as he stood facing them, Ms Rush holding his wrists out to his sides.

'So, you like being dominated do you, Julie?' Ms Rush asked, her eyes flicking up to his to await an answer.

'Er...no...Ms Rush...I...please?' He heard her switch his name to that of a girl's but it barely registered amidst the turmoil inside of his head.

'Kneel down please, Julie.' She pulled his wrists down, guiding him to his knees in front of her.

She let go of his arms and opening her legs wide she pulled her skirt up enough to reveal her black panties beneath. Julian stared open mouthed at her panty covered crotch, not sure how to react to this latest twist. His cock however knew exactly how to react and gave a forceful twitch between his legs.

'So you like my panties, do you Julie?' She paused just long enough for him to realise she'd begun to refer to him by a girl's name. 'Put your hand on your clitty and rub it for me, show me how sorry you are for making a mess in my office.'

Julian could barely breathe. He glanced up at her before his eyes were inextricably drawn back to between her legs.

'Rub your clitty, now!' She insisted in a firm tone.

Julian wrapped the fingers of one hand around his erection and began to stroke himself. The reality of what he was doing in front of these women seemed to dance on the edge of his consciousness, yet he was so transfixed by his first ever close up view of a woman's crotch, even one covered with panties, that he continued to do as he was bidden.

He could feel the telltale feelings of an orgasm building from within. His breathing was becoming ragged as he continued to rub himself in full view of his new boss and co-worker. A stifled laugh caught his attention and he glanced over at Lynsey who was watching wide eyed as he masturbated himself whilst kneeling in front of Ms Rush's panty covered crotch. He groaned at the ignominy of the situation but his natural subservience to such a strong woman wouldn't allow him to stop.

'I want you to tell me if you're going to spurt, Julie.' Ms Rush said, causing another giggle from Lynsey.

Julian's eyes had once more settled between the woman's legs and he imagined himself crawling forward to touch her there. He didn't of course move, but the thought was enough to drive him on and he felt his climax building inside. His balls began to tighten as his orgasm approached, and knowing that he was about to humiliate himself even further by cumming in front of them he dutifully owned up to the fact of what was about to happen.

'I'm...I'm going to sp-spurt, Ms Rush!' He said breathlessly as his little cock started to spasm in his hand.

And then the inevitable happened. Julian began to cum as his head drooped and he gasped aloud. The first jet of cum landed on the floor between Ms Rush's feet. Several more followed as he grunted and groaned his way through his solo performance, humiliation and shame mixed with arousal and release to create a conflicting mix of emotions as he spent himself right there on the floor of the woman's office, with his new colleague intently watching his embarrassment.

'Argh! I'm...I'm s-sorry...' He mumbled, unable to stop his orgasm from running its course but becoming acutely aware of what he was doing.

As his climax passed he sagged back onto his heels, unable to look either woman in the eye. There was silence in the room as both women gazed down at the spent boy, his shrinking cock still in his hand and his cum laying in several small pools at Ms Rush's feet.

'I think our little junior has a fondness for panties, don't you Lynsey?'

'I do, Ms Rush.'

'As it appears you have nothing to wear just now.' Observed Ms Rush. 'Lynsey, please take off your panties and give them to our new junior.'

Julian gasped as she said this. Despite himself he watched with fascination as Lynsey, without hesitation, dropped her wet clothes onto a chair and reached up underneath her skirt. He caught a glimpse of her lacy stocking tops as she fumbled for a moment, and then she was pulling down a pair of silky pink panties. His eyes felt like they were on stalks as he saw her step out of them before approaching him, grinning.

'There you are Julian. Please don't make them all wet and sticky.'

He realised both women were looking at him expectantly. Shifting his hands slightly he slowly raised one to take the proffered underwear in place of his own. Getting to his feet he

16

turned away from their eyes, accepting that they'd be seeing his naked bottom as he bent over. Placing his feet into the lacy leg holes he pulled them up his legs, feeling a little thrill run through him at the thought of wearing this girl's most intimate piece of clothing. His cock twitched as it was encased in the soft, sensual material. He could still feel the warmth from her body as they settled into place, causing his arousal to unexpectedly jump once more. He was forced to keep his hands in front of him lest his body's latest reaction became noticeable.

'Hmm, it appears they're a good fit.' Said Ms Rush. 'You're quite smooth but I'd still prefer to have you entirely hair free. It gives a much better impression and looks far nicer, don't you think Lynsey?'

'Oh yes, Ms Rush. Far nicer.' Agreed Lynsey, openly giggling at the sight of this young boy standing there in nothing but her panties.'

'Please make the necessary arrangements, Lynsey. It would be best if our junior were to have something else apart from his pink panties to wear also.'

Chapter 3

Lynsey gathered up his things and held the door open for Julian to leave the room. He couldn't believe they were about to have him walk outside like this, but he guessed as there was no one else about it'd make little difference just now. Once outside in the corridor Lynsey took his arm and led him back to the office.

'We'd better get you sorted out, hadn't we? We can't have you annoying Ms Rush again on your first day, can we?'

Julian was finding it hard to speak. He stood awkwardly next to his desk as the girl disappeared with his clothes in hand. He watched them go with something akin to despair as he wondered how on earth he was going to get through the rest of the day like this. She reappeared some five minutes later holding a tube of something in her hand.

'Right, take this and go and use it in the shower room at the end of the corridor. Make sure you get all of it as Ms Rush is very particular about this sort of thing.'

She held out the tube which he took from her curiously. It was a tube of depilatory cream. He looked at her open mouthed as if to question whether she were serious.

'You heard Ms Rush. She wants you to do something

about that boy hair of yours. I don't know why you're looking so worried, there's not much of it there any way so you won't miss it!'

He looked at the cream before letting out a low groan. He'd only been there a couple of hours and he'd already made a fool of himself, been spanked on his bare bottom by his new boss and forced to wear his co-workers pink panties, and now he'd been ordered to remove all of his body hair!

He walked self-consciously down the thankfully deserted corridor and into the bathroom that contained a shower cubicle. He slipped Lynsey's panties off before following the instructions to cover his hair in the thick cream. Twenty minutes later he was showering away his body hair as he wondered quite where this was heading and whether he shouldn't simply quit his new job.

Once dried off he ran his hands up his now smooth legs. It was a pleasant sensation, one that he hadn't expected. He fondled the silky panties, feeling his boyish cock becoming erect at the thought of pulling them on once more. He'd never experienced the feeling of wearing girl's clothing before, never even thought about it in fact. He felt himself becoming almost intoxicated at the idea of donning such an attractive girl's underwear. Deciding to put them on before his emotions got the better of him he sighed deeply as he felt them being drawn up his smooth hairless legs. It made them feel more appropriate somehow, having his legs looking and feeling so much more feminine. He admired his body in the mirror for a few seconds, taking note of the almost feminine curves of his slender form. He ran his hands through his long dark hair, allowing it to fall about his shoulders without his accustomed hair band that usually kept it tied into a ponytail. He'd always liked rock music and thought of himself as having the rock fan look, but he'd never quite looked at himself in this way before though.

He opened the door to the bathroom slowly, peering through the crack to ensure the coast was clear. Seeing no signs of anyone else he scampered outside and headed straight for his and Lynsey's shared office. As he hurriedly closed the door behind him he realised he was alone with a sense of relief. It was an odd sensation indeed, standing in the office in nothing but a pair of panties. He wondered what anyone else would think of it if they were to find him like that.

He began to search his surroundings for something else to wear, with the only thing presenting itself being a short leather jacket that clearly belonged to Lynsey. It wouldn't even cover his panties but he decided to slip it on anyway.

'You look cute!' Lynsey's voice came from the doorway to the filing room, he hadn't even realised she was in there. 'I see you like wearing my things then?'

'Um...no...I mean, it's not what you...I just wanted to...' He was flustered by the fact that she'd walked in to find him wearing more of her clothes. He was about to take off the jacket when he realised he was still naked apart from that and her panties.

'I thought you might need something else to wear, so I went out to the clothes shop across the road.' She said, smiling at his awkwardness.

Julian felt a wave of relieve sweep over him at the thought that she'd bought some more clothes for him to wear. At least he wouldn't have to spend the rest of the day in girl's clothing waiting for his to dry.

'Oh, thanks.' He said.

'So now I've changed into my new clothes you can wear these.'

Julian's jaw dropped as she held out a bundle of clothing which was clearly made up of the clothes she'd been wearing a few minutes ago.

'I thought...'

'It's okay, I don't mind, really.' She thrust them toward him leaving him little choice but to take them from her.

He looked down to see a pink bra that matched the panties he was already wearing laying on top. He swallowed hard, feeling his legs turning to jelly as he imagined being dressed from head to toe in her clothes.

'Let's take this off first and you can try my bra on. Oh...I see. You're getting a little excited at wearing my clothes, aren't you?'

Julian swiftly looked down to see his erection pushing out the front of her underwear. There was no denying his body's response.

'Just put my bra on and we'll worry about that later.' She said, taking the jacket from him.

Leaving the rest of her clothes on the desk, he fastened her pink bra about his chest as if in a dream before spinning it around and pulling the straps over his arms. The more embarrassing part was when she stepped forward and helped him to straighten it up.

'Now the stockings, but be careful, I don't want you tearing them.' She warned.

He sat down on a chair and very carefully rolled up one of her stockings as he'd seen women do on television. Poking his toes inside he immediately felt an excitement take hold as he began to roll the soft and sensual material up his smooth legs, watching as he encased himself within their embrace. He realised he'd stopped breathing as he reached his thigh, such was the intensity of these feelings. He took a moment to smooth the material out, sending an electric thrill up his leg and straight to his groin. By the time he'd managed to dress his other leg he was feeling breathless with emotion.

When he finally looked back up to where Lynsey was standing, watching, he blushed furiously at the idea of her seeing him wearing her lingerie. He wondered how on earth he'd found himself in such a position. He knew he should've just left at the point he'd been told to take off his clothes in front of the two women, but he'd somehow felt obliged to do as this fierce woman had instructed, regardless of how unconventional it'd seemed.

'Stand up then, let's have a look at you.' Said Lynsey, clearly enjoying his predicament.

Julian slowly stood. He heard and felt the stockings brush together, the sheer eroticism of which made his stiff little cock jump inside of his panties. Not for the first time he felt the need to cover his modesty. It felt as though his entire body was blushing, not just his cheeks.

A buzzer sounded and he realised this would be Ms Rush trying to get a hold of someone on the intercom. Lynsey answered, bending low to speak.

'Yes, Ms Rush.'

'Lynsey, can you send Julian in to clean up this mess please, right now!'

'Yes, Ms Rush. Straight away.'

Julian gave her a meaningful look regarding his current state of dress.

'Quickly, put my dress on and borrow these shoes.' Said Lynsey, moving to drop her black dress down over his head. 'Come on, she wants you in there now. You don't want to get into any more trouble do you?' She asked as he took half a step back.

Julian resigned himself to his fate with the thought that at least he wouldn't be half naked when he entered the woman's office. He pushed his feet into Lynsey's stiletto's as she drew the zip up the back of the dress. It didn't surprise either of them that the dress fitted perfectly as they were of such a similar build. Julian *was* surprised however that he was able to squeeze his smaller than average boy's feet into her shoes. He wobbled precariously out of the door as Lynsey handed him some cleaning supplies, feeling both demeaned and turned on by his current mode of dress.

Once inside his boss's office he was met with an approving look at the sight of him dressed in his female colleagues clothing. She allowed him to clean up the spillage before speaking to him again.

'I'd like another pot of coffee and this time do be more careful, won't you?'

'Y-Yes, Ms Rush.'

'And you could at least put on a little makeup, I do expect my girls to make the effort.'

Julian stared at her in amazement. He wanted to protest, to tell her that he wasn't a girl, but given how he was dressed and how his day had gone so far he couldn't quite manage to form the words.

'Hurry up girl, I don't like being kept waiting!'

He had to steady himself against the door frame as he left having never attempted to walk in such high heeled shoes before. He walked carefully back to his own office as if in a daze. Lynsey was back behind her desk carrying on as if everything were perfectly normal in the world, but for Julian his world couldn't be any less normal.

'Well, how did you get on?' Lynsey asked without looking up from her screen.

'Okay, I guess. She said I should put make-up on!' He said.

Lynsey looked up to study him for a moment. 'You would look better with a little make-up, most girl's wear it you know.'

'But...I'm not a girl!' He finally protested.

Lynsey slowly looked him up and down. 'Well, I'm sure no one would tell if you wore a little make-up, in fact, I doubt most people would realise you were a boy now. Come on, I'll let you use some of mine for now.'

'No, I don't want to.'

22

'Are you sure about that? After your little display in front of Ms Rush I'd've thought you'd want to avoid any more trouble. I mean, some people might think that what you did was some sort of sex crime or something.'

'Eh? But...it wasn't my idea.'

'But you're the naughty little boy that just masturbated in her office - naked. No one made you do it, did they? I mean, you could've just left the room with your clothes on, but now look at you. You're wearing my clothes instead and prancing around like the new office girl, I mean, what do you expect?'

Julian looked around wildly, feeling embarrassed and ashamed at what he'd done in his new boss's office. She was right in a way, he could've just walked out but he didn't. For some reason he stayed and humiliated himself in front of them. Suddenly the thought of being reported to the police for such a lewd act struck him and he wondered whether anyone would believe him that he'd simply been doing as he was told. He felt the need to sit down and pulled up the nearest chair, peering down at his stockinged legs he was almost oblivious to the fact that Lynsey was now removing her make-up from her bag and preparing to complete his transformation.

Chapter 4

Lynsey set to work on a compliant Julian as he ran through that mornings events in his mind, trying to work out at what point he'd lost all semblance of control over his fate and indeed his male identity. He moved his head around as instructed by Lynsey and before he knew it she was drawing a lipstick across his lips and talking of how good he looked.

'You look terrific! You're a natural girl. Go on, take a look in the mirror.'

She held up a hand mirror for him as his eyes slowly focused on the image staring back at him. It came as a shock just how feminine he now looked. Gone was any masculinity that may have been holding on despite being dressed in girl's clothes. He knew he would pass easily for a girl and wondered just how long he'd have to endure such treatment before he was allowed to return to his male identity. Maybe this was their idea of hazing. He'd read about such things in colleges before where the new students were purposefully humiliated and made to undergo embarrassing treatments at the hands of their peers. Maybe this was something that they did to new staff, to test how willing they were to endure such things in order to work there.

24

The thought seemed to brighten his mood slightly and he began to think that maybe this really would all be over soon, and he'd find himself as an accepted member of the team as a result of his willingness to be subjected to their initiation practises.

'I do look quite good.' He admitted, starting to see the funny side to his treatment at last. 'I'd better make another pot of coffee for Ms Rush.' He said, gathering himself together and tottering down the corridor to the kitchen determined not to blow his initiation.

He began to enjoy the sensation of walking in high heeled shoes. The constant brushing of the stockings together was keeping him in an aroused state as he hurriedly placed Ms Rush's coffee onto a tray and with a determination to impress her, click-clacked his way back down the corridor before knocking at her door, admiring his reflection in the stainless steel coffee pot as he waited for a response.

'Come in!'

He heard a voice calling through the closed door, but it wasn't Ms Rush. Feeling a tingle of anxiety he hesitated. He wondered for the briefest of moments whether he should simply turn around and come back when the woman was alone, but before he could make a decision the door was opened from within. Standing in the doorway was Miss James, the senior P.A. to Ms Rush that he'd met earlier. Any thoughts of whether this woman would be shocked at his appearance, or whether she'd even recognise him were dismissed almost immediately as a smile spread across her face.

'Ah, Julie.' She said, eyeing up his feminine appearance. 'Don't just stand there girl, come in.'

He let out a little groan at her referring to him as Julie and speaking to him as a girl. He tottered into the room, desperate not to have any more accidents.

'I see what you mean, Ms Rush. She does appear to be a natural.' Commented Miss James as she watched him pouring their coffee. 'A little more work and I don't doubt that she'll be one of our best yet.'

Julian was wondering what they were talking about as he placed a cup of coffee in front of Ms Rush. He assumed they were talking about his prospects as the new office junior and felt a pang of pride at the thought that they were already impressed with him in the role. He must have demonstrated a good level of determination to see his first day at the office through, regardless of what they'd thrown at him.

'I do wonder just how obedient and loyal she's willing to be. We've had so many disappointments over the years, I'd hate to think we were wasting our time with another fickle employee who wasn't up to the job.' Added Ms Rush.

Julian looked up to see Miss James nodding her agreement as they both observed him closely. A desire to speak up, to let them know that he was willing to do what was necessary to continue in his new job overcame him and he turned to face both women.

'Um...Ms Rush, I'd really like to do well in my new job. I won't let you down, I promise.' As both women continued to stare at him with questioning expressions he felt his confidence waning. 'I'm...I'm sorry about my accident earlier, it won't happen again and I'll make up for it in any way I can.' He finished by giving a little curtsy, much to the amusement of Miss James.

'She is sweet, I'll give her that.' She said, 'Maybe we should let her show us how good she can be?'

Julian just looked at them, a feeling of apprehension growing as he tried to predict quite what these women had in mind for him now. He calmed himself with the idea that it could hardly be more humiliating than stroking himself to an orgasm in plain view.

'Shall I let her perform service on me?' Asked Miss James, uncrossing her legs.

'No, that won't be necessary. Julie showed great interest in my own panties earlier, I think it's time for her to get to know them better.' Said Miss Rush.

She turned her chair sideways on to the desk and beckoned to Julian.

'Come around here, Julie.'

Julian looked from one woman to the other before making his way across the office. He passed Ms James as he rounded the desk and came to a halt in front of this woman once more. He was half expecting her to tell him to strip his clothes off again and was trying to decide whether he should continue to follow her orders or to extricate himself from this ever deepening hole.

'Kneel down and crawl over to me.'

This wasn't quite the command he was expecting and

although he was feeling uncertain about what was about to happen he found his knees bending as he automatically dropped to the floor. Feeling a little silly he began to crawl the last few feet toward her, just as she pulled her skirt upward to reveal her pantied crotch. He hesitated for a second as she adjusted her position before opening her legs wider.

'Come and kneel between my legs, Julie. That's a good girl. Now, as you were so interesting in my panties, I'm going to let you take a closer look. Put your face here and smell them.'

Julian felt his insides turn to jelly as his belly flipped over and he was overcome with a desire to do as he was bid. He slid in between her legs and slowly leaned inward, his cheeks brushing against the woman's stockinged thighs as he came within an inch of this woman's most intimate of places. Just as he'd been told to, he slowly inhaled. Her musky scent of arousal was clear and his cock began to harden inside of his own panties. He admired the mound between her legs, imagining touching her pussy lips. He'd never been this close to a woman's vagina before, it was a thrilling experience.

'Now taste my panties. Lick them, gently.'

He trembled at her words, bracing himself for the most sexual experience of his young life. He pushed his tongue out and ran it up the front of her silky underwear. They were becoming damp and he could taste her juices. He was surrounded by her scent, cloaked in her femininity as he pressed his face into her crotch, feeling her swollen lips beneath the thin satin covering.

'Ooooh!' He quivered as he took in another deep breath, inhaling of her womanhood as he pressed his tongue into her, driving the panties in between her lips and pushing at her slick hole.

'I think she's enjoying herself, Ms Rush.'

He heard Miss James' voice as if from a distance, all sounds being muffled by the woman's thighs either side of his head. He began to lap at her more frantically, his own boy cock stiff with desire. He wanted to stroke himself once more, to bring himself towards an orgasm as he sucked at this woman's ever more sodden underwear.

'I do believe she'll be squirting into her panties soon.' Said Miss James as she calmly watched the boy suckling desperately at her boss's crotch.

'You're not to squirt in your panties, do you hear me Julie?' Commanded Ms Rush from above.

'Mmm, yeth Mith Ruth.' He said obediently, his mouth still on her pantied pussy.

He felt disappointed to not be allowed to touch himself, but he didn't want her to stop him from tasting a woman's pussy for the first time, and so he was quick to acknowledge her orders.

'You may pull my panties aside and drink from me, if you like Julie.' Offered Ms Rush.

Julian's excitement increased as he heard her words and his fingers were soon pulling the panties to one side in a bid to gain direct access to her. He breathed her in deeply and stared in fascination at her engorged pussy lips in front of his face. Her juices were glistening at her entrance, enticing him in even further. He could barely contain himself as he opened his mouth wide and leaned in to her. His tongue was immediately covered in her nectar. He rolled it around his mouth as he tasted her, his cock twitching with a desperate need for release as he found himself burying his head in between her legs. He thrust his curious tongue into her hole and penetrated her with his soft and eager mouth organ.

'Oh yes, Julie. Just like that!' Moaned Ms Rush as he continued to pleasure her. 'That's a very good girl.'

He could hear her breathing deeply and erratically. Her hands were on his head, holding him there as her pussy began to pulse and her climax build. Julian's face was slathered in her juices. He could smell, taste and feel her sex as he ate greedily from her. His cock was aching but he knew he couldn't allow himself to cum, and so he kept his hands away and hoped that his body didn't betray him.

'That's it Julie, make me cum on you!'

Ms Rush's voice was hoarse with arousal as her legs closed about him and she thrust her groin into his face. He could barely breathe as she began to grind into him, rubbing herself against him and leaving his face slick with her juices. He couldn't help but feel as though she were using him for her own pleasure, taking advantage of his vulnerable situation and deepening his position of submission. He didn't mind though. Right now he was tasting a woman's sex for the very first time and he was hooked.

'Oh...Oh...Ohhhhh!'

Ms Rush came hard against his face, her juices pulsing out

28

of her as her pussy contracted and she ground her way through an orgasm. Julian was forced to swallow her copious fluids. He thought he would suffocate if she didn't release her grip on him soon, and much to his relief she did amidst a waning climax.

'Oh...yes. Very good Julie, you're a very good girl. Now clean my pussy for me.'

He slid his tongue across her quim, causing her to spasm once, twice, three times as he licked her clean before reluctantly pulling her panties back into place and covering the woman's sex. He slowly knelt back onto his heels and looked around self-consciously. He saw Miss James looking a little flushed as she continued to watch him. Ms Rush straightened herself up and pulled her skirt back down, signalling the end to his latest ordeal.

Chapter 5

Julian pushed himself to his feet, swaying unsteadily on his high heels for a moment before heading toward the door as he was duly dismissed from the room. From the satisfied smiles on the women's faces he guessed he'd done enough to please the pair of them.

Miss James told him to get back to work and said she'd be in to see him before the end of the day about his continuing induction. This seemed to almost confirm his suspicions about them testing him. It was certainly an unconventional way of breaking in a new employee, but he couldn't quite bring himself to resent the entire episode. Despite feeling embarrassed, humiliated and just a little degraded by his treatment at the hands of these women, he'd also experience some of the most erotic events in his life, and all within the first morning of starting a new job.

He looked down at himself, dressed as he was in female clothing and knowing he was sporting make-up, although quite what it looked like after his latest adventure between the boss's legs he had no idea. His rampant arousal was still evident in his panties and his stiff gait was as much to do with that as the high heeled stilettos he was wearing.

Returning to his desk he found that Lynsey had given him some more work to do and with no sign of her presence he went about his assigned tasks just like any other office girl would, except he knew that despite appearances he was no girl. He couldn't quite fathom why he was beginning to feel as comfortable as he was walking about dressed as a girl, but it was feeling nowhere near as alien to him now as it did at first. In fact, his underlying arousal being continually fed by the touch and feel of Lynsey's stockings and the knowledge that he was wearing her panties too was amounting to a constant state of sexual awareness and desire that he'd never experienced before. It felt increasingly intoxicating.

He'd become quite lost in his work when Miss James eventually reappeared in front of him. He looked up to find her smiling down at him.

'So, how are you enjoying your first day at the office, Julie?' She asked.

He registered the fact that the two women were now constantly referring to him by a girl's name, but given his situation it seemed almost normal.

'Yes, it's been very...interesting, Miss James.' He said, unsure of what else to say.

'Good. I think it's time you went for lunch, don't you? Shall we say an hour?'

'Oh, thank you.' Said Julian. 'Just one thing, Miss James. I should probably change back into my normal clothes before I go outside. Do you know where they are?'

'Nonsense, Julie. You look perfectly fine the way you are. I'll see you after lunch, although you may want to freshen up your make-up a little. I believe Lynsey has some in her desk.'

With that the woman left the room. Julian stared after her, wondering if she were serious about him leaving the building dressed as a girl. When there was no sign of her returning he figured she wasn't coming back and feeling rather bewildered by the idea, made his way to his co-worker's desk to look for her make-up. He found it without much trouble and was soon tidying up his face as best he could, it being the first time he'd actually handled make-up himself. Fortunately there wasn't too much to do and he decided he still looked perfectly passable as a girl.

He couldn't help but take a quick look around in case his clothes were nearby, but there was no sign of them. He considered skipping lunch despite being hungry, but the need to get out for a breath of fresh air and think more clearly about what was happening to him was a compelling one. Besides, it might be fun going outside dressed as a girl, just to see if anyone noticed of course.

It was a surreal feeling, opening the door out onto the street and stepping outside as Julie for the first time. He'd never had any interest in dressing as a girl before, but something about the feeling of wearing the sensual underwear and taking on a feminine appearance was beginning to fascinate him. He tried to take small steps as he began walking away from the building, trying not to topple over. There were more people about than earlier and he half expected a great cry to go up, drawing attention to the boy dressed up as a girl daring to walk amongst "normal" people, but nothing happened.

He caught a couple of looks from passing men, but something about the way they looked him up and down told him this was nothing to do with recognising him as a fellow male and more to do with sizing up a potential female mate. He smiled to himself as he continued on his way, grateful for the anonymity that a busy city centre offered. He quickly grew in confidence and found a nearby cafe to have his solo lunch. It wasn't until he was about to order something from the menu that he grew nervous of speaking in a man's voice, but he needn't have worried, he'd never had the deepest of voices anyway and no one seemed to notice anything out of place.

It was an exhilarating experience, sitting there knowing that to anyone casting a look in his direction he would appear as a perfectly normal office girl. It felt exciting, as if he were doing something daring and just a little naughty.

'Enjoying yourself?'

The unexpected voice from behind startled him and he looked around quickly. It was Lynsey, and she was grinning at him madly.

'I thought you looked a little too comfortable in my clothes.' She giggled. 'How're you enjoying being Julie?'

'I...don't know, I mean, it's not like this was my idea.'

'Does it matter? Besides, if you carry on like this then I'm sure you'll find yourself with a permanent position in no time.'

'Do you think so?' Julian screwed up his face, 'It's just

32

that...this is all a bit strange, don't you think? Did they do something similar to you when you started?'

'Oh yes. I wouldn't still be there if I hadn't proven myself in the same way you're doing.'

'So this is a way of testing new employees?'

'Of course. They won't take just anyone you know. You have to be a natural to some extent, and I'm guessing that you are.'

Julian felt himself swell with pride at the thought of having proven himself to his new employers. It would certainly make all of this worthwhile in the end, and he'd certainly had the experience of a lifetime up until now. They sat together for a while making conversation. Julian could almost forget how he was dressed...almost. Every time he moved he felt his stockings rub seductively together, reminding him of his appearance. His constant semi-aroused state was beginning to take over his mindset as he tried to keep his mind on other things.

They were soon back in the office, with Julian feeling almost disappointed to not be out as a girl any more. He doubted he'd ever experience anything like that again. They were settling into their work just as Miss James found them.

'Ah, Julie. Did you enjoy your lunch?' She asked pleasantly.

'Yes, Miss James.' There was no need to pretend as it'd surprised him how pleasant he'd found being a girl for an hour.

'Good. I see you're settling in well. Ms Rush was very pleased with your servicing earlier and she's agreed to reward you.' She gave him a wicked smile, 'Lynsey, I think we'll see how she gets on with a little "Hole Punching". I think we'll try her with the small one first.'

Julian looked at Lynsey, wondering why using a Hole Punch was considered as a reward. Lynsey looked quite excited by the prospect, leaving him even more confused. She rushed across the office to a set of drawers and began to rummage through the unseen contents.

'Stand up, Julie.' Commanded Miss James. 'You may take off your dress for this, we don't want it getting in the way do we?'

The idea that he was about to be asked to operate an unsafe piece of machinery struck him, yet he still couldn't see why he'd be asked to take off his dress.

'Hurry up girl, we haven't got all day and I need to know whether you can handle it correctly.' The woman insisted, placing

33

her hands on her hips impatiently.

Julian slowly pulled the dress up over his head, feeling acutely aware of revealing his lingerie clad body to this woman. He knew there was nothing that Lynsey hadn't already seen on his first day, but even so it felt quite wrong to be stripping off his clothes once more. As he discarded the dress onto the desk next to him he felt awkward, standing there in just his borrowed girl's underwear. He was tempted to ask when his initiation into the office would be at an end, but it didn't feel like the right time. He tugged the panties up a little further before turning to look back at what Lynsey was doing.

Lynsey closed the drawer and trotted back toward him and Miss James, who was busily eyeing up Julian's feminine body. He couldn't look her in the eye and studied the floor as he felt his face burning. His throat had gone dry and he doubted he could even speak at that moment as he awaited his next test.

'I found the smallest one, Miss James. And I've got some oil for lubrication.' Said Lynsey.

'Good girl, Lynsey.' Said Miss James. 'You may start when you're ready. Julie, I'd like you to bend over the desk please.'

Julian saw Lynsey place a small bottle of baby oil down next to him. He couldn't see what she had in her hand but he was beginning to realise that whatever was about to take place it was unlikely to be the traditional use of an office Hole Punch. He tried to say something but he was struggling to get the words out as an impatient Miss James took hold of his shoulders and guided him to the edge of the desk. She pushed him over the desk and held him in place with one hand.

'M-Miss James, what...what's going on?' He finally managed to ask in a croaky voice.

'I told you Julie, we're trying you with a little "Hole Punching". Now, when I tell you to, I want you to relax as much as possible. Don't worry, it won't hurt much and I'm sure you'll do fine.'

Chapter 6

He tried looking behind him but his only clue about what was about to happen was when Lynsey picked up the baby oil and poured some into her hand. With her free hand she took hold of his panties - sending a shiver up his spine as she did so - and pulled them to one side, exposing his bottom. He gasped as he felt her oiled up fingers touch him, spreading his bottom cheeks slightly apart before pressing into his virgin rosebud and spreading the oil across his hole. He squeaked anxiously as he felt her finger pressing into him, forcing its way inside a little way as she slicked his bottom hole with oil.

At this point he was in little doubt that something was about to be pushed into him, he just didn't know what. He'd never had anything inserted into his bottom before and he feared the pain of such a thing, wondering just how far these women would really go in order to find out if he were worthy of a position in their employ. Lynsey's finger pulled out slightly before she pushed it in a little further this time, helped by the slick baby oil.

'Just relax, Julie. You'll be fine.' Miss James reassured him as she continued to hold him across the desk.

Julian whimpered girlishly, not knowing what to do about

35

this latest humiliation. This was not how he'd expected his first day in an office job to go. Lynsey pulled her finger back out of him slowly. He could feel a slight burning sensation where she'd opened him up, but it was quite bearable. He wondered if that would be the extent of his latest test. He was wrong.

'Just relax, Julie. It's only a small one so it shouldn't hurt that much.' He looked around at Lynsey as she spoke, seeing a small penis shaped dildo in her hand.

It would've been smaller than most men's erect cocks, but this did little to assuage his anxiety. He realised that he was about to be penetrated by a toy penis, laid over a desk in nothing but girl's underwear by these women. He knew he should fight them, put a stop to such degradations, but he didn't. There was a confusion in his mind, one that meant he didn't know whether he wanted to stop this or not. It'd be yet another first for him in a day full of them, one that he'd no idea whether he wanted to experience or not.

He felt himself beginning to tremble as she parted his bottom cheeks and pushed it between them, nudging it up against his tight rosebud. He whimpered pitifully as he felt the pressure grow, pressing in to him, urging him to open up. He drew in a ragged breath, gripping the desk with his fingers and feeling the added pressure of Miss James' hand as she kept him firmly in place.

'We're going to make a real girl of you now, Julie. Isn't that exciting?' The woman said.

He didn't answer, his head was swimming with the realisation that he was about to have a penis shaped dildo thrust into him by another office girl. *Another office girl?* He thought. Since when did he start thinking of himself as an office girl.

The pressure increased against his bottom, and then he was opening himself to Lynsey. He felt the dildo begin to enter him, slowly prizing him apart.

'Just relax, girl.' Commanded Miss James, giving his bottom cheek a light slap and sending a shiver of embarrassment through him.

Lynsey gave another push from behind and he felt his bottom burning as he was penetrated. He tried to do as he was told and relax his muscles, trying not to fight against being entered in such a way. With some surprise he realised it was helping as the fake penis slid further inside of him. It stopped for a second before Lynsey withdrew it almost entirely, before once again pushing it back inside of him.

'Oh! P-Please...I can't...' He stammered as his breathing became ragged.

'Of course you can girl. The first time is always the hardest.' Said Miss James firmly. 'Now stop making a fuss and just let it happen.'

He bit his lip as he felt himself being slowly fucked with a dildo for the first time. It started off as an unpleasant experience, but as Lynsey continued to push and pull on the now slick dildo it was no longer causing his bottom to burn anywhere near as much as it had at first. He was still fighting to get used to it, but the more he relaxed the easier it was becoming.

'Good girl. Insert it fully now Lynsey, let her feel its full length.' Instructed Miss James as she watched her subordinate penetrating the boy's virgin rosebud.

Julian gasped as he felt the full length of the dildo inserted inside of him. As it began to massage him on the inside he was surprised to feel a deep arousal beginning to build. His cock was semi-erect, partly due to being pressed against the desk and partly because of this new form of stimulation.

'Mmm, arrghh...' He began to moan as Lynsey continued to move the silicone cock in and out of his stretched hole.

He managed to peer around behind at one point, seeing his panties pulled to one side and Lynsey holding his cheeks open with one hand whilst the other guided the sex toy in and out in a slow, methodical rhythm. She was focused entirely on his exposed bottom, making him feel vulnerable and demeaned by having someone a similar age carrying out such an act upon him. He gritted his teeth as he turned back around, glimpsing Miss James as she also had her eyes trained on his violated bottom hole.

Lynsey's pace was increasing and he could feel the inner stimulation causing his arousal to increase. It was a kind of arousal that he'd never experienced before. It felt different somehow, almost as though it were coming from a deeper place inside of him. He could hear a slight squelching sound from behind as he was being fucked toward an orgasm that he never would have expected from such an act, but was developing swiftly inside of him.

'Oh...oh...oh...' He began grunting with every thrust of the dildo, knowing he was about to shame himself by cumming onto the desk beneath him. He thought then that he may be in trouble if he did, that it would only make things worse if he spilt his seed carelessly once again. 'Miss...Miss J-James. I think I'm going to...to c-cum...' He mumbled with his head lowered as he felt his climax approaching swiftly.

His body tensed, his balls tightened as he felt his cock begin to pulse and much to his horror he found himself debasing himself on his own desk with a fake cock penetrating his bottom whilst he was still wearing Lynsey's bra, panties and stockings. It almost seemed to take him by surprise, as if he had little control over his body's reaction to the enforced stimulation inside of him. He began to spurt onto the desk below him, crying out with a mixture of ecstasy and complete and total shame at what he'd been made to do.

His cum coated the desk below him and as he slumped down onto it in mid orgasm he felt his belly being coated in his own juices. Without thinking he thrust his bottom back toward Lynsey, forcing the dildo all of the way inside of him as he climaxed, no longer aware of where he was or who was there, even his own identity seemed to blur as he felt himself being brought to a fierce climax by being penetrated from behind. He squirmed around on the desk, not knowing what to do with himself as he became lost in the sensations of a blissful and shameful release.

As his orgasm subsided he quivered violently as he emptied himself of the last remaining drops of his seed, laying exhaustedly in his own cum.

'Well, I think she grew to like being toyed quite quickly, don't you Lynsey?' Asked Miss James as she withdrew her hand from his back and stepped away to observe the young boy lying across the desk.

'Oh yes, Miss James. I think she liked it very much.' Agreed Lynsey, still holding the dildo inside of him with her other hand resting on his bottom. 'Should I take it out now, Miss James?' She asked.

Julian didn't hear a reply through the post orgasmic fog that now muddled his brain, but he assumed she must have agreed because it was then that he felt Lynsey gradually pulling the dildo from his bottom. As the fake head reached his sphincter he could feel himself being opened wider and groaned as the burn returned. It was soon over with as he felt himself being emptied of the sex toy's presence.

He knew he'd be sore for a while afterwards, but he couldn't help but feel a little empty without having his bottom filled up in such a way. His strength seemed to have been eroded with every thrust of the dildo as he could barely lift himself from the desk. Raising himself up he look down at his belly and saw the cum that'd been spread across him and the desk. He kept his eyes lowered, unwilling to look up at either of the women.

'My, My. You do seem to have made a mess on your desk, young lady. I'll leave you two to clean up shall I.' Said Miss James, before reaching out and taking hold of his chin. She turned his face to hers as she spoke directly to him. 'You've been a very good girl today, Julie. I'm sure you'll prove a perfect candidate.' She smiled at him before nodding to Lynsey and strutting out of the room.

There was an awkward silence as Julian imagined what he looked like right now to Lynsey. He straightened himself up and flinched slightly as the girl pulled his panties back into place for him.

'You did seem to enjoy that, Julie.' She commented, grinning at him with the glistening dildo still being held nonchalantly in her hand.

Julian cast a quick glance at the toy that had so recently been inside of him. It was a strange feeling seeing such a thing, now knowing how it felt to have something like that thrust into him by a girl. He forced a slight grin back at her as he tried to decide what to do with himself.

'I'll just clean this up while you wipe yourself down.' She said, giggling at his cum covered belly. 'And you'd best wipe your desk clean as well.'

Chapter 7

By the time Julian had finished cleaning himself and his desk he was feeling utterly shamed at what had happened to him. Part of the problem in his mind was that he couldn't honestly tell himself that he hadn't enjoyed what had happened, even on some deeper level. He slipped Lynsey's dress back on and sat down, flinching as he put his weight onto his sore bottom. Considering what he'd just been through it didn't hurt nearly as much as he imagined it might have.

Lynsey made sure he had some work to do for the rest of the day. It was nothing particularly taxing, and as he sat at his desk, shifting his position every so often so as to relieve the pressure on his bottom, his mind had plenty of spare capacity to mull over what he'd experienced over the course of the day. He could hardly believe it himself. He found it hard to engage in conversation or hold eye contact with Lynsey, knowing that she'd been the one to not only witness him degrading himself after being spanked in Ms Rush's office, but that she'd also loaned him her clothing and inserted a dildo into his bottom under Miss James' direction. He couldn't imagine that he could do anything else to further embarrass or humiliate himself in front of her.

It was soon getting to the end of the day and his thoughts turned to changing back into his own clothes and heading to his apartment. It wasn't much and it hardly felt like home as yet, but at least it was a roof over his head. He'd have to give some serious thought to whether he'd be returning the following day, although even a job that entailed such unconventional treatment as this one had was still a job, and it was a job that he needed right now.

'Lynsey, can I have my clothes back please?' He asked just as the clock on the wall was signalling the end of the day. 'I'll need to get changed to go home.'

Lynsey looked up at him with a surprised expression.

'Don't worry, you can still wear mine.' She said brightly. 'Besides, I'm not sure that'll be the plan for you. Miss James usually likes to continue the training at her home.'

Julian's jaw dropped. 'What? No one said anything about training in the evenings!'

Lynsey was about to respond when Miss James walked into the office, cutting their conversation short. Lynsey immediately turned to her.

'Miss James? Julie was asking about her old boy clothes and whether she'd be leaving tonight. Won't you be continuing her training overnight as with the other girls?' She asked, her face a picture of innocent curiosity.

'Quite right, Lynsey.' Miss James admitted before addressing Julian's look of surprise. 'You'll be accompanying me back to my apartment for further instruction. I have a room ready for you and a change of clothes will be available, you needn't bring anything. Any questions?'

Julian was almost too stunned to reply. This seemed to be taking things a little too far, assuming that he'd simply accompany her to her home with no thought of his own plans. The fact that he had no plans and nothing but a mostly empty apartment to go back to wasn't entirely lost on him. He didn't know anyone in the city as yet, so he wouldn't have been spending a particularly enjoyable night on his own anyway.

'I...I...suppose...' He tried to decide whether to go along with the woman as he spoke.

'Good, that's agreed then. Follow me and we'll be on our way. I'll see you later Lynsey.' She moved to the doorway and waited for him to follow, her expression telling him that she wasn't

41

used to being kept waiting.

Julian rose from the desk and looking around realised there was nothing for him to pick up before leaving. He tottered after Miss James with a resigned glance back at Lynsey. She waved him off with a grin.

He had no idea what Miss James's intentions were for his training. He click-clacked his way down the corridor behind her as she led the way from the building. They took the elevator to an underground car park and he was soon climbing into her car and being driven away. He watched as they drove out of the business district and headed into one of the more expensive residential areas. He found himself growing nervous as they pulled into another underground car park and she led him away, taking the elevator to the tenth floor. The building was clearly the preserve of those with more means than the average P.A., and he began to wonder how this woman could afford such surroundings.

'Here we are, Julie. This'll be your home for the next few days whilst you're in training.'

Julian followed her inside without a word. She hadn't mentioned anything about staying here for more than one night until now and it already seemed too late to refuse. He hoped that it would all prove worthwhile in the end.

It was an impressive apartment. Far more extensive than his own modest rental. She gave him a brief tour, ending with one of the smaller bedrooms at the end of a hallway.

'This'll be your room, Julie. You'll find everything you need in here, including several changes of clothes.' He looked at her with surprise. 'Don't worry, they should fit you perfectly, I'm an old hand at judging my girl's sizes.'

Her constant references to him being a girl was playing on his mind now. He imagined that this part of his initiation into the firm would be ending about now, but she seemed almost oblivious to the fact that he was a boy in the way she was speaking to him.

'Miss James?' He ventured, thinking he best tackle his uncertainty as quickly as possible. 'Will I be changing back into some normal clothes now?'

'Normal clothes? My young girl, you are wearing perfectly normal clothes already. Now I've left some things out on your bed that you'll be required to wear tonight, and I expect you to be shaved and made up again within the next hour, so hurry along now.' Taking hold of his shoulders she spun him around and patted his bottom before sending him into his temporary room.

Julian turned back around in amazement as she closed the door, leaving him alone in a strange room to contemplate his fate. He didn't know whether to laugh or cry just then, so surreal was the entire experience to him. He peered down at his feminine appearance and felt the strangeness of it all threatening to overwhelm him. Staggering slightly he made his way across the room and dropped onto the bed with a anxious sigh.

He took in his surroundings for a while, taking note that the room was clearly decorated for a female. Gripping the bed with his hands he felt something next to him and looked down, realising these must be the clothes he was expected to be wearing in less than an hours time. His eyes roamed across the neatly laid out garments with a sense of resigned inevitability. As he took a closer look his heart skipped a beat as he saw the overtly sexual lingerie that he was being expected to wear. He groaned as he ran his hand across the lacy bra and panties. The garter belt matched them perfectly with a pair of sheer stockings to match. He looked over at the dressing table to see a bright red lipstick along with a full set of make-up laid out ready for him. It seemed his sudden immersion into a world of femininity and sexuality was destined to continue unabated. He felt breathless with the sheer pace at which he was losing control of his own body and what he'd thought was his natural gender and sexuality.

He stared at the back of the door for several seconds trying to make up his mind whether to simply leave or allow his new employers to continue to play with him. Annoyingly he found himself tingling inside with an inner desire to put on the underwear laying next to him. It was as if he'd had his eyes opened to a whole new world of pleasuring, and bizarrely it involved him being dressed up as a girl in order to enjoy it.

Trying to convince himself that this was simply the latest in a line of personality tests designed to test his suitability for a new role, he slipped off the dress and Lynsey's underwear. His body was perfectly smooth and hair free from the head down, which only seemed to add to his current feelings of femininity. Taking himself into the en-suite bathroom he ensured there was no trace of male facial or body hair before returning to the bedroom. He'd taken the opportunity to freshen up with the floral scented products at his disposal, adding further to his descent into a girl's world.

He sat at the dressing table and took his time with his makeup. It was surprising how little it took to complete his female appearance and he was soon admiring his bright red pouting lips as he turned from side to side, checking that everything was in place. A quick check of the clock on the bedside table told him he had little more than five minutes left. A mild panic began to grip him as he nervously thought of what was about to happen and he quickly skipped over to the bed to pull on the lacy panties. He barely had time to acknowledge the sexual thrill it gave him pulling on such a feminine and intimate piece of underwear before he was hurriedly fastening the bra into place followed by the garter belt. He tried not to rush pulling on the stockings too much lest he tear them, but by the time he was struggling to fasten them to the garter belt he was wishing he'd been quicker. He'd never had to come to terms with such an awkward piece of underwear before and it was a relief when he'd successfully fixed the last strap into place.

Stepping over to the full length mirror he took a moment to smooth out the underwear and fluff out his hair. Something came over him then, as if he were seeing himself for the first time as a girl. He whimpered to himself as he looked himself up and down, seeing little evidence of the boy that'd crawled out of bed that very morning, despite the revealing nature of the lingerie that he was now sporting.

For a moment he felt a little silly, then grew quite self-conscious at the idea that someone else was about to see him like this, regardless of how this domineering woman had already seen him on that day. In a moment of sheer panic he glanced around, thinking that he should find something else to cover himself with. It was too late. The door opened with a flourish and then Miss James was standing there looking in at him as his body stiffened in response.

Chapter 8

'Very nice, Julie. I'm sure you'll be a real hit with our guests.' She said, admiring his underwear clad body.

'Guests!'

'Oh indeed. Don't look so worried you silly girl, that's not all you'll be wearing tonight.' With a flourish she pulled out a small white frilly apron from behind her back. It would cover the front of his panties but little else. 'Slip this on and meet me in the kitchen, you'll need to learn how to provide service to our clients.'

'Clients?' Julian's mouth dropped open as he tried to get his head around the idea of prancing around dressed in nothing but lingerie and a small apron in front of his supervisor's guests.

'It's okay, they're not real clients. We'll try you out with someone you know first and Ms Rush's partner. They'll be able to ascertain if you truly are suitable for a place with us.' She stepped into the room and wrapped the apron around his waist, tying it up with a large bow that draped across his pantied behind. With a little touching up of his hair and the addition of some high heeled shoes that he was struggling to balance upon she deemed him ready to leave the room and led him out to the kitchen.

He fought to keep pace with her without over-balancing as

he moved through the apartment. He wanted to ask what was going on. Why was he being expected to serve people dressed as he was, but Miss James began informing him of the correct way to serve people at the table and how to pour their wine correctly, leaving few gaps for him to fill with his own questions. Before he knew where he was he was standing in the kitchen preparing a tray of starters for the two guests that were about to arrive.

The doorbell rang and Miss James popped her head around the door.

'Go and answer the door, Julie. Don't forget to give a little curtsy as you greet them before taking their coats.'

'Um...yes, Miss James.' He felt his insides turning to water as he trotted daintily toward the door, feeling a little nauseous at what he was about to do. Hesitating with his hand on the door he took a deep breath before tugging it open. To his absolute relief the first person that he saw was Lynsey.

'Oh, hi!' He said, letting his breath go as he realised he'd little to worry about with her being a guest.

'Wow, don't you look sexy!' She said, examining him from head to toe.

Julian began to feel a familiar heat spreading across his cheeks as he tried to imagine just what he looked like to her eyes. He was hardly boyfriend material dressed like this. Realising for the first time that he was actually attracted to Lynsey didn't help his embarrassment levels, so he meekly stood to one side to let her in. As she brushed passed him another figure appeared from around the corner. The man stepped into the doorway with undisguised amusement on his face. Feeling a sudden urge to run Julian held himself firm and remembering what Ms James had said he gave a little curtsy, keeping his eyes firmly on the floor.

'Lynsey's right, you do look very sexy. Julie, isn't it?' He asked.

'Y-Yes, Sir.' Julian's throat seemed to be closing up as he realised just how ridiculous this entire situation was.

'Welcome aboard. I'm sure you'll make a fine addition to our little team. I look forward to getting to know you and seeing what you can do.'

The man shrugged his coat off and handed it to Julian without being asked. Julian quickly closed the door and hung it up on a nearby hook, feeling that he was truly at the bottom of the pecking order at this point.'

As the two guests took their seats at the dining table, Miss James joined him in the kitchen.

'Now Julie. I have something else I'd like you to wear tonight. Dexter - that is Mr Cooley to you - likes his girls to display a certain decoration during these kind of events. He feels it adds a certain class to the overall appearance.' She produced from her bag what was obviously a butt plug.

Its metal plug was finished with what looked like a large red gemstone. He wondered if it were real for a moment before quickly dismissing this. As realisation dawned upon him that she was expecting him to wear it his eyes grew wider.

'I wouldn't normally expect my girls to wear these on their first service, but as you accommodated Lynsey's efforts so well earlier, I think you'll be absolutely fine, and Mr Cooley will be most impressed with you. Now turn around and bend over, Julie, whilst I just pop this in for you.'

Julian stared at her in mild disbelief at this latest ignominy. The reminder of his earlier performance on the end of a penis shaped dildo quickly suppressed any fight that he had in him to resist her intentions. He bent as if in a dream and felt his panties being pulled to one side, much as Lynsey had done earlier that day. He began to tremble slightly as he felt her touch his rosebud with her finger, pushing it in slightly in order to introduce a little lubrication. Then he felt the cold metal tip pressing into him insistently before he was being forced to open himself once more. This time he did his best to relax straight away and let himself be penetrated without resistance. It made it easier although he gasped loudly as he felt the full width of the plug spreading his tight anus apart, and then, in an instant it seemed to be in as it slid into place, filling him up with its bulbous end and leaving him with a bejewelled bottom hole as his panties were gently pulled back into place. He knew the sheer see-through material would do little to hide his new decoration, especially if he were to bend over.

'There, all done. It looks very sweet on you too. Try walking around a little.'

Julian straightened up uncertainly before trying out a few tentative steps. It was a strange feeling having something lodged inside of him as he walked. It seemed to be holding itself firmly in place, although he was having a little difficulty in walking normally.

Its presence very quickly began to have an effect, stimulating him from within - especially as he walked - and causing his penis to become semi-erect. He was thankful that the apron was hiding his reaction from Miss James.

'Perfect! You may pour the wine now and we'll take our starters in five minutes.' The woman left the room looking pleased with her handiwork and leaving Julian feeling like a new toy in their hands.

This was certainly not on the job description, although come to think of it there'd been very little in the way of a description given to him.

The dinner began to proceed with Miss James guiding him as to what to do at every turn. The evening seemed to settle into its own rhythm, with Miss James and her two guests being served at the table by Julian in his frilly apron and lingerie. He tried to keep his mind focused on the job in hand but it was difficult not to become distracted when he was constantly aware of his nylon covered thighs brushing against each other, and a jewelled butt plug moving around inside of him at every step. He was suffering from a constant underlying arousal that kept him partially erect inside of his panties the entire time and turned every action into an erotic experience.

By the time he'd served them their dessert he'd counted at least five occasions when Mr Cooley had managed to brush his hand against his bottom as he leaned over the table. It was as he was topping up their glasses that Miss James decided it was time for him to undergo the next stage in his training.

'Have you noticed Julie's little decoration, Dexter?' She asked innocently.

'Decoration?' He looked from Miss James back to Julian as a smile played across his lips. 'I don't believe I've had the chance to admire it properly.'

'Oh you must, she looks so sweet with her flower in. Julie, Please turn around and show Mr Cooley your little decoration.'

Julian caught a look from Lynsey that said he should do as he was asked. The girl nodded encouragingly.

Feeling like some kind of exhibitionist, Julian slowly turned his back to Mr Cooley and bent forward. Reaching around he took hold of his lacy panties and feeling utterly exposed, pulled them down to reveal his bejewelled bottom.

'Pull your little cheeks apart so Mr Cooley can see it properly.' Miss James said.

He did as he was asked, spreading his cheeks with his fingers so that his bottom hole was clearly on show to the room, including his unorthodox jewellery.

'Very nice, very nice indeed. She seems perfect for the job, and I'm surprised you've been able to progress her so quickly. It's normally at least three days before they're able to show themselves in this way.' Said Mr Cooley.

'Oh, I think you'll find Julie is an absolute natural. She seems to have taken to her training with no problems at all.'

'In that case, why don't we see if she's ready for her first oral test.' Suggested Mr Cooley with a glint in his eye.

Julian was beginning to feel like some kind of exhibit, but something about having his lingerie clad body admired in such a way was managing to increase his latent arousal even further.

'I'm not sure that she's ready for something like that quite yet, are you Julie?' Asked Miss James, smiling at him sweetly as he turned his head toward her whilst still spreading his bottom cheeks.

'Um...I might be, Miss James.' Offered Julian uncertainly.

He didn't like to say no, lest they decide he wasn't up to the job, but by now he'd realised that an oral test was unlikely to involve a simple act of verbal questioning. His mind flicked back to when he'd found himself in between Ms Rush's thighs earlier in the day, tasting a woman's sex for the very first time as he brought her to orgasm. He speculated that a similar task could await him, but if so it was strange that Miss James would question whether he were up for it considering she'd watched him perform on Ms Rush already.

'In that case, I think it'd be best if she practised on Lynsey first, don't you Marlie?' Suggested Mr Cooley.

Julian gaped at Lynsey as she turned to face him. She grinned happily, clearly unfazed by the idea of having her new male co-worker performing a sexual act upon her whilst dressed in women's lingerie.

'Stand up Lynsey.' Ordered Miss James. 'Now come and kneel in front of Lynsey please, Julie. I think you know what you have to do.'

Chapter 9

Julian stopped displaying himself to Mr Cooley and slowly moved in front of Lynsey who was standing next to the table expectantly. He couldn't help but become excited at the idea of performing a sex act upon the attractive young woman, and his erection was quickly growing in anticipation. He lowered himself to his knees and looked around nervously, wishing he didn't have an audience present, but knowing it was because they were there that he was being given such an opportunity. He gazed up at Lynsey, feeling himself blushing profusely.

Lynsey looked to Miss James. 'Should I take my skirt off now, Miss James?' She asked.

'Yes, Lynsey. You may take off your skirt, but let Julie remove your panties, please.' The woman replied almost formerly.

Lynsey nodded and turned back to Julian, peering down at him seductively as she slowly, teasingly unfastened her thigh length skirt and gradually lowered it to the floor. Julian's breath caught in his throat as his anticipation grew. His cock was quite stiff inside of his panties now and he knew it would be clearly on show if he wasn't still wearing the small apron. Lynsey bent forward as she stepped out of her skirt, letting her small yet pert little breasts brush Julian's upturned face for the briefest of moments. Julian inhaled her scent as she came close to him, mesmerised by her sexual presence. Having stepped out of her skirt she slowly straightened back up, discarding the skirt onto her chair at arms length.

Julian's eyes moved from her face to her crisp pink blouse, seeing her young mounds rising and falling with every breath she took. As he continued to lower his gaze he came to her black lace panties, not dissimilar to the ones he now wore himself. He could see a pronounced pussy bulge between her legs where he imagined her lips would be swollen with desire. Her stockings were similar to his own other than the fact that she didn't need a garter belt to hold them up. He admired her shapely, feminine legs all the way down to her stilettoed feet and back up again. Breathing rapidly he shuffled forward slightly and hesitated, his hands midway toward Lynsey's pantied crotch. Taking her lead he also looked to Miss James for directions. He was about to ask permission to take down her underwear when the woman nodded her approval, signalling that he should proceed with revealing the girl's most private of places.

He licked his lips involuntarily as he continued to reach up to the waistband of Lynsey's underwear. He heard her gasp a little as he took hold of her panties and they both paused as if in joint anticipation of what was about to happen between them. He gripped the lacy material and slowly began to pull her panties down, growing ever closer to the point where her sex would be revealed to him. As he tugged them over her pert bottom cheeks they slid down the rest of the way in a flourish as his eyes stared uncomprehendingly between her legs. At first he didn't understand what he was looking at, but as the small yet growing cock unfolded itself from between her legs he realised that she wasn't at all what he'd expected.

'Wh-What?' He gaped at the quickly stiffening little cock between her legs. It was as hairless as his own, and somehow given her overt femininity and demeanour it managed to take on an almost feminine appearance, despite it being a male organ. 'You're...' He didn't finish the sentence. Instead he just gazed at her bald penis in absolute shock.

'Yes Julie, she's just like you, one of our "special" girls.' Explained Miss James in the background. 'She's obviously been with us for longer, but she was able to prove herself just as you have done. Now, I think you know what to do, don't you?'

Julian froze. This clearly wasn't what he'd expected at all. He recalled the fact that it was Lynsey who'd witnessed his first humiliation at Ms Rush's hands as he was spanked then told to masturbate himself in front of them. It was her who'd given him her clothes to wear, and her who'd penetrated his virgin bottom with a penis shaped dildo.

'You do want to, don't you?' Asked Lynsey with a pout. She looked as though she were feeling hurt at his sudden reluctance to continue.

'I...I...' He looked up at her and felt his sexual urges returning at the sight of this pretty young woman, despite the fact that she had a little extra between her legs, just like he did. He glanced around at the others, seeing the raised eyebrows that told him they were about to find out if he was indeed suited to their employment. The idea that he could find himself out of work by tomorrow if he displeased them wasn't a pleasant one, but he also realised this was a defining moment as far as his prospects were concerned. He studied the semi-erect cock in front of him, realising that he was still quite turned on by the whole situation. 'Um...Yes, I d-do.' He heard himself saying as he forced his hands into action again and continued to slide Lynsey's panties down her legs.

She stepped out of them daintily before planting her feet firmly in position and resting one hand on the chair next to her for support. Julian took a slow steady breath before returning his gaze to between her legs. He reached up and gently cupped her hairless balls. She took a sharp intake of breath as he did so, causing both of their cocks to jump in response. It was as though an electric current had sparked between them. With his other hand he touched her with his fingers, gently running them up and down her length and watching with fascination as she grew to her full size. He noted that she was no bigger than him, causing him to feel a certain comradeship with this person that was so similar to himself. His fingers were soon wrapping around her phallus as he began to masturbate her at eye level, watching as his hand moved up and down her shaft.

'Why don't you try tasting her, Julie?' Suggested Miss James from a distance.

Julian glanced in the woman's direction as if surprised that she were still there. His eyes darted back to Lynsey's erection as he bit his lip, trying to imagine what it would be like to have a cock inside of his mouth. He leaned forward, opening his mouth and decided to try licking the bulbous end first, as if this would tell him whether he could take the rest. He noticed how shiny it was, with the opening at the tip seemingly widening in anticipation of his tongues arrival. He pushed his tongue out and with the slightest of hesitations licked the end of the glans. He heard Lynsey moan from above as he increased her stimulation. It hadn't tasted unpleasant, and nothing had happened to make him rethink his actions, and so he began to roll his tongue around the bulbous end, making it slick with his own saliva and causing Lynsey to rock back and forth with pleasure.

He continued to lick around it as if it were a meaty kind of lollipop, before he realised he'd have to go further if he were to prove himself, and indeed, he realised he was now wanting to experience more. He gave Lynsey's balls a little squeeze before sliding his fingers back along the shaft and opening his mouth wider. It was a decisive moment in his life, one that he'd never before anticipated. Right now he simply felt like a sexual being. There was no male or female in him just now, simply a person who's sexual awareness was growing by the hour and who'd experienced his sexuality as a kind of boy-girl hybrid in such a way that he was no longer sure he wanted it to stop.

Committing himself to the act, Julian plunged forward and took Lynsey into his mouth, sucking her in and feeling the sensation of taking a fully erect cock into his mouth for the first time. He started gently, taking in barely a third of its length to begin with. As he started to move it in and out he experimented with how far he could take it and before long was going down on Lynsey as if he'd been doing this for years. He felt Lynsey's hand come to rest on the back of his head, adding to his submissive feelings.

'Oh...yes, J-Julie. Oh!' Lynsey moaned seductively over him, pushing her hips forward in a bid to urge him on.

Julian's own arousal was building once more as he began to feel quite slutty in his lingerie whilst sucking off another in front of his bosses. He wondered quite what they were making of the little show being put on in front of them, but then that's why they were here in the first place.

He became aware of Lynsey oozing precum into his mouth as he tasted it. He'd not really thought of what would happen when she orgasmed until now, and now the thought of having a boy's cum being ejaculated into his mouth was a frightening one. His hand was resting against Lynsey's stockinged thigh, adding to his arousal. He was beginning to question whether he should pull away, return to masturbating Lynsey by hand in a bid to avoid a mouthful of boy cum, but his inexperience at servicing another in this way meant that he still had his mouth filled with Lynsey's stiff little rod at the point she began to convulse, her moans growing louder and her body stiffening. Before Julian could make a decision he felt her cock spasm inside of his mouth and then the first jet of cum was coating his tongue. It's warm gooey consistency was a first for him and he went stiff with surprise as a second then a third stream of cum came pulsing out into his mouth. He was forced to swallow hard as he tasted the full effects of Lynsey's orgasm.

Julian tried to push Lynsey away in order to remove her from his mouth but she was too far gone in her climax to be able to do anything but buck against his face and continue to fill him with her seed. He could feel it escaping his mouth, running down his chin as he opened his eyes and stared up at her in shock at what was happening. Lynsey was biting down on her lip, looking more sexy than ever as her orgasm washed over her and she slowly came down from her climax. Her cock sent several more small ejaculations into him, before the last of her cum dribbled onto his tongue and she was able to steady herself once more. His mouth was still quite full and with no other option available he swallowed as much down as he could, feeling it slip down the back of his throat. The slightly salty tang staying with him as he gently took her out of his mouth and closed his lips.

Chapter 10

There was an excited atmosphere in the room, as if an important moment had just come to pass. Julian looked around self-consciously, seeing all eyes upon him as he continued to kneel in front of Lynsey's now flaccid penis. He realised he was still resting his hands against her legs and sat back slowly, not sure quite what to do with himself. Sensing a trickle of cum on his chin he tentatively wiped it away. There was nowhere to wipe it from his fingers so he quickly sucked them clean, seeing Miss James watching him intently as he pulled his now clean fingers from his mouth. He grimaced at his own act before looking down at the floor between Lynsey's legs.

'Well, I think she did very well for her first oral test, don't you Miss James.' Said Mr Cooley, his voice a little croaky.

'Indeed, Dexter. I wonder if we shouldn't give her a reward for being such a promising employee.' Replied Miss James. 'You may put your panties back on, Lynsey.'

Lynsey giggled breathlessly as she retrieved her clothes and stepped back into her own lacy lingerie. Julian couldn't help but watch as she covered her limp cock with the feminine underwear before pulling on her skirt and gathering herself together. She seemed perfectly at ease with what had just happened, but then he guessed she'd become used to experiencing such things if she'd been working at the company for some time.

'Stand up, Julie.' Commanded Miss James softly. 'I've no doubt that your little clitty is requiring some attention of its own by now, and as you've passed your latest test so well I think you should get to choose your own reward.'

Julian met her eye, wondering what he was about to be offered. He felt a pang of pride that he'd managed to please his new employers so much with his latest performance, even though he was still trying to come to terms with what he'd just done.

'Mmm, let me think.' The woman looked thoughtful as she apparently considered what would constitute an appropriate choice of rewards. 'I'm sure Lynsey would be more than willing to return your favour if you'd like, or you if you'd prefer we can progress to the next stage a little earlier than planned. What would you prefer?'

Julian caught Lynsey's eye as they exchanged a look. She was clearly more than happy to use her mouth on him in return by the look on her face. He wondered what the next stage of his training would entail but was almost too nervous to even ask. He shifted his weight from one leg to another and felt the butt plug move inside of him, bringing a girlish squeal from his lips. His own little rod was stiff inside of his panties, demanding a release.

'I...I wouldn't mind if Lynsey would...like to...' He couldn't quite bring himself to say that he wanted her to suck him off as his voice trailed off. Not certain if this was what he wanted but given he didn't know the alternative at least he'd be sure of relieving his own sexual tension.

Lynsey flashed a grin at Miss James before turning back to face him, all smiles.

'I'm quite certain that Lynsey would be more than happy to oblige. Go ahead, Lynsey. Mr Cooley and I would like to talk in private so you may go back to Julie's room.'

Julian felt a certain relief that he was being allowed to have some privacy. Lynsey was quickly on her feet again and taking hold of his wrist led him from the room and down the hallway. He was pulled into his new temporary accommodation before she closed the door behind them, a hungry look on her face.

'Why don't you sit on the bed and take your apron off. You'll be more comfortable there.' Lynsey suggested.

Julian did as she asked whilst Lynsey took off her clothes, leaving herself in just her underwear. He untied the apron and threw it to the floor, revealing his swollen penis as it pushed against the front of his panties. He was beginning to have second thoughts about having this girly boy suck him off but sensing the intensity of his own arousal he simply sat down on the edge of the bed and allowed Lynsey to push his legs apart. She slid in between them without a second's hesitation, pulling his panties aside and eliciting an excited cry from him as she released his stiff cock. Her hand was on him immediately as she began masturbating him. It was all he could do to look down in amazement as he found himself being massaged so intimately.

He noticed her watching his face as he felt himself being stroked toward an orgasm. With a seductive wink she lowered her head and brought a loud gasp of pleasure from him as he felt himself being drawn into her warm wet mouth. She was soon sucking on him fervently, cradling his balls as she returned the favour with outright gusto.

As his sexual arousal began to overtake him he rocked back and forth on the bed, causing the butt plug to move within him and add even more stimulation to his already overloaded mind. His head rolled back as he felt himself being moved quickly toward a climax.

'Oh...Oh...Oh no!' He moaned, remembering how it'd felt to have a mouth full of cock as he felt himself beginning to tense throughout.

It was as if his mind exploded at the same time as his cock. His balls tightened and his penis spasmed before sending a huge stream of cum into Lynsey's mouth. His body bucked on the bed, with every movement of the butt plug creating another bolt of excitement within as he came hard inside of his co-workers receptive mouth. Finally reduced to a quivering, moaning wreck, he slumped back onto the bed as Lynsey studiously sucked him dry before licking him clean.

He found himself in a kind of daze, no longer quite sure as to his own identity or place in the world. It was as though he'd been transported into another world, one where Julian no longer existed, and in his place a girly boy named Julie. A sexual creature that knew little of sexual boundaries or gender lines. His whole world had been turned upside down, and it was a thrilling

REBECCA STERNE -- TURNED INTO GIRLS!

adventure.

He seemed to come to a little while later, with Lynsey lying next to him on the bed. They were both dressed only in their lingerie, and they both bore a satisfied expression upon their faces.

'I think Miss James likes you.' Said Lynsey, 'I'm sure they'll keep you on after that.'

'After what?' He asked stupidly.

'After sucking on my boy clitty like that, silly.'

Julian found he still had the ability to become embarrassed over his own actions.

'What's going to happen now?' He asked.

'You'll stay here with Miss James while she trains you. You'll come to work in the office of course, with me. Don't look so nervous. You'll forget all about wearing nasty boy clothes in no time, and you'll get to have plenty of fun with the clients.'

'What do you mean - fun?' He pressed. 'What am I supposed to do?'

'Oh Julie! You're so naive. That's what's so cute about you. You'll learn, don't worry. They might even let me help train you, you know, show you what to do and stuff. Some of the clients like to have more than one of us attending to them.'

'I've not seen anyone else at the office like us. Are we the only ones?'

'No. Most of them are out with clients. Miss Rush likes to have me in the office though, she's my aunt.'

'Your aunt! And she did this to you?'

'You make it sound as though I was forced to be a girl. It's much nicer than being a boy, don't you think?'

Julian thought about this for a while. The trouble was he'd never really not wanted to be a boy, but now he knew what it was like to feel like a girl, at least on one level at least, he wasn't at all sure that he wanted to go back. He turned to look at Lynsey as she lay next to him, gazing at the ceiling with a contented smile upon her face. This day had proved to be a far more life-changing experience that he'd expected only that morning. He squirmed into the mattress, feeling the butt plug move inside of him once again, it never failed to send a sexual thrill through his body as it stimulated him from within.

Despite knowing that Lynsey was a boy just as much as he was, he couldn't quite bring himself to think of her as such. She gave every impression of being a girl. He noticed that she even had small budding breasts underneath her sheer black bra.

'Do you like them?' She asked, seeing his eyes settling on her chest. 'I've been on tablets for a few weeks now. I'm sure once they make you permanent that you'll get to grow your own titties too.'

Julian's eyes widened at the thought of developing breasts like a real girl. It was a surreal prospect, one that both scared and excited him in equal measures.

He heard movement in the apartment and realised that Miss James and her guest were heading toward his room. He sat bolt upright as if he were about to be caught doing something bad when the door opened and Miss James and Mr Cooley peered inside at the two girly boys in their lingerie.

'I see you're finished playing, girls.' She said, smirking at the guilty look on Julian's face. 'Mr Cooley will be leaving soon. You may take your meal in the kitchen when you're ready, Julie. Lynsey can clean up the table before finishing for the night.' She took a step back, eyeing Julian expectantly.

It took him a moment to realise that she was waiting for him to see her guest to the door and he quickly slid off the bed. As he reached Miss James he suddenly realised he was still in his underwear and turned back to look for his apron.

'Don't worry about that, girl. I assure you that Mr Cooley is quite content with you as you are. Now get his coat and see him out please.'

Julian scurried passed the man, feeling his eyes roaming across his body and settling on his pantied bottom as he went. Handing the man's coat to him he curtsied once more, feeling small and exposed in his presence as the man loomed over him.

'It was nice seeing you Julie. I'm sure I'll be seeing much more of you soon.' He winked before leaving the apartment, causing Julian's face to heat up and his insides to flutter self-consciously.

Chapter 11

Julian awoke the following day in a confused state. It took a while for him to recall the events of the previous day and to understand quite where he was. He pushed the bed covers from his body and saw that he was wearing a sheer black nightdress that barely came to mid-thigh. He sat bolt upright, the memories of the day before flooding back in a whirlwind of mixed emotions. Miss James had directed him to one of the drawers in his room to retrieve his nightwear. There was a selection of night clothes, all of which was along the lines of what he now wore.

Realising he had none of his boy clothes to wear he pushed himself from the bed and walked over to the closet. Opening the doors revealed a wardrobe of young girl's clothes. From short skirts for the office to slinky evening wear. He sighed nervously, feeling overwhelmed by the position he now found himself in. He knew there'd be little choice but to dress as Julie again that morning, and so he took himself into the bathroom to prepare as best he could.

An hour or so later Julian stared back at his reflection in the dressing table mirror, surprised at how easily he'd transformed himself into Julie once more. He was wearing a set of cream coloured lingerie, complete with garter belt and stockings. A thigh length white skirt was draped over the side of the bed alongside a pink top. He wasn't sure if his selection would be seen as appropriate for office wear or not, but he'd no experience of choosing girl's clothes to attend work in. He quickly slipped on the remaining items, feeling a thrill run through him as he tugged the skirt up his stocking encased legs. A familiar arousal was already rearing its head as he admired his feminine form in the full length mirror. Slipping on a pair of high heeled shoes, he tested himself out with a few steps before taking a deep breath and approaching the door.

Miss James was already up and sitting in the kitchen eating breakfast when he made a tentative appearance.

'I was about to come and get you, Julie. You really should be up earlier than this in future.' She looked him up and down as her expression softened. 'My my, you do look nice. You've done very well for your first full day. Now, hurry up and eat as we'll be leaving in fifteen minutes.'

Julian rushed his breakfast, noticing the occasional look he was receiving from Miss James. She seemed perfectly satisfied with his appearance, smiling to herself as he sat awkwardly in front of her at the table. Before long he was following on behind as she led the way to her car, and then once again into the elevator that would take them from the underground car park to the office. It almost felt like revisiting the scene of a crime, where Julian had met with an unexpected fate, only to be replaced with Julie, as he now appeared.

He was soon joined by Lynsey as they both began what appeared to be a normal day's work in the office, apart from the fact that he was now dressed as a girl. He took Ms Rush her morning coffee, meeting with an approving look as he went about serving her in her office without incident.

'I'm glad you're settling in, Julie.' She said as he poured her coffee. 'One of our more important clients is visiting this morning, and I'm sure he'll want to meet with our new office girl.' She smiled.

'Yes, Miss Rush.' Said Julian obediently with a rush of nerves at having an outsider meeting him as Julie.

The morning seemed to pass easily enough, until such time as Lynsey was required to escort their client through to Ms

Rush's office.

'He's very rich.' She said as she left her desk. 'He usually expects one of our VIP services.'

'VIP services?'

'Don't worry, they won't expect you to do anything like that yet, you have to be a permanent member of the team first.'

Julian watched her go curiously, wondering what she was alluding to. He had a niggling suspicion it was somehow related to the way they'd been testing him up until now, but he tried not to think of it too much. He heard Lynsey pass the office on her way to see Ms Rush with the client in tow. Julian found himself alone with his thoughts as he tried to focus on his admin tasks for the day.

'Good morning, young lady.' He looked up with a start as he heard the voice from the doorway. 'Well, aren't you a sight for sore eyes!' A strange man was standing there looking directly at him, he was a good six feet tall and handsome with it. He had an athletic build and emanated power and wealth to the point of being an imposing figure. He must have been in his thirties, with well groomed blond hair and piercing blue eyes. Julian became flustered, not sure how to react to such an enthusiastic greeting.

'Um, good morning, Sir.' He said, trying to speak as femininely as possible. To Julian's surprise the man walked into the room and made his way directly to his desk, sitting down on the edge of it as he perused the office girl in front of him.

'Oh, there you Mr Deveraux. I wondered where you'd gotten to.' Miss James was suddenly at the doorway, her eyes flicking to Julian and back to the man now clearly undressing Julian with his eyes.

'Tell me, has this young lady been made a permanent member of the team yet?' The man asked, his eyes never leaving Julian.

'Well, no, not yet. She's yet to progress as far as that, we only started preparing Julie for her full duties yesterday.'

'I'm sure she's more than capable of passing the final test, isn't that right, Julie? I'd be more than happy to oblige her as a little complimentary bonus to our deal.'

Julian felt light headed. His belly was somersaulting under the man's intense gaze, making him feel like a young girl in the spell of a Lothario.

'Um...I...I don't really know, Sir.' He murmured softly. 'I'm very new here.'

'Come, come, Julie. I'm sure you're keen to prove yourself in this most prestigious of companies, and I'm sure Miss James would hate to lose a promising young thing like yourself.'

'We wouldn't normally expect our girls to provide client services for at least another week, Mr Deveraux, as you well know.' Miss James looked a little uncomfortable with the situation, but she looked at Julian with something of an expectant expression. 'But it's really up to Julie. If she would agree to her final entrance exam, then I'm sure she's more than capable of passing to yours and our satisfaction.'

Julian heard the man's words, suggesting that he may be let go and the idea of having to find another job so soon was an unpleasant one. Something told him he'd been lucky to find something so quickly and he knew he needed to hang on to it, even if it did mean a rather unconventional way of working.

'I...I wouldn't mind taking my final exam, Miss James.' He interjected as the two exchanged looks. 'I'm sure I'd be up to it and I'd like to be made permanent if possible.' He realised he was sounding a little too keen to please but he didn't care at that point, he just wanted to be sure of having a job in the city.

There was a pause as both people studied his eager face before Miss James nodded. 'I suppose it's okay if you agree, Julie. I'll leave you in the capable hands of Mr Deveraux - one of our top clients. He'll let me know if you pass the exam.' She smiled at Julian in a way that made him feel as though this wasn't an unexpected outcome and he began to wonder if he hadn't been manoeuvred into agreeing to this deliberately.

'Well, Julie. I think it's time we gave you your final test. First of all I'd like you to take your top and skirt off.' He sat patiently waiting as Julian realised for certain that this was going to involve something else of a sexual nature.

He got to his feet and with the man's eyes firmly locked upon his body, slowly removed his top. He caught a glimpse of Mr Deveraux grinning as he set eyes on his lacy cream coloured bra underneath. Unfastening his skirt he allowed it to fall to the floor before stepping out of it, revealing his matching panties, garter belt and stockings. He felt extremely sexual at that point and couldn't resist running his hands up his own legs to feel the pure sensuousness of the smooth material, sending an erotic thrill shooting straight to his own groin. He looked up at the man, his eyes dropping to between his legs as he noticed the telltale bulge in his pants.

Unsure of quite what the man expected he hesitated, his hands behind his back looking demurely at his boss. The man got to his feet and unfastened his own clothing before dropping his pants to the floor. He kicked them away, grinning at Julian as he waited for the girly boy to make the next move.

There seemed little choice as Julian finally stepped forward, unable to tear his eyes away from the man's concealed erection as he took hold of either side of his underpants. He drew a breath before pulling them down. He had to stretch them toward him to get past his bulging cock and then he was tugging them down the man's hairy legs as he knelt in front of him.

He pulled the underwear clear, discarding it to one side as he looked back up. He gasped audibly as he saw the size of the man's engorged penis. It was far bigger than his, or indeed Lynsey's which was a similar size to his own. He felt positively girly in comparison to such a figure of a man. He felt a pang of fear as he reached up and wrapped his fingers around it's shaft, feeling the weight and girth. With a stunned expression he began to move his hand up and down, gripping it firmly as he wondered anxiously whether he'd be able to get it in his mouth. This was a different experience altogether to touching Lynsey. There was little doubt that he was in the presence of a real man, one that eclipsed any maleness that still existed within himself.

He leaned forward to taste the man's glans. Running his tongue around the tip he gazed upward, seeing Mr Deveraux watching him with undisguised pleasure, his eyes half closed. He cupped the man's balls in his free hand, surprised at the weight of them. Then he was leaning inward, opening his mouth and allowing the tip of this man's cock to enter him. It was more of a stretch than when he'd taken Lynsey. It felt like this was the first man he'd ever been with, as if Lynsey didn't count as one, and he guessed then that neither did he anymore.

With a certain amount of abandon he began to suck on Mr Deveraux's phallus, intending to make the best job of it he could and leave him in no doubt as to whether he should get the job. He could barely get half of it into his mouth before he had to pull back again, so long and thick was it.

'That's a good girl, make it nice and wet for me.' Moaned Mr Deveraux as he began to move his hips back and forth.

Julian pumped his one hand up and down the shaft as his other squeezed the man's balls at the same time as sucking him in and out of his mouth as far as he could manage. He wondered how long it would be before the man came, anxious of just how much man juice he would be forced to swallow. He needn't have worried too much about this, as just as he sensed that the man's precum had started oozing out into his mouth, the man pulled his hands away and withdrew his still hard cock from his mouth.

'Bend over the desk, Julie. It's time for your final entrance exam.' He said, guiding Julian to his feet and toward the desk as he took his place behind him.

Chapter 12

Julian whimpered as he was bent over, realisation dawning that this so-called "entrance" exam really was about entering him.

'Such a sexy bottom!' The man said, just as his hand landed against Julian's pantied behind.

SMACK!

'Ooh!' Squealed Julian, feeling his own arousal building at the thought of being taken like a girl.

Mr Deveraux wasted no time in pulling his panties aside before forcing his legs apart and nudging up against him. Julian could feel something heavy resting between his bottom cheeks and realised this was the man's erection. His insides turned to water as he waited with bated breath for what was about to come. The man spread his cheeks apart, exposing his pink little rosebud as he pushed in closer, his cock head pressing into him. The pressure increased and he could feel the man's hand between his legs, helping to guide his own cock to the target that was Julian's exposed bottom hole.

For a moment he didn't think the man would be able to enter him, but then the tip began to force his rosebud to open and then he was pushing into him, causing Julian to squeal as he felt the burn. Neither the dildo nor the butt plug had felt quite this big, and yet this was different somehow. The fleshy man meat seemed to enter more easily and he was soon being filled by Mr Cooley.

'Oh...Oh no...' Julian began to squirm against the desk as the man's shaft continued to enter him.

The man stopped for a moment before pulling back a little, and then pushing even deeper with the second thrust. He took his time to start with, moving gradually in then out, getting his stretched bottom hole used to being invaded in such a way. By the time he was thrusting in and out with something akin to a normal paced fucking, Julian was fast becoming aroused by the incessant inward stimulation. As if this wasn't enough, he couldn't help but look down at himself dressed so provocatively in women's lingerie and receive an extra thrill at the sight of such a thing. He was feeling so powerless just now, and yet there was an inner power that he'd somehow never experience before, in fact, it seemed most likely that this was something that could only ever be experienced whilst creating such sexual desire in another, especially a man.

'So tight! Such a sexy little thing.' Muttered Mr Deveraux as he lost himself in the act of taking the new office girl.

Julian could feel his own orgasm building under the constant stimulation inside of him. He gripped the desk hard and began to thrust his bottom back into the man, meeting flesh against flesh, slapping together as they both began grunting heavily. At one point he looked up through misty eyes and at first wasn't sure what he was seeing, but then realised it was Lynsey, standing in the doorway watching. She smiled at him encouragingly as her hand stroked the front of her own skirt, clearly becoming turned on by what she was seeing. Julian was too far gone to be embarrassed, but he knew in the back of his mind he'd feel the shame later when he had time to reflect on being taken in the bottom by a client in nothing but sexy lingerie in the middle of the office like this.

'Oh yes...yes...yes!' Mr Deveraux thrust himself inside as deeply as he could with one final push. Julian knew the man was cumming inside of him, thinking he could feel the man's juices being pumped deep inside of him.

It proved the final straw for himself as he felt his climax wash over him, cumming into his panties and no doubt onto the desk as he'd done so on the previous day as a result of Lynsey using the dildo on him. This time it was a real man that had taken him there, this time he'd been made into a proper girl.

As Mr Deveraux slowly pulled himself out of Julian, having gotten his breath back, Julian sagged forwards onto the desk. He realised that he felt more girl than boy now. Something inside of him had been changed forever, it felt as though he'd passed a point of no return. He was distantly aware of Mr Deveraux putting his clothes back on behind him as he spoke.

'I think I speak for everyone when I say welcome to the office, Julie. You certainly have what it takes to keep your company's clients happy. I'll let Miss James know that you've passed your final exam, shall I?'

'Th-Thank you, Mr Deveraux.' Julian muttered, wondering quite what he'd gotten himself into.

Lynsey helped him to clean up as he moved about stiffly, his bottom sore from having its first real cock. She seemed pleased and more than a little excited at the prospect of him joining her in the office. The rest of the day passed in a blur. There were no more tests or sexual adventures that day, it was as if they were allowing him time to get used to the idea of embarking on what was a whole new existence for him. By the time he lay his head on the pillow that night - staying once more at Miss James's apartment - it was as if he'd said goodbye to Julian, knowing that he'd be waking up to a new day and a new life as Julie, the office girl with a certain something extra to most other girls.

It'd been a whirlwind adventure over the past couple of days and he had little doubt that he'd be in for a great deal more by the time he finished his so-called training. Just what would be waiting for him as a fully trained office girl he didn't know for sure, but it would be a thrilling ride finding out just what Julie would be capable of along the way.

REBECCA STERNE -- TURNED INTO GIRLS!

REBECCA STERNE -- TURNED INTO GIRLS!

Turned into a Female Nurse

A Young Male Nurse's Tale of Feminization and Sexual Awakenings

Rebecca Sterne

Chapter 1

Michelle Beaufort was a young man about to make his way into the world. He was standing at the side of the road having waved his mother and sister off as they drove away, wishing him luck in his chosen career. The truth be told, it wasn't entirely his choice. He came from a dynasty of medical professionals and there'd always been an inevitability about where his future lay.

In a bid to at least save himself from the responsibility and dedication that came from training as a doctor, he'd opted instead to train as a nurse, much to the amusement of his older sister who'd teased him mercilessly about just how good he'd look in a dress with his long fair hair and blue eyes. At five feet five he was shorter than the average man in his family, and with a slender build he was always conscious of how he took after his mother far more than his father in appearance.

He turned toward the grounds of the teaching hospital and took a breath, steeling himself for the moment he'd have to present himself as one of the new batch of student nurses that were due to start their training that very day.

He noticed a couple of young girls getting out of a nearby

car with bags in tow much as himself and wondered if they'd be in his class. They were about the same age as his nineteen years, and they looked a little uncertain of themselves. At least they new each other he thought, feeling quite alone for the first time in his young life.

With a sigh of resignation he checked his hair was tied back in its usual ponytail and heaved his bag onto his shoulder. Staggering slightly under its weight he set off after the two mystery girls, seeing them heading toward the same building beyond the main hospital.

He began to absently wonder how many other male nurses there would be in his class. It was clearly no longer a female dominated profession but he still had the distinct impression that in this hospital at least, he'd be in the minority.

His hunch proved right as he trailed behind the two girls as they entered the teaching block. Despite the fact that this wasn't part of the main hospital it still managed to retain that clinical smell that was so familiar to him, having spent so much of his time around medical establishments growing up amongst a family of medics.

There were a number of people milling around in the reception area, clearly waiting for some kind of direction as to what would happen now that they'd arrived. He found a space against the wall, smiling self-consciously at the girl standing next to him as he peered around the room. He had to scan the assembled group for a second time before realising he was indeed the only male present.

'Attention please! Can I have your attention.' A loud voice silenced the group as a woman in her mid forties entered. She smiled a friendly greeting as she surveyed her latest batch of students before taking her place behind a desk. 'Thank you, girls.' She said, clearly forgetting that there was at least one male in the room in his view. 'I'm Mary Seeley - one of the senior nurses here - and I'd like to welcome you to Eastbrough Hospital and its nursing school. When I call your name you may collect your room key and information pack. This will tell you where your first class will be in the morning and provide you with all the information you need about your course.'

As the woman started calling names, Michelle watched as the individual girls approached this woman to receive their instruction. He'd convinced himself that more boys would turn up at any time but as the numbers dwindled it was seeming less and less likely.

'Michelle Beaufort?' He heard his name and instantly scurried forward to collect his key and information pack.

The woman barely looked up at him as just then another member of staff entered the room and began to speak to her. She directed him to sign a piece of paper and pushed his papers along with his room key toward him, barely acknowledging is presence.

'Thank you, dear.' She said without looking at him.

He nodded politely before leaving the room, busily reading the directions to his new accommodation. The student nurses block was easy enough to find, set back behind the main hospital as it was. He stopped for a moment to look up at the building, knowing he'd be spending the duration of his training living alongside his fellow students. With a pang of nervousness he entered the building and took the elevator up to the fourth floor. His room was towards the end of the corridor and he began to wonder who he'd be sharing with. They were all double occupancy rooms but as he'd not seen any other boys joining the class he suspected his roommate would be an existing student. That was okay though, he'd be able to enlist their help along the way.

At first it didn't quite register as he let himself into the room, but the fact that the walls were a pale shade of pink, and there was a poster on one of them of what appeared to be a young man showing his half naked chest as he sang into a microphone seemed a little out of place. He stopped to peer around his new surroundings, realising his roommate was already moved in he stared uncomprehendingly for several seconds at the pink bathrobe draped across one of the beds and an assortment of makeup scattered across their chest of drawers.

Listening for any sounds from outside for his roommate approaching, he slowly walked across the room having discarded his own bag and studied the girlish bedding and soft toys on the opposite bed. Something was clearly not quite right here and alarm bells began going off in his head. Drawing a breath he stepped over to this mystery persons closet and pulled the doors open. To his surprise it was filled with girl's clothes, leaving no doubt that his roommate was in fact ... female.

How could this be? They wouldn't have mixed sex rooms

like this, would they? There must be a mistake. They must've given him the wrong room he decided, as his eyes roamed across the array of feminine attire. A noise from outside startled him and he realised someone was pushing a key into the door. With a flurry of panic he closed the closet doors and sprung across the room to stand next to his bag.

The door swung open and a young girl walked in. She didn't notice him standing there at first, deep in conversation with another girl who trailed behind her as she was.

'Apparently they're the last being sent here. They're changing the way they teach the course ... oh!'

Both girls stopped dead as they became aware of someone else in the room. He could almost see the realisation dawn on them that there was a strange boy in the room. The first girl who was slightly taller than him with long blonde hair and blue eyes to match, looked as though she was about to greet her new roommate before something struck her as being odd. She studied him closer for a second before her eyes went wide and her hand moved up in front of her to point at him.

'You're a boy!' She exclaimed, just as the door closed behind them with an ominous click.

'Um ... I ... yeah.' Was all he could think to say at this point.

'What're you doing in my room?' She asked, looking as though she was about to get very angry. Her friend stepped up next to her as if to emphasise the fact that he was outnumbered, and with them both being of a similar height to each other he was feeling at a clear disadvantage.

'I ... they gave me a key.' He waved it in front of him as proof, 'I was told this would be my room. I'm ... I'm sorry, it must be a mistake.' He eyed the door behind the two girls, knowing he should pick up his bag and leave.

'You're one of the new class?' The second girl asked incredulously.

'Y-Yes.'

'You can't be, it's an all girl class.' Stated the first one. She frowned at him for a moment before holding out her hand. 'Let's see your papers, that should clear this up.'

Both girls expressions softened as they realised there'd been some kind of mistake that'd led to this male interloper being in one of their rooms. Michelle hurriedly picked up the information pack he'd been given with all of his paperwork and obediently handed it over.

'I'm Tanya, Tanya Kensit by the way. This is Lisa, Lisa Feelgood. She's next door.' The first girl introduced herself and her friend.

Lisa was a stark contrast to Tanya with her short black hair and brown eyes. They both stood a good inch taller than him but where Tanya was a similar slim build to himself, Lisa was considerably more curvaceous.

'I'm Michelle, Michelle Beaufort.' He said.

Both girls examined his paperwork. They seemed to do a double take as they read his documents before Tanya looked up at him with a wry smile spreading across her face.

'Did you read your own paperwork?' She asked, holding it out for him to see.

'Um ... no. Why?' He asked as he moved closer to read it.

'Because it seems they have you down as a girl.' She giggled as he read the paper, his eyes growing wide.

'But ... how? I'm ... I'm a boy. They saw me at the interview. How could they think I was a girl?' He spluttered, confusion reigning.

'I suppose whoever completed your information assumed having a name like "Michelle", meant that you were a girl.' Explained Lisa with undisguised amusement as she reread the paper still being held in the air by her friend.

'I ... I'd better tell them, get them to move me to a boy's room.' His face felt flushed as he realised how silly this must look. 'My parents are French, that's why I've got a French name.'

'Are you sure you're supposed to be here at all?' Asked Tanya, her face turning from amusement to concern. 'I'm sure your class is only supposed to be girls, and they're not starting any more after this. They're moving the nursing school to somewhere else. It's unlikely there's any boy's places available now.'

Michelle looked from one to another, feeling his future career coming apart before it'd even begun. He'd no idea what he'd do if they told him there'd been a mistake and he had to leave the course. He imagined returning home with no plan b, having invested everything in this one future career.

'Don't look so worried, Michelle.' Tanya said, 'I'm sure we

can sort this out between us. You wait here whilst me and Lisa go and find out the situation for you, you look like you could do with sitting down for a while.' Michelle gave them a weak smile as they turned to leave. 'Oh ... and don't go trying on my clothes whilst we're gone!' They both laughed as they left the room.

Michelle watched the door close behind them before sitting down heavily onto the bed. He knew that he should really be the one finding out about his situation, but he'd never been the most confident of people and he just felt like burying himself under the bedclothes at that precise moment and waiting for everything to sort itself out. Tanya's words came back to him and his eyes wandered toward her closet. It felt odd being in a strange girl's room all alone. He'd never really had a proper girlfriend before, so the female world still held a certain mystery to him despite having an older sister at home. He decided the best thing to do was simply wait for the girls to return, and so he lay back onto the bed, hoping that this whole thing could be straightened out - without him having to change his plans at the last moment.

Chapter 2

Michelle had no idea how long he'd been lying there when he finally heard the two girls returning to the room. He sat up just as they walked in. He couldn't read much in their expressions, but there was clearly something to their demeanour that told him it hadn't just been a case of being allocated a different room. He waited for the door to close before studying their faces expectantly.

'So ... what happened?' He asked, unable to contain himself any longer.

'Well, the main thing is not to worry. I'm sure there's a way around this.' Said Lisa, clearly trying to look positive but failing miserably.

'What? What's wrong?' He pressed, 'Can't they just give me another room?'

'It's not quite that simple.' Tanya exchanged a look with Lisa before continuing, 'They said if a boy had been accepted into the latest class then he'd have to leave, but I don't think they believed us when we asked.'

'Why not?'

'We didn't like to tell them your name in case they just said that you'd have to leave, so we kind of made it into a hypothetical question.' Lisa picked up the explanation from Tanya, 'The thing is, there weren't supposed to be any boys in your intake and they've not got any other accommodation. They said it would be impossible for something like that to happen, but if it did we should tell them so they could take action immediately.'

'Like I said, don't worry.' Said Tanya, 'We let them think we was just looking into a hypothetical situation, they don't know anything ... yet.'

Michelle opened his mouth to speak before closing it again. He wasn't sure what to make of it all. They'd avoided telling the staff that he was there as a girl by mistake, but where did that leave him? As far as they were concerned, Michelle Beaufort was still a girl and was now sharing a room with Tanya.

'You know, they clearly didn't realise you were a boy when they gave you a key, and to be honest, it took me a moment to realise you weren't a girl myself.' Said Tanya.

Lisa nodded her agreement as if this were a good thing. 'With a name like "Michelle" and looking like you do, I bet you could easily pass for a girl if you wanted to.'

'What? But ... I don't want to. I can't do that, that's ... that's ... mad!' He said, feeling insulted at the very idea that he looked like a girl. This combined with the fact that he was about to be sent home without a job or college place only served to make him feel wretched. He put his head in his hands and fought back the tears, feeling embarrassed, humiliated and alone.

There was an awkward pause before he felt the two girls' presence on either side of him. They both sat down, putting their arms around his shoulders to console him. It felt nice being between the two girls like this, having them be supportive even though they'd only just met him.

'It's got to be worth a try, hasn't it?' Said Tanya eventually, 'I mean, if no one ever found out you were really a boy, you'd still be able to qualify as a nurse and your real name would still be on the certificates and everything. If you think about it, it wouldn't make any difference in the long run. No one else would need to know that you trained as a girl.'

Michelle just groaned, wanting them to stop teasing him with a ridiculous scenario. He shook his head as he tried to imagine himself confessing to his family that he'd been sent home because they'd thought he was a girl until he'd pointed the truth out to them. He felt Tanya stand up and leave the bed as Lisa continued to console him. This was not how his first day as a student nurse was supposed to have been. He took a few breaths as he heard the girl bustling about the room, and then his attention was taken by hearing Lisa giggling from beside him. He slowly lifted his head to find Tanya standing in front of her bed, holding up a pair of panties and a bra.

'I think it's time you tried some of my clothes on, Michelle.' She said, 'I reckon you'd make a very convincing girl, don't you?'

'Eh? No ... I can't do that, it'd be wrong.' He protested in shock as he realised she really was serious, 'I don't want to be a girl.'

'What's wrong with being a girl?' Asked Lisa with a hurt expression on her face, 'Don't you like girls?'

'Of course I do, I just meant that ... I mean it's just ... '

'If you don't think there's anything wrong with being a girl, then why won't you put my panties on?' Tanya pouted as she waved her pink satin panties in front of her for emphasis.

The absurdity of her question and the fact that he was now sitting in this strange girl's room watching her dangling her underwear in front of him was starting to have an effect. He'd never been intimate with a girl before, and the idea that this one was now trying to convince him to put on her most intimate pieces of underwear was stirring something deep inside of him. He gaped at her open-mouthed, unsure of how to react.

'Go on, Michelle, try my panties on. It'll be fun. If you don't look like a girl then you can just go and tell the senior nurse and she'll let you go home, if that's what you want?'

'I ... I don't want that.' He stuttered, his young cock twitching inside of his undershorts as he continued to stare at Tanya's panties.

'Then you've got no choice, have you?' Said Lisa, placing her hands on her hips as if losing patience with him. 'Most boys would jump at the chance to put her panties on!'

He looked at the other girl, feeling bewildered by the choice being offered him. He knew this was a ludicrous thing to do, but his only other choice would be to simply leave the hospital in the most humiliating of ways. He felt himself becoming breathless as he turned back to Tanya as if mesmerised by her underwear.

'You know you want to, so you may as well just take your clothes off and give them a try. They probably won't fit you anyway, but it's worth a shot.' Said Tanya, dropping the underwear onto the bed and nodding to Lisa.

They approached him from either side and before he could ask what they were doing they were taking hold of his shirt and pulling it up and over his head.

'W-Wait!' His voice became muffled as the shirt was tugged over his head. He tried to grab a hold of it as they pulled it clear but he missed his grip and was immediately left bare chested. 'What ... what are you doing?' The question was unnecessary as it was perfectly clear what their intentions were.

'Stop whining and take your jeans off. It'll be a lot easier if you just help us.' Said Lisa impatiently as they approached him once more.

In an effort to avoid them undressing him any further he stood up as if to make for the door. It proved to be the wrong choice as they both took hold of his jeans and between them began to unfasten them.

'No ... d-don't ... p-please?' He cried as they succeeded in opening the front and began to tug them down his legs. He tried to hold onto them but they both swatted his hands away before one final effort succeeded in dragging them down to his ankles. His legs were unable to move and he quickly covered himself between the legs, suddenly aware that he was sporting a partial erection as a result of their attentions.

They pushed him backwards so that he collapsed onto the bed before snatching his shoes away and tugging the jeans clear off along with his socks. He was now mostly naked, with only his underwear left to cover himself.

'I'll put these out of the way in my room, shall I?' Offered Lisa as she picked up his bag and confiscated clothing before darting out of the door momentarily. She reappeared in no time, empty handed and with a wicked grin on her face. 'There, now you just need to take those silly boy shorts off.'

Michelle half sat up, desperately holding his hands in front of his underwear clad privates lest he show them too much. He was at a complete loss as to what to do now. He was practically naked without access to his boy clothes. He knew he couldn't just run back out into the corridor without landing himself in an even worse position. He could just see himself now, explaining to his parents and hospital staff that he'd been overpowered by two girls and stripped of all his clothes having been mistaken for being female and allocated a shared room as a girl. He whimpered pathetically.

He looked from one to another, seeing a determination in their eyes to see their plan through to completion. His options seemed severely limited as he considered the prospect of being further overpowered by the two girls.

'Um ... okay, I'll ... I'll put them on.' He tried desperately to think of a way not only to satisfy the two student nurses, but also to extricate himself from the situation with as little harm to what remained of his self-respect and dignity. 'But just for a moment. Then you'll give me my clothes back, right?'

'If you don't pass for a girl ... yes.' Tanya agreed with a glint in her eye.

Something told him that they were unlikely to agree to anything they didn't want to, but at least it'd buy him some more time to think of a way out of this - he hoped.

'You've got to turn around though.' He told them. He'd never been naked in front of a girl before and it was a disconcerting thought.

'Oh no you don't! You'll just run out the door in your shorts.' Said Lisa, looking suspicious. 'You turn around if you want to, but you'd better take them off quickly.'

With a final look of despair, Michelle got to his feet and turned his back on them. He could feel his belly doing somersaults as he pictured himself being made to put on this girl's underwear. At this point he didn't know whether it excited him or just plain terrified him. With a reluctant sigh he slowly pulled his shorts down his legs, kicking them off as he straightened up with his hands firmly in front of his still semi-erect cock. He was wishing fervently that it'd go down, as the last thing he felt right now was turned on, but despite how he thought he was feeling his embarrassing condition just seemed to continue unabated.

'Here you go, Michelle.' He heard Tanya say from behind and turned his head to look at her. She was holding out her pink silky panties at arms length, but still far enough away that he'd have to turn around in order to take them.

Trying his best not to expose himself he carefully turned about and reached out with one hand to take them. She pulled them back out of reach with a giggle before placing them into his outstretched fingers.

'Th-Thanks.' He said, puzzling to himself why he'd just thanked her for pushing him into wearing her panties.

He turned back around amidst several giggles and held out the soft, sensual underwear in front of him. He felt his arousal jump at the thought of putting on this attractive girl's underwear. Trying his utmost to control his own thoughts and feelings, he bent forward and lowered them down. As he stepped into them a thrill ran through his entire body and he felt his cock twitch forcibly with approval. He heard himself groan quietly as he began to slide them up his legs. By the time they'd reached his crotch he was feeling breathless with excitement. He tried to tuck his stiffening little rod between his legs but knew his state of arousal was barely hidden beneath the thin silky panties.

Chapter 3

'I like his bottom, it's very ... cute.' Lisa commented as he tried to compose himself.

'Turn around then, let's have a look.' Ordered Tanya in a commanding voice.

There seemed little point in putting off the inevitable. He slowly swivelled around to face his tormentors, thoroughly expecting them to continue their teasing until satisfied that they'd had their fun.

'Take you hands away, we can't see my panties.'

Letting out his breath slowly, Michelle moved his hands to his sides, bracing himself for the humiliation that would swiftly follow.

'Very cute, and they're a perfect fit aren't they, Lisa?'

'Yep, he looks very cute in your panties.' Lisa agreed, nodding.

When the expected humiliations never came, Michelle looked up at them to see them both admiring his panty covered crotch. His cock twitched as a result of seeing where they were gazing.

'I think wearing your panties is getting him all excited.'

84

Grinned Lisa.

'They are super cute panties I suppose, I don't blame him.' Said Tanya. 'Now, put my bra on.' She lifted her bra from the bed and held it out to him.

He hooked his fingers into the bra strap and took it from her, feeling at complete odds with such a peculiarly feminine piece of underwear. He studied it for a moment before wrapping it around his chest and hooking it into place. Swivelling the garment around he pulled the straps over his arms before settling it into position, feeling embarrassed by how he must look. To add to his embarrassment, Tanya stepped forward to help him straighten it up with a slight adjustment to the straps.

'There, perfect! You just need some little titties.' Observed Tanya as she strode over to her drawers and began rummaging around in the middle one. She swiftly produced two pairs of pantyhose and proceeded to ball them up before stuffing them inside of the bra. 'Brilliant!' She took a third pair of thick pantyhose from the drawer and held them out to him. 'Put these on, we need to cover your legs. They're not very hairy but they could do with a shave.

As Michelle sat back on the bed and began to struggle with Tanya's pantyhose, the two girl's busied themselves in her closet. By the time he'd pulled them up his legs, feeling himself becoming encased within Tanya's femininity they were ready and waiting for him.

'You can wear this skirt and top for now, I'm sure they'll fit fine.' She gave him a thigh length denim skirt and pink top to wear.

In way he was relieved to be able to wear something over the top of her underwear, but there was no getting away from the fact that he would now be dressed from head to toe in girl's clothes. He breathed in her scent as he pulled the top over his head, adding to his arousal as he did so. He was just beginning to wonder how much further they'd be taking this when Tanya took his arm and had him sit on her bed.

'Did you shave this morning?' She asked. He nodded. 'Good, we can try a little makeup and then do something with your hair.'

'What?' The idea of having makeup applied hadn't occurred to him until now. It seemed a step too far.

'Don't look so surprised, it's the only way we'll know for sure that you look like a real girl, isn't it?'

She didn't wait for an answer, instead she began to apply a layer of foundation as Lisa selected some eyeshadow and lipstick to complete his look. He could feel his masculinity diminishing the further he allowed these girls to feminize him. He'd never done anything like this before in his life and it was a surreal experience. He was grateful at least that there were no other boys around to see him being so thoroughly emasculated.

He could feel his anxiety growing the longer the two girls spent applying make up and restyling his long hair to a more feminine look. He was on the verge of crying out in protest, to put a stop to this madness and have them let him go when both girls stood back with self-satisfied looks upon their faces.

'There, all done. You look great!' Said Tanya.

'Wow, I'd never know he was a boy!' Said Lisa, looking amazed by their efforts. 'Take a look in the mirror, Michelle.'

He wasn't at all sure that he wanted to, but he knew he'd have to before they'd be satisfied. With an effort he got to his feet. He glanced in the direction of the mirror as if his very fate lie in its depths. Forcing himself to take the four or five steps necessary in order to view his full length reflection, he kept his eyes on his stockinged feet until he was in front of it. With a strange sense of anxiety he lifted his head, seeing what appeared to be a nineteen year old girl looking back at him. His jaw dropped as he realised just how convincing he looked as a girl.

'Well, what do you think?' Asked Tanya.

'I ... I dunno. It's weird.' He said, trying to make up his mind if he should be pleased by the transformation or horrified.

'You look brilliant!' Cried Lisa excitedly, 'You could easily pass for a girl.'

'What? How? I ... I can't pretend to be a girl.' He felt unable to look away from his female reflection. 'Can I have my clothes back now?'

'I think he needs a bit more convincing.' Said Tanya, sounding disappointed by his reaction.

'I know, let's take him out. That'll prove that no one'll know he's not a girl.' Tina was clearly getting more and more excited at the prospect of pulling off such a ruse.

Michelle looked at her in absolute shock at the idea that he should go outside dressed as a girl. His protests seemed to die in his throat as it closed up in fear with his legs turning to jelly. The entire unfortunate situation was now getting way out of hand but he'd no idea how to put the breaks on, not now that he was clearly in their power.

'I'll find you some shoes.' Said Tanya as she rummaged in the bottom of her closet. She'd soon reappeared with a pair of black high heeled boots. 'These'll look great with that outfit. Come on, put them on.'

As if in a dream, Michelle found himself pulling on a pair of slinky knee length boots. Standing up with their help he took a few tentative steps. Much to his own surprise he found that he could walk in them without too much trouble.

'Let's go!' Shouted Lisa before throwing the door open and taking his hand.

'No ... wait!' Before he could stop himself he'd been launched into the hallway. The door was swiftly closed behind them as the two girls took up position on either side. With no key to let himself back into the room he was now trapped outside dressed as a girl in Tanya's clothes.

'Stop looking so scared and just act naturally, no one will notice a thing.' Reassured Lisa.

'If I don't like it, can I have my own clothes back?' He asked timidly, trying not to raise his voice and draw any attention to himself despite there being no one else around.

'Of course you can, Michelle. We're not *making* you do anything.' Said Tanya as if answering a rather silly question.

They were soon propelling him down the hallway toward the elevators as he tried to come to terms with what was happening to him at the hands of these two girls. He supposed that regardless of how he got on, once they'd returned to the room he could simply demand to have his own clothes back and make his exit, hopefully none the worse for wear despite this most bizarre of ordeals.

Riding the elevator to the ground floor, they marched him back toward the reception area where he'd been handed the keys to Tanya's room in error. For a moment he feared they'd bump into the same woman and that she'd immediately recognise him as a boy in girl's clothing, regardless of the fact she hadn't noticed he was a boy even when dressed as one, albeit in a somewhat androgynous fashion.

His fears seemed to be coming true as he scanned the room and immediately set eyes on Miss Seeley, the woman who'd allocated everyone to their rooms earlier. He was about to head in the opposite direction when Tanya began to steer him straight toward her, with Lisa taking her lead and following suit. He had to stop struggling against them so as not to draw attention from the few girls that were milling around the room.

'Good morning, Miss Seeley.' Chimed Tanya as they drew nearer.

'Oh, good morning girls. How are you?' The woman looked up with a smile.

'We're well, thank you.' Said Lisa.

'I'm not sure we've met have we?' The woman's eyes quickly settled onto Michelle as he stood between the two girls, wishing desperately to be somewhere else.

'I think you met Michelle earlier, Miss Seeley. This's Michelle Beaufort, one of the new intake. She's sharing my room.'

'Of course, Michelle. I'm sorry I didn't recognise you dear, I was a little preoccupied this morning. How are you settling in? I hope Tanya and Lisa are looking after you?'

He felt their eyes upon him as all three awaited his response. He cleared his throat nervously, expecting to be exposed as soon as he opened his mouth. In a last ditch effort to avoid being completely and utterly humiliated, he tried to soften his voice as he spoke.

'Oh yes, Miss Seeley. They're taking good care of me, thank you.'

'Very good, Michelle. It's always nice to familiarise ones self with ones students. I look forward to seeing you in class first thing in the morning.'

Michelle smiled coyly as the woman had a brief chat with Lisa about her classes. He felt as though he was in shock having fooled this woman into thinking he was a girl. He realised then that she would recognise him as Michelle Beaufort from now on, a young nineteen year old female student. How on earth could he now confess to her that he'd been placed in an all female class by mistake, and that he was really a boy who'd shown up in front of her dressed as a girl in a bid to deliberately fool her? The full weight of the situation he now found himself in seemed to come crashing in on him and he had a powerful urge to sit down. He gave Tanya's arm a tug to get her attention.

'I need to sit down.' He said quietly.

'Okay, let's go to the restaurant shall we?' Said Tanya, loud enough for Lisa to hear.

It wasn't quite what he'd had in mind, but he needed to be away from Miss Seeley as soon as possible. He allowed the two girls to lead him out of the building and across the hospital grounds until they reached the large restaurant on the ground floor. It was bustling with people. Staff, students and members of the public were all there, making him feel even more exposed. It was a relief to finally sit down in a discreet corner away from the worst of the crowd as Lisa went to get some drinks. A bizarre situation had just turned into a complicated deception that he was now struggling to see an easy way out of.

Chapter 4

'I don't see what you're so worried about, Michelle. Miss Seeley believes you're a girl now, so all you have to do is play along.' Said Lisa, trying to calm down a clearly panicking boy who was sat in front of her dressed as a girl. 'Besides, you can't go back on it now. Just think of all the trouble you'll be in with the hospital and your parents if they find out you joined a class as a girl. I wouldn't want to be in your shoes if Miss Seeley finds out you pretended to be a girl in front of her either, she can be pretty fierce.'

Michelle groaned despondently. He wanted to shout and scream at the two girls over what they'd gotten him into but it'd only result in him being found out. He sucked on his straw, finding some solace in the refreshing soda that Lisa had supplied.

'Look, if nothing else we've just proven that you can stay here as a girl. If we can fool Miss Seeley, we can fool anyone.' Added Tanya, looking positive. 'You'll have to borrow some clothes for a while, but we can buy you some of your own when you've got some money. We'll even introduce you around so you can make some new friends.'

He groaned again, this time at the idea of their deception growing even wider as more people got to know him as a girl. He peered around the restaurant, seeing a number of fellow students gathered about in groups. He caught the eye of a male student, clearly older than himself and from an earlier intake. Their eyes seemed to lock for a moment before Michelle realised this boy thought he was looking at a girl. He looked away sharply, a feeling of dread washing over him at the idea that he was now for all intents and purposes sitting on the opposite side of the gender divide.

'Come on, let's go back to our room and get you settled in.' Said Tanya, pulling him to his feet. 'I'll sort out some clothes for you, and we can see if anyone else can spare some too.'

He looked at her with trepidation, visions of them traipsing around the student accommodation asking for clothing donations for the boy pretending to be a girl running through his mind. This didn't happen of course, and once they'd safely arrived back at their shared room, Michelle gratefully sank onto his bed having drawn little attention from anyone on his first foray into the world as a girl.

'Right, take off your top and skirt and we can try some other clothes on you.' Said Tanya almost immediately. She opened her closet as Lisa continued to watch him from the opposite bed.

'Go on then, take them off.' Lisa prompted with a grin. 'I'll bring your bag back once we've found you some girl's clothes.'

The idea that he'd soon have access to his bag again complete with boy's clothes brightened his mood. It seemed worthwhile allowing their teasing to continue for now until he could make his own decision on what to do. Looking away from Lisa he pulled Tanya's top up over his head, revealing the pink bra beneath. He could feel his embarrassment rising as he got to his feet and unfastened the skirt, wriggling his way out of it until he was standing there in just the girl's underwear. He was grateful that the pantyhose were there to help hide his boy's privates.

'Do you like wearing girl's underwear?' Asked Tina almost innocently. She waited for an answer.

'Um ... yeah, I guess it's okay.' He said after an awkward pause as he became acutely aware of how he was standing in front of them again in just Tanya's panties, pantyhose and bra.

'Is your little thingy getting hard?' She continued to look directly at him, although her eyes soon drifted down to his crotch. 'It seemed to excite you earlier.'

As much as Michelle was trying not to focus on anything between his legs, his attention couldn't fail to switch as a result of Tina's deliberate questioning. He felt his cock twitch in response to her gaze, as if her eyes were physically touching him. Much to his increasing embarrassment he felt his penis begin to engorge. He was helpless to stop it and was caught in indecision about whether to draw more attention to it by covering himself, or to hope that his body's reaction wasn't yet showing.

'Look Tanya, his little peeny's getting all stiff again. I think he likes your underwear.'

He glanced down as if to confirm for himself that his budding erection was showing before squeaking girlishly and covering himself with his hands. Tanya turned around and joined her friend in observing his covered crotch.

'Take your hands away, Michelle. It's okay, we're all nurses together here, there's nothing to be embarrassed about.' Said Tanya.

'I ... er ... ' He felt his belly flip-flop as his body continued to betray him. The more he tried to turn his mind to other things, the more conscious he was of his growing erection as a result of these two girls tormenting him.

'Take them away silly!' Said Tanya, walking over to him and taking hold of his wrists. 'I want to see if your peeny's getting stiff in my panties.'

He didn't feel as though he had any strength in his body to resist her as she pulled his hands away and stared openly at his nylon covered crotch. He let out a little gasp, feeling her eyes studying his crotch with his cock growing stiffer as a result. He didn't understand why he was becoming erect with them humiliating him like this, but no attempt at controlling his own body seemed to have the slightest effect. His penis began to straighten itself out as it continued to grow stiff underneath Tanya's pantyhose.

There followed an interminable few seconds where the two girls just continued to watch as his cock grew to its full size. Another furtive glance downward confirmed that despite his small size for a man, it was still outlined perfectly clearly by the smooth feminine underwear. He realised he'd started to breath shallowly, as if he were being stimulated by more than just the feel of Tanya's panties.

'Is that as big as it gets?' Asked Lisa, looking a little surprised by the idea.

Tanya raised her eyebrow as he stood stiffly in place, unwilling to answer the question. He felt her hand let go of one of his wrists and looked down just in time to see her reach toward him. As her hand gently cupped him between the legs he gasped as and electric thrill ran through his body. He'd never been touched like this before. He felt excited, vulnerable and demeaned all at the same time. He could feel his face flushing hotly as he tried to process the fact that this girl was now touching him through her underwear. She looked up at his face as if to gauge his reaction before returning her attention further down. Her hand began to move up and down his shaft, her fingers probing further between his legs and underneath his tightening balls before once again tracing his erection all the way to his swollen glans.

Michelle began to shiver with excitement feeling himself being slowly, delicately massaged. He wanted to protest at his treatment, at how he was being used for their undoubted amusement, but his voice had abandoned him and his body felt as though it were paralysed into inaction. The powerful feelings of eroticism that now ran through him were threatening to blow his mind. He'd never experienced anything like this. He imagined how Tanya had worn these very panties herself, how the silky soft material had cosseted and cupped her young pussy so intimately. He couldn't seem to take his eyes off the sight of her hand as she continued to stroke him, caress him.

'I hope you're not going to have a boy accident in my panties, Michelle.' Said Tanya distractedly as she observed closely the effect that her hand was having on him.

'Oh ... oh ... ' Was all Michelle could manage as he imagined himself cumming in front of these two girls. It was all proving too much to bear as his body shuddered forcefully, his rigid cock pulsing, pushing out against her fingers.

Tanya seemed to sense he was about to lose control of himself and increased the speed that her hand was massaging him. She pushed into him, rapidly masturbating him toward a climax as he began to grunt and groan with his ever building arousal and a desperation to hold onto at least a small shred of dignity. It wasn't to be. He began to squirm against her as his orgasm threatened. He looked around the room through misted eyes, catching sight of

Lisa as she watched him being brought to a climax in her friends underwear, grinning broadly. His mind wandered briefly over how his day had brought him to such a climax - literally.

'Oh ... please? I-I think I'm going to ... to ... ' He couldn't bring himself to say the word. He thought for a moment that he would simply pull away from her, stop the torment, but it was already too late. His body tensed and his balls tightened. His knees went weak as his orgasm rushed forward. He squealed girlishly as he began to thrust his hips into the girl's hand, grunting with resignation as he felt the first jet of cum being pumped outward into the panties.

All he could do now was try and stay upright as he shot load after load of warm cum into Tanya's underwear, knowing that both girl's were watching his humiliating performance. Tanya could undoubtedly feel the warmth of his seed as it soaked into her panties and pantyhose, making him feel like a little child who was in the process of wetting himself in front of the adults. He was surprised at how forceful his climax proved to be, ejaculating a copious amount of cum until finally his orgasm began to subside, his cock pulsing with the final few drops as he became fully aware of how the girl was still cupping him with her hand.

'He's made your panties all wet, Tanya!' Giggled Tina from across the room, breaking the momentary tension as all three seemed to realise just what'd happened.

'I know, *and* my pantyhose. I wish I hadn't given him clean ones to wear now!' Said Tanya.

Michelle glanced at each girl in turn, quickly returning his gaze to the floor as he felt himself sagging from the effects of his climax and the added weight of his humiliation. Tanya was slow to withdraw her hand, looking down as if to check if it were covered in boy juice. It wasn't, but the panties that he wore were now soaked through with it.

'I'll go get your things, shall I?' Offered Lisa eventually. Forcing her fascinated gaze from Michelle's wet and sticky crotch to the door. Tanya smiled at him before sinking back onto her own bed.

Michelle wasn't sure what to do with himself. In the absence of a better idea he followed Tanya's lead and sat back onto his bed, grimacing at the feel of his cum filled panties being squished against him as he did so. The only thought he had now was to retrieve his own clothes and make a hasty exit as soon as he could. He'd have to deal with the consequences later.

Chapter 5

Lisa returned several minutes later, much to Michelle's relief. He wondered what'd taken her so long to simply pick up his bag from the next room, but at least she was back and with his bag in her hand. She brought it over to him and dropped it onto the bed. He looked at her sheepishly as she giggled at the sight of him sitting there in just Tanya's cum soaked underwear, still made up to look like a girl.

'I still wouldn't know you was a boy, even in your underwear. Especially as your little dicky's not swollen any more, not that it was that obvious anyway.' Said Lisa.

He looked down at himself, feeling degraded and shamefaced at what'd become of him since arriving at the hospital. He reached over to his bag and unzipped it, hoping to don some more appropriate clothing before deciding how best to extricate himself from the situation. Staring down at its contents he pulled it closer to get a better look inside. For a moment he was confused before realising that Lisa had removed all of his clothes, only leaving behind his study books and equipment.

'Where ... where are my clothes?' He looked up at the two girls in surprise.

'Your clothes?' Repeated Lisa. The two girls looked at each other quizzically, as if the question made no sense at all. 'I thought we agreed you'd have to borrow some of ours for now. You can't go walking around dressed as a boy, not now.'

'We'd best get you tidied up. You'll need to get rid of any boy hair of course.' Added Tanya.

Michelle stared at them as if they'd gone mad. He hadn't really believed they'd go through with their plan to have him stay in the nursing school as a girl, but now it appeared they were perfectly serious.

'Come on, throw my robe on and we'll take you down to the bathroom.' Said Tanya, picking up a pink fluffy bathrobe and throwing it onto his lap.

They both stood waiting by the door, fixing their gazes on him until he began to feel uncomfortable. Standing up stiffly he pulled the robe on, covering his cum soaked underwear. Tanya threw him a pair of fluffy pink slippers that matched the colour of the robe. Pushing his feet into them he found himself being led out of the room and to the very end of the hallway. They entered one of the shared bathrooms together before Lisa locked the door behind them.

'You can use this to make your legs nice and smooth, then we'll freshen up your makeup for you.' Tanya handed over a tube of depilatory cream and ushered him toward the shower. 'Take off my underwear first, silly!'

He felt as though he'd lost all control over his own fate. Locked in a girl's bathroom in nothing but Tanya's soiled underwear he passively submitted to the two girls' wishes. Unfastening the bra, he handed it back to Tanya before turning his back to them and working the pantyhose back down his legs. Much to his surprise he felt a tinge of disappointment at taking off the sensual nylons. The panties quickly followed, causing him to whimper as he tugged the wet sticky panties down his legs, trying desperately to hide himself from view. Balling them up with the pantyhose he awkwardly held them out behind him for Tanya to take.

'Eeew! They're all wet.' She announced, adding to his embarrassment.

It was almost a relief to step behind the shower curtain out of sight for a while. The two girls chatted patiently as he busied himself with the cream. He stared with fascination as he washed what little boy hair he had away down the drain, running his hands over perfectly smooth and feminine looking legs. It wasn't until he'd dried off that he realised he had nothing but the bathrobe to cover himself for the short walk back to Tanya's room.

'Can I have the robe, please?' He asked, peering out from around the curtain.

'You'll need to put some panties on first, Michelle.' Said Tanya.

'Oh ... I didn't bring any clean ones.' Said Lisa, 'Did you?'

'No. We'll have to improvise I suppose.' Tanya looked thoughtful for a moment before her lips spread into a cheeky smile. 'You can wear theses for now.'

Michelle swallowed hard as he watched, mesmerised, as Tanya lifted her skirt enough to take hold of her panties and begin to slide them down her legs. As she slowly stepped out of them to hold them up for him, he couldn't help but notice a small dark patch in the crotch.

'Sorry, they're a little damp, but not as wet as the others.' She apologised with a shrug of her shoulders.

Knowing there was little choice but to go along with their plans, Michelle reached out and took them from her hand. He pulled the curtain across as he prepared to put them on, feeling the warmth of her body and detecting the aroma of female arousal. Bringing them closer to his face he inhaled her musk as his fingers touched where she'd dirtied them with her girl juice. Realising what he was doing as his cock jumped forcibly between his legs he pulled them away and stepped into them, trying not to think of where they'd come from. He trembled at the feel of the soft panties being drawn up his smooth and noticeably more sensitive legs. As they reached his crotch and he tried to tuck his little manhood between his legs he could feel a distinct dampness between his legs, making him acutely aware of wearing her soiled panties.

He had to take a few breaths to steady his reaction before appearing once more from behind the curtain. Much to his surprise he found Tanya presenting him with her bra which she'd clearly taken off whilst he was immersed in the act of putting on her panties. As he finished fastening it into place, Lise whipped the curtain aside to expose his underwear clad body.

'Your legs look nice and smooth. Let's get you back to the room, shall we?' Said Lisa.

They soon had him shuffling back along the corridor in Tanya's pink bathrobe and slippers. His mind wanted to focus its attentions between his legs and the warm damp feeling that was a constant reminder of Tanya's panties that'd been soiled by her arousal. He fought against himself in a bid to avoid becoming blatantly turned on once more, giving up any fight to maintain control of what was now happening to him.

The girl's got him fully dressed back in the room before declaring that it was time they found something to eat and led him outside once more. This time he felt a little less self-conscious as he realised no one was taking much notice of the three girls leaving the building. He wondered just how far this outlandish ruse would be taken before he found himself the subject of a very public denouncement as a boy passing himself off as a girl student.

-o0o-

The rest of the day was spent following Tanya and Lisa around as they took him to the restaurant for something to eat before showing him around the hospital. Michelle caught the odd look from others, some of them were from men who were clearly eyeing up the trio of young medical students, others from fellow students wondering who the new girl was who'd started hanging out with these two second years.

He felt himself tense as Tanya and Lisa greeted another couple of girls who they knew. They introduced him as Michelle, Tanya's new roommate and first year student. He nodded shyly, thinking that at any moment they would realise his true gender and announce it to the world but they never did. By the time they'd introduced him to a fourth and fifth group of girls he'd stopped worrying so much. He still didn't trust himself to speak openly, knowing that he was coming across as rather shy and withdrawn. This didn't seem particularly important just now, the main event being the fact that he was increasingly becoming known as a girl by the resident student population.

It was with a great sense of relief that the night drew to a close as they sat in the recreation room of the building, watching

T.V. as Tanya and Lisa shared stories of their first year of training. Tanya turned to him, unable to resist checking his female persona out for a moment before speaking.

'We'd better go to bed, you'll have an early start tomorrow I guess. I checked your timetable and after your induction session you'll be picking up your uniform.' Said Tanya.

Michelle suddenly felt a little light headed as he imagined waking up with the prospect of starting his first full day as a student nurse - and as a girl. They were soon entering their shared room having said goodnight to Lisa. He sat down on his bed, feeling suddenly awkward about spending the night in the same room as a girl for the first time, despite them having separate beds. Tanya rummaged about in her drawers before turning toward him, holding out a slinky looking black nightdress that he realised would barely reach mid-thigh.

'You can borrow this tonight if you like?' She grinned, 'We can't have you sleeping naked, can we?'

Michelle groaned at the sight of such a feminine garment, but he couldn't completely ignore the subtle urge he was feeling to put it on. He shifted his weight self-consciously, remembering the fact that he was still wearing her soiled panties.

In an unspoken yet mutually agreed effort to preserve each other's dignity - not withstanding his earlier humiliations - they both turned their backs to one another as they undressed and donned their nightwear. He kept her panties on underneath the sheer nightdress, telling himself that it was to help keep himself covered but knowing there was an underlying desire inside of him to continue feeling the presence of this girl's panties hugging his little cock and balls.

Having crawled into bed with Tanya flicking off the lights, he found himself alone with his thoughts for the first time that day. He tried to make sense of all that'd happened, to rationalise the events and the reason why he was now lying in bed dressed in a nightdress and panties with a girl on the other side of the room. He wondered quite what his parents and sister would make of it if they found out he'd entered the nursing school as a girl. Sure, it'd been a mistake on the part of the hospital, but how could he explain why he was still there having spent the day dressed as a female student?

A noise from the other side of the room drew his

attention and he turned his head, listening to what sounded like a rhythmic movement against Tanya's bedclothes accompanied by her audibly heavy breathing.

'Are you okay?' He asked without thinking, hearing a little squeak of surprise emanate from her at the sound of the question.

'Um ... yeah. I was just ... thinking.' She said, her voice sounding a little strange. 'It was kind of cool, seeing you in my underwear today. I just need to ... you know ... '

He wasn't sure he did know. He was about to ask what she meant when he heard her getting out of bed before she suddenly appeared next to him. Much to his surprise she lifted up the covers and slid in next to him. He was forced to move over in the tight confines of the single bed as she shuffled up beside him.

'As I did you a favour today, I think it's your turn.' She whispered in a hoarse voice.

He jumped a little as he felt her hand touch his before drawing it across her body and down toward her crotch. He breathed in sharply as he felt his fingers being placed on top of her panties, sensing the heat from within and realising then that he'd heard her masturbating under the covers. He'd never even come close to such a level of intimacy before and he felt himself freeze out of nervousness. She didn't seem to take much notice as she gently began to guide his fingers up and down the front of her panties. He could feel her engorged pussy lips and the wetness that already pervaded the soft material as he was made to stroke her.

'Ooh ... that's it, touch me like that.' She moaned as her entire body seemed to squirm around next to him.

He had to force himself to start breathing again as he continued to massage her privates. He could feel her wetness growing, seeping through the thin panties and beginning to coat his fingers. She pressed them in further, almost to the point of entering her slick hole before increasing the speed with which she was using his hand to masturbate herself with.

'Oh yes, Michelle, yes!' She mewled into his ear, her breathing becoming heavier, more rapid.

Michelle couldn't quite believe what he was doing or where his fingers were. He'd never seen a girl have an orgasm in real life. His own little cock quickly became rigid at the sight, sound and feel of this girl approaching her climax under his own fingers. He could hear a distinct squelching sound emanating from

REBECCA STERNE -- TURNED INTO GIRLS!

between her legs as her juices flowed freely within her panties. Then she was arching her back and quivering throughout her entire body as she cried out in mid climax. Her legs clamped together, trapping his hand between them as her soaking wet pussy was pushed against his hand. She grunted several times, writhing against him as her orgasm broke over her like a wave of sexual release.

It took her a while to come down from her sexual high, breathing hard next to him as he kept his hand between her legs trying to absorb the moment into his mind. He wanted to touch himself, to have her touch him, but something about the moment seemed too sublime to interrupt. When eventually she seemed to gather her senses, she lifted herself up onto her elbow and looked at him.

'I think it could be quite fun, having you as a roommate. The last girl was a bit boring. I'm sure you're going to be much more fun.'

She pecked him on the cheek before sliding back out of the bed and heading back to her side of the room. He stared up at the ceiling for a long time before sleep eventually found him, his mind a whirl of emotions, not the least of which was a raging erection that refused to diminish, especially as he couldn't completely ignore the fact that he was wearing Tanya's black nightdress and borrowed panties.

Chapter 6

The next morning was a surreal awakening for Michelle. He awoke to the sound of Tanya heading off to the bathroom, telling him to make sure his face was hair free before leaving the room. It seemed her pink bathrobe and slippers were now his to wear as he took himself discreetly to the bathroom for his morning ablutions.

By the time he returned Tanya was already dressed and applying her makeup. She'd thoughtfully laid out a set of her underwear on his bed, along with a flouncy skirt and matching top. He picked them up and examined them with a sense of trepidation. Everything seemed different in the early morning, and he wondered - not for the first time that morning - what on earth he was doing going along with the girls' crazy deception.

As he picked up the panties it seemed obvious that they'd already been worn. She must have noticed his questioning look as she was soon standing at his shoulder.

'After yesterday you're only allowed to wear my dirty panties, I'm not having you make my clean ones all wet and sticky.' She said, giggling at his shocked expression.

Contrary to what she probably thought, it was the fact that

he actually wanted to wear them that was confusing Michelle and not the idea that she was pushing him into doing so. He tried to hide his arousal as he stepped into her white coloured satin panties. His smooth hairless legs seemed to amplify the effect of the girl's underwear. His diminutive boy cock was semi-erect by the time he'd pulled them into place. He was almost grateful for the addition of another pair of flesh coloured pantyhose in order to keep his reaction under control. The tight sensuous feel of the nylon as he worked them up his legs did nothing to assuage his sexual feelings, and by the time he'd fastened the bra into place he knew there was a distinct outline between his legs of his stiff little shaft.

'It's a good job that skirt isn't too tight, otherwise someone might notice your little mound.' Tanya seemed to find his situation perfectly amusing as he quickly stepped into the skirt, pulling it up to cover his embarrassment. The way she described his erection as a "little mound" managed to make it sound like he had girl parts instead of boy's.

She talked him through applying his makeup as quickly as she could, leaving him in no doubt that he'd be expected to put it on himself as soon as possible. With the addition of some borrowed jewellery, including some large hooped earrings which he was fortunate enough to have two pierced ears to accommodate, he was soon looking every bit the young female student about to embark on her new career.

Breakfast was an anxious time as they met up with Lisa and her roommate Phillipa. If he'd any doubts as to whether this new girl had been let in on their little secret, they were dismissed almost immediately as she leaned into Tanya and spoke loud enough that he could hear.

'You'd never know she wasn't a ... *she*, would you?' She said, her eyes wandering up and down his body with interest.

'He's ... I mean *she's* a natural girl, don't you think?' Said Tanya proudly, as if she'd created him herself (which in many ways she had).

Michelle looked down at the floor from embarrassment, wondering just how many others would be told his true nature and knowing that with every person who found out, his risk of discovery was heightened.

It was with great anxiety that he finally made his way to his very first class. All alone for the first time since meeting Tanya, he walked stiffly into the classroom and found a seat at the back, desperate to avoid as much attention as possible. The class began with them being asked to complete their induction forms. Having filled out his name he came to a box that specified gender, his pen wavered over the top as he tried to decide what to do for the best. If he marked himself down as female then he'd be complicit in his own fate, and with documentary proof that he'd claimed to be a girl there'd be no denying his part in all of this.

'Are you okay ... Michelle?' The tutor was hovering by his side as she made her way around the new intake's classroom. 'Just tick that box and write down the rest of your details, Dear.' She said, watching him.

Feeling the woman's eyes upon him his hand automatically moved to the box on the piece of paper and he watched as if from a distance as his pen put a tick against "Female". He felt something inside of him snap, as if he'd just sealed his fate and committed himself to living the next three years as a girl. The woman drifted off as he forced himself to fill out the rest of the form, feeling his insides flipping over at what he'd just done.

He tried to concentrate on what the woman was saying for the rest of the time but his mind was reeling with the implications of his fraudulent act. He gazed about the classroom, seeing other girls looking somewhat nervous on their first day but knowing with absolute certainty that they'd far less to be nervous about than himself. Following the class he traipsed out of the room and out of the building as they were led toward the place where they'd pick up their uniforms. It wasn't until he'd squeezed into the tight confines of the room in between two of his new classmates that he realised he was about to be issued with a female uniform. He could see several piles of clothing behind the counter. He watched as one girl was issued hers by the officious looking woman and she held the knee length nurses dress up against herself. With little else to do he filed forward alongside the other girls until he was next in line.

'Name?' The woman asked, peering up at him from her list.

'Um ...'

'Hurry up young lady, what's your name?' She said, clearly wishing to get through the task as quickly as possible.

'M-Michelle, Michelle Beaufort.' He said in a slightly shrill voice, much to his increasing embarrassment.

The woman raised her eyebrows before checking the list. He saw her tick his name off before searching through the few remaining piles behind her. They already had his basic measurements, something that he'd been tasked with providing before arriving the day before, so he hoped that everything would be as it should and there'd be no awkward questions or delays. She barely even looked at him as she presented him with his bundle of hospital issued clothing, dismissing him with a curt nod of the head as she moved on to the next girl in line.

He followed the girl in front as they made their way back to the nursing school. The girl turned around and waited for him to draw level before speaking.

'I thought they might give us some of those scrubs that most nurses wear now, I'm so glad we get to wear a dress like a proper nurse, aren't you? I'm Keelee, by the way.'

'Oh ... I'm Michelle.'

'Well, do you like your dress? And it's such a cute little hat as well.'

'Oh yes, it's very ... nice.' He agreed as she waved the little nurses hat in front of her.

It was hard to imagine himself wearing such a thing, but he guessed he wouldn't have to imagine it for very much longer. As they arrived back inside the classroom, the rest of the girls were milling around, showing off their new uniforms.

'Now girls!' The tutor clapped her hands together to get their attention. 'We'll be taking a tour of the hospital shortly so that you can get your bearings, and then we'll start your tuition this afternoon. Please change into your uniforms now.'

Michelle's jaw dropped as he looked around to see a number of girls starting to take their tops off, eager to try their nurse's uniforms on. His mind seemed to freeze from the shock of being surrounded by a bunch of unsuspecting girls undressing down to their underwear in front of him, and the sudden fear of having to do the same himself. He froze for several seconds, unsure of what to do.

'Hurry up, Michelle.' The tutor said in passing, seeing him hesitate. 'Don't worry, there's no boys around to see you, we're all girls together here.'

He tried desperately not to look at anyone, but the appearance of several girls in just their bras and panties was a powerful distraction. Moving close to the wall he realised he'd have no choice but to follow suit. Looking around nervously to check that none of the girls were paying him any real attention, he turned to face the wall in an effort to hide any give away signs of being a boy and quickly dropped his skirt. He could feel himself reacting to being surrounded by girls dressed only in their underwear and feared he'd soon be giving himself away. With a flourish he whipped his top off, glancing down to ensure that his pantyhose stuffed bra was positioned so as not to display his lack of real breasts. His eyes were drawn lower for a moment, expecting to see his penis outlined by the pantyhose. Much to his relief there was little to see other than a slight bulge that could easily pass as a female one.

He fumbled with the nurse's dress with outright panic lurking just below the surface. Unzipping it quickly, he stepped straight into it before pulling it up and slipping it over his shoulders. The relief was palpable as he drew the zip up in front to once again conceal his boy's body underneath the female clothing. It was only at the point where he began to smooth down the dress, concentrating on slowing his breathing that he realised it was a perfect fit. The white dress reached to just above his knees and its cut gave him a suitably feminine outline.

'They're nice, aren't they?' Said one girl from behind him.

He turned to look at her just as she was drawing the zip up the front of hers, giving him a brief glimpse of her young milky breasts being pushed up seductively by her white lacy bra. He swallowed hard, feeling his little manhood twitching with approval.

'Here, let's help each other with the hats.' The girl continued, picking up his traditional looking nurses hat and moving behind him to help pin it in place. 'There, it looks cute on you.' She said.

Michelle smiled awkwardly before realising she was waiting for him to do the same for her. As he took the girl's hat he stepped behind her, watching two other girls nearby to see how they were fixing the hats into place. He grappled unsuccessfully for several seconds, trying to pin the hat into place and becoming increasingly aware of his close proximity to his young female classmate. He could smell her perfume and had to focus his mind with an effort in order to get her hat to stay in place.

'All done.' He said, stepping back to look at her.

By now most of the girls were fully dressed. A room full of young female nurses, all in uniform, with him dressed identically in their midst. It was a strange feeling to realise how he now looked. He caught sight of his reflection in a glass door to the rear of the room and turned for a moment to check his appearance. He knew it was wrong, but he couldn't help but feel a little sexy in his new uniform. A loud clapping of the tutors hands brought him back to reality and he self-consciously shuffled back to his desk, picking up his discarded skirt and top on the way.

This was certainly going to prove an interesting day.

Chapter 7

Following some further orientation within the classroom and an overview of their course, the class was taken on a tour of the hospital. Trailing behind the group of female nursing students, with him dressed identically took some getting used to. He couldn't help but notice the amount of attention the girl's and him were receiving from not just the male patients in particular, but also the male doctors that were floating around. One particular doctor who must've been in his thirties eyed him up lasciviously for several seconds before smiling broadly. It took a moment for him to realise his group had moved on and he had to scurry along the ward to catch up, feeling the man's eyes upon him the entire time.

Far from blending in with the crowd he was beginning to feel like he was a piece of meat in a butchers shop being measured up for the taking. He wondered if the other girls felt the same in their new uniforms, or whether as natural girls they'd grown used to such male attention.

At some point in the afternoon they were told they'd be shadowing established staff for the rest of the day to see how a typical day in the life of a nurse was like. As they passed through one of the wards he was introduced to a couple of nurses in their mid twenties.

'This is Wendy and Jenna, they'll take care of you for the remainder of the day.' The tutor nudged him toward the two nurses that were grinning at him. He had the uncomfortable feeling that they were looking forward to amusing themselves with a fresh student. 'Just follow their instructions and you'll be fine, Dear.'

He watched as the rest of the group wandered off, a slight sinking feeling inside of him.

'Hi, Michelle.' Wendy said, 'It's good to have some help for the day, we're just about to do some patient care.'

He smiled at them nervously as the two nurses exchanged a look.

'We thought we'd start with Mr Greening. He's in a private room and he needs some ... *personal* care.' Said Jenna, appearing to stifle a laugh.

They both linked arms with him and started to question him as to where he was from and how he was finding the nursing school. He answered as best he could, trying not to say anything that would raise any awkward questions. Fortunately it seemed they were less interested in his background and more interested in whether he'd ever worked in a hospital environment before.

'Well, the important thing is to make sure that your patient's needs are always taken care of. They come first, even if it's something you're not used to doing.' Instructed Wendy, 'Remember, a nurse's primary responsibility is the patients day to day care and well being, whatever that entails.'

They led him off the main ward and into a private room where the man was laying asleep in his bed.

'As you can see, Mr Greening has two broken legs so he's unable to do anything for himself.' Said Jenna quietly into his ear. 'He can be a little ... demanding sometimes, but I'm sure he'll be quite happy to have you take care of him. The first thing we need to do is strip him down and give him a wash. We'll take his top half and you can concentrate on his lower half.'

He watched as they woke the man up. He was a handsome man, perhaps in his late thirties. His eyes quickly settled onto Michelle as the two nurses introduced him. Realising they were expecting him to wash a grown man's genitals he baulked at the very idea, but quickly realised this was a task that he would've performed when necessary as a male nurse anyway, he just didn't expect to be doing it in a dress and wearing makeup! He forced himself to approach the bed, catching the man's eye and looking away quickly.

'You can pull the covers down Michelle. You'll find soap and water over there by the basin.' Directed Wendy.

He was soon placing a bowl of warm water next to the man's plastered legs and exposing him below the waist. Something about seeing another man naked whilst dressed as a girl made him feel quite strange about the entire business. He placed a towel underneath the man as he tried to ignore his rather large cock and balls staring up at him. The two girls stood back a little.

'As Mr Greening can manage his top half I think we'll leave you to carry on. We'll be back in a while to check on your progress.' Said Jenna as she leaned into his ear on passing, 'Don't forget.' She whispered, 'You're here to take care of *all* of his needs.'

There was clearly a hidden meaning to the emphasis on "*all*", but he was far too nervous to ask what it was. He suddenly felt abandoned as the two nurses retreated from the room, giving him an encouraging nod as they did so with what could only be described as mischievous grins.

He tentatively began to wash the man as his patient laid back and observed him. As he reached his groin he hesitated before taking hold of the man's penis and beginning to gently bathe him. To his growing horror he realised the patient was getting an erection as he held him between his fingers. At first he was shocked that it was happening before remembering that as far as this red blooded male was concerned, he had an inexperienced young female nurse in the process of manhandling his most intimate of areas.

Trying to ignore the effect he was having on the man he continued as if nothing was wrong, but it was becoming harder and harder to ignore the man's blatant arousal. It was then that he felt a touch from behind as the man placed his hand on Michelle's bottom, stroking him through the stiff cotton of his newly acquired nurse's dress.

'That feels nice, Nurse. I'm afraid it's been a while since I've been able to ... relieve myself. Feel free to help me if you wish.' The man said, his voice croaky with sexual arousal.

'Um ... I ... shouldn't really ... I mean ...' Michelle didn't know what to do as he looked down at the fully erect cock that was sitting proudly in his hand. He wondered if this was a normal part of a nurse's day, being seen as more than just a mere medical person.

'Don't worry, no one else will mind. Just use your hand like a good girl.' The man said, squeezing Michelle's bottom with his strong fingers.

Michelle gasped as he felt himself being touched sexually. Without thinking, his hand gripped the man's phallus tighter, causing him to groan with pleasure as he felt the young nurse beginning to pleasure him. Michelle realised what he'd done and slowly loosened his grip just as the patient lifted his bottom and pushed his cock upward through his fingers. He began to thrust himself up and down as far as he could, masturbating himself with Michelle's hand as the nervous young nurse just gazed down with shock at what his hand appeared to be doing.

'That's it, Nurse. I won't tell your colleagues if you keep going just like that, I promise. Oh, that feels nice.'

Michelle had a vision of being exposed for carrying out a sex act on a male patient and subsequently having his true identity discovered. The consequences were too great to imagine and he whimpered as his hand began to move up and down the man's meaty shaft. He'd never touched another man before and he couldn't help but watch what he was doing with a sense of curiosity.

'Keep going, young lady. Make me cum and I won't tell anyone, I promise.' The man said, his hand massaging Michelle's bottom in return.

It was a confusing moment for Michelle. He'd never had any feelings of being attracted to men before, but something about being dressed as a girl somehow made this feel less ... wrong. He knew he couldn't afford to have this patient telling tales on him, and so he made the decision to get this out of the way just as quickly as possible and do as the man wanted.

He tightened his grip and purposefully set about masturbating the man to an orgasm. He was clearly far more masculine than Michelle himself. His thick veined cock was easily twice his size, making him feel even more feminine in response. He sensed the man's hand working its way down his leg. Stroking his

112

stockinged thigh and beginning to creep up underneath his dress. He used his free hand to pull the man's probing fingers away and with little idea of what else to do, simply placed them back onto his pert bottom once more. The man seemed to understand that this was as far as the young nurse would allow him to go and contented himself with probing the girl's soft bottom cheeks as she used her willing hand upon him.

Michelle peered closely at the shiny bulbous glans as his hand pumped up and down the shaft, seeing a small amount of precum beginning to ooze out. He quickly realised it was now on his fingers and he could feel it's wetness on his hand. He felt his belly flip over at the thought of having another man's cum on his hand. A powerful spasm seemed to pulse through the man's cock and he heard his breathing becoming more rapid, shallower. He knew from his own experiences of masturbating himself in private - which was the only experience he had to draw on - that the man was nearing his climax. He wondered how to deal with it, whether he should find something to catch his cum in or whether to cover him over. In the end he did neither of these in time to avoid having the man cum openly in his hand.

As Mr Greening tensed, half raising himself from the bed he felt his hips buck and his manhood spasm even more forcibly, and then the first load of cum came spewing out of him. It still managed to take Michelle by surprise as his eyes went wide and he gasped aloud. He watched as if in slow motion as the stream of thick cum flew up toward him, before falling back down and landing across the back of his own hand. He could feel its warmth as it began to run down his wrist just as a second load was ejected into the air.

He couldn't take his eyes off the sight of this man's orgasm. The thought that he was directly responsible for making this man cum by his own hand was a bewildering one, yet he couldn't deny the underlying feeling of pleasure that he'd created such arousal in another, regardless of gender.

The patient continued to ejaculate as his orgasm ran its course. Michelle was surprised by the amount of cum now running down over his hand. He gave his shaft a quick squeeze as something he found pleasurable for himself as he'd climaxed, making the man shudder as he emptied the last of his seed onto the young nurse's hand. Michelle stopped moving but kept his fingers wrapped around the cock that was now slowly softening. His eyes didn't want to leave the sight of what he'd done, this rather unconventional and no doubt outlawed act of personal care. He realised he was breathing a little too fast, his own penis partially swollen with an unexplainable arousal of his own.

'That ... that was very nice of you, Nurse. You're a very good girl.' Said Mr Greening as he laid back onto the bed with half closed eyes.

Suddenly aware that he was still standing there holding the man's cum covered cock in his hand with a copious amount of man juice coating his fingers, he pulled himself out of his stupor and began to look around for a way of cleaning the both of them up. It was as he was washing the last of the man's cum from his hand that the two older nurses walked back into the room, smirking.

He looked over at the patient and realised he was still lying there with his now flaccid penis exposed, evidence of his orgasm still glistening across his cock head. As the two nurses peered over, their faces taking on a look of surprise he quickly walked back over to the bed and washed away the evidence of his indiscretion.

'Have you quite finished with Mr Greening, Michelle?' Asked Wendy, her eyes giving away the fact that she knew exactly what'd occurred inside the room a few moments ago.

'Y-Yes, I think so.' Stammered Michelle, his face burning with embarrassment as he avoided any direct eye contact.

They led him out of the room once they'd helped to finish everything up and into a small staff room opposite. He wondered what they were about to say to him, dreading that he'd overstepped the mark with his actions.

'Did you just do what I think you did?' Asked Jenna, trying hard to hold back an excited laugh. He looked at her as noncommittally as he could. 'He always tries it on with the nurses, especially the younger ones. What did he get you to do?'

The two nurses were openly excited by what'd happened in the room between him and their patient. He realised he'd somehow been set up, that they knew exactly what the man was likely to do when left alone with a young female nurse.

'He ... he wanted me to ...'

'Yes? To do what?' Wendy prompted eagerly as he hesitated to tell her.

'To ... give him a ... h-hand job.' He whimpered as he heard his own humiliating confession.

'And you did it?' Jenna looked as though her eyes were about to pop out of her head as she gaped open mouthed at him, laughter threatening to take her. All he could do was nod his head in admission, feeling humiliated by what he'd done.

'Oh my god! We didn't expect you to actually do it.' Exclaimed Wendy. 'You little slut!' She laughed loudly, but something about her expression told him she wasn't angry or disgusted, only amused and at least a little impressed by the fact that this young nurse had gone through with such a thing.

'I think we owe you a drink, Michelle.' Announced Jenna, taking him by surprise by approaching him and pulling him into a tight hug. He didn't feel quite so bad about what he'd done now. At least it was clear that he wasn't to be in any trouble from these two. He sank into the older girl's friendly hug, sensing his own arousal being triggered once more between his legs. It was a good thing that he was wearing pantyhose as well as panties in order to hide his intermittent stirrings.

Chapter 8

By the time he made it back to his room Michelle was a mess of emotions. He still couldn't quite believe that he'd masturbated another man to an orgasm, least of all a patient. The two nurses had clearly decided not to torment him any further after that first incident and they'd had him follow their lead with some fairly mundane tasks afterward.

As he let himself back into the room he immediately spied Tanya draped across her bed, wearing nothing but panties and bra. At the sound of the door opening she looked up from her studying and smiled.

'Don't you look cute in your new uniform?' She said, grinning from ear to ear.

He smiled stiffly, feeling trapped by his roommate's ploy to have him train as a girl. Closing the door behind him he jumped slightly as he noticed Tina standing at the closet doors, clearly in the process of trying on some of her friends clothes. She was in the process of slipping off one of Tanya's dresses. He sat on the edge of his bed, not sure what to do with himself. His instinct was to strip out of the nurses uniform that he still wore, but the presence of the two girl's made him think twice. He tried to avert

116

his eyes from the sight of Lisa's plump bottom as she replaced the dress in the closet, now in just her underwear too.

'I think she's feeling shy about seeing us in our panties.' Said Tanya, an amused look on her face as she studied him from across the room.

'Why? We're all girls here. Aren't we, Michelle?' Tina stepped into the centre of the room as if to torment him further with her scantily clad body.

He tried to look elsewhere but he couldn't seem to stop himself from being drawn back to the two young nurses.

'I hear you frigged Tanya last night, through her panties.' Stated Lisa, watching as he turned beet red at the blatant reminder, and the idea that Tanya had told her friend what they'd done. 'It's okay, no one else needs to know.'

The girl sauntered across the room before sitting down beside him. She placed her hand on his knee, caressing him through the thin pantyhose and causing his cock to jump into life beneath the dress.

'I think it's time you helped me out. Don't you?' She asked. 'I'm in need of a tongue bath, and you're just the nurse to give it to me.'

He turned to look at her in shock, his eyes momentarily drifting down to her body before he forced himself to meet her eyes.

'Wh-What do you mean?' He asked, recent memories of his indiscretions with a certain male patient still running through his mind.

'I mean, I want you to use your tongue on me ... down there.' She flicked her eyes down to her own crotch by way of explanation. 'Have you ever done anything like that with a girl before?'

'Erm ... I ... n-no, I haven't.' He felt himself becoming light headed at the prospect of being made to perform a sex act on his fellow student.

'Well don't just sit there, Nurse Beaufort. Get down between my legs and help me out.' She pouted at him, 'You do want us to be friends, don't you. I'd hate to see you being found out.'

It wasn't entirely clear in his mind whether this was a direct threat or not, but his mind was too focused on the idea of coming face to face with a girl's real life sex to think clearly. He glanced over to Tanya, seeing her eager expression as she waited to see what he'd do.

'Go on, Michelle. If you're going to be a nurse you're going to have to learn about these things.' Said Lisa, spreading her legs wide enough that he could kneel between them.

Feeling as though there was little option but to keep the two girls happy - at least for now - he slowly slid from the bed and onto his knees. He crawled between her legs, his eyes settling between her legs and the cream coloured panties that were covering her sex, a damp spot already evident where he imagined her pussy hole to be. He reached up to take his hat off but was stopped when Lisa leaned forward to take hold of his wrists.

'Leave it on, Michelle. You look sexy in your uniform.' She said.

With trembling hands he reached out to steady himself against her thighs before slowly lowering his face toward her panties. This was as close as he'd ever been to a girl's sex and it was making his head swim. He looked up nervously, wondering exactly what she expected from him. Realising he was unsure of himself, Lisa slid her hands between her legs and took hold of her panties, pulling them aside to reveal her shaved pussy. He drew in a sharp breath and gazed curiously at her bare crotch, his own arousal building quickly at his close proximity to the girl's most private of places.

Lisa's impatience got the better of her as she took hold of his head and pulled him in toward her. He could smell her feminine musk the closer he came, and then he was within an inch of her mound. She paused for a second before pulling his face inward, pressing his mouth and nose into her crotch and gasping as she felt the sexual contact between them.

Michelle opened his mouth on instinct, pushing his tongue in between her lips and tasting her heavenly juices as she moved against him. He couldn't quite believe what he was doing and a vision of what he'd look like to Tanya, kneeling between her friends legs dressed in his female nurses uniform with his tongue lapping at her pussy. It would certainly make for an interesting sight. As if reading his thoughts, he sensed Tanya moving closer to him and then her hands were upon him, pulling his dress upward to reveal his pantied bottom. At first he didn't understand what she

118

was doing, and then he heard the audible click as her camera phone snapped the picture. He tried to cry out in protest but his mouth was full of Tina's pussy. Her juices were beginning to flow in earnest as she ground herself against him.

'Lick my clitty, Michelle, just here.' She directed his tongue upwards until he found her engorged clitoris. She moaned breathlessly as he began to flick it with his tongue, playing with it for all he was worth. His cock was fully engorged inside his panties and pantyhose. He wondered how long he could go without a release, having suffered a prolonged underlying arousal ever since the day before when he'd fingered his roommate to orgasm. He was aware that his bottom was moving of its own accord, wiggling suggestively as he tried to fully take in the taste and smell of Tina's wet pussy.

His face was soon coated in her juices as he slid back down toward her hole. He inserted his tongue as far as it would go before moving it in and out. He ate hungrily from her, losing himself in the moment and quite forgetting the fact that Tanya was watching the entire thing from behind, having already collected photographic evidence of his brazenly sexual act.

His hand drifted along his dress and up between his own legs. Without thinking he started to rub himself there, feeling the sensual touch of the satin panties and smooth nylon pantyhose as he caressed his stiff little cock. He didn't care that Tanya would see what he was doing, he was too busy lapping at her friend's slick pussy to think of anything else except that and his body's sexual response.

'Oh god ... yes!' Moaned Tina in a guttural voice as she pulled him tighter against her. 'I'm going to ... to cum.'

Michelle's entire world was reduced to that tightly confined and sex filled space between Tina's thighs. Nothing else existed for him as he felt the girl tensing her body. He realised through the fog of his own arousal that he was going to experience having a girl cumming against his face for the very first time. His hand paused in mid stroke as Tina thrust herself forward, burying his face into her fleshy wet mound as she climaxed against him.

He drank deeply from her, his tongue coated in her pussy juices and his cheeks and chin slathered in glistening girl cum. He was immersed in the sound, smell and taste of her as she orgasmed forcefully, grunting and groaning as she lost control of her body.

119

As she came down from her climax Michelle gradually pulled away, sitting back on his haunches with his hand still resting between his legs. He was desperate for his own release but now that he was fully aware of where he was he became too self-conscious to continue. He peered up at Tina with a bashful expression as she let out a contented sigh, pulling her panties back across her pussy. She smiled over at Tanya, causing him to turn in time to see her lick her lips with a clearly wanton look on her face. With a cursory glance at Michelle, she moved across the room and sat next to Tina on his bed.

'You can't do Tina and not me, Michelle. That wouldn't be fair at all.' She said, opening her legs to him just as Tina had done a few minutes ago.

Suffering from a rampant arousal of his own as he savoured the taste of Tina's juices in his mouth, Michelle was in no position to argue. He dutifully crawled up between Tanya's legs for a repeat performance. He didn't know how much longer he could go without relieving himself of his pent up feelings, and it was with a vain hope that the two girl's would take pity on him that he lowered his mouth toward his roommate's bared pussy, breathing her in as he remembered the feel of her through her panties and became acutely aware of how he was still wearing this girl's borrowed underwear.

His sexual torments at the hands of these student nurses was clearly not about to stop, and his unplanned journey into the world of female nursing was taking on an ever more sexual course into the unknown. He wondered what they'd say and do if they knew just what he'd allowed himself to be duped into doing with his male patient, and whether that would lead to an even more debauched existence for him as a female nursing student.

For now it was enough to gaze greedily in between Tanya's thighs, seeing her uncovering her moist pussy with a clear invite to partake of her feminine nectar. It wasn't what he'd expected upon his return to the room, but he was in no position to complain - nor did his body want him to.

Chapter 9

Michelle suffered the torment from his chronic state of arousal for the rest of the night. When he awoke the following morning it was with a stiffness between his legs that was made even worse as he ran his hands down Tanya's nightdress and panties. He peeked over toward her side of the room, wondering whether she'd notice if he were to relieve himself under the bed clothes. The thought that he might be caught out by her seeing his soiled sheets caused him to fight his urges and by the time he was starting to gently stroke himself through her panties, Tanya was waking up.

It was as if he was in a kind of a fog, with his pent up arousal and the constant stimulation of being dressed as a girl turning everything into an erotic experience. He spent that morning dressed from head to toe in Tanya's clothes once more, however, she'd insisted that he wear her soiled panties from the day before, having noticed his semi-erect state just as soon as he'd crawled out from the bed.

'You're obviously enjoying my underwear far too much. I'm not having you dirty my clean panties if you can't control yourself.' She said, throwing him her still damp underwear from across the room.

That afternoon he was due to join his classmates in full uniform to meet with some of the doctors. He was beginning to feel more comfortable with being one of the girls, as no one had shown any signs of realising his true gender. In fact, they'd been nothing but welcoming to the shy girl at the back of the class. Tagging along behind them he was soon joined by Keelee who'd taken it upon herself to befriend him.

'I can't wait to meet some of the doctors. Jennifer says that one of them is really good looking. She says that we'll be split into pairs so that we can watch them work. I hope we get a good looking one, don't you?' She rambled on excitedly, clearly expecting him to show a similar level of enthusiasm.

'Oh yes, I hope so.' He said, trying to sound even half as keen as she was. She was a nice girl and he couldn't help but like her. He wished in a way that she knew the truth, but there was no way he could risk telling anyone, not yet at least.

He was taken by surprise as the girl linked arms with him as she continued to chat away, merrily following on behind the main group. They were soon gathered inside a treatment room off one of the main wards, waiting expectantly for their doctors. When eventually three young junior doctors walked in, their entrance was met with several gasps of approval from the young female students.

Michelle tried to see what had them all so excited and as he perused the three men he had to admit that at least one of them would be considered rather good looking. His swept back blond hair and blue eyes seemed to fit perfectly with his six foot two inch frame. His eyes roamed around the room at the gathering of young girls, studying each in turn. Michelle barely heard what the tutor was saying as he waited with bated breath as the man's eyes made their way toward him. As their eyes met Michelle wanted to turn away, to break their connection but something about the man's gaze held him fast. It was only as he sensed a movement beside him as Keelee once again took hold of his arm, that his focus shifted and he realised his new friend was speaking.

'... be a pair, Miss.' The girl said.

He looked about himself in confusion for a moment before understanding that they'd split into pairs and Keelee had claimed him as her partner. His stomach did a somersault as he realised he'd probably given entirely the wrong signals to this doctor, who was now observing the tutor as she organised her group of girls.

As he continued to watch - wondering quite what he'd missed - he saw the first two doctors peer around the various partnerships and choose one couple each. He heard Keelee saying what sounded like a little prayer from beside him, wishing to be picked by the blond medic who'd stepped forward to make his choice. He seemed to peruse his options for a second, but it came as no surprise when the man looked straight at him and pointed.

'I'll take those two for my first pair.' He said, smiling politely. 'They look keen to get started.'

Michelle glanced around at Keelee to see her face positively light up when her wish was answered. He'd no idea what they were about to do with this doctor, but when the man beckoned to the pair of them with a sly smile, he had the uncomfortable feeling that the man had more than just medical training on his mind. He followed Keelee as she practically skipped across the room.

'Apparently he has a bad reputation for liking the student nurses!' Said Keelee, sounding excited by the prospect of being placed in is hands.

'You know him?' He whispered back as they squeezed between the other chosen pairs.

'Know him? It's Dr Lydon, you know - Dr Lie Down?' She looked at him as if in shock that he'd never heard of the man. 'He's only the most good looking doctor in the hospital. You wait, everyone's going to be so jealous of us.'

Their conversation was halted abruptly as they approached the man. He smiled down at them before standing aside.

'After you, ladies.' He said, gesturing toward the door he'd entered through.

Michelle could almost feel the man's eyes upon him as he followed Keelee out of the room. He thought he felt something brush against his bottom as he passed by the man, but a quick look over his shoulder only succeeded in catching Dr Lydon's eye once more, which only served to deepen the feeling that he was transmitting all of the wrong signals. There was an unusual atmosphere between the doctor, Keelee and Michelle. It felt as though there was something in the air, making him feel tense and uncertain. They were led across the hospital, eventually arriving at the man's private office.

There were few people about as they entered the room, with Michelle trying to avoid stepping too close to the man as he held the door open for his young uniformed charges. He stood next to Keelee, feeling like a schoolgirl having been summoned into a teacher's office. He peered down at his white nurse's dress and stockinged legs, knowing that this man had no idea of his true identity or indeed gender. He wondered what he'd make of it if he were to find out. He couldn't allow that to happen and decided to deflect any suspicion by going along with whatever he was supposed to do.

Dr Lydon closed the door behind them before turning to face the two young nurses. 'I thought we'd start with some basic examination techniques before we head out onto my rounds. Have you been taught any methods for examining patients yet, girls?'

Michelle looked at Keelee before shaking his head nervously. He could tell by Keelee's expression that she was looking forward to some close tuition.

'Well, let's run through a basic exam then, shall we?' Dr Lydon grinned, clearly pleased that he was able to move ahead as intended. He talked for a few brief minutes about basic observations of patients before moving to his desk and picking up a stethoscope. 'Now, let's see if we can pick up a heart beat, shall we?'

Keelee took a half a step forward. 'You can listen to mine if you like, Doctor?' She said, her eyes wide with anticipation.

'Alright then, Keelee is it? As you seem to be quite keen. I'll need to expose your chest a little I'm afraid. These nurses uniforms can be a little too thick to hear anything properly.' He moved across the room to stand directly in front of the girl. There was a pause as he looked Keelee directly in the eyes, having a visible effect on her demeanour. 'May I?' He asked, reaching out to take a hold of her dress and slowly unzip her uniform at the front.

Michelle was rooted to the spot. He watched as if mesmerised as Keelee's bra covered breasts came into view as her dress gapped open at the front. The next thought that ran through his head which quite took him by surprise, was that her bra was a delicate pink colour that he wouldn't mind wearing himself. He had to mentally shake himself before realising that this letch of a man would be wanting to carry out the same exam on him.

'Beautiful.' Said Dr Lydon, admiring the girl's plump milky white breasts. 'This may be a little cold.' He warned her as he breathed onto the metal end of the stethoscope, before gently placing it between her mounds.

Keelee breathed in sharply at the contact and so did Michelle. He watched with fascination as the man gently probed her chest whilst he supposedly searched for her heart beat.

'Your heart seems to be beating a little fast, but I'm quite happy it's perfectly healthy. Whilst I have you here, why don't we review the basic breast exam techniques?' He said, his eyes giving away his arousal as he gazed down at Keelee's bared chest. His hand stayed where it was, nestled against her right mound.

Keelee nodded as if unable to speak, her breathing rapid. Michelle couldn't look away as the doctor helped Keelee to free first one and then the other breast from her bra cups. His hand slid underneath her pert mound as his thumb brushed against her erect nipple. He began to explain what to look for during an exam, but the way his hands were caressing her flesh he wasn't convinced that this doctor was looking for anything in particular.

'Why don't you copy me, Michelle, and examine Keelee's other breast. I'm sure she won't mind.' The man looked at Keelee for her agreement but Michelle knew she wasn't about to disagree with anything this man said.

He hesitated, his eyes fixed on the sight of Keelee's young breasts. He knew this wasn't right. That this doctor was taking advantage of the two girls in his charge, but he felt unable to protest given his precarious position. Keelee smiled at him, nodding almost imperceptibly as if to give him permission to do as instructed. He moved closer before raising his hands. He held his breath as he gently cupped her warm breast, trying to copy what the doctor was doing but becoming quickly distracted by Keelee's stiff nipple.

'That's right, Michelle, gently squeeze your friend's breast and check if there's anything unusual to be found.'

Michelle noticed the man watching what he was doing, giving the firm impression that he was becoming more aroused by seeing this young female nurse massaging her classmate's bare tittie. He soon realised that his own actions were having a similar effect on himself as his cock began to swell inside of his borrowed panties. A touch from behind made him flinch as he felt the man's free hand on his bottom, stroking him through his uniform.

'You know, it's surprising how much more sensitive your tongue can be as compared to your fingers. Why don't you try using that on young Keelee here, see how much better that is?' The man squeezed Michelle's bottom bringing a little gasp from his lips.

Michelle was trapped in the midst of a situation that he felt obliged to see through, unwilling to risk exposing himself as anything less than an eager young female nurse. Keelee was looking at the doctor with misty eyes, clearly unconcerned by what her friend had been asked to do. He tried to tell himself that he was only doing this in order to keep up his pretence, but the stirring between his legs claimed otherwise as he lowered his head toward Keeley's left nipple.

He'd never handled a girl's breasts, let alone used his mouth on one. It was another first for him since joining the hospital. He flicked his tongue across her erect nipple as if to test her reaction. Hearing her gasp with pleasure he decided to take it further. Opening his lips he sucked her soft flesh into his mouth and felt himself grow light headed with desire as he began to suckle on his classmate. It took a while for him to realise that Dr Lydon was no longer caressing Keelee's other breast. Instead he was standing slightly further away, one hand kneading Michelle's bottom with his other snaking around his waist. He knew the man was about to move higher, intent on touching his breasts. He realised the man wouldn't need to be a doctor to tell that his breasts weren't real, that two pairs of rolled up pantyhose would offer a poor imitation of a girl's natural breast such as the one he was now busily sucking and licking upon. He needed a distraction. A way of diverting this man's attention away from his body. One that would occupy his mind fully enough that any suspicions would be allayed.

A thought came to mind that instantly made him take a mental step backward, but the continuing attentions of this man's hands and the sure knowledge that he was seconds from discovery left him little choice but to act on his one and only plan. He lifted his mouth from the soft milky flesh of Keelee's breast and reluctantly turned himself around, taking a hold of the man's hands and fixing him with a sultry look. It was time to convince this man just how much of a girl he was.

REBECCA STERNE -- TURNED INTO GIRLS!

Chapter 10

Dr Lydon looked at Michelle with surprise as he turned to face him, pulling the man's hand away from his chest.

'Doctor,' He began, not entirely sure of what he was going to say but knowing he needed to act quickly. 'I was wondering, are there any other types of examination we can try? I mean similar ones, possibly on you?'

'You ... you want to examine me?' Said Dr Lydon, an uncertain smile appearing on his face. 'With your mouth? Well, I can think of one but I wouldn't normally expect something like that so quickly. Of course, if it's what you want, young nurse?'

'Oh, yes ... please?' He said, realising he'd successfully managed to divert this man's attention elsewhere.

Dr Lydon was grinning from ear to ear as his hands dropped down and he began to unbuckle his belt. It wasn't until his clothing hit the floor and Michelle looked down to see the man's rampant arousal pushing against the front of his undershorts that he suddenly realised what he'd led this man to believe. He watched with absolute horror as he pulled his shorts down, revealing his large stiff cock standing rigidly to attention and twitching with the anticipation of having this young nurse going down on him.

'Maybe Keelee would like to help you with your first ... exam?' He suggested breathlessly.

Keelee was quick to step up to his side, and with a look of total amazement she slowly went down onto her knees in front of the man's erection, looking back up to Michelle as if to urge him to do the same. As if in a dream he found himself kneeling down next to her, watching as his friend wrapped her fingers around the thick shaft and began to move them up and down.

'You can go first if you like.' Said Keelee, her eyes fixed squarely on the shiny bulbous end of this handsome doctor's cock.

'I ... um ...' Michelle wanted to say that he'd never done this before, that he hadn't quite meant this when he'd asked to carry out a different exam, but his words died in his throat as memories of masturbating a male patient to orgasm floated back up to him. He realised that his own arousal hadn't diminished, if anything he'd continued to grow even more aroused by what was now happening. Swallowing his nerves he decided not to think about what he was about to do, other than to remind himself of how he was simply protecting his secret before leaning forward with his tongue out.

As he came into contact with his first penis, much to his surprise he didn't feel repelled by the sensation. He experimented by licking around the glans, then slowly wrapping his tongue around the shaft as Keelee continued to massage her hand up and down.

'Oh yes, that's nice. You're a good nurse, Michelle.' Moaned Dr Lydon from up above.

It seemed as though some innate inbuilt instinct took over as he opened his mouth wide, taking the man's head inside of him and sucking it in - much as he'd done with Keelee's breast. It was an entirely different sensation, having a hard cock in his mouth but he continued to suck on it, hoping to have him climax quickly in order to bring the situation to an end.

'My turn, Michelle. We're doing this together, remember.'

He opened his eyes to see Keelee looking at him expectantly. He pulled back, giving her a chance to taste the man's meat and watched closely as she began to suck and lick on him greedily. He could feel himself at full arousal inside of his panties and wished he could have Keelee doing the same to him, but he knew this was not to be, at least not now.

They started to take turns with the man's phallus. Whilst one sucked and licked, the other stroked and caressed. They even began to lick up and down the man's shaft at the same time, touching tongues and sharing themselves orally with each other at the same time as working the man toward a climax.

Michelle lost track of time after a while, amazing himself with what he was now doing. He'd never dreamt of doing anything like this in his life, let alone dressed as a female nurse. A sudden spasm of the man's cock and a thrust of his hips alerted Michelle to the fact that this man was about to cum. He'd just placed his mouth over his cock head when he felt a pair of hands on his head, pulling him further in and forcing him to take the man deep into his mouth. His eyes grew wide with fear as he realised he was about to have a man cum into his mouth.

Keelee seemed excited by the prospect of experiencing the results to their joint efforts. She squeezed the man's balls and increased the speed of her fingers as she pumped his shaft furiously. There was little doubt that her efforts would bring the man to his peak that much sooner.

Michelle was doubting whether he wanted this to happen. He hadn't really intended for this but somehow he seemed to have an ability to escalate a situation until he found himself in the most surreal of positions. He felt another spasm as the rigid cock was thrust even further into his mouth, almost making him gag. He placed his hands against the man's thighs, intending to push himself away and avoid what was about to happen in a last moment panic, but it was too late. Dr Lydon bucked and writhed against him, holding his head fast as his orgasm exploded inside of Michelle's mouth.

Michelle felt the first powerful stream of cum being ejaculated onto his tongue and toward the back of his throat. He grunted with surprise a second then a third jet of thick man juice began to fill his mouth. With no other choice he forcibly swallowed it down, just as another load was pumped into him. He could taste the salty tang of male cum for the first time. His tongue and mouth were coated in the warm gooey liquid and he was swallowing it down just as fast as he could for fear of choking. As the man's orgasm began to wane the last of his cum was squeezed out. Michelle was breathing hard through his nose with his mouth full to bursting with man meat.

He felt a wave of relief wash over him as he realised the doctor's climax had passed. As the man's hands left his head he pulled back, sucking off the remnants of cum from the still impressively sized yet gradually softening manhood. He felt like a pure slut. His face was glowing with embarrassment at what he'd done. Despite the man's lecherous behaviour towards two young female nurses, it was impossible to entirely divorce himself of blame. He could've extricated himself from the situation without going as far as sucking the man off and he'd no idea why he hadn't.

There was a strange feeling in the air as he pushed himself to his feet. Keelee covered up her breasts and zipped herself back into her dress.

'That was very good, girls. We'd better head out for some doctor's rounds now, but I look forward to giving you additional tuition in the future.'

The man patted them both on the bottom as they finally left his room. Keelee was grinning happily, but Michelle was experiencing some confusing thoughts and feelings as to what had just happened, and indeed over his entire experience as a student nurse so far. It was as if he were turning into a different person, a different gender, a different sexuality even.

-o0o-

By the time Michelle returned to the nurse's accommodation he'd had plenty of time to consider what'd happened between him, Keelee and Dr Lydon. He couldn't help but wonder how different his experience would've been had he been able to enter the nursing school as a boy. He needed to talk about what'd happened and so it was with Tanya that he confessed his indiscretions.

'So let me get this straight.' Tanya was looking more than a little shocked at the revelation that he'd performed oral sex on a male doctor. 'To stop him from touching your fake titties, you decided to distract him by sucking on his cock?'

'No ... well, not exactly. It wasn't really my idea to ... *suck* him off.' Saying the actual words again brought it home to him just how deep his deception had become. 'He just thought that's what I meant.'

'But you didn't say no?'

'I didn't know what else to do!'

'You could've just stopped him. Are you sure you didn't really want to. I mean, not only did you suck on your classmate's titties, but then you went down on the doctor *and* swallowed. It seems a little too much if you didn't really want to. You said it yourself that he didn't actually force you into anything.'

Michelle opened his mouth to refute what she was saying, but a dawning realisation that he could've just avoided the entire episode and the fact that he hadn't was now playing on his mind.

'I ... I didn't want him to know I don't have breasts!' He finally blurted out in self-defence.

Tanya seemed to take a moment to think about this last statement before responding.

'We could do something about that, I suppose. I know someone who works in the endocrinology department, I bet she could help us out.'

'The *what* department?' Michelle looked at her questioningly. He'd no idea what she had in mind, but he guessed if it helped avoid discovery it was worth a go.

-o0o-

Two days later Tanya came into the room just as Michelle was preparing to go to bed with an excited look on her face.

'She did it! Here, this should make a big difference.' She held out a bag of white tablets and a large pot of cream. 'You can put the cream on twice a day and take the pills at the same time. It'll take a while to get started but she says it's a new formula or something that they've been working on.'

Michelle took the bag of pills and cream from her feeling somewhat confused. There was nothing to say exactly what any of it was for.

'Go on, take a pill and rub the cream over your chest.' Tanya moved closer and without asking pulled the straps of his borrowed nightdress down revealing his bare chest. 'It'll be pretty cool if you can grow some little titties of your own.'

'WHAT? Grow my own breasts! I can't do that, I'm a boy.' He stammered. A picture of him sporting a pair of young girl's breasts flashed through his mind.

'Why not? You're sharing a room with me - *as a girl.*' She pointed out, her hands on her hips as she gave him a stern look. 'You're wearing *my* clothes most of the time, and the only clothes you have of your own are your nurse's uniform - which is a *girl's*! How much more of a girl can you be without actually having titties?'

'I ... um ...' He didn't have an answer. His entire life had turned into that of a girl. The thought of being found out and summarily thrown out of the hospital in the most publicly humiliating of ways was not a happy one, neither was the thought of his family finding out what he'd done.

'Come on, Michelle.' Tanya's tone changed as she saw the defeat in his eyes. 'No one has to know except us. It'll actually make it *less* likely that someone will find out the truth. So in a way it'll be safer for you, don't you think?'

'I ... suppose, in a way.' There was no denying the logic that growing breasts would make him a more convincing girl.

'Go on then, take the pill and I'll rub some cream on your chest.'

She took the pot of cream and dipped her fingers into it, pulling out a generous amount as she watched him pop one of the pills into his mouth. She smiled victoriously as he bent to her will, stifling a giggle as she began to rub the cream across Michelle's flat boy chest.

Chapter 11

For the next two weeks Michelle did his best to avoid any contact with Dr Lydon. He bumped into him on more than one occasion but was able to get away before the man had a chance to attempt another seduction. The look of lust in the man's eyes whenever he saw his favourite student nurse was a certain indication that he wanted nothing more than to try his luck again.

At first Michelle was sceptical of the effects of the pills and the cream that he was being coerced into using. He wasn't sure that he was too disappointed by this, uncertain of whether growing girl breasts was something that he wanted. The training had become the main focus of his new life as a nurse and on some days he could almost forget that he was really a boy, or at least that he was pretending to be someone other than who he really was.

It was as he was pulling on the latest pair of Tanya's panties that she'd lent him - worn just the day before by her, of course - that he caught sight of himself in the mirror and realised for the first time that his body was changing shape. His hips had become a little more pronounced, with his bottom appearing more girlish. The biggest surprise to him was when he noticed that his chest was starting to develop. His nipples had begun to grow in size and there was an obvious growth in breast tissue. If he'd ever seen a young teenage girl's developing chest he fancied that this is what it'd look like.

He was mesmerised by his own reflection for a time, standing naked apart from his panties, staring up and down at his girlish image. He knew now that his scepticism of the hormone treatment he'd been undergoing was misplaced. It was a startling revelation to realise that apart from his male cock and balls, he was taking on the physical appearance of a girl. He was so immersed in his own thoughts and feelings that he completely failed to hear his roommate and her friend entering the room.

'Ooh look, Lisa. Michelle's got little titties!' Tanya announced excitedly as she realised what he was looking at with such evident amazement.

Michelle spun around, immediately covering up his budding breasts as he felt his emotions taking over.

'What have you done?' He cried. 'I'm turning into a girl.'

'Not everywhere silly. Look, you're little peenie's still there.' Said Tina, pointing between his legs at the unexpected bulge in his panties. 'I think you like having titties really.'

'Don't look so worried, Michelle. You look lovely!' Said Tanya, approaching him. She pulled his hands away and admired his barely budding breasts for a moment. 'Can I touch them?' She didn't wait for an answer, instead she placed her hands on either side of his chest and gave his tiny mounds an affectionate squeeze. 'They're coming on very nicely, Michelle.'

'Maybe it's time you became a real girl.' Said Tina, giving Tanya a mischievous look. Seeing her friend looking confused she leaned over and whispered something into her ear.

'Alright, I'll help her get ready.' Said Tanya.

He looked from one girl to another before seeing Tina leave the room with an eager look on her face.

'I think you should get changed into something different. We're going to have a little party to celebrate your ... coming of age - as a girl!' Said Tanya. 'Take off my nightdress and panties and I'll give you something else to wear.'

He was about to refuse. To tell her that he just wanted to get into bed but he knew he was under her control, that there was nothing he could do that would not result in the ultimate of humiliating discoveries. Slipping off the nightdress he once again looked down at his budding little breasts, unable to deny a surge of pride of how feminine he was now looking. This only served to confuse his state of mind even further as he drew Tanya's panties down his legs, still conscious of being naked in her presence as he covered himself with his hands.

Tanya had been busily looking through her underwear drawer before pulling out several items. She turned back to him and held out a pair of sheer white panties for him to put on.

'These first.' She said. 'I'll help you with your bra.'

He knew the panties left little to the imagination and he hoped whatever he'd be wearing over the top would offer more dignity. He gasped as Tanya then picked up a garter belt that matched his existing lingerie. He stood passively in place as she wrapped it around his waist before retrieving a pair of white nylon stockings. He obediently sat down on the bed in order to roll them up his legs, feeling the soft touch of the material beginning to have its usual effect between his legs. Tanya was quick to help him fasten the garter straps onto the stocking tops before standing back and admiring him.

'You really do make a very cute girl you know?' She said, her eyes drifting down to between his legs where he'd quite forgotten how exposed he was in the sheer fronted panties. 'Even your little dickie looks quite girlie somehow.'

He followed her gaze and saw how his cock was stiffening under her scrutiny. It was as if he'd been conditioned to respond to entirely different stimuli since being inducted as a girl. Just then the door was practically flung open and Tina burst into the room, closely followed by Phillipa her roommate. He was acutely aware that he was the only one in the room wearing nothing but underwear, and not just underwear but a set of sexy looking lingerie. It was then that he looked down and saw what Tina was holding in her hand.

'What's that for?' He asked nervously.

Tina held up the penis shaped dildo that was held securely in a kind of harness.

'What do you think, silly. It's time you found out what it's like to have sex like a girl.' She said as if stating the obvious. 'Now that you *are* one.'

He could feel all three girls studying him closely from head to foot. He felt trapped, vulnerable and entirely at their mercy.

Then Tanya began to slowly take off her clothes, closely followed by the others. They were soon down to their underwear. Not as blatantly sexual as his, but just their bra and panties at least. As Tina stepped into the harness and pulled the dildo up between her legs, he swallowed anxiously as he realised exactly what this girl intended to do with him. Tanya and Phillipa were quickly at his sides, their hands running up and down his body, distracting his mind from what lay ahead as his arousal grew at their touch.

Then he was kissing Tanya, her mouth open, her tongue probing. Her hands were stroking him, first his pert little panty clad bottom and then his small mounds through the soft lacy bra. Phillipa too had her hands upon him. She pulled one of the bra cups down to expose his puffy nipple and sucked it into her mouth, bringing a surprised gasp from him as he felt himself being touched in all of his most intimate of places. Someone's hand was between his legs, pulling his own hands away to expose him to their touch. They cupped his sex, squeezing him gently as he grew stiff with desire. His mind was still resisting somehow, unwilling to succumb to their control, to give up his true gender, and yet he already knew he was losing the fight both physically and mentally.

They manoeuvred him to the side of the bed before forcing him down between them. Tanya had taken out her own breasts and was pressing a nipple into his mouth, forcing him to suckle upon her teat. He felt his hand being pulled between Phillipa's legs as she pushed her panties aside and had him finger her already wet pussy. His mind was being overwhelmed with sexual stimuli. He could barely focus on where their hands were or even where his own were. It was as if he'd been swamped in a deluge of femininity and sexuality. As they pushed him onto his back and positioned him at the end of the bed he tried to lift his head to see what was going on, but Tanya's leg appeared above him and then she was lowering her bare sex down onto his face, forcing him to taste her sopping wet pussy as she ground herself against his mouth.

It came as a shock to his system when he felt his panties being pulled aside and the weight of another girl sitting astride him. Her fingers were then wrapped around his stiff little shaft, stroking him up and down as his arousal built swiftly. As his legs were splayed apart he sensed the third girl moving in between his thighs. It took a moment to understand the significance, but the feeling of her fingers between his cheeks, exploring his virgin rosebud as she lubricated his tight little hole was enough to remind him of the strap-on dildo that Tina was wearing, and the sure knowledge of where she intended to put it.

He tried to say something, to tell them to stop but his mouth was muffled by Tanya's sex, her pussy juices flowing onto his tongue and down his chin as he tried unsuccessfully to speak. He attempted to shift his position but Phillipa's weight was also holding him down. There was a weakness inside of him as a result of the girl's continuing masturbation that left him incapable of any real fight.

The dildo was then being pressed up against him, searching for his entrance and the ultimate emancipation of his former boyhood. He could feel a pressure, the head of the penis shaped dildo beginning to force his rosebud open and then it was pushing its way inside of him. He groaned into Tanya's wet pussy hole as he felt himself being penetrated for the first time in his life. It burned as it entered but the constant stimulation from the other two girls meant that his mind was unable to focus fully on the sensation of having a fake penis entering him. It seemed to slide in a long way before pausing, withdrawing a little way and then starting its journey inside of him once more as Tina slowly fucked him like a girl.

After a short while the burning sensation subsided and he was left to contemplate the fullness inside of him. He was no longer in control of his body, his mind or his destiny. It was as if he'd finally capitulated in the face of overwhelming odds, giving up his masculinity for the life of a female nursing student and the sexual plaything of his fellow students. He could feel a powerful arousal building from deep within him, different to anything he'd experienced before. He could feel Tanya's body beginning to tense as he plunged his tongue inside of her, tasting her sex and smelling her feminine arousal all about him. He could feel Phillipa's mouth upon him, sucking him toward an orgasm that was fast being overtaken by something bigger, more primal even.

It felt as though he was the centre of a writhing, moaning sexual coming together. Tanya spasmed against him, crying out as her orgasm broke. She pulled his head up into her, squeezing her juices out to be lapped up and swallowed by the former boy beneath her. Almost in tandem he could feel his balls tightening, causing him to clamp down on the dildo that still filled him to bursting. His climax rushed forward, starting deep down within and racing to the surface as he felt his entire body tense. He was caught in a limbo for what seemed an age, on the peak of a powerful orgasm before his cock jumped and he began to pump cum into Phillipa's warm receptive mouth.

His climax seemed to last a long time as he became lost in a world of bucking, squirting sexual highs. He felt Tina thrust into him one final time, causing him to empty himself of the last of his hot sticky seed. He spasmed and squirmed intermittently at every touch as he slowly came back down to earth from what had been the most all consuming experience of his existence.

The presence of the dildo inside of him, filling him up and stretching him apart became far more apparent as first Tanya and then Phillipa eased themselves off of him. By the look on Phillipa's face she'd reached her own climax, but whether this was by her own hand or someone else's he couldn't be sure. He began to whimper at the sensation of being impaled on the rubber cock. As Tina gradually pulled it free of him he felt it leave his body and gasped breathlessly at the sensation of being emptied. It was a strange feeling that followed, as he was both relieved to no longer have Tina's dildo penetrating him, but at the same time feeling empty as a result.

It took a long time before he could look any of the girls in the eye, and only then did he truly realise what had just happened and how this was now a point of no return for him. He knew there was no longer any escape from his new life as a girl. Not just a girl, but a female nurse and everything that that would entail.

Chapter 12

Michelle's deflowering at the hands of his roommate and her friends felt like crossing a gender divide. He couldn't get his mind off the feeling of being taken by another in such a dominant way. Tanya took to using him to pleasure herself whenever the fancy took her - which was most nights. More often than not he would be left in a state of painful arousal as she sated herself at his expense. This ongoing state of mind was only making matters worse for him as he went about his new life as a student nurse.

Nearly a week passed before he once again crossed paths with Dr Lydon, and the man had clearly not forgotten him. He was assisting Keelee as they were busily helping out on one of the wards. They'd just began their break and were taking a few minutes to relax in private. There'd been little spoken between them about what happened between them and Dr Lydon. Keelee seemed almost as embarrassed by the event as he was, but she couldn't quite conceal her pleasure at having been so intimate with the man. Apparently he was considered quite the catch by most of the female nurses.

'Michelle, Keelee!' Said Dr Lydon as he entered the small office behind the nurse's station. 'I've been hoping to catch up with the pair of you. I think we need to clarify our previous session together, just so there's no misunderstandings.'

Michelle was startled by the intrusion and looked around at Keelee in surprise. Keelee's eyes lit up at the sight of the man, clearly more pleased then he was by Dr Lydon's unexpected entrance. He gazed passed the man toward the door that was still slightly open until the man pushed it closed, flicking the lock across so they wouldn't be disturbed. Michelle swallowed nervously, wondering how he could get himself out of the situation. He didn't know if this man had any intention to continue their intimate tryst, but from the look in his eye it seemed more than likely he wasn't just interested in holding an innocent conversation.

'What misunderstanding, Doctor?' Asked Keelee, visibly melting at the sight of the man. 'I thought we understood each other quite well.'

Dr Lydon considered her for a moment. If he'd intended anything other than a sexual rendezvous when he walked through the door it'd clearly been superseded by Keelee's brazen flirting. A smile slowly spread across his face as he peered over his shoulder at the locked door. Something in his expression told Michelle that the man was wondering how sound proof the room would be and how likely it was he could get away with some personal time with these two young nurses. As he turned back toward Michelle and Keelee the grin gave away his conclusion.

'Can we ... um ... *help* you with something, Doctor?' Asked Keelee.

Michelle was feeling a powerful sense of deja vu, his knees suddenly felt weak. He shifted his weight and became acutely aware of how his pantyhose brushed together. He looked down at his feminine nurse's uniform, reminding him of the fact that he was still in borrowed panties and bra. He knew this man had no idea of his true gender still, why would he? After all, he was perfectly convincing as a girl and had only reinforced the man's opinion of him by sucking him off as if he were a young impressionable girl especially eager to please the handsome doctor.

Keelee stepped forward, keen to take control of the situation. She wrapped her arms around the man's neck and planted a kiss on his lips. Dr Lydon was soon joining in, kissing her back ever more deeply before apparently remembering the second young nurse standing nearby. Looking up he reached out with one hand and grabbed Michelle around the waist, pulling him into their three way embrace and pressing his lips against him. Michelle half opened his mouth to protest, to say that he didn't want to do this any more but he only succeeded in allowing the man's tongue to search out his own, stifling any words as he felt himself being pulled tightly against the pair of them.

When the man broke away he smiled at Keelee. Michelle missed the subtle communication that passed between him and Keeley and was taken by surprise once more as Keelee turned her head and covered his mouth with hers. He was taken aback, almost as though he were sharing an unexpected lesbian kiss before something in the back of his mind reminded him that he was in fact still a boy underneath. He kissed her back, delighting in her touch and the way she looked him in the eyes as their tongues battled sensually with one another's. He felt his arousal being brought to life. It was as if it were present just under the surface the entire time, needing little in the way of stimulation to release it. His little boy cock twitched inside of his panties, making him even more aware of what he was wearing which only increased the effect.

He sensed the doctor's hand sliding down his back to cup his bottom, squeezing both girls cheeks and pulling them into him as they each gasped at his firm touch. Michelle knew he was once more in danger of being inadvertently discovered by this man's wandering hands as he grew ever more stiff between the legs. He managed to force one hand in between him and Dr Lydon, attempting to push himself away but only succeeding in pressing his fingers into the man's crotch, feeling the doctor's erect manhood and causing the man to push his hips forward, embracing the touch of the nurse's slender fingers. Michelle squealed with a mixture of frustration and dismay at his inadvertent touching of the man's sex.

'I must have one of you ... right now!' Dr Lydon spoke in a low almost animalistic voice. He was hoarse with naked desire as he watched them continue to kiss each other.

Keelee broke away first, leaving Michelle feeling breathless and dumbfounded at how he'd managed to once again give off all of the wrong signals. He was beginning to wonder whether on a sub-conscious level he actually wanted all of this more than he realised. The attention that he was receiving as a girl was far more than anything he'd ever experienced as a boy and it was becoming intoxicating.

A tension settled over the room as all three paused for a moment. The man's hands started to roam back up the girls' bodies. He cupped Keelee's breast, causing a moment of panic in Michelle. He took the man's hand and quickly pulled it away. As Dr Lydon looked him in the eye Michelle's only response was to smile nervously, giving his hand a little squeeze as he tried to decide what to do now.

Dr Lydon smiled back and nodded. 'Alright, Michelle.' He said, turning toward Keelee. 'But I'd like to give you a nice oral exam at the same time, if that's okay with you?'

Both Michelle and Keelee looked confused for a moment before Keelee shrugged happily. She reached up underneath her dress and pulled down her panties and pantyhose in one motion, kicking off her shoes and stepping out of them as she prepared herself to be orally pleasured. She looked over at the nearby couch.

'Would you like to lay on the couch, Dr Lydon?' She said.

'Indeed I would, Keelee.'

The man stepped across the small office and unbuckled his belt before stepping out of his own clothes. Michelle couldn't help but whimper as the man's fully erect penis dropped heavily forward as it was released. His eyes were transfixed by its bulbous end and veined shaft. He was unable to avoid a natural comparison to his own rather puny looking cock. Once more he felt his diminishing manhood being swept away in the face of someone so evidently more masculine than himself.

As the doctor lay back onto the couch, watching the two young nurses expectantly, Keelee approached where his head lay and glanced back at Michelle. Her eyes tracked towards the man's exposed phallus before giving him a meaningful look. It seemed clear what was expected of him. He'd managed to give the impression that he'd volunteered to be taken by this man whilst his friend was serviced orally.

As he tried to think of what to do he automatically began to pull down his pantyhose, careful not to display himself as he lifted his dress upward to take a hold of his roommate's nylon hosiery. As he tugged them off his feet he watched as Keelee began to straddle the man's face and realised that she'd be facing away from him. With her crotch covering the doctor's mouth he'd have no way of seeing Michelle, only feeling him. The memory of having a penis shaped dildo being thrust into him flashed before his eyes and he realised there was a way of supposedly giving this man what he wanted, although he was not entirely convinced he wouldn't give himself away.

Feeling somewhat astonished at his own actions he sidled over to the couch as Keelee began to lower herself onto the man's face. He could see Dr Lydon's tongue poking out, eager to taste this girl's pussy. Feeling ever more self-conscious and uncertain of why he was in fact going along with the man's request, he lifted his leg and began to straddle the man's naked sex. He made sure his dress still covered him as he licked his fingers and slid them into his panties, wetting his rosebud that was already spasming as if wanting this more than he knew.

Taking hold of the man's thick hard cock, he began to pump his free hand up and down bringing a moan of pleasure from underneath Keelee's crotch. The other girl quickly glanced back over her shoulder to see that Michelle was playing his part in their menage a trois. He felt his own partially erect cock jump as he watched as if disembodied from himself, his hand working on another man's penis. The overpowering notion was that he was no longer a man himself - not entirely anyway - and that he was performing a sexual act on someone of a different gender.

He had no idea if what he was about to do was a good thing or not, but he gently lowered himself down, taking a moment to adjust himself into a comfortable position before directing the man's cock toward his tight little bottom hole. Pulling his panties aside he felt the man's engorged phallus pressing into his bottom cheeks before sliding in between them and nudging up against his hole. He held his breath as he tried lowering himself onto the man, feeling the cock pushing into him as his sphincter tried to resist being invaded. With a conscious effort he relaxed his bottom and slid lower still, feeling himself being parted as he opened himself to a real man for the very first time. He gasped a couple of times as he sensed how close he was to being taken, and then with one final lowering of his body he felt his rosebud being penetrated.

He burned as the man's cock began to slide into him, causing him to squeal girlishly as the bulbous head spread his

144

opening and he began to enter him. It was a different sensation to that of the dildo. Although this man was probably thicker than the toy that he'd been taken with by the girls, it didn't seem so unforgiving. Taking a breath he resolved to go all of the way and slowly yet determinedly kept dropping down until he felt himself being filled with man meat. It was thrilling, fulfilling and shameful all at the same time.

'Oh y-yesss! Baby!' The muffled words of Dr Lydon drifted up to him as he felt the man pushing upward to meet him. His bottom made contact with the man's crotch and he knew he'd taken the full length inside of himself. He paused for several moments to get his breath back before lifting himself up and starting to withdraw before reversing direction and having the man's cock begin to fuck him like a girl.

His eyes were half closed as he looked up at the back of Keelee's head to see her riding the man's face, clearly enjoying herself. She was trying to stifle her words, to stop herself from crying out as the man tongue fucked her toward a climax. Something about having both him and Keelee on top of the man suddenly felt as though they were the ones using him. That it was he who was being taken advantage of and not them. Michelle tried to ignore the mild burning in his bottom as he rode the man's cock, speeding up his rhythm as his bottom began to slap against the man flesh beneath him. He realised he was groaning with a mixture of pain and pleasure and tried to close his mouth. He could only manage to bite his own lip as his breathing increased.

His own cock was beginning to grow in response and he had to put a hand against the front of his panties to ensure that his diminutive erection didn't make its presence known. He could feel a deep arousal within him, similar to the one that he'd experienced when being fucked by the strap-on. He knew if he continued like this he would bring himself to an explosive orgasm and he began to hold on to a distant hope that the man would cum first, giving him a reason to remove himself before he risked his own release.

He could see, hear and feel Keelee beginning to buck her way through her own orgasm. Grinding herself against the man's face and chin as she came hard against him. Dr Lydon began to thrust upward more urgently as if his own climax would soon arrive.

'Oh ... so tight!' He moaned as Keelee lifted away from

him in a bid to stop herself from crying out with his continued stimulation. The doctor's hands moved downward and then he was gripping Michelle's thighs as he pumped himself in and out of his bottom. Michelle could feel his own orgasm beginning deep down inside of him as the man's intensity grew, and then with one final thrust into him the man paused as if on the brink for one memorable moment before bucking and writhing underneath him as he filled Michelle with hot cum.

Michelle thought that he could sense the warmth of the man's juices filling him up inside as he frantically held onto himself through his panties, trying not to let his own orgasm loose. In the end he couldn't quite avoid it and he started to pulse inside of his underwear. It wasn't as full blown an orgasm as he'd feared but he still managed to soil his borrowed underwear with two or three jets of boy cum.

As the man slowly came down from his climax underneath him, Michelle resolved to remove himself as quickly as he could. Lifting himself up he felt the man being pulled from him, his bottom burning as the still erect glans withdrew through his tight rosebud. Pulling his panties back into place he slid off the couch, his legs feeling weak and his bottom oozing with man cum as he did so. He was quick to pull his pantyhose back on in an effort to stop any man juice from running down his legs.

Michelle didn't know whether to feel pleased or embarrassed by what he'd done. He stood awkwardly by the door, his panties soiled both in front and back with a mixture of his own and Dr Lyden's cum. He'd no idea what he would say to either Keelee or Dr Lydon as he watched them slowly recover themselves from their latest sex session. In fact, he'd no idea how to deal with what'd just happened at all, it'd been such an extraordinary development in his growing femininity.

Chapter 13

It took Michelle several days before he could finally accept what had happened with him and Keelee. The other girl was beside herself with excitement, trying to get him to agree to another sex session with Dr Lydon as soon as possible. He declined to provide an answer one way or another.

When eventually he decided to confide in his roommate over his latest experience with a man, she was almost as excited as Keelee had been. To her it was yet another justification to have him continue taking hormone supplements in order to better develop as a girl. He could no longer put up much of an argument to the contrary, given that his every action seemed to be embracing his new found girlhood as a female nursing student. Her and Lisa even began to talk of finding him a boy more his own age to date. He reminded them of his true nature, which only drew a token amount of sympathy.

Michelle's life at the hospital had certainly not taken the direction he'd expected it to, but he was still training as a nurse at least. If he could just keep his secret safe from his family and the hospital management then he might just be able to pull this whole thing off and become a qualified nurse. He'd no doubt there would be many unexpected adventures along the way, now that he'd accepted his new life as a girl. It wasn't going to be as straightforward as he'd imagined life as a nurse to be, not now that he was living as a female student but it was certainly going to be an interesting journey nonetheless.

He began to idly wonder just how much his breasts would develop, and whether he'd be able to show them off to the male doctors when found himself the subject of some of their more unprofessional behaviours. From his experiences so far, girl's definitely seemed to have more fun than boys!

REBECCA STERNE -- TURNED INTO GIRLS!

REBECCA STERNE -- TURNED INTO GIRLS!

Turned into a Sexy Hotel Maid

A Young Man's Unexpected Journey into a World of Forced Feminization and Sexual Service

Rebecca Sterne

Chapter 1

Alex Bailey stared up at the imposing building before him. He'd been sent by an agency to fill an urgent vacancy in the hotel and he'd no idea what was expected of him. It looked like the kind of grand hotel that'd stood forever, a timeless establishment that'd seen the city grow up around it but paid little heed to the changing world. He spied the hotel doorman as he held the gleaming glass doors wide open for a client as they hurried toward a waiting car.

He'd never worked in a hotel before, in fact, he'd never worked anywhere much. A succession of temporary positions had followed his leaving college with little in the way of qualifications to support his ambitions. The end result being that he was happy to accept anything that the job agency could offer him right now, after all, he still had bills to pay.

Feeling apprehensive at entering such a well-to-do establishment, he walked up to the doors with the intention of finding the main reception desk.

'Just a moment, young lady!'

He stopped suddenly, confused by the fact that the doorman was looking directly at him but addressing him as female.

In truth it wasn't the first time this had happened to him. On several occasions he'd been referred to as "young lady" or "Miss" by bus drivers or restaurant workers who'd only given him the briefest of looks. He found it embarrassing at times, particularly if he was with a family member or friend. His face would grow hot and he'd become uncomfortably aware of the way people were looking at him, either with amusement or as they tried to work out whether he was in fact a *she*...or not, just as he was feeling right now.

'I'm sorry, are...are you talking to me?' He answered unsteadily, one hand already on the door.

The man looked down at him from beneath his top hat, his eyes narrowing as something told him the person in front of him was not quite what he'd initially thought.

'Oh...are you a...?'

'Boy...um...a man, yes!' He stammered. 'I've been sent by the agency, for a job.'

The man looked as though he didn't quite believe him, either about the agency or being a man - he wasn't quite sure which. He glanced down at himself as if to confirm that he was in fact dressed in male clothing. He realised his non-descript jeans and pale yellow t-shirt were somewhat androgynous in nature, but still, he didn't think he looked *that* unlike a boy.

'Right. You'll need to go around the side to the staff entrance then, *Sir.*'

The man pronounced the word "Sir" as if he was still unconvinced, pointing him in the direction of an alleyway that led around back. Alex nodded politely and let the door go, keen to get away from the man before anyone else witnessed his embarrassment. As he rounded the corner of the building he stopped to take a breath, willing the redness from his cheeks and trying to forget the look in the man's eyes as he'd confirmed his actual gender.

He let out a short groan before heading along the side of the building in search of another entrance. It was a stark contrast to the public entrance in the front. An unassuming doorway with the words "Staff Entrance" written above denoted where he'd be expected to enter and leave. He pushed the door open, walking into a small vestibule with a rather disinterested looking security guard sitting behind a desk. He approached the desk as the man continued to look down at something in front of him, hidden from Alex's view.

Letting out a little cough, he almost jumped as the man looked up at him.

'I'm from the agency.' He announced in a small voice. He was met with an uncomprehending frown. 'I'm supposed to be starting work here today.' He explained.

The security guard picked up a clipboard and began to check its contents.

'Housekeeping?' He grumbled.

'Um...yeah, I guess.' Said Alex, 'I'm Alex, Alex Bailey.'

'Take a seat, I'll get someone down.'

Alex peered around the small room and shuffled over to a chair in the corner. He heard the man speaking over the phone briefly before putting the receiver down and continuing to ignore him. This did nothing to assuage Alex's nerves. He wasn't the most confident of people at the best of times, especially not when in a strange environment such as this. He was beginning to think he'd be better off making his excuses and leaving as the minutes slowly ticked by, but then a woman came bustling in from an adjoining corridor. She looked around for a moment before her eyes settled back onto Alex. He grinned nervously.

'Are you Alexis?' She asked, looking confused.

'Er...I'm Alex.' He said, feeling uncomfortable with the way she was staring at him.

'Oh, I thought they said Alexis.' She looked at him accusingly, 'I thought we were getting a girl.'

Alex wasn't sure what to say to that, so he just shrugged apologetically.

'Well, can't be helped. Come along with me. We're short handed so I need you to start work as soon as possible.' She turned on her heel and began walking back up the corridor. Alex jumped up from the chair and scurried after her, feeling as though he should apologise for disappointing her.

The woman half turned toward him without breaking her stride and looked him up and down.

'Did you bring more suitable clothes to wear?' She asked, frowning.

'They...they didn't say anything about that at the agency.' He said, walking half a step behind.

'Oh really! We do have a standard dress code for our staff. You can't attend the public areas dressed in jeans and a t-shirt, young man.'

The day was clearly not getting off to a good start. He followed her through the maze of corridors under the main hotel before they entered what looked to be a staff room of sorts. There were a number of lockers lining two of the walls, with one young woman hurriedly taking off her coat and stuffing it into one of them before pulling out her uniform.

'Another two minutes and you'd have been late again, Cheryl.' The woman barked.

'Yes, Miss Tamworth.' The girl nodded obediently. She couldn't have been much older than his twenty years, with long dark hair and attractive features. He gauged they were about the same height at five feet six inches. He'd always been self-conscious of his short stature, something that didn't help matters with being mistaken for a girl on the odd occasion. The girl smiled at him, rolling her eyes as the woman looked away with a thoughtful expression.

'It'd be best if we could find you something to wear rather than sending you away. I really can't afford to be any more short staffed than I already am.' She pondered. 'I really need someone else in housekeeping.'

'He could borrow my clothes, Miss Tamworth. He looks about my size.'

Alex and the woman both turned to look at the girl across the room.

'Don't be silly, Cheryl. I can't have a boy running around in a maid's uniform.'

'No, Miss. I meant that he can wear my trousers and shirt. The trousers are black and the shirt doesn't look too girly. He'd be smarter looking than he is now.' She offered, tugging at her black trousers and white shirt as proof as she prepared to change into her working uniform.

Alex was about to laugh at her joke but thought better of it when Miss Tamworth turned her attention back to him, narrowing her eyes as she studied him for a moment.

'I suppose that might work for now.' She said, taking Alex by surprise. 'When you're both presentable you may join me in my office before starting work.' The woman strode out of the room, leaving Alex alone with the grinning girl.

'But...I...' He stammered, not sure what to say to the idea of borrowing this girl's clothes. He looked around at Cheryl to find her grinning back at him.

'Come on, take those off. She doesn't like being kept waiting.' She said, unbuttoning her top as she spoke.

Alex wasn't quite sure where to look as the girl exposed her white bra underneath. He turned around, trying to ignore the fact that there was a girl he didn't know undressing just behind him. He thought of walking out but his legs felt heavy and uncooperative. He wasn't particularly experienced with girls and this was certainly a new situation for him.

'Aren't you going to take your clothes off?' The girl's question made him jump. He couldn't help but glance over his shoulder to find her in the process of pulling up her traditional looking maid's dress. Her bra covered breasts were visible for a brief moment longer as she shrugged her way into the short black dress. Their eyes met as she zipped herself up.

'You'd better hurry or you'll be in trouble. Just take your jeans and shirt off.'

He felt his face beginning to flush at the realisation that she knew he'd seen her bra. He pulled his shirt over his head in a bid to find something to occupy him. As he unfastening his jeans he hesitated.

'Um...would you mind turning around?' He asked politely, not wanting to display himself in his underwear.

Cheryl flashed him a smile before rolling her eyes and turning away. It wasn't until he was standing there in just his underpants that he realised he didn't have anything to change into. He looked over towards the girl and saw her discarded clothing laying across a small bench beside her. He wanted to ask her for her clothes, but the thought that she'd have to turn around only to find him dressed in nothing but his rather faded underwear was an unsettling one to say the least. He'd never been in such an awkward situation before. Deciding to take her clothes as quickly as possible he scuttled across the room and reached out to take them. He couldn't quite shake the idea that someone might walk in at any moment.

'Eew! You're not wearing them, are you?' Cheryl said unexpectedly.

He was so focused on taking her clothes that he hadn't realised she was now watching him. He looked down at himself, trying to work out what she was talking about.

'You definitely need some nicer underwear.' She said, frowning.

Realising where she was looking he straightened up sharply and dropped his hands to cover his crotch.

'It's alright, nothing's showing!' She smirked, 'But I don't think I want you wearing those things under my trousers.'

'It's all I've got!' He protested, feeling annoyed at her comment but knowing her criticism wasn't entirely out of place. He could feel his face beginning to flush at the idea that this girl had seen him in just his underwear, particularly as it wasn't the finest looking pair of underpants in the world.

Cheryl looked thoughtful for a moment. 'Well, I suppose I could lend you mine. No one'll notice that I'm not wearing any.'

'Eh?' He said, just as she reached up underneath her skirt.

He just caught a glimpse of her stocking tops as her skirt lifted upward before seeing her tugging her panties down her legs. He swallowed hard, unable to take his eyes off what she was doing. He watched mesmerised as she pulled a pair of red satin panties down her legs and stepped out of them. He stared at her uncomprehendingly as she smoothed her skirt out and held them up in front of him.

'Go on then, put them on.' She said with a glint in her eye. 'Don't just look at them silly. Take them and I'll turn around while you change.'

His hand moved up as if it had a mind of its own and he saw himself taking the proffered panties from her hand. She was grinning as she turned her back on him. Without thinking he took hold of them in both hands and studied them for a moment. Running them through his fingers, feeling the warmth from her body still present. He noticed his fingers trembling slightly as he imagined putting them on. How could he possibly start his new job wearing this girl's clothes instead of his own?

'You'd better hurry up. Miss Tamworth will be waiting for us.' She said over her shoulder as if sensing his inactivity.

With a flourish he took hold of his own underwear and whipped them down his legs. Panicking at the idea that someone else might see him, he quickly held out the girl's panties and

157

stepped into them. He tried to ignore his feelings of arousal as he drew them up his legs. They seemed to send a spark of electricity up through his body as he felt them cupping his small penis. He could feel the beginnings of an erection, so he took her trousers and pulled them up his legs before she had a chance to turn around. He fumbled for a moment as he came to terms with them fastening on the girl's side before managing to settle them into place. There was a distinct lack of room in the crotch and they hugged him more tightly than any boy's trouser's would've.

He was so busy with his borrowed clothing that he barely noticed Cheryl retrieving his underpants from the floor until she spoke.

'We won't be needing these now.' She threw them in her locker before picking up his other clothes and doing the same with them.

There was no other option but to put her shirt on in order to cover himself up. It too fastened on the opposite side to what he was used to and he struggled to button it up until she stepped over to help him with the last few buttons. Without warning she slipped her fingers into the waistband of the trousers and pulled them outward.

'Mmm, nice panties, Alex!' She said, giggling as she looked down at him.

He pulled away - embarrassed.

Chapter 2

'I look silly!' Said Alex, eyeing himself up in the mirror on the nearby wall.

'No, you don't.' Said Cheryl, 'No one'll know they're girl's clothes. You're just wearing trousers and a shirt. They won't allow you to work here in jeans so there's not much choice, is there?.'

Alex bit his lip, trying to decide how obvious it was that he was wearing her clothes. He was acutely aware of her panties as they cradled his partially erect cock in between his legs. He kept thinking he could see an outline of his manhood in the tight fitting trousers, but it could've just been his imagination.

'Come on, we haven't got time to stand around.'

Cheryl took his arm and pulled him away from the mirror. He was still wearing his own shoes and socks, which would barely make the grade as far as the expected smart dress of someone working in housekeeping, but at least he wasn't entirely dressed in girl's clothes. Cheryl on the other hand was dressed in a traditional looking maid's outfit that barely reached mid-thigh. Her black stockings and shoes just seemed to draw the eye upward to where she'd slipped a white apron over her head that tied in the back. She even wore a small frilly hat that was clipped into her hair to complete the outfit.

They passed several other staff members on the way to Miss Tamworth's office, only one of which seemed to pay him any mind. The thought that he was being drawn further and further away from where his clothes were now locked away in this girl's locker was an increasingly unsettling one.

Eventually they stopped outside of a fairly nondescript office as Cheryl hurriedly rapped on the door. Without waiting for an invitation she turned the handle and led him inside. Miss Tamworth was sitting behind a desk working on some kind of staff rota as they approached. She looked up and immediately studied Alex's appearance. He waited for her to tell him how silly he looked wearing Cheryl's clothes only to send him home without any work.

'I suppose that looks acceptable.' She said, begrudgingly. 'Cheryl, you'll be showing Alex around today. He can work alongside you. I'll be up to check on his progress as soon as I can.'

'Yes, Miss Tamworth.' Said Cheryl, giving an almost imperceptible curtsy.

'We're a traditional establishment here, Alex. We expect our staff to perform to the highest standards of customer service. The guest is always right and nothing is too much trouble. Do you understand?'

'Er...Yes, Miss Tamworth.' He wasn't sure whether he was expected to bow or do something else. In the end he nodded his head as he bent his knees, performing a rather odd acknowledgement somewhere between a bow and a curtsy. Miss Tamworth couldn't quite control her face as she showed her amusement.

'We don't usually employ boys in our housekeeping department, but there's no reason you can't perform just as well as the girls. If you're up to the required standard you may find yourself with a well paid and enjoyable position.' She nodded at the pair of them. 'You may go.'

Alex looked to Cheryl and followed her lead as she curtsied once more before leaving the room. Alex's bow was just as awkward and uncoordinated as the first attempt and he found himself feeling somewhat silly as he rushed to leave the room. He was sure he caught the sound of Miss Tamworth giggling as he closed the door.

160

'Right, follow me.' Said Cheryl, leading him to a nearby staff elevator.

They were soon arriving at the twentieth floor of the building. As they stepped out into the public corridor, Alex marvelled at the stylish decor surrounding him. He'd never been in a hotel like this before, and he guessed he'd never afford to be a guest in such a place. He followed his mentor to a nearby cleaning cupboard and she began to talk him through what their duties would be as they entered the guest rooms. He helped her load up a trolley with clean linen and other supplies before they headed to their first room. A guest was coming out of his room and they walked passed him just as he looked up.

'Good morning, Girls.' The man said, smiling politely.

'Good morning, Sir.' Said Cheryl automatically.

As the man walked away, Cheryl turned to him.

'You should say "Good morning" to the guests, Alex.' She berated him.

'But...he thought I was a girl!' He said, feeling a little put out. 'You said I didn't look silly.'

'It doesn't matter, does it? You should still answer them politely, and you don't look silly at all. You just look a bit like a girl is all.' She laughed.

'I don't want to look like a girl.' He could feel himself growing red in the cheeks as he realised how much easier it'd be for people to mistake him for a girl now. 'I'd like to put my own clothes back on.'

'That's not very grateful, is it?' Said Cheryl, looking offended. 'I lent you my clothes so you could work here and now you're complaining about them. I even let you put my panties on!'

'I...um...' Alex's thoughts went straight to Cheryl's panties and how nice they felt against his skin. His little cock twitched in appreciation, throwing any further thoughts into disarray.

'Of course, if you don't want a job?' Cheryl crossed her arms as she gave him a stern look.

'I do...of course I do, I mean, I need a job.' His heart began to race at the prospect of being out of work again.

'So stop complaining and do as you're told, okay?'

'Yeah, okay.' He replied sulkily.

Alex followed her into one of the guest rooms. The bed was unkempt and there was an assortment of discarded clothing around the room. Cheryl immediately began to pull the bedclothes off.

'Pick up the clothes and put them on the chair, would you? Then you can clean the bathroom.' Said Cheryl.

As he scanned the floor he realised it was all female clothing. He felt a little uncertain about picking up some strange woman's underwear, but he bent to his task nevertheless. As he gathered up the rest of the clothing he couldn't help but admire the softness of the pantyhose, the cuteness of the lacy bra and panties. His mind was drawn back to the fact that he was wearing Cheryl's clothes and he felt himself becoming aroused inside of her panties. It was a strange feeling, being turned on by the feel of a pair of girl's panties and he began to wonder at these newly discovered sensations. He walked stiffly around the room as he felt his arousal growing ever further at the thought of being dressed in this attractive girl's clothing.

'You'd better hurry up and clean the bathroom, Alex. We don't have long.' Cheryl said from across the room.

He quickly piled the clothes onto a nearby chair before heading through the door and into the bathroom. It was still steamy and warm from where the shower had been running. Without thinking he stepped over to the bath where the shower curtain was still drawn. As he grasped a hold of it he heard a noise and realised someone was there just as his hand yanked the curtain out of the way. Stood in front of him was a woman with a stunned expression on her face, she was quite naked.

'Oh ... um ... s-sorry, Miss. I didn't realise you ... um ...' He stumbled over his words as he took in the sight of the female guest. Her body was rather curvaceous and she was clearly in the process of finishing her shower. Her mouth dropped open for a moment as she stared back at him.

The moment seemed to stretch onward as he froze in place, unsure of what to do. Realising he was still gazing openly at her bare breasts he tore his eyes away from her, just as Cheryl appeared in the doorway.

'Oh! I'm really sorry, Miss. We didn't realise you were still here.' She explained apologetically.

The woman looked over at her and back to Alex as he backed away from the bathtub.

'I'm sure you didn't, girls.' The woman said, sounding

annoyed. 'I'd appreciate it if you'd knock first, next time.'

'Of course, we're sorry.' Said Cheryl.

The woman seemed to study Alex more closely, her expression one of uncertainty.

'You are...a girl, aren't you?' She asked, raising an eyebrow as Alex looked away anxiously. 'Young lady?'

As Alex was forced to look her in the eye he knew his guilty expression had given him away almost immediately.

'You're a boy, aren't you?' The woman still appeared unsure of her own conclusion.

'I...um...y-yes, Miss.' He said croakily, trying desperately not to look at her naked body. 'S-Sorry.'

Alex felt himself being pulled from the room. Cheryl stepped into the bathroom and closed the door behind her, leaving him to contemplate his embarrassing encounter alone. He couldn't get the picture of this older yet attractive woman's body out of his mind. He'd never seen a woman naked before and this was certainly not how he'd expected it to happen for the first time. He looked down at himself and wondered exactly what had given him away as a boy, before having to remind himself that he wasn't supposed to look like a girl anyway. The fact this woman had also mistaken him for a girl at first only served to increase his own feelings of confusion and embarrassment.

He busied himself by tidying the room as best he could, trying not to listen to the conversation between Cheryl and the guest. He could hear that she wasn't happy having a boy walk in on her, although he was sure he heard her comment on how he could easily be taken for a girl instead. It seemed like an age before the bathroom door finally opened and Cheryl reappeared. She closed the door softly behind her before indicating that he should follow her out of the room.

'She's not happy about you walking in on her.' She explained as they walked away. 'She's going to report us to Miss Tamworth. We'd better head down there to see her. I don't think she'd've worried if you'd been a girl though. Our guests aren't used to boy housekeepers.'

Alex didn't say anything. He followed Cheryl back down into the lower depths of the hotel with a growing feeling of despondency. It seemed inevitable that they'd let him go, telling the agency that he wasn't suited for the position. It'd just make things even harder for him. Finding work wasn't easy and now it could prove impossible with a poor reference from such a prestigious hotel.

By the time they entered Miss Tamworth's office she was already on the phone to the woman. She scowled disapprovingly at Alex as they were summoned forward to stand in front of her desk.

'Once again, I do apologise for our housekeeper's behaviour. I can assure you that it won't happen again.' She listened for a moment, her angry expression giving way to a look of surprise, and then much to Alex's amazement - amusement. 'I do understand that if he'd've been a girl this would not have been so upsetting for you, and it's of no surprise that you were initially mistaken.' Alex felt a familiar warmth flooding his cheeks as he listened to the woman discussing him with the guest. 'That's an interesting suggestion, one which I'll give due consideration to, Mrs Hatton ... well, it's a little unconventional but I see your point ... Indeed, I'm sure it would pass quite unnoticed. If you're sure this is what you'd want, we'd be more than happy to oblige you as one of our most valued guests ... Yes, goodbye, Mrs Hatton, and thank you for your understanding.'

She slowly placed the phone back onto its cradle before looking up at Alex.

'I'm sure you realise whom that was on the phone?' Both Alex and Cheryl nodded nervously. 'Mrs Hatton is one of our most valued clients and I am obliged to take into consideration her wishes.' Alex felt his stomach sinking as he prepared for a swift dismissal. 'It appears that she has a somewhat different idea to myself as to what action we should take. Personally, I would normally be sending you on your way, but our guest seems to think that you'd benefit from some additional ... training, shall we say. It seems that your appearance may be of benefit. In order to avoid any future awkwardness she has suggested that we fore-go your current mode of dress ... and employ a more traditional uniform.'

Alex heart jumped as he realised he wasn't being dismissed in his first morning. It would be a relief to get out of Cheryl's clothes as well, as Miss Tamworth had clearly agreed to let him dress more normally in future. He wondered if they did in fact have some male clothes that he could use. Although why that hadn't been the case to start with he couldn't quite fathom, but at least he still had a job.

Chapter 3

Miss Tamworth picked up the phone once more and asked someone else to join them. Within a few seconds a brief knock on the door was heard before another woman in her mid to late twenties entered.

'Ah, Kelly. I need something from the staff supplies.' Said Miss Tamworth.

The new woman glanced at both Alex and Cheryl before approaching the desk. Miss Tamworth wrote a list of items onto a piece of paper and scribbled a note underneath. Kelly looked at her and her mouth fell open as she looked back at Alex.

'A boy?' She said, looking him over, 'I thought he was a *she.*'

'Yes, a number of people seem to have made that assumption, which is why Mrs Hatton has made this request of us. A little unconventional I give you, but I think it'll work under the circumstances.'

Alex could feel himself being studied intently by both women. He was beginning to get a bad feeling about what was coming. He looked down to the floor, feeling even more aware of how he was dressed. It'd be a relief to get into something more

REBECCA STERNE -- TURNED INTO GIRLS!

appropriate.

The new woman soon left the office and Miss Tamworth asked them both to wait in the staff room. Cheryl seemed far less worried than he, but then it was him that'd created a difficult situation. Cheryl plopped down next to him on the bench seat and patted his leg.

'So, how do my panties feel? Comfortable?' She asked brightly.

'Eh? Oh ... they're okay, I guess.' He said, trying not to think of her underwear lest his arousal start up again. He shifted his position, feeling the softness of the female clothing against his skin and to his annoyance, a budding erection inside of the panties as a result.

'So you don't mind wearing girl's clothes then?'

'No ... I mean, yes. I don't know!' He became flustered as he sensed her closeness to him.

'It's alright if you do, most people think you're a girl anyway, even without makeup or anything.' She looked a little closer at his face before stroking his leg. 'I wouldn't normally lend my clothes to a boy, in case you're wondering, and I don't normally walk around with no panties on either.'

His little cock jumped at her reference to the panties, he recalled the warmth from her body as he'd put them on and couldn't help but think of her exposed crotch underneath her maid's dress. The sooner he was out of these clothes the better, he thought.

They both looked up as they heard footsteps approaching, just as Miss Tamworth and Kelly walked in. They stood up in unison, Alex covering his crotch with his hands in order to hide any signs of his arousal.

'Right, Alex.' Began Miss Tamworth, 'You're in luck, we've been able to find just about everything you need with the exception of some underwear.'

'It's okay, Miss Tamworth. He's wearing my panties.' Said Cheryl, bringing a groan of embarrassment from Alex.

Both women looked from Cheryl to Alex in mild surprise before Miss Tamworth nodded. 'Good. Then you can get changed into these before Cheryl helps you with some makeup. We don't want any more unfortunate incidents with guests now, do we?'

'Makeup?' Asked Alex, feeling confused.

'Of course. Now put these on, quickly.' Miss Tamworth nodded to her assistant.

The woman stepped forward and opened a bag that she was holding. She pulled what was unmistakably a maid's dress from inside and hung it up on a nearby hook, before producing a matching apron and hat that were identical to Cheryl's. Alex's mouth dropped open as he watched her then produce a pair of sheer black hold-up stockings and a black bra. To finish it off she then took out a pair of girl's shoes from a second bag with small heels.

There was a pause as both Alex and Cheryl starred at the apparel now hanging up waiting for him.

'Brilliant!' Said Cheryl, breaking the silence. 'You're going to be a real maid.'

'What! I can't wear that.' Alex protested, unable to take his eyes off the dress. 'I'm ... I'm not a girl. I thought you were going to give me boy clothes.'

'It was Mrs Hatton's idea, Alex.' Said Miss Tamworth, grinning. 'I couldn't exactly say no to her, given what'd just happened. Besides, you'll have no problem passing for a maid given you almost do that now. Cheryl, you can help him change and come to my office when he's ready to start work.' She narrowed her eyes impatiently. 'Hurry up, you've got work to do!' She turned around and swiftly left the room. Her assistant hesitated for a moment, watching him for a moment before following.

In a moment of panic Alex spun around to look directly at Cheryl. 'I can't do this! I'll look silly. I'm a boy, not a girl.'

'Most people seem to think you look like a girl.' She responded - quite unhelpfully in his opinion. 'What're you worried about? No one else needs to know. Look, if you want to keep this job you'd better do what Miss Tamworth says.'

Alex looked across to where the maid's dress was hanging, with a pair of stockings and a bra laid across a chair underneath. He couldn't imagine walking around dressed in such an outfit, but it seemed his only option. For the first time in his life he was grateful for the fact that he was so easily mistaken for a girl. With his legs feeling weak he walked across the room and examined the bra and stockings. A thrill of anticipation ran through him as he felt the sensuous material of the stockings as he ran them through his hands.

'Go on, get undressed then. Quickly!' Said Cheryl, closing the door.

He thought of the panties he was wearing underneath Cheryl's clothes, but as they belonged to her anyway he decided he had little to lose by stripping down to them. Turning away from her he unfastened the trousers and slid them down his legs. As he stepped out of his shoes he kicked them off along with his socks. The shirt followed and he was soon standing with his back to her in nothing but her shiny red panties. He was about to put the stockings on when Cheryl placed a hand on his arm.

'I think you'd better shave before you put them on. Come on, we've got a shower just through here.' She took his hand and led him into a small room complete with shower cubicle and basin. She rummaged around in a small cupboard before producing a razor and some scented shaving cream. 'Make sure you shave everything!' She ordered him, pushing him into the shower.

Once hidden behind the curtain he removed her panties and flung them onto a nearby stool. He felt as though he was in some sort of a dream as he proceeded to shave all traces of boy hair away. He kept wondering why he was going along with this, but the constant thoughts of not having a job to pay his bills nagged away at him, forcing him to continue regardless. It didn't take very long due to his light hair growth, but he still marvelled at how smooth and silky his legs felt afterwards. He'd been diligent in removing every trace of hair from his face down. Wondering what Cheryl would make of it he peeked out from behind the curtain to find her sitting down with her red panties in her hand.

'Let's have a look then.' She said eagerly.

She jumped up and before he could say anything she'd ripped the curtain aside. He gasped with surprise as she looked down at his naked and hairless body.

'Very nice.' She said quietly, 'Are they nice and smooth?'

Without waiting for an answer she moved closer and reached out, touching his thigh and stroking his leg to test for any hair. Alex's cock began to engorge at her touch and he quickly tried to cover himself, wishing he hadn't shaved quite so thoroughly as he was now entirely bald between the legs also. Her eyes drifted up to his covered crotch as her hand continued to brush up and down his leg. He'd never been touched like this before, let alone be naked in the presence of a girl.

'Perfect.' She muttered as she felt his smooth skin. 'I hope you're not getting a stiffy, you can't put my panties on if you're hard.'

Alex grimaced, letting out a little squeak of embarrassment.

'You are, aren't you?' She asked, smiling. 'Let me have a look. Maybe we can do something about it.'

She took hold of his hands and tried to pull them away. Initially he resisted her, but his resolve was weak and he quickly submitted to the inevitable humiliation. His stiff little cock was pointing directly at her and he felt completely unable to do anything about it. She let go of his hands and reached between his legs, causing him to jump as her fingers wrapped around his slender shaft.

'It's not very big, is it?' She observed without thinking.

Alex began to tremble as he felt himself become fully erect in her hand. She began to move her fingers up and down, her eyes meeting his as she watched his reaction.

'I think you looked quite sexy in my panties. You should dress in girl's clothes more often, don't you think?'

Alex tried to answer her, to argue that he wasn't that sort of boy, but all that came out was a pathetic whimper as he felt himself being gently masturbated. He was struggling to get his mind around the fact that this was happening at all. Things like this just didn't happen to him. He was breathing fast as he felt an orgasm growing inside of him. He felt a pang of fear at the idea of ejaculating in her hand, of having her see him disgrace himself in such a way, but all he could do was stay where he was and let it happen. Her hand was moving faster now, her eyes watching him closely with a faint smile on her lips.

'It's okay, Alex, you can cum in my hand if you like?' She said, teasing him. 'Alex. That's a girl's name as well, isn't it? That's quite lucky really.'

Alex could feel himself about to blow. His climax was fast approaching and he knew there was nothing he could do to avoid it now. He groaned at the thought of how he was about to humiliate himself, just as his arousal surged and he felt his hairless little balls tightening between his legs.

'Oh ... Oh ... N-No!' He squealed, just as he felt his cock

spasming in Cheryl's hand.

He glanced down with narrowed eyes to see that her fingers were already coated in his precum. It glistened back at him, causing his embarrassment to deepen even further. Then he felt himself begin to cum. He teetered on the brink for several moment's as if to stretch out the inevitable point of humiliation, and then he felt the first jet of cum escaping him. It shot out from between her fingers and he watched as it arced before falling to the floor of the shower cubicle. He heard Cheryl giggle as another stream of cum escaped him, and then he was bucking and squirming his way through the most powerful orgasm he'd ever experienced. It was the first time he'd cum under another's hand. He could see the girl's hand being covered in his thick juices as she continued to milk him, her eyes never leaving his glistening cock head.

As he regained control of his body he had to lean against the wall to steady himself. He quivered several times as Cheryl squeezed his now softening cock in her hand, draining him of any remaining boy juice. He felt a strange sense of humiliation and relief as she let him go and studied her cum covered hand.

'Mmm, I think you've been saving it up, haven't you?' She said, laughing at his shamed expression. 'You'd better clean yourself up. Then you can put my panties on and finish getting dressed.'

He felt as though he was moving through treacle at first. His energy seemed to have been drained along with his seed. Cheryl left him alone to clean up. As he stepped into her silky panties once more he was struck by the sensuous feeling of pulling them up his now perfectly smooth legs. Despite the fact that he'd just experienced a powerful orgasm he realised he was actually semi-erect by the time he pulled the panties into place. Determined not to embarrass himself again, he pushed his little cock back between his legs in order to hide it before tentatively walking out of the bathroom to face his ordeal, careful to check that they were still alone in the room before making an appearance.

Chapter 4

'Put this on.' Said Cheryl, holding out the black bra.

Alex looked at her bashfully. He could barely look her in the eye after what'd happened in the bathroom, and now she was telling him to put on a bra. He felt himself flushing from head to toe but knew he'd already allowed himself to come too far to back out now. He told himself he was doing this to earn some money. To keep a roof over his head, but something was niggling at the back of his mind. Every time he found himself slipping into a pair of girl's panties, or even pants, he felt an unexpected thrill running through him. He'd assumed it was a normal reaction, one which all boys would experience in such a situation, but something was telling him this wasn't entirely true.

Ignoring the voice at the back of his mind, he stepped up to Cheryl and took the bra without looking at her. He held it up, wondering what the best way of getting into it was.

'Come here, I'll help you!' Said Cheryl. 'Anyone'd think you'd never put a bra on before.'

'I haven't!'

'Yeah, okay.'

She sounded unconvinced by his denial, a denial that was

entirely truthful. She guided his arms into the shoulder straps before pulling it tight around his chest and fastening it into place.

'We'll need something to fill it with, hold on.' She said.

He peered around as she looked about the room before shrugging her shoulders and picking up the stockings. She balled them up before stuffing them into the bra cups.

'There, that'll do. You can borrow mine for now. Miss Tamworth won't mind me not wearing any today, I'm sure.'

He watched mesmerised as she reached up underneath her dress, this time taking hold of her stocking tops one at a time and rolling them down her legs. She held them out for him.

'Go on, put them on, and be careful you don't snag them.'

He caught her eye and quickly looked down. Taking the stockings, he sat on the bench and pushed his foot into the first one. As he worked it up his leg he could sense the warmth of her body lingering in the soft sensuous material. He was becoming breathless as he experienced the sensation of having his smooth hairless legs being encased in a pair of nylons for the first time. It was a heady experience and he had to pause for a moment before getting to his feet.

'I suppose you're going to tell me you've never put a pair of stockings on either?' She crossed her arms as if to challenge him.

'I ... I haven't.' He said in a weak voice.

She scoffed before taking hold of the dress and holding it out for him. He gingerly stepped into it and she was soon zipping him up at the back. He knew he was now trapped in this maid's uniform. Sitting down to slip the shoes on he was surprised at how well they fitted him. Before he could get to his feet again, Cheryl had pulled some makeup out of her locker and was preparing to complete his transformation.

'You've got quite a pretty face, Alex. You'll look great with a little makeup.' She said.

He sat rigidly in place as she began to apply a light covering of foundation before moving on to his eyes. He could feel himself becoming more anxious as he tried to imagine just what he'd look like as a girl. It was a strange feeling, being transformed in such a way. He could almost feel his masculinity dwindling away as this girl he'd only just met continued to feminize him. He flinched as she began to apply eyeliner, causing her to hold his face steady as she continued unabated. By the time she was running her lipstick along his lips he was feeling weak with nerves.

'There, all done. I'll just tidy your hair up a little and you can take a quick look before we go to Miss Tamworth's office.'

She pulled his hair band out and began to rearrange his hair. A little hairspray followed before she finally pinned his lacy maid's hat into place.

'You look great! Take a look.' She said, stepping back.

He stood up nervously and walked over to the mirror. As his face came into view he gasped at what he saw. Gone was the boy that'd started work that morning. In truth there were no drastic changes to his features apart from a little makeup and a girlish hair style, but it was all that was needed to bring out the girl in him. He felt himself quivering slightly as Cheryl tied his apron into place.

'Come on, Miss Tamworth will be waiting.' She said, before pulling him out of the door.

He didn't have the strength to resist. His stomach was performing somersaults as he anticipated facing the next few hours dressed as a girl in public. Not just a girl, but a hotel maid. He became aware of the brushing together of his stockinged legs as he followed his mentor along the staff corridor. The feel of her panties, the presence of the bra and the slight swishing of the maid's dress that barely reached mid-thigh. It was proving to be a heady concoction, one that was beginning to have an unwanted effect between his legs. They paused outside Miss Tamworth's office whilst Cheryl checked his appearance once more, and with a wide grin she led him inside.

The woman was engaged in conversation with another maid as they entered. She glanced up at the intrusion and did a double take as she realised who was now standing before her.

'Well, I have to say that's a definite improvement, Alex.' She said, looking a little shocked. 'You make a very pretty young maid, don't you think, Cheryl?'

'Oh yes, Miss Tamworth. It's a definite improvement.' Said Cheryl.

The other maid looked from one to another, clearly confused by the tone of the conversation.

'He looks much better as a girl.' Added Cheryl, giggling at his obvious discomfort.

'*He?*' Exclaimed the other maid, staring back at Alex as she tried to comprehend the situation. 'You mean, she's a ... *boy?*'

'Oh yes, Lynsey. Although he looks far better now than when he came to us a couple of hours ago.' Confirmed Miss Tamworth. 'It's a little unconventional, but considering our guest's suggestion and the fact that we're so short staffed, I think we'd best go with it for now. Off you go then, Alex. I'll be checking in on you later today, so please don't upset any more guests. Remember, the guests are our highest priority.'

'Yes, Miss Tamworth.' Said Alex, trying not to catch the eye of the other maid who was still openly staring at him with a look of astonishment.

This time he'd no doubt what would be expected of him, and he gave a meek little curtsy in unison with Cheryl before exiting the room. Cheryl was quite happy to lead her feminized co-worker back up to their assigned floor, seemingly oblivious to his state of anxiety. They passed two more guests as they stepped out of the elevator, neither one showing any signs of recognising him as a boy in a dress.

'We've got some time to make up now, so you'll have to start the next room without me. I'll come and check on your work when I'm finished with mine, okay?' Said Cheryl, pointing him to one of the nearby doors.

'But ... what if someone realises I'm a ... *boy.*' He whispered this last part for fear of anyone overhearing.

'Don't be silly, you look perfectly natural as a girl. If in doubt, just do what you think a girl would do in your place. Now hurry up and get back to work.'

He hesitated next to the trolley as Cheryl gathered some clean bed linen and hurried away from him. He suddenly felt even more exposed and vulnerable now that he was standing there alone, dressed as a maid. Despite her assurances he couldn't quite bring himself to believe that he looked that convincing, in fact, he wasn't sure that he even wanted to be that convincing as a girl. Hearing one of the doors being opened further down the hallway he grabbed some linen of his own and let himself into the room behind him, wanting desperately to be out of sight of any other guests or even fellow staff members. He wondered fleetingly what the woman at the agency would think if she knew quite how his first day was going, and that one of her male clients was now dressed as a female maid in such a prestigious establishment.

The room was in semi-darkness as he entered. Seeing the curtains still closed, he dropped the linen into a nearby chair and slowly made his way toward the windows, trying not to trip on anything as he went. He could just make out the pile of bedding laying across the bed as he fumbled his way passed before reaching the window. As he took hold of the curtains he heard a noise from behind, startling him. As if on instinct he whipped one of the curtains aside before spinning around. The pile of bedding moved.

'I didn't order room service, but as you're here.' A man's voice spoke up.

As his eyes settled onto the bed he saw the man lying there, the bedclothes pushed to one side to reveal his naked body. Alex drew in a sharp breath, locking eyes with the male guest before he inevitably peered down at where the man was holding his erect cock in one hand, clearly already in the process of pleasuring himself.

'Oh! I ... I'm sorry, Sir. I'll go ...' Alex flushed bright red as he realised he was looking down at another man's erection.

'Go? Why? I'm sure you'd like to make up for walking in on me ... in *flagrante,* as it were. After all, we wouldn't want you to get into trouble would we, young lady?'

Alex couldn't take his eyes off the sight of this man lying there entirely naked, with his fingers still wrapped around his impressively sized phallus. He felt small and quite feminine in comparison. It was hard to tell how much of this was due to his appearance and how much was due to his diminutive penis size. He swallowed hard, trying to make his brain work so as to extricate himself from this uncomfortable situation.

'I ... I really should be going, Sir.' He said in a small voice, but his legs refused to move.

'Come and sit down.' The man patted the side of the bed with his free hand, still slowly stroking his cock with the other. 'I'd like you to perform a little personal service before you go.'

Alex was caught in indecision. He knew he could simply leave, but if the man complained about him walking in on him unannounced it would be the second such complaint. He doubted he'd keep the position any longer. He swallowed again and without making any conscious decisions he found himself shuffling nervously over to the bed. He saw the man smile, his eyes lighting up as he realised this young maid was about to grant his wish. He had a muscular physique and was a good ten years older than Alex. He seemed to exude a powerful presence. The man was clearly used to getting exactly what he wanted.

Finding himself standing next to the bed, Alex looked up at the man's face for a moment before his eyes were drawn back down his body. The man patted the bed once more and indicated for him to sit. It was as if he'd lost control of his own actions as he slowly lowered himself onto the bed. The man reached out and placed his free hand onto his stockinged leg, gently caressing him before letting go of himself and guiding Alex's hand in between his legs. Alex watched as if from a distance as his fingers curled around the man's shaft, feeling the firm cock in his hand. He whimpered as he realised exactly what he was doing.

'That's a good girl. You know what to do now, don't you?' Said the man, his voice cracking slightly as he half closed his eyes. His hand continued to stroke Alex's leg, sending a shiver up his body at the sensual feelings of having his stockings stroked in such a way.

He began to move his hand up and down the man's length. He'd never even thought of touching another man in this way before, let alone actually done anything remotely like this. His mind was struggling to comprehend what his body was now doing as he stared blankly down at his own hand as it began to masturbate the male guest. He felt a kind of fascination with the feel of such an impressive cock between his fingers and gave it a little squeeze, bringing a moan of pleasure from the male guest. He continued to move his hand up and down, rubbing the glans with his thumb as he reached it before moving back down the shaft. He could tell the man had already brought himself close to a climax, so engorged was he. He began to increase the speed, sensing that it could all be over quite soon. He could feel a wetness on his thumb and realised the man was oozing precum. Alex's breath caught in his throat as he anticipated what was about to happen.

The man began to grunt and groan, his hand squeezing Alex's thigh as his climax built. Alex could only watch as his hand continued to masturbate the man's hard cock towards orgasm. His fingers were slick with precum now as he tightened his grip a little and continued to pump his hand up and down. The man's body seemed to go rigid and he grunted heavily, moment's later his cock exploded as a huge jet of cum was sent gushing into the air. Alex jumped as it happened, watching as it fell down to land across the back of his hand and wrist. He could feel the hot, sticky man juice running down his skin as another stream was ejected into the air, closely followed by several more diminishing loads. His hand was now slathered in the man's cum as it dripped down onto the bedclothes between the man's open legs.

Alex didn't know quite how to react, so he held onto the man's cock as he continued to ooze the last of his cum. The man's glistening glans seemed to look up at him accusingly. He whimpered to himself as the reality of what he'd just done dawned. He'd just given a hand job to a hotel guest, dressed as a female maid. This day was turning out to be quite surreal.

Chapter 5

Alex didn't know what to do or say as the man's breathing slowed and he relaxed back onto the bed with closed eyes. He slowly let go of the man's penis, peering down at his own cum covered hand. The man's hand gave his leg one more affectionate squeeze before sliding back onto the bed.

'I'd ... I'd better go, Sir.' He mumbled, forcing himself to stand up.

His legs felt weak and he was ashamed of what he'd just done. He'd no idea how he'd managed to put himself into such a situation. It just felt so inexplicable all of a sudden. Holding his hand out in front of him he walked quickly into the bathroom and began to wash the man's seed away, wondering whether this guest would say anything, or whether this would remain their little secret.

He briefly checked his appearance in the mirror before smoothing down his dress and gathering himself together. It was as though he'd turned into a different person by putting on these girl's clothes. Taking a deep breath he left the bathroom, intent on exiting the room as quickly as possible.

'Well, I have to say that was very good guest service.' The man's voice stopped him in his tracks and he looked up to see him laying on the bed, still naked and gazing at him with a smile of satisfaction. 'I look forward to receiving more from you.'

'I ... I'm sorry, Sir. I shouldn't have done that.' Alex stammered, 'I'd best be going now.' He turned to rush out of the room but hesitated, looking back at the man with a coy expression. 'You won't say anything, will you?'

The man's smile grew as he studied the young maid in front of him. 'I'm sure I can keep this between ourselves.' He raised an eyebrow thoughtfully. 'Especially if you plan to provide more services like *that* during my stay.'

'I ... um ...' Alex was struck be a sinking feeling as he heard the man's implied threat. He could feel himself turning red in the face at the thought of doing such a thing again. Unable to speak coherently he found himself giving a little curtsy before turning around and letting himself out of the room.

His legs turned to jelly as he closed the door behind him and he was forced to lean up against it. He looked down at his hand as if not quite believing his own actions.

'What's wrong with you? And why were you in there, the guest's still in the room.' Cheryl appeared in front of him, replenishing her supplies before starting on the next room.

'I ... I went in by mistake.' He said breathlessly, expecting her to know precisely what he'd been up to. She gave him a suspicious look before shrugging dismissively.

'That's the room you need.' She pointed to the next door along. 'So hurry up.'

He began to perform an obedient curtsy before catching himself in time. He quickly immersed himself into his maid's duties, all the while thinking about the feel of his hand rubbing another man's cock until it came all over him. The entire incident was already seeming less and less real, as if it'd been nothing more than a fleeting day dream. He realised that his own cock was partially erect inside of his panties. He couldn't be sure if this was related to the other man or whether it was simply the effect of walking around in girl's clothing with his stockings constantly gliding against each other to remind him of what he was wearing under the dress.

Pausing in front of a full length mirror, he began to admire how feminine he looked. It was no wonder the man in the next room had believed him to be a girl. There were no outward signs of his hidden masculinity apparent, and he suddenly felt the need to raise his dress up as if to check that he was indeed still a boy. As he did so he could see a slight bulge in his borrowed panties, but he knew it was nothing like the size of the man he'd just given a hand job to. He gave a little twirl, watching as the dress rose up to show off the lacy stocking tops. The surreal situation that he now found himself in suddenly came home to him and he stopped to stare back at his reflection. After a while he gazed about the room, knowing he had work to do. In an effort to feel normal he steadied himself before tackling his duties, trying desperately to ignore the feel of his female clothing as he bustled about the room - with little success.

-oOo-

With his mind being fogged by sexual thoughts and feelings, he drifted into an almost unthinking routine of cleaning. With Cheryl offering direction as to which rooms to attend, he followed her lead with a nagging arousal that refused to diminish. He was struggling to understand his own reaction to such an ignominious situation. He'd never even considered wearing girl's clothing before.

It was in this befuddled state of mind that he reentered a room that both he and Cheryl had been in earlier that morning. It wasn't until he faintly recognised the pile of women's clothing on a nearby chair that he remembered that very first encounter with a certain Mrs Hatton, and his resulting change of clothes at Miss Tamworth's insistence. Hearing a noise at the door he looked up, feeling a sense of deja vu at the idea of this female guest walking in on him. At least he wasn't about to discover her naked and unawares this time, he thought. To his enormous relief it was Cheryl, carrying a fresh pile of towels.

'What're you looking so worried about?' She asked, pausing in front of him.

'I ... I thought it was Mrs Hatton coming in. This is her room, isn't it?' He asked nervously.

'Yes it is, and you'd better do a good job this time. You don't want her reporting you a second time.' Cheryl frowned at him.

Alex nodded as he turned around, busying himself by

tidying up the bed. He took no notice when he heard the door opening again a few minutes later, assuming Cheryl had finished the bathroom.

'Well, what do we have here!'

The woman's voice startled him and he straightened up in a hurry. Turning around his eyes settled on the sight of Mrs Hatton, standing with her arms crossed as she studied the maid in front of her.

'I hope you checked the room before entering. The last *person* simply strode into my bathroom unannounced.' She said.

Alex realised then that she hadn't recognised him from earlier. He did his best to calm his expression, giving her the briefest of curtsies before speaking softly.

'Yes, Mrs Hatton.'

'Oh, you know who I am, girl. That's good, very good.' She said haughtily, just as Cheryl stepped out of the bathroom and locked eyes with this formidable woman. 'You again?' She added, raising her eyebrow.

'Oh! Yes, Mrs Hatton. Sorry to disturb you again, we'll be on our way if you'd like the room.' She took a step toward the door, indicating for Alex to follow. 'Once again, we're very sorry about earlier. Alex here didn't mean to walk in on you like that, it won't happen again.'

Mrs Hatton looked confused for a moment before turning back to Alex and fixing him with a stern expression. Alex stopped in his tracks. Hearing Cheryl reveal his true identity made him go cold for a moment. He could feel his face turning red under the woman's intense stare.

'You're ... that boy?' Said Mrs Hatton, squinting at him as if to see him clearer.

Alex cast a fearful look at Cheryl before directing his gaze to the floor. His feet were rooted to the spot as he felt his insides flip over and his cheeks burn. The sight of his stockinged legs and female shoes only served to increase his discomfort as he became even more acutely aware of how he was dressed.

'Um ... Yes, it is.' Cheryl answered for him. 'Miss Tamworth found a spare uniform for him, as you ... requested, Miss.'

Mrs Hatton looked vacant for a moment before appearing to recall her telephone conversation.

'Indeed I did.' She nodded firmly, 'Although I have to admit, I didn't really expect the hotel to be quite so ... accommodating.' A smile slowly spread across her face as she looked Alex up and down. 'You make a surprisingly fine girl. I hope this has taught you a lesson in manners.'

Alex screwed his face up in a pained expression but said nothing. He didn't trust his own voice not to crack under the circumstances. He felt weak with embarrassment and powerless to do anything lest he make this humiliating experience even worse for himself.

'Alex?' Prompted Cheryl.

Alex opened his mouth to answer but nothing came out, instead he opted for what he thought to be an agreeable nod of the head.

'I see our girly houseboy has still to accept his true place.' Mrs Hatton scowled at him. 'Come over here ... *Girl*.'

The woman strode over to the bed and planted herself down, watching Alex expectantly. Alex didn't know what to do at this point and looked up at Cheryl for guidance. He was met with a sympathetic expression but little else. In the end she nodded in the direction of the woman who was sitting neatly on the edge of the bed. Alex had to physically and mentally force his body into action. He slowly moved across the room, not knowing what to expect or how this situation could get any worse for him. He was soon to find out.

'Hurry up ... *Girl*. I haven't got all day.' Said Mrs Hatton, impatiently.

As Alex stepped up beside her he avoided making eye contact. Every movement of the maid's dress, every touch of his stockings as they brushed softly against each other seemed to increase his humiliation even further.

'Right, over my knee, *Girl*. It's time you were shown some discipline.'

Alex's eyes went wide. In his astonishment at the woman's order he flashed a look of surprise toward Cheryl before looking straight at Mrs Hatton.

'But ... I ... You can't ...' He stumbled over his words as his throat constricted and his mouth turned dry.

'Oh yes I can, and I will.' Mrs Hatton reached out to take hold of Alex's arm. She pulled him down roughly, meeting little resistance from the feminised boy.

Any thoughts of resisting came too late as Alex found himself across her lap. As an afterthought he tried to push himself back up but the woman simply slapped his hands away before holding him firmly in place with a hand upon his back.

'If you value your position you'll do as I say, is that understood, *Girl*!'

Her emphasis on the word "Girl" felt like a physical dig every time, serving to further weaken his position and crush what little fight he had in him. To his horror he felt the woman's other hand lifting his dress up and draping it across his back, exposing his pantied bottom. He whimpered as his eyes met those of Cheryl, who was watching events with unabashed amazement, a curious smile upon her lips.

'You're even wearing panties, very good.' Said Mrs Hatton, running her hand across his bottom cheeks. 'I dare say it's not for the first time.'

Alex wanted to protest but any words died in his throat as the woman lifted her hand away and brought it back down with purpose. He let out a surprised squeal as he felt the blow land. Before he'd had a chance to process the fact that he was now being spanked by this woman a second blow landed, bringing a whimper of humiliation from him as he felt himself being subjugated against his will. He began to squirm an her lap, trying to gain some kind of purchase in order to break her hold on him.

'Stay still, Girl! It'll be far worse if I have to spank you on your bare bottom.' Threatened Mrs Hatton as she tightened her grip and brought her hand down once more, this time driving his crotch up against her leg.

To Alex's horror he felt his little cock rubbing against the woman's thigh, becoming stiffer as a result. Realising he'd only make matters worse the more he moved, he froze in position, determined not to increase his own humiliation any further.

SMACK! Another blow landed bringing a grunt of embarrassment from him. He was now fully aware of how his crotch was pressed into this woman's leg, with every single movement intensifying the entire experience. SMACK! He sobbed loudly as he felt himself submitting to this woman's will in front of his colleague. Any vestige of dignity that remained to him was now being spanked out of him, one slap at a time. He soon lost count of how many times her hand landed against his bottom, it was beginning to feel a little numb, but the pain was dulled by the thin nylon covering of his panties and was nothing compared to the abject humiliation that he now felt.

'Well, I see our newly acquired maid has gotten a little excited by all of this.' Said Mrs Hatton as she finally stopped spanking him. She patted his pantied bottom with amusement as Alex realised she could undoubtedly feel the presence of his partially erect cock pressing into her. He groaned softly, feeling himself trembling. 'I have to say, having a young - *Girl* - such as yourself over my lap, and seeing that cute little bottom quiver under my hand has quite created a certain need in me too.'

Alex felt his dress being pulled back into place before the woman's hand was lifted from his back and she began to push him off her lap.

'Kneel down for me, Girl.' She said. 'I expect I can rely on your total discretion, young lady. After all, I am a most valuable client of this establishment.'

'Yes, Mrs Hatton. Discretion is guaranteed.' Replied Cheryl from across the room.

Alex turned his head to look at her. She was standing in the same spot, her eyes never leaving him as he knelt in front of the guest. He wondered quite what she was making of his treatment. He knew she would offer no help in ending the situation, seemingly satisfied to continue watching his shaming at Mrs Hatton's hands. Sensing a movement behind him he turned back around just in time to see the woman slipping a pair of panties down her legs. She kicked them off before smiling sweetly at him, a lustful look in her eye as she tugged her skirt upward to reveal her naked sex. Alex gasped with shock at this brazen display, feeling even more lost than he already was. He stared open mouthed as she slowly spread her legs apart in front of him.

'Now that you've made me a little ... damp, I expect you to attend to your duty as a maid.' Alex's eyes settled on the thin strip of pubic hair between her legs. He could see her swollen lips, with a slight glistening at where he assumed the entrance to her hole would be. 'Don't be shy, Girl. Crawl in between my legs and put your girly tongue to good use.'

He'd never been intimate with a woman before. Never even seen one naked before his eyes like this. As if on auto-pilot he crawled forwards until he couldn't get any closer, staring between her legs with a mixture of fear and fascination.

'You're quite shy aren't you? How cute.' Said the woman, her voice a little croaky. 'Just put your mouth between my legs and use your tongue.'

He forced himself to take a breath before leaning in to her. He could smell her musky scent as his face drew nearer to her mound. His heart was beating rapidly as he hesitated, and then he opened his mouth. Pushing his tongue toward her lips he ran it up each one in turn, tasting her flesh before sliding in between them and lapping at her wet hole. He could taste her pussy now, feel her warmth and was enveloped in her aroma as he delved deeper in between her legs. He felt her move against him, moaning with pleasure as he began to dutifully tongue her most intimate of places.

'Oh my, you are a good little maid, aren't you?' Said Mrs Hatton as her hands began to run back and forth through his hair, pulling his head inward and almost displacing his maid's hat at the same time.

With his mouth pressed up against her warm, fleshy mound he began to delight in the taste of this woman's sex. He recalled the feel of the male guest's penis in his hand and found himself almost comparing the two with each other.

'A little higher, my girl. Lick my clitty, there's a good girl!' Mrs Hatton's voice was hoarse with desire as she tried to guide his mouth upward towards her swollen clitoris.

As soon as Alex's tongue found it he heard her let out a cry of pleasure and he began to flick at it with his tongue, curious as to the enhanced effect it was having on this woman. Her legs tightened against his head and her hands pulled him ever deeper into her crotch as she began to ride his face. He was beginning to feel like nothing more than a sex toy at this point. Something to be used for another's pleasure. He could feel his cock straining against his panties as his own arousal built. He wanted to touch himself, to pleasure himself but it was all he could do to hold himself in position and avoid being entirely smothered by this womans pussy.

Her juices were running down his chin, his mouth was full of her fleshy lips. Slipping back down her crotch he thrust his tongue deep into her slick pussy hole, bringing an instant reaction from her.

186

'Oh yes! Oh! Ohhh!' The woman was bucking her hips against him as her climax built.

Somewhere at the back of Alex's mind he began to wonder what would happen when she came on his face. He wasn't sure what to expect but he knew her orgasm was fast approaching. He could imagine in his mind's eye, Cheryl standing open-mouthed behind him as she watched, mesmerised, as her feminised colleague performed such a lewd sex act upon a hotel guest.

'Oh! I'm ... I'm cumming ... Oh god, YES!' Screeched Mrs Hatton as her entire body stiffened and then began to convulse.

To Alex's amazement an initial jet of pussy juice was sent forcefully into his mouth, followed by copious amounts of her nectar oozing out as her pussy pulsed under a forceful orgasm. His mouth and chin were coated in glistening pussy juice as she came against his face with some force. He swallowed her juices down as he struggled to pull in a breath. It felt like an absolute age before the woman's climax began to abate, and even then she writhed and twitched with every touch as her legs loosened their grip and was finally able to come up for breath.

His eyes focused onto her glistening pussy lips, seeing her wetness spreading down onto the bedsheet below. Not knowing quite how to respond to what'd happened, he sat back on his heels and looked bashfully around to find Cheryl standing awkwardly against the bathroom door. Seeing him peering up at her she quickly moved her hand away from her own crotch, as if he'd caught her in an act of her own. Her cheeks were flushed as she returned his gaze, giving him a weak smile.

As he looked back at Mrs Hatton he saw that she'd lain back onto the bed, her legs still parted in a most unladylike manner. He felt his embarrassment rising once more and decided to get to his feet.

'You'd better fix your makeup before you leave, Girl.' He heard Mrs Hatton remark.

Checking his own reflection in the mirror he could see the woman's juices on his face, his lipstick smudged. He groaned at the sight of himself, still dressed as a maid with his lacy hat now sitting at a jaunty angle on his head. With an anxious look at Cheryl, he caught her pointing him into the bathroom. Shuffling across the room he closed the door behind him before attending to his dishevelled appearance.

REBECCA STERNE -- TURNED INTO GIRLS!

Chapter 6

'I can't believe what just happened!' Said Cheryl, sounding shocked as they walked away from Mrs Hatton's room. 'You let her spank you and then you ... did that!'

Alex felt as though he was in a state of shock. His slender cock was still swollen inside of his panties having not received any relief of his own. His body felt hypersensitive, every brush of his stockings, every touch of his dress as it swayed against his body sending tiny electric shocks straight to his crotch. His face was still burning with embarrassment and his mind was tormented by the idea that he'd so easily been manipulated, not once or even twice since arriving at the hotel, but at least three times.

'What ... What could I do?' He whined girlishly as he tried to think of how he could've extricated himself from the situation without degrading himself in such a way. 'I was scared to say "no". After that man made me ... *service* him, I couldn't risk more trouble with Mrs Hatton, could I?'

Cheryl stopped abruptly, pulling him around to face her. 'What man?' She asked.

'The man in that other room that I went into by mistake. He was still in bed and he was touching himself and ...' Suddenly he realised he was making a full confession and stopped talking. It must've been the effects of what'd just happened, muddling his brain and causing him to speak without thinking.

'And?' She asked.

Alex tried to shrug it off, trying desperately to think of a way of diverting the story.

'And ... nothing, really. I just found him there and had to leave.' He looked at the floor, unable to meet her eye.

'You're lying. You said something about him making you *service* him. Did you do something with him too?' Alex couldn't think of anything to say. 'You little slut, you did, didn't you? Tell me what you did with him, now!'

'I ... he just ...' He swallowed hard, plucking up the courage to admit to performing a sex act on another man. 'He got me to ... use my hand on him.' His voice trailed off into silence.

'Oh my god! You gave him a hand job.' Cheryl burst into laughter. 'I thought some of the other maids were bad, but you're a complete slut!'

'Shhh, not so loud.' Alex tried to quieten her as he imagined other people overhearing this young maid being accused of being the hotel slut. 'And I'm not a slut!' He hissed back at her, feeling every bit the slut that she'd accused him of.

'What if he tells someone? I mean, Mrs Hatton won't say anything as long as she gets what she wants, but if this other guest makes it public then we could both be in trouble.' Said Cheryl, looking concerned. 'We'd better go and see him. Make sure he doesn't tell anyone.'

'What? I can't go back there.' Alex felt horrified by the idea of seeing this man again. He wrung his hands nervously before smoothing out the front of his apron. The look and feel of his female uniform brought home to him just how vulnerable he was.

'Come on, we're going to see him. Hopefully we can stop him from spreading this around.' Alex caught a look in her eye that told him she had more in mind than just talking, but before he could question her she'd taken his hand and was pulling him down the hallway. 'Let me do the talking. If you do as you're told then maybe we won't get into any more trouble.' She shook her head as she looked at him. 'You're not the girl I expected you to be, that's for sure.'

'Eh? But ... I'm not ...' He didn't have time to finish his sentence as she continued to pull him unceremoniously down the hallway.

Silence descended between them. Alex was desperately trying to make sense of what was happening to him. He touched his bottom through his dress, remembering the spanking he'd just received. He fancied that he could still taste Mrs Hatton's sex on his tongue. His mind was a whirlwind of emotion as he studied his reflection in a mirror as they passed it by. It was easy to see how other's were fooled into thinking he was a girl. There was no outward sign of his masculinity, even his still partially erect cock was hidden under the folds of the black maid's dress and apron. For a moment he found himself thinking that he actually looked quite sexy in his uniform, before mentally pulling himself back to reality.

'Right, just follow me and do as you're told.' Cheryl commanded. He felt entirely out of control as he meekly allowed himself to be led back to the scene of his crime.

'Young lady!'

The call from behind made both he and Cheryl stop. He spun around to find a middle aged woman stepping out of her room, looking straight at him.

'Can you bring me some additional towels please, when you're ready?' She asked politely, looking him directly in the eye.

'Oh ... Yes, Miss. C-Certainly, Miss.' He curtsied on instinct, looking down at his feet as he did so.

'Oh, how sweet!' Smiled the woman as she turned away.

Alex was beginning to wonder quite where his masculinity had disappeared to. The ease with which he'd stepped into his enforced role as a female maid was disconcerting and more than a little frightening to him. Cheryl gave his arm a tug.

'Come on, Maid Alex. We've got a certain man to see.' Said Cheryl, looking perfectly amused.

He followed on behind without protest, trying to ignore the sensual brushing of his stockings. Before he knew it they were once again standing outside the male guest's room. His heart was in his mouth as Cheryl knocked on the door, something he wished he'd done himself before entering unannounced earlier. They both heard a muffled reply which sounded like "Come in.", so Cheryl smoothed her own uniform out before briefly checking Alex's appearance. She then led him inside.

'Well, I see you came back with a friend.' The man's voice came from the bathroom. He walked through the doorway in nothing but a towel and a broad grin on his face.

'S-Sorry to trouble you, Sir.' Began Cheryl, sounding slightly breathless. Alex looked at her, seeing the lustful look in her eyes as she pored over this man's fit body. 'It's just, I wanted to ensure my colleague here hadn't given you cause for complaint in any way.'

Alex was experiencing a sense of foreboding as he saw Cheryl's eyes widen with admiration as the man turned away and sauntered over to the bed. As his eyes were drawn to the man's thinly covered bottom, the towel dropped and he gasped with surprise as the man turned around to face them.

'Well, I suppose she did help me out with a little ... something.' He grinned at Alex as his hand moved to take hold of his meaty cock. 'Although, she did walk in on me without even knocking.'

'Erm ... Yes, we're sorry about that, Sir. She's new I'm afraid.' Continued Cheryl, her eyes firmly fixed on the man's phallus. 'I was hoping we could settle the matter between us. If there's anything else we can ... do for you?' She raised an eyebrow questioningly.

Alex could sense the tension in the room. He dared not move lest he simply draw the man's attention back to himself.

'Well, actually, I could avoid making any complaints if she were to put that pretty little mouth to good use, perhaps.'

Cheryl looked around at Alex. He trembled as he gazed down upon the man's slowly engorging cock. He could clearly recall the feel of it between his fingers as he'd stroked the man to orgasm, but to actually use his mouth on it seemed a different matter entirely. Cheryl smirked at him before meeting the man's eyes once more.

'And perhaps, while my friend here does that, you'd like to do the same for me? Just as a little thank you to us.' She said.

The man's smile grew even wider as he contemplated the two young maids standing before him. Alex felt himself shrinking under his gaze, his legs turning to jelly once more as he thought about what Cheryl was pushing him into. He cast a furtive look behind him at the door as he considered making a sharp exit.

'Come on, Alex. The man's waiting. You don't want to get into trouble, do you?' Asked Cheryl as she took his hand and pulled him toward the bed.

Finding himself positioned within reach of the man once more he tried to tell his legs to move, to get him away but nothing happened. He just stood frozen to the spot as Cheryl reached up underneath her skirt as if to pull her panties down.

'Oh, that's right, I'm not wearing any.' Cheryl shrugged and grinned at the man as he slid onto the bed and laid flat, a look of expectancy on his face. She turned to Alex. 'Well, don't keep our guest waiting, Alexandra. You know what to do.'

Alex's cock twitched at the reminder that he was still wearing her panties underneath the dress, causing his arousal to grow even further. His mouth dropped open as he heard her extend his name to that of a girl. He could see the man's cock growing ever harder as he anticipated having this maid's mouth on him. Cheryl crawled onto the bed and with a mischievous grin positioned herself above the man's face. She gave a pointed look towards the man's crotch as she waited for him to position himself on the bed in front of her. With a resigned whimper he crawled up next to the man's crotch and looked down with trepidation.

'After you, Alexandra.' Said Cheryl, clearly waiting for him to make a start on pleasuring the man before she lowered herself to receive her own reward.

Alex groaned softly as he moved his hand across and just as he had done earlier that very morning, wrapped his fingers around the man's thickening shaft. He drew in a sharp breath as he felt the firm flesh grow in his hand. Slowly he began to move his fingers up and down in a repeat of his previous actions as he peered up at Cheryl. She'd lowered herself onto the man's face and was giggling as he used his tongue on her pussy. Her dress was covering the man's head and Alex could only imagine what was going on between her legs.

'Oh, Sir!' Cheryl mumbled, biting her lip as she stared straight at Alex. 'Go on Alex, do as you're told.' She said breathlessly.

Alex returned his attention to the man's erect cock, now fully engorged in his hand. He swallowed hard as he peered down at the swollen glans peeking out from between his thumb and forefinger. His stomach somersaulted at the thought of what he

193

was about to do, but despite his reluctance he found himself slowly lowering his head toward the man's naked crotch. Pausing within inches of another man's penis, he swallowed hard as he tried not to think too much about what he was doing. His own cock twitched forcefully inside of his panties. Realising he was still being turned on by the situation came as a shock to his system, and with another despondent groan he decided to test the water and taste another man's cock for the very first time.

Pushing his tongue out, he bent lower and ran it cautiously along the tip, tasting the fleshy glans. It didn't seem too bad, and so he began to lick around the tip as his hand continued to move up and down the shaft. He could feel his own stiff little cock bouncing inside of his panties as he moved, increasing his own desire and overcoming any reluctance to continue. Sinking lower he opened his mouth wide and took the man's cock inside of him, feeling his mouth being filled with thick, fleshy man meat as he sucked it in.

'That's it Alex, suck him off like a good girl!' Cheryl spoke between pants as she rode against the man's face, her eyes half closed yet closely watching him going down on the man's cock.

Alex tried to ignore what she'd said as he took more and more penis into his mouth. The man's hips had started to move with him, trying to force himself further into Alex's mouth as he held onto the thick shaft. He had to focus on breathing through his nose as he was filled with another man's phallus. His entire being seemed to be focused on pleasuring another once more, his femininised form preying on his mind, allowing him to convince himself that he was merely acting the part of a girl, but in truth he knew that something deep inside of him was changing.

As he pumped the man's shaft with his hand he became aware of something oozing out into his mouth. He could taste precum on his tongue and his anxiety built as he anticipated what would surely happen if he continued to suck this man toward a climax. He felt debased, humiliated and thrilled at this new experience. His mind was too confused to think straight and so he simply continued what he was doing.

'Oh god! Oh god! Y-Yessss!' Cheryl cried out as she began to climax, throwing her head back as her entire body tensed.

Alex's own cock responded to the sound of this young maid orgasming next to him and his cock jumped again. He sensed

194

something wet in his panties and realised that he too was leaking precum. In a bid to finish the man off he increased the speed of his hand as he pumped it up and down furiously, his mouth still filled with his cock head. It was then he sensed a tightening of the man's balls and a tenseness in his body. He thought of pulling back but the man thrust his hips upwards, forcing his cock deep into his mouth as the first jet of cum gushed forth. Alex's eyes went wide as he realised what was happening. He felt the hot thick cum spewing out onto his tongue and down the back of his throat. Thinking he was going to choke he swallowed hard, taking the man juice down just as another stream filled his mouth. He could taste the cum on his tongue and had to continually swallow it down in order to avoid choking.

It seemed to go on for an age, but finally the last drops were squeezed out into his mouth and he was able to slip the man's cock out from between his lips. He still felt close to an orgasm of his own, so aroused had he become after performing successive sex acts. He whimpered as he wiped some escaped cum from his lips, feeling debased by his own actions. For a moment he dared not move, worried that even the slightest stimulation would send him over the edge and have him cumming into his own panties.

All he could hear was the heavy breathing coming from both Cheryl and the man as they both recovered from their orgasms. Cheryl slowly lifted herself from the bed. Alex followed suit to stand next to her, his legs feeling like jelly with a desperate need for his own release nagging away at him.

'Well, if that'll be all, Sir? I trust everything has been to your satisfaction.' Said Cheryl as she smoothed down her uniform.

The man laughed wearily from the bed. 'Oh yes, young lady. Quite satisfactory.' He turned his head to look at Alex. 'You're clearly quite practised at your work, Girl. Maybe I'll see you again on a future visit.' He winked.

Alex smiled politely, not knowing what else to do or say. It was a relief when Cheryl led him back out of the room into the bright hallway. She sighed happily.

'That was nice. Have you done that before, Alex?' She asked absently.

'No!' He said defensively, but even he would have trouble believing him after that.

Chapter 7

They both looked a little shocked at what they'd done as they stood in the hallway together. Cheryl's face was still flushed from her climax.

'Oh my god!' She said under her breath, as if not quite believing what'd happened. 'I've never done anything like that before. You're such a naughty little slut, Alex.'

'Me?' Alex was nonplussed as to why he was being accused of such a thing.

'It's because of you that we were in there. If you hadn't already jerked him off, Alexandra!' She giggled as he shifted his weight uncomfortably, wishing he could get rid of his erection. 'Did you like it?' She asked, almost as an afterthought.

'What? I ... N-No, I ...' His face grew even hotter as she watched his expression.

'Let's see.' Her hand shot up his dress and before he could react she'd cupped his stiff little cock in her hand. 'You did, you little slut!' She giggled harder as he groaned loudly.

'P-Please ... let go ... I'm ... I ... argghh!'

The touch of her hand through the panties was all it took to send him over the edge. He felt his balls tighten and then he was spurting into his underwear, soiling himself as he shuddered his way through the most humiliating orgasm of his life.

'Oh my god!' She said again, this time looking quite shocked as he filled her panties with cum. 'I don't believe it.'

Alex felt himself on the verge of tears as he was forced to support himself against the wall. He couldn't stop what was happening and had no choice but to stand there and allow his climax to run its course. This was the second time that he'd cum in her hand and was undoubtedly the most embarrassing. When finally he'd stopped cumming, he felt her hand slowly withdraw from his crotch.

'I'm ... sorry.' He said in a quivering voice.

He could feel the wetness between his legs. A trickle of cum was running slowly down the inside of one of his thighs to soak into the stocking top.

'Well, we've still got work to do, you know? Come on.' Cheryl took his wrist and forced him to follow her.

He walked stiffly, acutely aware of how wet his panties were and desperately hoping that they'd contain enough of his juices to avoid any embarrassing leaks in public. By the time they were approaching their trolley he was having serious doubts as to whether this would be the case. Cheryl stopped by the trolley and studied him for a moment.

'What's wrong?' She asked.

'My ... panties. I need to change them.' He spoke softly, his humiliation deepening at the admission that not only was he wearing panties, but that he'd made them sopping wet too.

Cheryl looked up and down the hallway for a moment before having an idea.

'We don't have time to go back downstairs to change, we've too much to do here. Follow me.' She said before knocking on the door opposite. When no answer was heard she opened the door and waited for him to enter before closing it behind them. 'We can borrow some from in here. I saw the two girls leaving earlier and I doubt they'll miss a pair of panties.'

'What? I can't take someone else's panties!' He whispered frantically.

'Well you took mine and you made them all dirty, so you haven't got much of a choice, unless you *want* to walk around without any on under your dress.' She said, looking him up and down critically.

'I ... well, no.' He knew he needed something to keep his diminutive manhood hidden away, so he shrugged disconsolately and peered around the room. There were a number of articles of clothing lying around, amongst them at least three pairs of panties. He wondered if everyone was so untidy when staying in a hotel before watching Cheryl cross the room and bend over to pick up the nearest pair.

'What about these?' She asked, holding out a pair of black lacy panties.

Catching sight of her stocking tops as she bent over and knowing that she wasn't wearing any underwear herself made his heart skip a beat. He shrugged his shoulders once more, unable to put up any further resistance to this young attractive maid.

'Right, go clean yourself up and change your panties ... quickly!' She threw the underwear to him as she pointed to the bathroom. 'I'll tidy the room so they don't notice them missing.'

He walked stiffly into the bathroom, his cum soaked panties feeling uncomfortable against his skin. He caught sight of himself in the mirror and immediately looked away. It was still a peculiar experience, seeing himself in the form of a female maid. Pulling his wet panties off he lifted his dress and quickly cleaned himself up, feeling a little ashamed and incredibly embarrassed by what'd just happened. He knew he'd lost all control of the situation and was entirely at the mercy of Cheryl and Miss Tamworth now. A feeling of helplessness overcame him as he lifted up the black panties in front of him. He was now resorting to wearing a complete strangers worn underwear, the feminine aroma evident as he studied them for several seconds before resigning himself to the act of putting them on. He quickly pulled them up his stockinged legs and felt a familiar thrill at their touch as he settled them into place. He wondered who they belonged to and hoped they'd not be missed.

By the time he exited the bathroom, Cheryl had made good progress at tidying the room. He joined in without another word and between them they finished their work and stepped back out into the hallway.

'Oh good, you've cleaned our room. Thanks girls!'

Alex looked up to see two young women walking toward them from the elevator. They looked like sisters, although one was blond and the other brunette. They were both attractive girls and he immediately began to blush at the thought that he was surreptitiously wearing a pair of panties that belonged to one of them.

'Yes, Miss. All cleaned and ready for you.' Cheryl smiled before pulling him away toward their trolley.

As the two girls disappeared into their room he held out the soiled panties to Cheryl, having been holding them with a pile of dirty towels. She grimaced slightly as she took them before shaking her head in amusement and dropping them into the laundry bag.

'I'll deal with them later.' She said. 'Let's finish our work and we can take a break.'

-o0o-

By the time the two maids had completed their work Alex was feeling tired both physically and emotionally. There'd been several more encounters with guests along the way, although none of them developed into sexual encounters. No one seemed to notice anything out of place in this young maid going about her duties. He was even becoming accustomed to the occasional admiring glances from the male guests. Having sent the laundry down the shoot they made their way back downstairs for a break. It was as they were sitting together in the staff room that Miss Tamworth found them.

'Ah, Girls!' She said, marching toward them. She took a moment to check that no one else was present before looking at Alex. 'I assume there've been no further problems performing your duties?'

'Um ... no, Miss Tamworth.' He answered, visions of his performing sex acts on Mrs Hatton and the male guest flashing through his mind.

'Good. In fact, I have to tell you that one of our guests - a certain Mr Mahoney in room 2010 - has phoned reception to offer his compliments to a young maid fitting your description. Would that be you do you think?'

Alex exchanged looks with Cheryl, knowing full well who it would be. He turned back to Miss Tamworth and nodded guiltily, wondering just what the man had said to her.

'Well don't look so downbeat about it, Alex. You've done well. It's not many maids that receive such compliments on their first day.' She looked at him thoughtfully for several seconds as Alex sat there feeling increasingly uncomfortable. 'I don't suppose you have any girl clothes at home, do you?' She asked, quite taking him by surprise.

'Er ... no, I don't.' He said, unsure whether to be offended by the question or not. Suddenly aware of the clothing he was wearing he pulled his dress down as far as it would go and straightened his apron.

'Mmm, we'll have to do something about that. You'll need clean underwear of course, and a change of uniform too.'

Alex looked up at her, feeling bewildered by her words.

'But ... why?' He asked. Seeing the impatient reaction in her he added quickly, 'I ... I can come as a boy tomorrow, can't I?'

'A boy? Of course not, Alex. Don't be silly. I can't have guests recognising you as a boy when only the previous day you were going about your duties as a girl, can I?' She said firmly. 'No, you'll just have to continue working as a girl and that's all there is to it, young lady!'

'I can lend her some underwear, Miss Tamworth, if that'll help.' Offered Cheryl.

'Yes, that would be most helpful, Cheryl. I should be able to find another spare uniform, and who knows what we'll find in the lost property cupboard, there's usually some clothing in there too.'

Alex looked from one to another in disbelief. Could they honestly be planning to have him work there as a female maid? It felt like complete madness, and no one had even bothered to check whether he was happy to go along with their plans.

'She could stay in the staff quarters, if there's room, that way I can help her get ready in the morning.' Said Cheryl excitedly. Alex wasn't aware of there being such a thing as staff quarters until now.

'Hmm, that sounds sensible. She'll obviously need a room in the female quarters but I'm sure that won't be a problem. We'll just keep this our little secret, shall we?' Said Miss Tamworth, giving them both a hard look.

'Of course, Miss Tamworth. I'll even let her borrow my clothes, until she gets her own that is.'

'That's decided then. Come and see me when you finish your shift and I'll arrange her lodgings. You'll still need to pay for them though, they're not entirely free.' With that Miss Tamworth nodded with satisfaction and left them alone.

Alex just stared after her, wondering at what point he'd agreed to such a plan. He turned to Cheryl.

'How can I ... I mean ...'

'Don't look so worried, Alex. You'll be fine. The rooms aren't that big but they're not bad, and the rent's really cheap.'

'But I'm already renting a room.' He said.

'I bet it's costing more than the staff rooms here, and you won't have to travel to work. Come on, it'll be fun. You can give up your other room and move in tonight if you like?'

Alex remained speechless for a time. His eyes drifted down to his feminine attire, trying to understand how he'd found himself in such a position. It seemed he had a simple choice to make, either accept the offer and move into the hotel as a girl, or leave his job. With little prospect of finding another position that easily he wondered just how long he'd have a roof over his head anyway. Letting out a resigned whimper he looked about the staff room as if seeing it for the first time. It seemed as though this would be his new home, and that he'd be living there as a hotel maid for the foreseeable future. It was a strange turn of events indeed, and given how his first day had progressed he doubted it his life as a female employee was going to be anything other than interesting for the foreseeable future.

How I Was Turned Into My Girlfriend's Little Sister

One boy's story of sexual feminisation

in the home

Rebecca Sterne

Chapter 1

Walking through the front door of my girlfriend Laura's house, I called out to her mom Theresa expecting to hear her usual reply from somewhere inside. Being met with complete silence I remembered that they'd told me that very morning they'd be visiting Laura's older sister – Nicole at her new apartment. They expected to be back later that evening, but until then I'd have the house to myself.

It seemed strange to be arriving home after college to an empty house. Theresa usually worked from home and would normally be there to greet me. I dropped my backpack in the hallway and skulked into the kitchen, fixing myself a drink from the refrigerator as I tried to forget my day.

I'd met Laura soon after starting at the local college and despite her being twenty-one and two years older than me we were soon an item. I counted myself lucky that a girl like Laura had seen something in me that made her ask me out on a date. It wasn't exactly a whirlwind romance but we quickly developed a close friendship that saw us hanging out together as often as we could. She was clearly the dominant force in our relationship and given that I normally struggled to form new friendships I was perfectly happy with this.

My first few weeks at college had not been a whole lot of fun for me, especially as not only had my father moved away soon after I'd started, but he'd made it clear I wasn't to go with him. My mother had left the family home several years earlier to start a new life and I quickly found myself facing the prospect of sleeping on the street. Luckily my new girlfriend had taken pity on me and convinced her mom to let me stay with them. Theirs was an all female household and had been since Laura was a young girl and their father had left them.

I'd never been that great at making friends and my college term was proving to be difficult. I'd hoped that the juvenile teasing about my size would not carry on into college, but that'd proved to be a false hope. Sure, it wasn't quite as bad as it had been at school, but my slight five foot three inch frame meant that I appeared more as a middle school kid than an older teenager. The fact that I seldom had to shave and that in a rebellious move I'd resisted having my hair cut for some time also drew comparisons with being more like a girl than a boy. I could see what they meant sometimes when I caught sight of my straight blonde hair laying across my shoulders, but I couldn't quite bring myself to concede defeat and have it styled to look manlier.

It seemed strange moving in with my girlfriend and her mom. Laura's sister had only recently left for a new job opportunity and was experiencing life as an independent woman of twenty-two. I found myself being given her room as their mom was unwilling to have me share with her daughter. It was clearly a girl's room. Pink walls and posters of her favourite boy bands covered the area above the bed. The bedding was ultra-feminine and apart from moving her old clothes and girlish paraphernalia out of the way it was pretty much as she'd left it.

Feeling a little lost for what to do I traipsed up the stairs to Nicole's room, intent on spending the rest of the day immersed in a video game. In a further bid to put my day behind me I quickly stripped my clothes off before putting on a bathrobe. As much as I tried over the next twenty minutes, I just couldn't seem to concentrate on the games at hand. I looked around my room feeling rather disgruntled before sliding off the bed and headed towards the bathroom.

As I reached the bathroom across the hall, I noticed the door to Laura's mom's bedroom had been left wide open. Pausing for a moment, it was as if my boredom and desire to find something different to do got the better of me, and I found myself changing direction towards Theresa's room.

Standing in the doorway I peered inside, seeing an array of boxes strewn across the floor I realised she had been busily sorting through her daughter's things. Stepping inside, I looked down into the nearest box to see some of her old toys and childish books neatly packed away. She'd written "Give away" on the side, clearly denoting that these were destined to be donated to the local thrift store. Moving further into the room I began to look inside the rest of the half dozen boxes.

It was then that I spotted a pair of pink cotton panties lying atop the contents of one box in particular. I didn't know it then, but what followed was about to change my life in a way that I could never have expected. I still wonder if I'd just left them where they were and returned to my games whether any of this would have happened. Don't get me wrong, I couldn't be happier than I am right now; it's just one of those fateful moments that depending on what action you choose can send you in one of two entirely different directions. In this case, I chose to pick them up.

As I lifted them up to dangle them from my fingers, I realised they must have been a pair of Nicole's panties from when she was younger. Holding the soft material in my hands I looked at the delicate pink trim and small satin bow at the front, and much to my surprise felt something stir deep inside of me. Glancing back into the box I couldn't help but crouch down next to it and start rummaging through its contents.

Theresa had obviously decided it was time to clear out all of her daughter's childhood clothing as it was full of underwear and nightwear. Moving to the next box along I spied several girl's dresses and skirts with tops piled into a third. I found myself wondering curiously as to whether her old clothes would actually fit me. If I'd been of an average height and build for a boy my age it would have been unlikely, but I suspected I could probably squeeze into them if I tried.

Rolling Nicole's panties around in my hands for several seconds I contemplated what I was tempted to do. I'd never worn girl's clothes before, although I'd be lying to myself if I didn't admit to feeling a certain curiosity when it came to seeing Laura's abandoned clothing around the house at times. We'd never tried much more than heavy petting so far in our relationship, apart from some brief touching through each other's underwear. I guess my sexual urges were beginning to get the better of me.

Eventually something inside of me gave in to the inevitable, and with the added knowledge that I had the place to myself for several more hours I allowed the bathrobe to fall to the floor. I searched through the boxes in turn with a more purposeful intent as I gathered what I hoped was a suitable bundle of clothing together before dropping them onto Theresa's bed.

With one last look at the pile of clothing that I'd retrieved, I picked up the pale pink panties and slowly stepped into them. I was fortunate that I possessed very little in the way of body hair, and as I drew them up my legs I found myself holding my breath as I felt the soft cotton panties being pulled slowly upwards. The feel of them cupping my twitching penis as I pulled them all of the way up sent a kind of thrill through me that I'd never before experienced. I realised that I was trembling, as if the very sensation of putting my girlfriend's sister's girlish panties on had somehow overwhelmed my senses.

Realising I'd been holding my breath all of the while, I finally let it out with a ragged sigh. I couldn't stop myself from running my hands across my pantied bottom, feeling the softness of the material as it clung sensually to my most intimate of areas. The joy of knowing that they fit me perfectly ran through me as if all my Christmas's had come at once. I wasn't sure why I was feeling so relieved and happy at this revelation, I only knew that I now wanted to go further, try more of her clothes on.

Looking down at the bed my eyes settled on a bra top that closely matched the panties I was already wearing. It was clearly designed for girls that were at that budding stage of development as there was little support evident. Hoping that this would also fit my slight frame I lifted it from the bed and pulled it over my head. Pushing my arms through the straps I pulled it down to cover my flat chest, delighted that this also fit my dimensions perfectly. Feeling the pink, silky straps and looking down at the girlish motifs on the front of the bra top I could feel my masculinity slipping away in favour of an innocent femininity that was in stark contrast to anything I'd ever felt before.

With an increased urgency I then pulled the white lace frilled ankle socks onto my feet. Admiring how they made my legs look so girly, I was soon lifting a baby pink dress from the bed. Holding it out in front of me I wondered if it would indeed fit, designed for a young girl as it was. The puffy sleeves and shiny pink bow that adorned the back were girlishness personified. For a moment I was thankful that my girlfriend's sister had always been such a girly girl. I'd only ever seen her dressed in the most feminine of items.

A real sense of nervousness arose inside of me as I actually began to worry that her dress wouldn't fit me. Lifting it above my head I slipped my arms through the holes and began to pull it downward. For a moment it became stuck as I struggled with the unfamiliarity of putting a dress on, panicking that not only would it not fit me but that I might find myself trapped within the material, hopelessly stuck until my girlfriend or worse, her mom returned to find me half dressed in Nicole's old clothes. When eventually I managed to pull it down a little further it quickly fell into place, draping me within its soft delicate embrace as I became buried in the very definition of girlish femininity.

With an irresistible urge to see myself, I scurried across the room to take advantage of the full length mirror. My breath was taken away for a moment as I saw myself in Nicole's juvenile clothing for the first time. My heart was beating fast as I took in the sight of the pretty pink dress and lacy ankle socks, knowing that underneath it all I had on an equally pretty set of matching underwear. As I looked myself up and down I caught sight of my own inane grin in the mirror, transfixed by my own reflection.

My entire body was tingling. Without thinking I lifted the hem of the dress to reveal the panties underneath, seeing the small bulge of my arousal showing through. For a while I just turned this way and that in front of the mirror, not wanting to let go of the image of myself as a girl. I soon realised that I bore an uncanny resemblance to my own girlfriend now that I was presenting myself in her sister's clothes. Studying my unkempt hair for a moment, the urge to dress even more girly came upon me and I hopped over to the boxes for another search of their contents.

I soon located several hair bands and other accessories and pulled them out onto the floor for closer examination. Spotting the girl's hair band with a pink bow on top I knew immediately this was the one that I wanted. Looking through the various accessories I was surprised to find some rather infantile looking dressing up jewellery, including some pink clip on earrings and a matching necklace. Taking my small haul over to the dressing table I retrieved one of Theresa's hair brushes and brushed through my hair until it was presentable. Pushing the hair band in and adding the jewellery, I finally presented myself back to the full length mirror for a final inspection. I looked every bit the pretty young girl, much to my own amazement.

-o0o-

Feeling as though I were walking on air, I decided to take a stroll around the house in my new found persona. It felt strange, emerging from my girlfriend's mom's room dressed in her sister's old clothes. It also felt naughty somehow. I had an undeniable arousal between my legs, feeling the dress moving against my bare thighs as I walked out into the hallway. Swishing my way back into Nicole's old room, I looked around with a feeling of disinterest and decided to make my way downstairs for something to eat.

I couldn't resist pausing in front of the mirror in the downstairs hallway, admiring my girlish look and wondering at how it was making me feel. A mixture of sweet femininity and underlying arousal in the headiest of combinations. Almost without realising it I walked into the kitchen with my hands clasped sweetly in front of myself, as if to fool anyone watching into believing I really was just an innocent young girl. I was of course quite alone, but for one fleeting moment I did wonder if I would look convincing enough to fool anyone who might see.

My beastly day seemed to slip gently away as I padded around the room, busily fixing myself something to eat. Opening the cupboard to find a tin of alphabet spaghetti, one of my girlfriend's favourites when she was younger and something her mom had never gotten out of the habit of buying every so often. I decided to have this on toast as a way of extending my temporary regression into a childhood that I'd never experienced as a girl.

By the time this was ready I'd poured myself a glass of milk and took my childish meal into the living area to watch television. Somehow I was overcome with the desire to continue experiencing things as if I were of a younger age, and was quickly settled in for a night of cartoons. As much as I was enjoying the sensation of acting as a young girl, my grown up feelings of arousal at being dressed in Nicole's old clothes would not go away, and I was acutely aware of my erection straining against the front of the panties as if to demand its own attention.

Eventually I lay back upon the couch, lifting the dress up to reveal the soft pink panties below with my small yet rigid penis underneath. Placing my hand onto Nicole's underwear I gently caressed myself, gazing down at the clothes I now wore and becoming lost in the sensations that were coursing through me as I touched myself through the girlish panties. With my eyes slowly closing I began to squirm from my own ministrations. Imagining my girlfriend seeing me in her sister's clothes, and being the one to touch me down there as she became turned on herself.

Several minutes went by in this way as my arousal continued to grow inside of me, causing my breathing to become shallow with desire. As my thoughts penetrated further into my mind I paused, worried at what I was doing in these clothes and conscious of how it might look to another, but then I calmed myself with the notion that neither my girlfriend nor anyone else would ever know, and it wasn't as if I were doing anyone any harm.

Relaxing into my own rhythm, I began to slowly thrust my hips upward against my hand, imagining myself to be a girl in the throes of her own self-induced arousal. I could feel a sensation building inside of me, as if I were fast approaching the point of no return. I could hear my own whimpers of pleasure escaping as I felt a tightening between my legs, as if my body were preparing to explode its pleasure outward. The idea that I would soon climax into my girlfriend's sister's panties if I continued to stroke myself in this way came to the fore, but it already felt too late to stop it as I pushed any concerns away in favour of reaching what I now knew would be the most explosive climax of my entire life.

I could feel the panties becoming wet with precum. Suddenly my whole body went rigid, held in time and space for one excruciating and tantalising moment as my orgasm rushed through me and my little cock began to spasm inside Nicole's underwear.

'LOUIS!'

I only heard the voice as if from a distance at first, as my climax surged forth and I began to spew hot cum into the cotton panties, gasping as I did so.

'What are you doing?'

It was then that it registered that someone else was now in the room and talking to me. A split second later it also registered that it was Theresa's voice, and that despite the situation I could not stop my orgasm from continuing onward. As my eyes fluttered open in shock, I caught a glimpse of her standing in the doorway, her eyes fixed upon where my hand was pressed firmly against the front of her daughter's panties, her expression one of shock and disbelief at what she was now witnessing as the underwear became increasingly sodden with my cum.

As I tried to respond I could only groan despondently as the last few spasms rushed through me, squeezing the last of my climax outward only to deepen my humiliation even further. By the time my orgasm was subsiding my face was already a deep shade of red, a combination of post orgasmic flushing and acute embarrassment at my own actions that had been witnessed by my girlfriend's mom.

I shakily sat up on the couch and pulled the dress down to cover myself. For a while she simply stood there, watching me as if mesmerised by what she'd seen. Then, walking tentatively around to the side of the couch she looked me up and down as if trying to understand what I was wearing.

'Are you wearing Nicole's clothes?' She asked uncertainly, her eyes never leaving me. I gazed down at myself, knowing I'd have to admit everything as she could plainly see for herself that I was. I nodded timidly before answering in a quiet voice.

'Yes. I...I'm sorry Theresa. It's just that...I mean...I was bored and...' I had no idea how to explain what I'd been doing to her. My voice trailed off into an embarrassed silence whilst she looked at me, and I looked down at my feet.

'Stand up!' She suddenly ordered in a firm voice. As I complied I could feel the wet panties clinging to me underneath the dress. Without warning she stepped forward and lifted the dress up above my waist.

'Wait!' I protested instinctively, trying to pull it back down again but she simply batted my hands away with an annoyed expression. She looked me in the eyes for a moment as if to dare me to object any further. Seeing my resistance crumble as I moved my hands behind my back she cast her eyes downward once more to study my sodden panties.

'I take it you found these in my room?' She asked.

'Yes.' My chin gave a little wobble as I saw myself being thrown out of the house, losing my girlfriend and becoming homeless because of one moment of madness.

'Well, I was going to give these away, but I can't very well do that now.' I was unable to speak as I tried to hold back my emotions. 'I assume you weren't expecting us back for some time.' She said, dropping the dress back into place.

I turned my head to peer anxiously out of the room, wondering where my girlfriend was. Then she appeared in the doorway. It was as if she didn't realise the situation for a moment as she breezed into the room.

'I'll just go and find Louis; he's probably playing his computer games again.' She said. Her eyes flicked over to me as she realised someone else was in the room. 'Oh. Hi. I didn't realise someone...' I could see the realisation wash over her as she processed the sight of me standing across the room, dressed as a girl. 'Louis? What...what are you wearing?' She stared open mouthed, waiting for someone to explain the situation to her.

'It appears your boyfriend has been into my room and decided to wear Nicole's old clothes. Which surprisingly seem to fit him quite well.' Theresa looked me up and down, confirming that the clothes did in fact fit me.

There was a pause whilst everyone seemed to consider what needed to happen next. Swallowing hard I decided to break the silence.

'I-I'm sorry, Laura.' I began croakily, 'I'd better go and take these off.'

'You're not going anywhere!' Theresa said firmly, drawing a look from both myself and Laura. 'Laura, it seems that Louis here was quite excited about wearing girl's clothes. So excited that he managed to dirty Nicole's old panties.' She looked at me accusingly. If the ground had opened up into a large cavernous expanse right there and then, I would gladly have leapt in without a moment's hesitation.

Pausing for a moment, Laura approached me before copying her mom's earlier actions and lifting the dress up. She studied the wet, sticky panties that I was wearing for several seconds before letting go.

'If you're going to act like a naughty little girl then we'll just have to treat you as such. Won't we?' Theresa glanced at her daughter before looking back at me. My lips moved but nothing came out as I tried to formulate a response. I had no idea what she meant by this. 'It appears that your boyfriend here is one of those little sissy boys that likes to dress in girl's clothes.' I studied her expression, trying to work out whether this was a derisive remark or whether there was something else behind it. Her face didn't appear angry as such, more thoughtful than anything.

'Is this true Louis? You like wearing girl's clothes?' Laura asked inquisitively.

'I...um...' I didn't know what to say. It would seem ludicrous to attempt some kind of denial given what I was wearing, and my one overriding thought at this time was not to do or say anything that might result in my spending the night on the street.

'I think that's self-evident, don't you Laura?' Theresa said. 'The question is, what do we do about it? Louis, stand over there please. I'd like to speak to Laura.' I followed her pointing finger and realised she was directing me to the corner of the room. Feeling as though there was little choice but to comply, I did as I was told as Laura and her mom left the room.

The next few minutes were possibly the longest of my life as I contemplated what was about to happen. It seemed quite certain that I'd soon be looking for somewhere else to live and that my relationship with my best friend was now over.

Chapter 2

It seemed as if I'd studied every inch of the wallpaper in front of me several times over before my girlfriend and her mom eventually reappeared in the room. At first I was nervous of turning around to face them, suddenly wishing that my corner time could go on even longer as I dreaded what they were about to say to me.

'Turn around Louis.' Theresa ordered firmly. As I did so I was met with her stern expression, but as I glanced at Laura I was surprised to see a smirk of amusement upon my girlfriend's face. I was still uncomfortably aware of the damp panties between my legs which served as a reminder of just how badly I'd embarrassed myself already.

'We've had a little talk about your dressing up.' I opened my mouth to speak, thinking to nip this in the bud with a planned explanation of why I'd been caught wearing Nicole's old clothes and why it'd never happen again if they were to give me a second chance. Theresa simply raised her hand. The assertive look in her eyes was enough to still my tongue. 'I'm not happy that you snuck into my room and took Nicole's clothes, despite the fact they were being thrown out.' Again I opened my mouth to speak but was

214

silenced by her hand; her look of impatience was enough to stop any further protests from me. 'However, I understand that you must have been suppressing your own desires to be dressed as a girl, and presented with the opportunity you were unable to stop yourself.' She took a step closer to me, her expression softening slightly as she looked me up and down. 'We've decided that you can be dressed as a girl and you can even have Nicole's old clothes, but if you want to be treated as a girl you'll be punished as one too.'

Confusion reigned in my mind as I tried to understand what she was saying to me. Had I heard her right? Had she really just said that I can have her daughter's clothes for myself? What did she mean by being treated and punished as a girl? It seemed that they'd misinterpreted my unusual act of boredom for one with more of a purpose than was really there.

Theresa stepped towards me and taking hold of my wrist she led me over to a chair, sitting herself down in front of me. She pulled me towards her and as I stumbled forward to find myself standing against her legs she began to pull me down across her lap.

'On my lap. Now please!' She demanded as I stopped resisting and allowed her to position me across her legs. It was then that I realised she intended to spank me like a child! 'Stop squirming or you'll get even more.' She said as I mumbled an apology as if this would ward off her attentions.

I felt the dress being lifted up at the back as she placed one hand firmly on top of me, holding me in position. She had on a reasonably short skirt that rode up her legs. I realised my cum filled panties were now pressed against her bare thigh, causing my embarrassment to deepen even further as I knew she must feel their wetness against her skin. My plight wasn't helped by the fact that at thirty nine years old, she was an attractive woman whose daughters had clearly both inherited their looks from her.

I held my breath, trying to remain as still as I could so as not to move my manhood against her. To my absolute horror I felt her take hold of the waistband on the panties and pull them down just far enough to expose my bottom cheeks.

'No...Please?' I reached around to pull them back up again, only to have my hand slapped away.

'Mom, what are you doing?' I heard Laura question her mom.

'If she's going to be treated as one of my girls she's going to get an appropriate punishment. A bare bottom spanking is definitely called for here.'

'She?'

'Well, we can hardly refer to her as him, can we? Not now.' Theresa seemed to be throwing herself into the idea that I was now one of her girls as long as I was wearing Nicole's clothes. I felt her adjusting her position underneath me, causing my little cock to twitch against her leg through the panties. I hoped desperately that she hadn't felt anything. 'You do not take something that is not yours without asking in future. Is that clear?'

'Y-Yes.' I squeaked breathlessly. I wanted to protest, to argue against what she was doing and demand that I be treated like an adult, but every time I looked down at myself I realised just how pathetic this would seem to both my girlfriend and her mom.

SMACK!

The first blow landed and I felt my soft flesh stinging in response. I managed to stop myself from crying out, more from the humiliation than the pain. I couldn't manage to stop my hips from jerking away from her hand and forcing myself up against her leg, knowing that my panty covered penis was grinding against her but unable to stop it from happening.

SMACK!

The second blow struck my other cheek and began that one burning. Once again I jerked against her leg and not only felt myself pushing into her, but also growing partially erect as a result.

SMACK!

I'd no time to recover from the last blow before the next one landed. By now I was more focussed on my unwanted erection inside the panties than the spanking itself. I knew she must have been able to feel it, my face burned even more than my bottom.

SMACK!

Once again I found my little stiffy grinding against my girlfriend's mom's leg. This time I let out a little yelp as the heat in my bottom grew more apparent.

SMACK!

A full grown sob escaped me this time. I wasn't certain whether it was from the stinging blow that had just landed or my overall feelings of complete and utter humiliation at this woman's hands. The fact that it was entirely my own fault did not escape me.

SMACK!

'Aaarrggghhh!' I cried out as the stinging in my bottom cheeks reached a new level. The blows stopped and I waited uncertainly for the next one to land. When several seconds passed by without another smack I began to wonder if it was over. My own embarrassment saw me stay precisely where I was, unwilling to face either Theresa or my girlfriend. Then the panties were being pulled back up and the dress lowered to at least offer a small amount of dignity.

'You may stand.' Theresa said. It was an awkward moment as I slowly tried to push myself from her lap, knowing that my still partially erect cock had brushed against her bare leg as I did so. 'You may take those wet panties off.' She added as I stood unsteadily, my eyes fixed forlornly upon the floor. I expected she would have me strip her daughter's clothes off before having me leave the house. Resistance seemed pointless at this stage and I reached underneath the skirt to take down the cum stained panties.

I pulled them down my legs and stepped out of them. Balling them up self-consciously as I prepared to be told to remove the rest of the clothes.

'As you're unable to keep your panties dry, you can put these on underneath your dress for now.' I looked up as Theresa pointed to what Laura was holding in her hand. It took me a moment to realise what they were. 'Laura used to wear them when she was younger sometimes. They're pull-up diapers.' Her explanation only served to confirm what I already knew. From the fairy design on the front I could tell they were girl's diapers. I found myself frozen to the spot as Laura headed towards me.

'It's okay, they're quite comfy really.' She said, as if this would make me feel better about being diapered. As she bent down in front of me, holding the legs open I was suddenly overcome with the surreal situation that I now found myself in. Far from taking Nicole's clothes back, they'd actually decided between them that I would be spanked and put into girl's diapers for my transgressions. In a daze I lifted each leg in turn to allow my girlfriend to slip them on me. She was bigger than me and a good three inches taller which meant it was no surprise to find that her old diapers fit me perfectly. As she drew them up my legs I stood with a slightly wider stance, allowing her to tug them all of the way up. It wasn't until she pulled them up underneath the dress

217

that I realised I still had a partial erection. As she maneuvered them all of the way up I knew she'd noticed as she finished dressing me. Her little smile as she looked me in the eye was a clear indication of that.

The softness of the diaper between my legs actually felt quite reassuring in a strange way. Realising that Laura had never seen my manhood before I looked away coyly.

'You actually look quite cute in my sister's clothes.' Said Laura, grinning.

I looked at Theresa, wondering what my next move should be. She clearly had no intention of having me put my boy clothes back on again.

'I'm sorry for taking the clothes.' I said weakly, 'It's just that I had another bad day at college and I was looking for something to do...and...'

'Well, you won't be returning to college just yet Louis; I think you need some punishment time for what you did.' Said Theresa as she rose up from the chair. 'You can stay here for now as I have some changes to make upstairs. Laura, you can keep an eye on her, make sure she doesn't do anything else.'

I watched as she left the room. Laura made herself comfortable on the couch, patting the seat next to her as an invitation to join her. Seeing little option I lowered myself down next to her, trying to keep the dress from riding up and showing off my girlish diapers.

'How long have you been wearing girl's clothes?' Laura asked after a short while.

'I haven't, I mean...I've never done it before.' I shrugged. 'I don't suppose you want to be my girlfriend anymore.' I seriously doubted that she would want to continue in a relationship with a boy that had worn her sister's clothes and been spanked by her mom for it.

'Well...I'll carry on being your girlfriend...if you'll be mine?'

Her response surprised me and I looked back at her, 'You still want me as your boyfriend?' I asked, relieved.

'No silly, but you can be my girlfriend if you like.' She giggled as she watched my face turn from hope into confusion. 'If you're going to dress like a girl I can't exactly call you my boyfriend, can I? You do look quite convincing.' She seemed to study me more closely for a moment. 'I think if I saw you outside

I'd have been convinced that you were just a young girl.'

I gaped at her for several seconds, her reaction to my indiscretions completely unexpected. Her eyes drifted downward to where we both knew I was now wearing a diaper. Without another word she slipped her hand underneath the dress and lifted it up before resting her palm lightly against the front of the padding. I breathed in sharply as I felt her pushing against my diapered cock.

'What are you doing?' I whispered. I felt as though I were trapped in my girl's clothing, unable to escape from the attentions of Laura or her mom as long as I was dressed this way.

'I saw you earlier, when I put your diaper on.' She said. Hearing my own girlfriend telling me that she'd put a diaper on me sounded strange to my ears. 'I saw your little stiffy.' She smiled as I squirmed from embarrassment. 'If I'd known you liked wearing girl's clothes I'd have lent you some of mine. Although they'd have been a bit big on you. You're lucky Nicole's old clothes were still here.'

Her hand began to move up and down the front of the diaper, causing me to become aroused once more. I sat rigidly in place, dumbfounded by what was now happening. The feel of her hand rubbing me through the diaper quickly had me fully erect. As she detected the telltale bulge below the padding she squeezed it between her fingers as much as the diaper would allow, sending a thrill of excitement right through me. Realising I'd soon be climaxing under her hand if she continued I wanted to stop her from deepening my shame any further.

'Please stop...Laura.' I said breathlessly, trying desperately to control my own reactions. 'I...I'm going to...' Suddenly I had to squeeze my eyes shut as I felt myself fast approaching another climax. Taking some deep breaths I made one last plea to my girlfriend. 'L-Laura...please...no!' She turned to look at me as I began to writhe under her hand.

'It's okay Louis; you've got a diaper on now. It's not like you'll wet your panties again.' She whispered this last part in an almost conspiratorial tone, as if to keep my little secret between us.

'Oh god!' I whimpered as I felt a familiar tightening between my legs. I couldn't believe quite what was happening right now as I cast my eyes back to the infantile looking diaper that Laura's hand was massaging me through. I knew it was already too late to avoid the inevitable as precum began to leak into the soft padding and my orgasm rushed forth. 'Oh no!' I cried, turned on and humiliated in equal measures by my predicament I felt my stiffened cock start to spew cum into the diaper as Laura pressed her hand into me. I jerked uncontrollably as I filled the diaper with my boy juice. Laura was giggling furiously as she watched my reactions, squirming under her hand in her sister's clothes and one of her old diapers.

When eventually I came back to earth from my climax, I felt my face reddening once again at the thought of being masturbated to an orgasm in a diaper. Laura continued to gently rub the front of the diaper as if fascinated by it for several seconds before finally removing her hand. She pecked me on the cheek with a broad smile upon her face.

'Naughty girl!' She said, laughing at my plight as I sagged visibly in front of her. I looked down between my legs and was relieved to see that there was no outward sign of what I'd just done inside of the diaper. 'Stay here. I'm going to see what Mom is doing.' She bounced out of the room leaving me thoroughly deflated and spent.

Sitting myself up I tried to focus on what was happening. I'd managed to get myself into a most surreal situation, and to say that I was surprised by both my girlfriend's and her mom's reactions was a serious understatement. It appeared that I wasn't about to be thrown out onto the street for wearing Nicole's old clothes, nor even for masturbating into her panties. It seemed a long way back to reinstate my position as Laura's boyfriend, or at least one that she could see as proper boyfriend material at least. I cast my eyes down at myself once more as if to confirm that I was in fact still wearing a girl's pink dress with frilly ankle socks and a diaper underneath.

I couldn't stop the despondent moan that escaped me as I reflected on what I'd actually done and how I now looked to Laura and her mom. What was I thinking? One moment of absolute madness and I'd landed myself in a whole heap of trouble that I suspected would not simply go away anytime soon. If I was honest with myself there'd been an underlying curiosity within me for some time when it came to girl's clothing. I'd picked up Laura's panties on more than one occasion, turning them over in my hands and wondering what it would be like to wear them. I'd even come close to doing so on one occasion, when I'd been alone in the house previously but something had stopped me. I guess it was the idea of being caught, worrying about the consequences and what Laura would think of me if she knew.

Shaking my head I felt the need to move around, to clear my head somehow. As I rose from the couch I was conscious of the dress brushing against my thighs and the feeling of the plump diaper between my legs. Walking into the hallway I looked at the front door for a moment, but one glance at my reflection in the mirror was enough to quell any thoughts of leaving the house.

Turning away I was forced to look back again, studying the girl that now looked back at me. The more I looked the more I realised that I really could quite easily pass for a girl. It was a moot point of course, as I'd never have to pass myself off to anyone, but I did secretly gain a certain satisfaction from the idea.

'Louis?' I heard Laura calling from upstairs, 'Come up here.'

With a final look at my reflection I started towards the stairs, forcing the grin off of my face. I couldn't let them know that I'd actually liked what I'd seen in the mirror.

Arriving at the top of the stairs I wondered where they were and why I'd been summoned. Presenting myself to them still dressed as a girl felt embarrassing but there was little option just now. Besides, it was still not as humiliating as being spanked over Theresa's knee like a little girl.

I could hear some movement from Nicole's room, or what was now my room at least temporarily. As I pushed the door all of the way open I saw Laura and her mom applying what looked like some finishing touches to the bed, which was now strewn with childish soft toys. Still unsure of what they'd been doing I peered around the room. The first thing that I noticed was one of the boxes that had previously been in Theresa's room now sitting empty upon the floor. As my eyes settled upon the various surfaces I realised that they'd put back a lot of Nicole's possessions that had been destined for the charity shop. It now resembled a young girl's bedroom, not just in decor but with all of its associated paraphernalia included.

I spotted some makeup arranged on one of the surfaces with a pink brush and comb set and assorted costume jewellery for a teen girl. My first thought was that they were about to throw me out of the house and had decided to put Nicole's room back to how it was before I'd arrived.

'There you are.' Laura said, looking up from the bed. 'Come and have a look.'

I stepped further inside, my belly doing somersaults as I dreaded what was to come. I noticed a pink fluffy bathrobe hanging on the back of the door in place of my own, although the last time I'd seen that was when I'd entered Theresa's room. Laura walked over to the chest of drawers and opened the top one, waiting for me to approach so as to look inside. As I did so I noticed that instead of my own underwear it was now full of girl's panties and bra tops. As she opened the next one I saw girl's socks and pantyhose all neatly arranged within, but not a single pair of my boy socks.

'And look!' Laura bounced over to the closet, flinging the doors wide open. To my astonishment it was now filled with what I knew were all of her sister's old clothes, dresses, skirts and tops of various feminine and girly colours. As my eyes dropped to the bottom of the closet I saw a host of girl's shoes lined up with not a single pair of my own amongst them. This seemed to confirm my worst fear, that I was now officially out of there following my ill thought out and spontaneous act of dressing up. Laura seemed to notice my downcast expression as she closed the closet doors.

'Don't you like it?' She asked.

'I'm sure Nicole will be pleased.' I said with a resigned expression, 'I suppose I'd better get changed and go then.'

'Go?' She looked confused, 'Go where?'

'You're throwing me out...aren't you?' I could feel myself getting annoyed at her playing this game. I just wanted my humiliation to be over and done with, even if it meant sleeping outside tonight.

'What? Don't be silly.' She said, looking exasperated, 'This is for you.'

'Silly girl!' Theresa added as she came to stand beside me. 'You wanted to be a girl, so now you are.' I gaped at her, lost for words as I tried to comprehend their intentions. 'Don't even think of trying to find your boy clothes because they're locked away. As further punishment for your actions you'll be spending the next few days as a girl whether you like it or not. Then we'll see if you still like the idea. Your nightdresses are in the drawer so you'd better put one on, then you can join us for something to eat downstairs.'

Laura pecked me on the cheek before leaving the room with a broad grin upon her face.

'You can keep your diaper on as well for now, I don't want you messing another pair of panties tonight.' Her mom added as she followed her daughter. I had the distinct impression that they were both enjoying my ongoing humiliation, especially Laura's mom.

Chapter 3

I stared at the back of the door for several seconds feeling stunned. As if in a dream I walked over to the drawer that contained Nicole's nightwear and pulled out a cotton nightdress with some kind of cartoon characters emblazoned across the front. It was a struggle to pull the dress back over my head, but once it was off I caught sight of myself in the mirror in just my bra top, diaper and ankle socks. In an effort to hide the sight of the diaper I quickly pulled the nightdress over my head.

I spent some time looking around the room at the girlish accessories now on display. It was as if I'd been plunged into a world of girly femininity. I felt out of character, as if I were becoming someone else entirely. Slumping down onto the bed I picked up one of the soft toys and held it in my lap, there was something strangely comforting about the experience that was made all the more so by the feeling of having a soft plump diaper on underneath the nightdress.

Before leaving the room I quickly searched for any signs of my own clothes but they'd clearly been removed for safekeeping. Resigned to my fate I left the room to rejoin my girlfriend and her mom. As I made my way back down the stairs I reasoned that they probably intended to prolong my punishment over the weekend before relenting. I hesitated outside of the kitchen as I heard them talking. I was sure I heard my name mentioned and crept closer in order to listen.

'But mom...you can't do that to him. I'm sure he didn't mean any harm. I know he's not very manly but he's like my best friend.' Laura was speaking as if to defend my position.

'You're right about him not being very manly. He's quite the sissy boy as we've just found out.' Theresa sounded as though she was laying down the law to her daughter. 'If he wants to be dressed like a little girl then he can be treated like a little girl as far as I'm concerned, besides, I never was too happy about having another man in the house. This way it's just us girls again, it'll be like you've got a little sister. It might actually be fun, and you have to admit he looks quite cute as a girl.'

'I know he does. To be honest I think he looks better as a girl than he does as a boy.' Laura's voice gave away her own surprise at this revelation. 'But what about college and stuff?'

'Let me worry about that Laura. I think he's a little messed up right now and he could do with a firm hand for a while.' Theresa said, 'It might even be fun, having Louis as a girl.'

I couldn't believe they were actually plotting to keep me dressed as a girl. For a moment I was caught in indecision, wondering whether to join them or go on a frantic hunt for my own clothes in order to make an escape. Reality soon intruded into my thoughts as I wondered quite where I'd be escaping to. It was whilst I was nervously trying to decide what to do, that Theresa stepped into view in the doorway.

'There you are Louis.' She cast her eyes over me as she noticed my presence, 'The nightdress looks cute on you. Come and take a seat.' With the decision made for me I padded over to the table where Laura was already seated and made myself comfortable beside her. I caught her smiling at me.

'What?' I asked. A slight defensiveness creeping into my voice.

'Nothing.' She said with a little giggle. 'You do look cute though...especially when you pout.'

I was acutely aware of sitting on a plump diaper as I ate my meal. Laura and her mom made conversation whilst I sat self-consciously at the table, feeling as though I were a naughty child in some kind of punishment clothing. I detected a source of amusement between the two of them as Theresa went to fix us all a drink. As she set down her's and Laura's glasses she returned to the counter to fetch mine. I glanced up as she leaned over to my side of the table, setting down a pink plastic sippy cup in front of me filled with chocolate milk.

'What's this?' I asked dumbly. It was apparent that they'd decided to make use of more than just Nicole's old clothes.

'You don't deserve to drink from an adult glass after your earlier performance, so you'll be using this amongst others for the time being.' Theresa stated.

I looked around at Laura to find her grinning all over her face. 'That was mine when I was little, but I don't mind you using it, Louis.' She said.

'Hmmm, we can't really call you by a boy's name at the moment, can we?' Theresa added before I could protest. 'We could just call you Louise instead. What do you think Laura?' Laura giggled at the suggestion, and seeing my face drop she quickly nodded.

'I think that's perfect.' She agreed with her mom.

'No!' I blurted, having finally found my tongue. 'You can't. My name's Louis and I'm not a girl.' I stared at the pair of them defiantly.

'You look like a girl, and you like dressing as a girl.' Laura said, crossing her arms.

'You like dressing as a girl a little too much from what I saw.' Theresa glared down at me, challenging me to put up a fight. 'Do you need another spanking, Louise?' I knew she was deliberately using the girl's name to taunt me. The memory of her witnessing my shameful abasement in her daughter's panties was enough for me to purse my lips tightly together. I could feel my face heating up as I realised just how humiliating all of this would be if anyone at the local college were to find out. There was a long pause whilst they both watched for my reaction.

'That's what I thought.' Said Theresa finally. 'You'd better do as you're told from now on young lady. I won't have you acting like a spoilt little brat in my house.' With that she sat back down and continued her meal. Laura did the same, leaving me to contemplate my precarious situation.

Despite my sudden thirst I tried holding out for the rest

of the meal without resorting to using the infantile looking sippy cup, but in the end I relented. I knew Theresa would have her way eventually and so I lifted it up to my lips when I thought they were more focussed on the meal than me. I'd quite forgotten the experience of using such a thing and it took several experimental sucks before I seemed to get the hang of it. Every time I made a noise trying to extract the liquid it made me even more conscious of my diminished status in the eyes of my girlfriend and her mom. I did catch a little satisfied smile on Theresa's lips as she looked over at me in mid sip.

When finally my ordeal at the dinner table was over I found myself being dismissed to the living area. Laura actually followed me into the room and without a word flicked the cartoon network onto the television. Before leaving the room to help her mom clear away she came over to stand in front of me, looking me up and down. I was about to speak when she put her head to one side and beat me to it.

'I've always wondered what it'd be like to have a little sister.' She said. 'I think this could be really nice. Don't you?'

My mouth opened and closed several times before I could actually speak. 'You don't really want me to stay like this, do you?' I asked.

'Why not? Don't pretend that you don't like dressing in my sister's old clothes. We both know that wouldn't be true, don't we?'

I felt flustered and lost for words at that point, wondering what on earth this would mean for our relationship. How could my girlfriend want to have a boyfriend that she also treated like a little sister? I swallowed hard as I tried to think of something to say, but nothing came to mind other than my ability to undermine my own manhood in such a spectacular fashion.

'Just relax, Louise.' She continued, sounding as though she were trying out my new name for the first time. 'Louise...I think it suits you.' She gave me a peck on the cheek before prancing out of the room, leaving me to watch her go in stunned silence. I collapsed onto the couch in complete defeat. The nightdress rode up my legs enough that the diaper was visible beneath. I let out an exasperated groan, feeling like Alice as she first entered the rabbit hole to find a rather surreal and baffling world beyond.

-o0o-

It was later that evening that my ongoing humiliation took another turn for the worse. It was barely eight o'clock when Theresa turned to me as I sat next to Laura on the couch, watching a chick flick that she'd chosen for us.

'I think it's time you were in bed, young lady.' She announced. I wasn't sure if she were referring to myself or Laura as I looked around. Her steady stare was clearly directed solely at me.

'I'm sorry?' I said. I still felt a little insulted that she was treating me like such a child.

'You heard me. Now up you go and I'll be along in a moment.' I stared back at her in disbelief before turning to Laura. She seemed to have taken little notice and simply shrugged at me as if to say there was little choice.

'But...' I began to argue.

'But nothing!' Theresa said firmly. 'You can take your little diapered bottom up to bed right now.' The mention of my diapered bottom was enough to deflate any further argument from me, and so I pushed myself to my feet and skulked out of the room.

My feelings were pretty mixed up as I made my way to my bedroom. In some ways it almost felt comforting to be put back into a position of immaturity. One where I had little say over anything of importance. On the other hand I felt embarrassed and emasculated by the entire situation, even though I'd not exactly been the epitome of masculinity to begin with.

Entering the bedroom I took another look around at the girlish environment that I now inhabited. There was nothing to indicate that a boy currently occupied the room, in fact, it would be difficult to envisage anyone other than a young girl living amidst such femininity.

I crawled under the covers and sat back, my mind a confusion of how to proceed. As much as I kept telling myself this was simply a deserved punishment for my actions, it was feeling more and more as though there was an element of permanency to all of this. The conversation I'd overheard in the kitchen certainly added to this in no small way.

Just as I was building myself up to marching back downstairs and confronting my girlfriend and her mom about how

228

ludicrous this all was, Theresa entered the room without so much as a knock on the door.

'Good girl.' She said, seeing that I'd obeyed her command. She approached the bed as I scowled at her. Sitting down next to me she fixed me with another of her looks that soon caused me to look away. 'There's no point in sulking Louise, this is entirely your own fault, isn't it?' She waited patiently for an answer. I knew there was a truth to her statement that couldn't be entirely denied.

'I suppose.' I offered begrudgingly.

'Right, so stop pouting you silly girl.'

As I turned back to her she raised her hand and pushed something against my lips. As I partially opened my mouth to object I found a pacifier being forced in.

'If you spit it out you'll be in for another spanking.' She said before I could do just that. I hesitated, feeling the rubber teat in my mouth.

'But...you can't expect...' As I tried to talk around the pacifier, not daring to take it out at this point, the words came out poorly formed and indistinct.

'Stop talking, please.' She said. Once satisfied that I was no longer attempting to speak she continued. 'I wouldn't normally do this if one of my girls had been naughty, but I'll make an exception in your case and hopefully this will calm you down a little.'

I gave her a bemused look as I wondered what on earth she was about to do now. When she leaned over to a nearby shelf and pulled down a book to read to me I breathed a sigh of relief whilst at the same time groaning inwardly at the idea of being read a story. She sat back next to me and pulled me into her before she began. I have to admit, something about that experience felt quite warm and comforting. Despite the fact that she was my girlfriend's mom and not my own, I found myself giving in to the moment and just relaxing down as she read the book out loud. I didn't realise it at first, but I caught myself gently sucking on the pink pacifier that she'd popped into my mouth as I drifted slowly towards sleep.

When she came to the end of the book I was even a little disappointed when she'd finished. Standing up she lifted up the covers for me to scoot further into the bed.

'I said Laura can come and say goodnight to you. After that I expect you to go to sleep. You'll not be going to college

229

tomorrow, I've decided. I have other things planned, so don't worry about that.' She actually kissed me on the forehead before leaving the room, switching on a small night light before closing the door behind her. Even though she was no longer there to observe me, I still didn't remove the pacifier. Preferring instead to suck thoughtfully upon it as I thought through the day's events up to that point.

It was as I was slipping towards sleep that I heard the door being pushed open and someone else entering the room. I opened my eyes and realised it was Laura, no doubt come to say goodnight to her emasculated boyfriend. Without a word she crept towards the bed and slipped under the covers to lie next to me. Ordinarily I would have reacted like most eighteen year old boys, but being acutely aware of the fact that I was not only wearing a girl's diaper and nightdress but also still had a pacifier in my mouth I felt supremely coy with her closeness. I raised my hand to my mouth to remove the pacifier but she took hold of me before I could do so.

'Leave it in.' She whispered. 'I'm feeling quite turned on by having my boyfriend wear my diapers and using my old pacifier.' I looked at her wide eyed at such a revelation. I'd imagined she'd have been feeling quite the opposite by now, but surprisingly she seemed to be enjoying my treatment as much as her mom. 'Look, it's made me all wet.' She added, directing my hand underneath the bed clothes and under her own nightdress that she now wore. She still had panties on underneath but I was immediately aware of how wet they were underneath my fingers.

My breath caught in my throat as I'd never had the opportunity to touch Laura so intimately before. I could feel the warmth of her arousal under my hand and the soft mound of her sex. She started to slowly move my hand across her swollen lips, causing the thin cotton panties to become even wetter with her juices. I squeaked a little sound around the pacifier as I felt my little cock becoming stiff once more inside of my diaper. I could hear her breathing change as she slowly began to masturbate herself with my fingers, her head dipping towards mine and her breath playing across my neck.

'Mmmm, that's it baby.' She moaned softly into my ear as her arousal grew. I sucked harder upon the pacifier as I moved my other hand to press against the front of my own diaper, wishing for her to touch me also. She began grinding her hips slowly in

230

response to my touch, my entire body was tense, not entirely sure how to proceed but loving the feel of her body even through her now sopping wet panties.

I could hear her breathing becoming shallower, more rapid. In an instant she lifted my hand further up her belly and plunged it back down underneath her panties. For the first time in my life I was touching a girl's naked pussy. My fingers ran easily between her puffed up lips as her juices quickly coated my fingers. I could hear her stifled moans of pleasure as she tried not to alert her mom to what was going on in her sister's room. Finding her slick hole I tried pushing my finger inside of her, bringing a little squeal of pleasure from her as I did so.

I knew that with or without her help I would soon be cumming into my diaper once again as I grew intensely aroused by the experience. She clamped her hand over mine at one point and redirected my attentions slightly further up. It was then I found her swollen clitty, just waiting to be teased by my fingers. As I started to gently flick my fingertip across it her arousal seemed to jump to another level as she began to squirm under my hand. She began to pant against my neck as her climax approached. In an effort to please her I redoubled my efforts at stimulating her clit, sending waves of pleasure through her as she moved steadily towards an orgasm.

The very thought of bringing a girl to orgasm by my own hand was enough to tip me over the edge at this point, and I felt my own climax rushing forward. As I spasmed against her leg I felt myself explode another load of cum into the girl's diaper. It was then that Laura experienced her own orgasm with my fingers pressed in between her lips. We both climaxed together, writhing as one until both of our orgasms slowly subsided. Each of us spasmed several more times before we were both completely spent.

As we lay next to each other, my hand still resting inside of Laura's panties with my other hand touching my own diaper, I sucked contentedly on the pacifier. It was certainly not the way I would have expected to have first touched Laura's cunny. Lying in her sister's bed dressed as a girl and sucking on a pacifier, but in that moment I didn't mind in the least how I was dressed. It seemed that somehow it had turned my girlfriend on to such an extent that I'd experienced the most significant moment in our relationship so far.

'I'd better go.' Laura finally whispered into my ear. I turned to kiss her, but still having the pacifier in my mouth I just made out her smiling at me before kissing me on the forehead, much like her mom had done before slipping out of the bed. She padded across the floor, blowing me one last kiss before leaving me alone for the night.

Bringing my hand to my face I inhaled Laura's scent from my still wet fingers before tasting her juices. I wondered what it would be like to lick her between her legs, but I was still more than happy at what had occurred between us. I was aware of the stickiness inside of my diaper but not knowing what the reaction would be if I were to take it off overnight, or indeed where I could find a clean one. I decided to stay as I was. It had been a strange day indeed, and I knew my experience wasn't over as yet. It didn't seem as though Laura's mom could do much else to punish me than she already had, so I expected to be kept in Nicole's clothes over the weekend before being allowed to return to being a boy. I resigned myself to my fate at that point, wondering how much else would occur between me and Laura whilst I was in punishment clothing.

It turned out that I'd underestimated my girlfriend's mom somewhat, as she had no intention of letting me off the hook that easily or quickly.

Chapter 4

The next morning I lay awake for some time before deciding to get out of bed. The diaper between my legs was feeling particularly plump and so I pulled down the covers to have a look. To my horror I realised I'd wet myself overnight, filling it up so that it'd expanded noticeably. The pacifier was still in my mouth and I pulled it out with a flourish, annoyed as to why I'd done such a thing.

The idea of Laura or her mom finding out about my childish accident was not a pleasing one, and so I jumped out of bed with the intention of taking it off and putting some panties on in its place. No doubt hearing me moving about within my room Theresa chose that moment to enter, catching me as I lifted the nightdress up above my waist in order to pull the diaper down.

'What are you doing?' She asked. I froze in place for a moment before hurriedly dropping the nightdress back into place. 'Let me see that.' She said, stalking towards me.

'It's nothing.' I said, 'You don't have to see.'

It was a useless attempt at avoiding her finding out as she grabbed the nightdress and pulled it back up again. I thought better of trying to prevent her from doing so, knowing it would prove to be a futile gesture.

'You've wet your diaper.' She announced to the room. 'It's a good job you were wearing it, isn't it?'

'I...um...yeah.' I reluctantly agreed despite suspecting it was precisely because I was wearing a diaper that I'd used it subconsciously.

'You can put a clean pair of panties on when you get dressed. Come and have some breakfast first.' She held the door open for me, waiting until I'd led her out. It seemed a cruel start to the day to have humiliated myself before I'd even left the bedroom that morning. I was acutely aware of the fullness between my legs as I made my way downstairs, hoping it wasn't showing too obviously at the back as Theresa followed me down.

Laura had apparently already left for college that morning, and so I breakfasted alone whilst Theresa went about her morning chores. I felt reluctant to even move when I'd finished. Not wanting to remind myself or Theresa of my embarrassment at wetting my diaper.

'Stop looking so guilty, Louise.' Theresa said as she walked back into the kitchen. 'Laura used to do the same thing until she was at least fifteen. It's lucky we still had some of her nighttime diapers left.'

It didn't make me feel any better knowing this, but at least she didn't seem particularly concerned by it. It was a relief to remove the wet diaper when I returned to my room before getting showered. I was feeling considerably better about myself once I'd shaved the small amount of hair growth from my face and showered. I noticed my blue towels had been replaced by pink ones since the previous day. Despite this I returned to my room with one draped around me ready to get dressed for the day. For whatever reason it wasn't until I was standing there, wondering what to wear that it fully dawned on me that the only clothes available to me were Nicole's.

I went around opening all of the drawers and the closet, glancing inside only to confirm that this was very definitely the case. I could feel myself shrinking in defeat, imagining presenting myself to Theresa in girl's clothes once again. The thought crossed my mind to ask where my boy clothes were once again, but I knew this would be pointless. It was clear that she intended to continue my punishment for at least a couple more days.

Accepting my situation I rooted through the underwear drawer and picked out a pair of lemon coloured panties with a little pink bow at the front. Pulling them up my legs I tried to ignore the pleasurable feelings I was experiencing as I once again began to dress as a girl, only this time with the full knowledge of Laura and her mom. A white bra top followed before I pulled on a pair of ankle socks with a frilly lemon trim to them.

As I opened the closet I ran my hands across the assorted dresses, tops and skirts. There was clearly nothing in the least bit boyish to any of Nicole's old clothes, and so I picked out a knee length yellow gingham print dress. As I slipped it over my head I could feel my masculinity retreating out of sight as I felt myself being transformed into a girl again.

I spent quite some time brushing my hair out before placing a yellow hairband upon my head to complete the look. Standing up from the small dressing table I stepped in front of the full length mirror, anxiously looking myself up and down. Once again I marvelled at just how convincing I appeared to be as a girl. Spinning around I actually felt pleased at my appearance, although somewhere at the back of my mind I was wishing I was wearing something more akin to my age group, even if it were girl's clothes.

Taking a deep breath I forced myself to leave the bedroom, knowing I was simply putting off the inevitable the longer I hid myself away. Walking through the hallway towards the kitchen it felt like I was somehow walking into a new existence, one that didn't include my male self.

'You look lovely, Louise!' Theresa looked up to see me standing nervously in the doorway. 'I'll just need to find you some shoes.' She paused in the doorway to look me up and down, smoothing out my dress and making a slight adjustment to my hair before moving past me. I hung around the kitchen for the next few minutes, unsure of what to do with myself until she returned carrying two pairs of shoes.

'You'd better try these on. You've got quite small feet so they might still fit. If not you can borrow a pair of Laura's.' She explained. I took the first pair of shoes off her before examining them. They were basically a pair of black Mary Jane shoes that looked a little on the small side. I assumed these were once Nicole's as well. Thinking this was her idea of completing the outfit; I dropped them to the floor and pushed my foot into one of them. To my complete surprise it almost slipped straight on. With a little effort I was able to squeeze my foot in and fasten the strap across the front. The second one was a similar fit.

'Perfect.' Theresa said. 'Can you walk in them?' I demonstrated walking up and down the kitchen several times to confirm that I could in fact walk without difficulty. 'Excellent.' She said, clearly pleased at discovering my smaller than average feet.

'Well, I think you look fine. Let's go.' Theresa said, and without stopping to explain she took hold of my hand and began pulling me towards the front door.

'Wait!' I shouted, suddenly fearful of being exposed in the street. 'I can't go out like this.' I pulled back against her, trying to dig my Mary Jane heels into the floor.

'You will do exactly as I tell you.' She declared. 'No-one will know that you're not really a girl, silly. Now you will do exactly as you're told unless you want to be punished even more severely.' I tried standing my ground as I considered what a more severe punishment than being taken outside dressed as a girl would entail. 'I will not have you throwing a tantrum young lady.'

'I'm not a young lady...I'm a boy.' This last part sounded rather weak given my current appearance.

'Really? Then why do you want to dress as a girl?' My throat tightened as I realised there was very little to be said as far as my obviously absent masculinity was concerned. With a powerful tug she pulled me off balance and dragged me through the door before I could dig my heels in once again. Before I knew it I was standing outside of the house with a locked front door behind me and nowhere to run to.

'Unless you want to make a scene I suggest you start acting a little more respectful and do as you're told.' She scolded me. My eyes searched the surrounding area for anyone that might be watching. I noticed a man and a woman on the opposite side of the street glancing in our direction. I immediately averted my eyes.

'Sorry.' I said quietly. After a pause Theresa seemed to be mollified by this and took my hand once more. Leading me down the drive to where her car was parked. Once inside I felt somewhat less vulnerable, although I knew I'd be expected to leave the safety of the car once we reached our destination.

The destination turned out to be somewhere that I tended to avoid even dressed in my boy clothes, let alone as a girl. The local shopping mall. Anxiety seemed to be weighing me down as I reluctantly allowed her to lead me from the car and into the shopping centre. I suspected it was part of her punishment that others would see me being paraded in girl's clothing and add to my humiliation.

This wasn't quite how things turned out in the end. It took a good twenty minutes or so before I really caught on, but I then realised that no-one had taken the slightest notice of me since I'd been walking around with Theresa.

'I don't think anyone's noticed.' I mumbled half to myself and half to Theresa. My eyes began to lift a little as I found myself relaxing somewhat.

'Of course they haven't, Louise.' She answered from close to my ear. 'I told you, you make a very convincing girl. In fact, both Laura and I agreed that you look much nicer as a girl than a boy.' She added with a smile.

Theresa's motive behind taking me to the mall wasn't in fact part of my punishment as such. She had decided to buy me another pack of girl's diapers, but in addition to this we spent some time purchasing some items of girl's clothing that were more of my own age. It was a strange experience entering the girl's fitting rooms in order to try them on, but despite the odds I managed to actually enjoy the experience. I did try asking her how long she intended to have me wearing girl's clothes but she seemed quite vague with her response, telling me not to worry about such things.

I had a shock of sorts when she actually led me into one shop and asked the assistant to pierce my ears for me. Nervous of causing a scene if I were to object to such a thing, I simply sat down and yelped slightly as the woman fired the earrings into my flesh. They didn't sting too much and despite Theresa telling me that plenty of boys had both of their ears pierced nowadays it still had the effect of making me feel as though I were falling further and further into that rabbit hole.

As much as I was glad to return to the house, I knew that something inside of me had actually enjoyed being taken out as a girl. We carried the assorted bags inside between us, with me anticipating trying on some new clothes. It felt different somehow knowing that they'd been bought especially for me. That they were my girl's clothes.

'Thank you, Theresa.' I said, as I reminded myself of the

new outfit that she'd bought me along with some teenage underwear. 'I guess I've got something of my own to wear this weekend.'

'You'll only wear your new clothes when you're in company. The rest of the time you'll be dressed as today.' Her response surprised me.

'But...I thought...'

'Don't worry about thinking Louise. For the time being you'll simply do as you're told. When I think you've learnt your lesson I'll let you start making your own decisions again. Okay?' Her voice was firm but not unkind. As if she was doing this for my own good, which I couldn't help but wonder at. 'Now. We've still got a couple of hours to ourselves before Laura gets home, so why don't we have another look at your new clothes?'

We took the bags into the living area with me expecting to peruse the items we'd bought before putting them away. The first item I pulled out of a bag was a new red dress. I still thought it looked a little short and clingy, but Theresa insisted I would look good in it. Next came a white skirt that also only came to about mid-thigh along with a matching top. She held them up to me before once again saying how good they'd look upon me. It was when we got to the new underwear that things took an unexpected turn, at least in my mind.

Of course you can see many things in hindsight, and it seems abundantly clear to me now that Theresa already knew what she wanted to happen. I on the other hand, was blissfully unaware of her inner desires that had been growing since seeing my little performance in her daughter's panties.

Holding up the skimpy looking red lace thong in my hands I felt a little embarrassed. I also wondered at why my girlfriend's mom would be buying me such things as these. There was a matching bra and even a pair of red stockings and garter belt to go with them. I was about to put them back into the bag when she stopped me.

'Why don't you try them on?' She asked, smiling at me with a definite glint in her eye. We'd tried the majority of the clothing on in the shops, with the noticeable exception of the underwear. I looked at her uncertainly for a moment, not sure if I wanted her to see me that way. Don't get me wrong, she was an attractive woman. It just felt a little wrong to be flaunting myself in skimpy lingerie in front of my girlfriend's mom. 'Go on, don't be shy.' She prompted, 'I've already seen you in Nicole's panties and a diaper.' This last comment felt as though it destroyed any pretence at holding on to even a shred of dignity. With a reluctant nod I got up from the couch, intending to change in another room.

'Don't be silly.' She said. 'I'll just turn around if you're that shy.'

Hesitating as she turned away from me, I felt trapped into doing what she said once more. I knew there was now no getting away from this, and so I blushingly pulled Nicole's dress over my head. The socks and bra top were next before I paused once more, my hand on either side of the panties. Theresa was still facing the opposite direction as I made myself slip them down my legs and quickly swapped them for the thong. As I stepped into it, it seemed even skimpier than when I'd looked at it earlier.

I quickly pulled it up my legs and felt the thin material slipping between my bottom cheeks as I covered my little cock. In an effort to feel more covered I fastened the bra around my chest and swivelled it into place before sliding my arms through the straps. I'd never put stockings on before, and feeling the delicate material in my hands I was careful to roll them up my legs so as not to tear them.

'Are you dressed yet?' Theresa asked, clearly becoming impatient. Her use of the word dressed seemed a little generous given how little of me would be covered by the lingerie.

'Nearly.' I said. Wrapping the garter belt around my waist I spent a good deal of time struggling with the clasps in order to fix the stockings into place. Eventually and with a sigh of relief I was finished. It felt strange indeed to be standing there, clad only in sexy red lingerie. I was reluctant to announce that I was ready for her inspection, feeling anything but ready given how exposed I now felt. I quickly pulled the hair band out of my hair and shook my hair loose in an attempt to appear more adult.

'I'm dressed.' I said softly.

She turned around slowly as if wanting to draw out the moment of reveal. A smile spread across her face as she took in the sight of her daughter's boyfriend standing in front of her, dressed in women's lingerie. Her eyes wandered brazenly up and down my body as if to take in every last inch. I'd never felt so bare before.

'You look very nice.' She said finally. 'Very nice indeed. Turn around, let's have a look at you from behind.'

Knowing that my bottom would be on full display to her I hesitated. She continued to stare at me expectantly. Giving in to her forceful will I slowly began to turn around. I could feel her eyes burning into my bottom cheeks as I displayed myself to her. My face grew warm, knowing I'd lost yet another piece of my masculinity to this woman.

'You have a very cute bottom, Louise.' I heard her say a split second before she playfully slapped me, making my fleshy cheeks jiggle in front of her. I flinched in surprise, spinning back around to face her. 'We're going to have to do something about that I feel.' She stated, looking down between my legs. As I followed her gaze I realised I'd become aroused by the situation, my partially erect manhood was showing itself from beneath the small covering of red lace.

'Oh!' I quickly tried to cover myself with my hands.

'Don't be silly, Louise.' She admonished me, 'We'll just have to get rid of that I'm afraid.'

For one panicked and irrational moment I thought she meant to cut it off, but then she raised her hands and gently pulled mine away. The look in her eyes was enough to tell me that she had something quite different in mind. My body almost became numb as I watched with trepidation as she slid to the edge of her seat, her face only inches away from my thong covered penis.

I had to force myself to start breathing again as I wondered what I should do. It felt as though all control was now with her and that I had none. Her hand slid across the thin lace and rested against the front of my privates. I tried to will my erection to diminish, to think of other things, anything but what was happening right now. My body betrayed me as her touch sent my hormones racing; my erection began to grow even more under her fingers.

'Your clitty's all swollen, Louise. Do you like me touching you?' She asked. The sound of her voice and the reference to my clitty only served to worsen the situation as I became fully erect in front of her eyes. 'We'll have to keep this just between us two girls. I don't think Laura would like it if she knew you were doing this. We don't want her throwing you out, do we?'

I couldn't find my voice enough to answer, so I simply

nodded compliantly. She grinned up at me before returning her attention to between my legs. Her fingers took hold of the edge of the thong and slowly pulled it aside, allowing my stiff little cock to drop down in front of her. She smiled for a moment before her other hand took hold of me, sending a shiver down my spine as I felt her fingers wrapping around me.

She gently caressed my shaft, studying it closely in her hand as she moved her face closer. I could feel her warm breath playing across my head as she flicked her eyes upwards for a brief moment. It was then that she opened her mouth and enveloped me. I gasped at the feeling of having her moist tongue rolling around my cock as she sucked me into her. I'd never experienced anything close to this before, my mind felt like it was going to explode as I watched as if hypnotised.

I whimpered pathetically as I furtively glanced at the door, half expecting Laura to walk through it to find her mom sucking on my cock. I then looked back down as she began to move her mouth up and down my erect penis, sending waves of pleasure through me. I knew that I wouldn't last long, that I'd soon be shaming myself again if she continued with her unexpected act of fellatio.

'P-Pleeease.' I moaned. Half of me wanted her to stop, but the other more carnal side just wanted to submit to her wants. I peered down at my lingerie clad body, feeling the sensual material of the stockings hugging my legs. Seeing the red bra and garter belt that spoke of pure sex, and I felt something that I'd never felt before. A sexuality that I hadn't even known was there. I felt myself to be a sensual being that in that single moment simply adored the way that I was now dressed. I began to groan softly, moving my hips in time with her mouth as I felt my climax building swiftly. It was like a freight train heading to the surface with no way to stop it. Confused thoughts crowded through my brain, telling me this was wrong but savouring every last sensation as my body began to stiffen in readiness for its ultimate release.

'I...I'm going to...to cum...' I squealed breathlessly before biting my lip. She seemed to slow her movements. Sucking firmly but gently as if awaiting the arrival of my climax, and climax I did. 'S-Sorry...' For some reason I felt the need to apologise as my balls tightened and my little cock spasmed in her mouth. As I began to spurt I expected her to recoil, but instead she held me firmly in her

241

mouth as she drank my boy juice down. Several large spurts were forced into her as I shivered and shook my way through the most extraordinary orgasm of my young life.

Theresa swallowed every last drop as I filled her mouth. I felt as though she were draining me physically. Milking my very masculinity out of me as I ran my hands up and down my body, touching the lingerie and grasping my own bare bottom cheeks as I allowed myself to be used for her pleasure.

When finally I came down from my climax I shivered as she licked the last remnants of cum from my cock, placing it gently back inside of the lace thong.

'Well, I think you enjoyed having your little clitty licked, didn't you?' Her question seemed to reinforce my subjugation to her. I could only nod weakly before unsteadily taking a seat next to her. I wished I could cover myself up, suddenly feeling vulnerable and exposed to her eyes. She stroked my stockinged leg reassuringly before preparing to leave the room.

'I think you should put your other clothes back on for tonight. We can save your new lingerie for another occasion. Put it away for now, there's a good girl.' She kissed me on the cheek before leaving me to consider the latest abasement in my ongoing punishment. Although if I were honest at the time, I knew then that it was feeling less and less of a punishment and more and more like a journey.

Chapter 5

By the time Laura arrived home from college I was once again dressed in her sister's old clothes and busily helping her mom to clean the house. She pranced into her bedroom to find me in the process of emptying her small waste bin.

'Hi, Louise.' She said, as if calling me by a girl's name was perfectly natural to her. 'You look cute.'

I glanced down at myself before blushing slightly.

'It's just like having a little sister in the house.' She said with a sarcastic grin.

'By the way, I've got a couple of friends coming over tonight.'

'What?' I looked at her in surprise. 'I'd better get changed back into my own clothes.' I said quickly.

'Those are your own clothes now silly. Don't worry; I'm sure they won't mind my little sister being around.' I gave her a puzzled look for a moment. 'Oh, didn't I tell you. Mom's going out tonight and she said I could have a girl's night.'

The idea of being in a house full of girls, with me dressed as I was sent shivers of fear down my spine. I wondered whom she was having over and whether they were girls that would recognise me. I'd never really met many of her friends and I didn't know how much they'd know about me.

'But...they'll know I'm not your sister and won't they wonder about your boyfriend...and what if they recognise me or realise I'm not a girl?' I could feel an inner panic starting to rise up within me. It felt like this whole episode was starting to go too far. As if it would reach a point of no return and I'd be trapped in a female guise from where there'd be no escaping without losing everything.

'Stop worrying so much. You look perfectly fine as a girl. I'll tell you what; we'll put a little makeup on you and dress you in something a little older. If we tell them that you're my half-sister they won't think anything of it.' She seemed quite pleased with her own idea.

I imagined being dressed in my red lacy lingerie and short dress for a moment, wondering what Laura would make of the new clothes that her mom had bought for me. Before I could say any more she began rummaging through her own closet, looking for something to lend me for the evening. In a way it felt an improvement to be dressed in an older mode, but at the same time I couldn't imagine being part of a girl's night in and playing the part of my own girlfriend's sister. I dithered for a while before heading towards the door.

'Don't go. You've got to try some things on for tonight first.' Laura said over her shoulder as she pulled three or four dresses out of the closet and headed to her underwear drawer.

Over the next thirty minutes or so I found myself trying on several of her dresses. Most of which were slightly too big for me although we did find a couple that seemed okay. Settling on a little black dress that came above my knees, she rooted through her underwear before pulling out a matching set of black panties and bra. The outfit would be completed with a pair of pantyhose. She sent me into the bathroom to rid myself of any boy hair that may be present before I was summoned back into her room.

So far I'd tried her clothes on whilst remaining in her sister's girlish underwear, but now she intended for me to change completely.

'Right, take those off and put my underwear on.' She ordered, indicating the bra, panties and pantyhose piled on the bed. She watched as I slipped the bra top off. As I came to the panties I looked at her, expecting her to give me some privacy despite her being my girlfriend. Being as the only time she'd ever seen me naked between my legs was when she helped put the diaper on me the previous night; I still felt a little shy about being completely naked in her presence.

Hesitating with my hands on the waistband of the panties I realised she had no intention of turning around. I elected to turn away from her before pulling them down my legs, putting my bottom on display for the second time that day. I quickly took her panties from the bed and stepped into them. Unlike her sister's underwear, these were of a silky material and gave me an entirely new sensation as I tugged them up my legs. Feeling the soft satiny material hugging my penis I fought against my latest feelings of arousal, having not worn a pair of Laura's panties before. As I tried to focus on fixing her bra into place I became aware of her standing next to me, her hand brushing my pantied bottom seductively.

'They look sexy on you.' She giggled. 'You'd better tuck that away; we don't want my friends noticing your little boy bulge between your legs, do we?'

I looked down to see a slight protuberance, mainly because I wasn't completely soft any more. Self-consciously slipping my hands down the front of the panties I tucked myself back between my legs enough to hide any evidence of my boyhood. Laura watched with a slight smile upon her face as I sat on the bed and carefully rolled the pantyhose up my smooth legs. The feeling of having them cosseting my entire lower half in their soft yet firm embrace was enough to leave me a little breathless. I wanted desperately to run my hands up and down my own legs and feel my nylon encased bottom, but in an effort to not let Laura see just how much I was beginning to enjoy my coerced feminisation, I resisted the urge.

She had me sit at her dressing table whilst she began to apply makeup to my face. Allowing me to watch my subtle transformation in the mirror. She was careful to use as little as possible, just enough to leave me looking like a natural girl. I couldn't help but smile as she used her hair curlers to put a little more shape into my hair. Some additional pantyhose to fill out my bra followed before she had me step into her dress. With the addition of some jewellery I was now ready to face her friends, although I would have to face her mom first.

Laura got herself changed whilst I waited in her room, having been discreet enough to turn around whilst she changed her panties and bra, much to her amusement, I watched with interest as she applied her own makeup. She looked more like she was going on a date than having a girl's night in by the time she led me from her room. We found her mom downstairs already dressed for her own night out and she immediately clapped her hands together as she set eyes on her daughter and me.

'You look lovely, the pair of you.' She said, 'Hold on, let me get a photo of all three of us together.'

Before I knew it I was being pushed into the middle of Laura and her mom as she set the camera's timer and we posed for a group picture. I worried quite how far this would circulate as I knew both of them were keen social media buffs, but my concerns were simply brushed off without much credence by the pair of them.

Theresa was quick to say her goodbyes and wish us a lovely evening with our friends. I tried to question whether it was a good idea me being seen dressed as a girl by Laura's friends but she didn't seem to think there was a problem.

'Stop worrying, Louise.' She said, 'You look lovely and I'm sure Laura's friends are all very nice.'

I watched as the door closed behind her, nervously anticipating the evening ahead. I even thought about shutting myself away in my bedroom, but with no actual lock on the door this seemed a pointless plan as Laura would no doubt decide to drag me out to meet her friends at some point. It was with growing anxiety that I waited in the kitchen with Laura as she pulled out some snacks and a bottle of alcohol that she'd secreted away somewhere.

When at last the doorbell rang and I heard several girls talking and laughing on the other side, I went cold with fear, feeling rooted to the spot. I waited as Laura answered, hearing her friends entering the house amidst much babbling and giggling as they looked forward to the evening.

As they came trooping into the kitchen I counted five other girls in total, all dressed up in similar fashion to Laura and myself. When she noticed a couple of the girls looking in my direction she wasted no time in introducing me to them.

'Girls, this is Louise.' She gestured in my direction as I tried to smile back at them. 'She's my half-sister.'

'You didn't tell me you had a half-sister.' One of the girls complained as they all chorused a greeting.

'Sorry.' Laura apologised for her imagined oversight. 'She's actually staying with us for a while.'

I glanced at her for a moment, wishing she hadn't made it sound as if Louise would be around for longer than one night. They seemed friendly enough and much to my relief, none of them seemed to think anything amiss with the new girl in their midst.

Laura slipped her arm into mine to lead me into the living area with them. She clearly had no intention of letting me sit this evening out on the sidelines. As they all found places to sit the snacks were quickly opened and the drink passed around to fill everyone's glasses. With the music channel on the television they launched into their girly chat, beginning with college and veering onto the various boys they knew. I felt like an outsider to some extent but they tried to include me as much as possible when they noticed I was quietly sitting to one side. If only they knew the truth as to why I was so reticent to join in!

I have to admit, after my second drink I was starting to feel far more relaxed and actually found myself joining in where I could. I was feeling pleased with myself that none of them had shown any suspicion over my gender not quite being what it appeared to be. They were a friendly group and I could almost have forgotten my true identity as a boy after a while...almost.

After an hour or so everyone began to get hungry for something more than just snacks, and pizza seemed to be the order of the day. A quick phone call followed and the evening continued as we awaited the food delivery. Whilst we waited the suggestion of a game of truth or dare was made by one of Laura's friends. This didn't seem a good idea to me but in the end I had little choice but to join them in a circle upon the floor, hoping that they wouldn't test me too much.

Laura decided she'd go first to get things moving and immediately pointed to Kelly, the attractive dark haired girl sitting opposite her. She declared that she'd take a 'Truth'. Laura thought for a moment before coming up with her question.

'How many boys have you kissed?' She asked, grinning. Kelly paused to count in her head before responding.

'Six...I think.' She seemed none too sure but was greeted with a round of laughter as she tried to run through the list of names. Now it was her turn and she looked around the circle for the next victim. I could feel myself shrinking down into the floor, hoping that I wouldn't be picked out.

'Tanya!' She announced, turning to the redheaded girl on her left much to my relief. Once again it was decided she'd take a 'Truth' and we all waited expectantly until Kelly came up with her question.

'How many boys have you let touch you under your bra.' It seemed the tone of the questions had now been set.

I dreaded it coming to my turn. Unfortunately I didn't have too long to wait. Tanya picked out Jasmine who was sitting next to me for the next go, she also elected to answer a 'Truth' question and found herself confessing to having sex with two boys. After looking around the circle she finally settled her gaze upon me, clearly deciding it was time to bring the new girl into the game.

'Louise, truth or dare?' She asked. Fearing that a dare would involve something that might reveal myself to them I opted for the 'Truth' question. I caught Laura looking at me curiously, clearly wondering whether I'd actually tell the truth or make up a story.

'How many blowjobs have you given?' I was immediately on the back foot with Jasmine's question and realised I'd started to blush. Knowing I'd probably look incredibly guilty if I tried to make up a number I chose to tell the truth, hoping they'd simply think me a little shy with the boys.

'None.' I said, looking down shyly.

The assembled girls thought this to be a surprising revelation as they clearly expected me to have had some sexual experiences with the opposite gender. I had to listen to them telling me about their first time of putting a boy's cock into their mouths and how it felt. They seemed quite fascinated when Kelly admitted to swallowing a boy's cum as a result, the others said they'd avoided that particular act. Then it was my turn to redirect the questioning, and so I picked a blond haired girl sitting next to Laura. I was taken by surprise when she asked for a dare, I had no idea what the group of girls would normally expect for this, but the general theme was all too clear.

'Well? What should she do?' Prompted Jasmine with an eager glint in her eye as I hesitated, trying to think of what to dare her. I would come to regret my choice of challenges later, as I managed to set myself onto a course for something I would not have believed myself capable of until now.

'Kiss...Kelly.' I heard myself saying amidst much amusement from the other girls.

'With or without tongues?' Questioned Laura, a broad smile upon her face as she nodded approvingly at my dare.

'Um...With.' I said. It seemed unlikely that they'd expect anything less than this. I watched in awe as the blond haired girl Mandy, got to her knees and crawled over to Kelly with a slight scowl upon her face. As much as she tried to feign disgust at the prospect of kissing one of her friends in such a way she showed little hesitance in meeting the challenge. Kelly watched her approach with an amused look on her face until they were looking directly into each other's eyes, mere inches between them. Then Mandy leaned in and started to kiss her friend. Their lips were soon parted as they allowed their tongues to invade each other's mouths whilst I tried desperately not to become aroused inside of my panties.

They took a little longer to complete the task than was strictly necessary, to much jeering and giggling from the other girls. Having completed her dare it was now Mandy's turn to continue the game. Much to my growing horror it was now apparent that the name of the game had become 'Dare', as everyone was expected to follow mine and Mandy's lead. I knew with absolute certainty that I would now be expected to take a dare on my next turn as I watched Laura being dared to fondle Jasmine's breasts. I couldn't stop myself from watching as my girlfriend slipped the other girl's dress down from her shoulders and began to massage her plump little breasts in front of the group.

I was grateful that I was wearing a snug pair of pantyhose over my panties to keep my growing cock hidden securely between my legs. I was becoming quite uncomfortable as a result of my increasing arousal, but it was preferable to showing an unexpected bulge through the tight fitting dress. I sat through one more dare where Kelly actually went as far as to put Tanya's breast in her mouth for an entire minute, suckling at her friend's exposed chest in such a way that left the other girl clearly turned on if her erect

REBECCA STERNE -- TURNED INTO GIRLS!

nipples were anything to go by. This did nothing to assuage my own arousal, or indeed make me dread my own turn any less as I wondered what would happen if I were expected to expose any part of my body in a similar way.

The inevitability of my encroaching doom was such that it came as little surprise to me when Tanya looked in my direction and denoted me as the next one in line. I wanted to ask for a 'Truth' question but I knew from the rising atmosphere that this would be seen as a cop out and they'd likely push me into a dare anyway. I listened to myself say the word 'Dare' and waited nervously for the challenge to be announced. I glanced at Laura, seeing what I thought was a shared anxiety as to what I'd now be expected to do, but there was also something else in her expression, an eagerness to see me carrying out a similar dare to the others on one of her friends.

We all heard the approaching sound of a scooter coming up the driveway at the same time. For a moment I thought I was about to be quite literally saved by the bell, but I was soon jolted out of any sense of relief when Tanya spoke up quickly.

'I know!' Her mouth spread into a mischievous smile, 'You can give your first blowjob...to the pizza boy.' My mouth dropped open as I processed what she'd just said. Several excited screams went up as they all looked to me for an answer. I looked at Laura for help but even she was giggling away at the suggestion. They didn't really wait for an answer as they all began to stand up. I was quickly pulled to my own feet and lead out into the hallway amidst much excitement.

This was certainly not something I was prepared for. I couldn't imagine taking another boy's penis into my mouth, let alone sucking him off to an orgasm.

'I...I don't know about this.' I tried to say to Laura as she moved passed me towards the door. Kelly overheard my words and was quick to offer her support.

'Don't worry, it'll be fine.' She said, 'Just don't put it in too far to start with.' She actually put her arm around my waist to give me an encouraging hug. My only hope at this point was that either the delivery person was actually female, or possibly an older man that would have none of it, or that if it was a boy that he would simply refuse to take part in any such activity. This last hope seemed unlikely as most red blooded young men would struggle to refuse such an offer from a group of inebriated girls such as us.

As Laura opened the door wide I looked past her to the delivery person approaching the door, pizzas in hand. As he took his crash helmet off I saw that he was indeed male and probably about Laura's age or a little older. Seeing his face light up at the sight of a group of girls watching him from the house I knew then that I was unlikely to get a reprieve from this particular red blooded male.

'Hi girls.' He greeted the assembled group, flashing a broad smile.

'Hi there.' Said Laura, 'Can you bring them in?' She stepped to one side and I found myself being hustled into the kitchen by the other girls as they led the way through for him. I caught sight of a slightly bemused look on his face before he shrugged happily and carried the pizzas inside. Laura brought him with her and had him put the food down upon the counter before picking up some money for him. I could see him looking from one girl to the next. He was clearly enjoying the view.

'We only have the right money I'm afraid.' Kelly began apologetically, 'But we can still tip you if you like?' The delivery man smiled at her, clearly curious as to her suggested payment.

'What did you have in mind?' He asked.

Chapter 6

'Well, you can say no if you like.' Kelly continued. I suspected she knew full well that no refusal would be forthcoming when he heard her idea. 'But Louise here would like to try giving her first blowjob.' I blushed as I heard her words. As I looked up I saw the boy looking at me questioningly where Kelly had indicated which girl she was talking about. I blushed even more furiously. I couldn't believe the position Laura and her friends had now put me in.

'What...in front of everyone else?' He asked, peering around the room at his assembled audience.

'Don't worry; we'll give you some privacy.' She said.

I looked at Laura once again and was surprised to see her nod encouragingly to me. What was she thinking? Had she forgotten that I was her boyfriend? I was speechless for a moment, not sure how to deal with the situation.

'Come on.' Kelly said as she came over to me and took my arm. I think I was too shell shocked to put up a fight as I let her lead me into the utility room behind me. As we stepped through the door she leaned close to my ear and whispered. 'It's okay, it's easy. It doesn't take much to get them to blow their load.' She giggled, clearly thinking this was a great opportunity for me to try out oral sex for the first time.

I turned around as she pushed me further into the room, only to see the boy being ushered in behind me. He looked as though he couldn't believe his luck as he grinned from ear to ear. Kelly squeezed past him to leave the room, pulling the door closed behind her.

'I'm Rick.' He said as he stepped towards me. He seemed unsure of the etiquette needed in such an unexpected situation. 'So...should I just...?' He brought his hands up to his waistband and slowly unfastened his belt. 'You're pretty cute.' He said, his fingers now drawing his zipper down. I just watched him without moving. Feeling shocked by the fact this boy was about to reveal his penis to me. Then he was unfastening his button, allowing the jeans to slowly slide down his legs. I could see the pronounced bulge of his erection inside of his boxer shorts.

I tried to make my voice work but my throat had tightened up. I desperately looked towards the door behind Rick and saw that the girls had pushed it open slightly, their eyes watching our every move through the gap. I swallowed nervously as I peered back down to Rick's crotch. He was grasping the waistband of his shorts and in one swift motion he tugged them downwards. As he straightened once more I got my first clear view of his engorged cock as it stood straight out, twitching every so often of its own accord.

Still enthralled by his stiff manhood in front of me I jumped slightly as he reached out and took my hand. Pulling it towards him he gently laid it against his pulsing cock. Without thinking I instinctively wrapped my fingers around it, feeling its fleshy hardness in my hand. It was obviously bigger than my own and I could feel the weight of it as I lifted it up slightly.

I heard Rick let out a breath as I gave it a tentative squeeze. It felt as though my head was about to explode as I watched myself as if from afar handling another boy's erection. With little thought as to what I was doing I begun to move my hand up and down his shaft, bringing a guttural moan from his lips as I did so.

I looked up to his face, seeing his eyes closed and his head lolling backwards as he gave himself over to my ministrations. One more glance in the direction of the doorway was enough to confirm that my girlfriends were avidly watching my every move. I bit my lip for a second, wondering whether I should simply do as they expected or bring this to a premature end. It crossed my mind that the game of dares would in all likelihood come to an end after this, and that by performing an act of fellatio I would be satisfying them as to my credentials as one of the girls. Of course, I'm sure I could have simply refused and sometimes I wonder why I didn't. I think I just wanted to deflect any questions over my unwillingness to be with a boy and do my best to fit in.

Casting my eyes back down to between Rick's legs I made my decision. I slowly lowered myself towards the floor and was soon at eye level with his thick veined cock. Taking a breath to steady myself I moved my face closer. Before attempting to take him into my mouth I decided to find out what it was like to taste another boy's cock and gradually poked my tongue out. As I licked the bulbous end I caught the taste of precum as I wrapped my tongue around him. To my surprise I wasn't repelled by the experience and plunged on with my next move.

My only experience of a blow job to date had been earlier that very same day when Laura's mom had sucked me off whilst I was clad in the lacy red lingerie. Emulating her technique I guessed would produce the desired outcome in no time at all, and so I tried to draw on this as much as possible to guide my own fumbling attempt to perform oral sex as a girl.

Opening my mouth wide I moved myself forward, engulfing his cock with my mouth before closing my lips around him. I heard another moan as Rick felt me taking him in. Starting to suck him further in I kept moving my fingers up and down the rest of his shaft, driving his arousal continually forwards.

I struggled to get my head around the fact that I was now sucking off another boy. It seemed an almost surreal experience, one that I'd never planned for or expected to happen...ever! My eyes drifted back to the gap in the doorway to see Laura watching me wide eyed. I wondered if she'd really expected me to go through with it or whether she'd just assumed I would point blank refuse. It was too late to worry about it now, but I couldn't help but wonder whether this would work for me or against me when it came to our increasingly strange relationship.

Suddenly Rick moved his hands to the back of my head. 'Oh yeah...that's good baby.' He murmured to himself, his hips starting to thrust his cock deeper into my mouth. The taste of salty precum was growing more evident as his arousal built. I wondered at what point I should pull away in order to avoid having him cum into my mouth. Assuming as a boy that I would easily recognise the signs I continued as I was, focusing my attention on moving my mouth up and down his hard cock as my fingers did the same only nearer the base.

I did of course know what it felt like to experience an orgasm as a boy, but I now wondered how I'd recognise the signs in someone else. Lifting my free hand to cup his balls I tried to feel for them tightening up as mine always did just before I climaxed. This had the impact of increasing his arousal even more and his body became rigid, his breathing more intense. As he began to moan and hunch over me I decided to pull away, but his hands held me firmly in place as his cock started to spasm in my mouth.

I realised then that I'd left it too late and I was about to have my mouth filled with cum. I could feel a certain panic rising within me as I anticipated what was about to happen. He lurched forward slightly, bucking his hips as he began to unload into me. A huge spurt of warm cum jetted into my mouth, closely followed by a second and a third. I could feel the thick boy juice pooling on my tongue and coating the inside of my mouth. Squeezing my eyes closed I tried not to gag as I felt it oozing down the back of my throat. In his throes of orgasm Rick pulled my head in closer, pushing his spasming cock deeper into me. Just as I thought I couldn't take any more his climax began to subside, several smaller spurts of cum were ejaculated into my mouth before he slowly released his grip on my head.

I could hear his ragged breathing above me. His hands brushed through my hair affectionately before his body relaxed and I could sense his cock starting to soften in my mouth. I took the opportunity to pull away, sucking the remaining cum from his manhood as I sat back onto my heels. Keeping my lips pursed I was acutely aware of the fact that I now had a mouthful of cum that I still had to deal with.

Opening my eyes I glanced over to the doorway, seeing the girls watching me closely as I tried to consider what to do. I could feel some of Rick's boy juice running down towards my chin and I held my hands up to catch any that may drip. For a few moments I looked about myself, wondering what to do before I faced the inevitable. Allowing the still warm cum to roll towards the back of my throat I swallowed it down. I couldn't quite believe what I'd just done at that point as I continued to take down the remnants of Rick's juices. Wiping what still remained on my face with my hand I licked it off, more because I wasn't sure what else to do with it than anything else. At this point I realised I probably looked incredibly slutty to all those present, lapping up my reward for a blowjob well done.

'Wow!' Rick said finally as he'd gotten his breath back. 'That was great, thanks.' He made it sound as if I'd just carried out a rather mundane favour for him, but then I guessed the situation was probably just as weird for him as it was for me, well...almost. I smiled up at him weakly before getting to my feet. His penis was considerably smaller than it had been a couple of minutes earlier as he pulled his shorts and jeans back up. I caught a movement from the corner of my eye and realised the girls had vacated the doorway, clearly not wanting him to know that they'd witnessed the entire act.

We shuffled self-consciously back into the kitchen to find the group innocently standing around with drinks in their hands as if they'd been there the entire time.

'How was your tip, Rick?' Asked Kelly with a smile upon her face.

'Yeah, it was great. Thanks girls.' Rick said. He was clearly feeling a bit awkward having emerged from our sexual endeavour to a room full of girls. He took his pizza money gratefully and made his way out with little else to say. The grin plastered across his face was evidence enough of his satisfaction over this particular delivery.

As the door closed behind him a cheer went up from the girls as they thrust a drink into my hand. They found the whole thing most amusing and were positively impressed by my performance with my first blowjob. I could feel myself blushing furiously, but at the same time I was feeling pleased at being such a hit within the group. As I expected, the game of truth or dare had come to an end and we spent the rest of the evening eating pizza and finishing off the bottle of drink. I was actually a little disappointed when it came time for the girls to start heading home; I was having an unexpectedly good time with them.

'Well...I think you pulled that off quite well. Don't you?'

Laura said to me as she returned to the couch having seen the last of them off. We were both quite tipsy as I looked her in the eyes, hoping that she wasn't mad at what had happened. The fact that she was as complicit in setting up the entire episode as anyone else escaped me for a moment.

'It was a bit weird, but I think I did it okay.' I said, thinking of Rick's explosive climax. 'I only did it because it was a dare.'

'I was talking about you being a girl for the evening, but you did a good job with that as well.'

'Oh!' For a moment I'd almost forgotten that I was actually pretending to be a girl. I looked down at myself as if to confirm that that was still the case. Any thoughts of having a penis of my own hidden between my legs had disappeared after my escapade with Rick and a couple more drinks besides.

'I'm quite jealous actually.' Laura continued with a mock frown upon her face. 'You've never had your head between my legs before.' My mouth dropped open at what she was saying. I wasn't sure what to say and so I gave an apologetic shrug. She took my hand in hers and drunkenly pushed it underneath her dress. As she pressed my fingers against her panties I could feel a definite wetness there. 'You see how turned on I am now. I think it's my turn, don't you?' I glanced down to where my hand was and back up to her face. I knew she was serious and having had her watch me commit an act of oral sex already that night, I wasn't about to refuse her.

I suddenly felt a tingle of nervousness as I realised I was about to go down on my girlfriend for the very first time. Shifting my attention lower, I slid off the couch and pushed her dress upwards with both hands. She breathed in sharply as she realised I was about to do as she'd asked. As her panties became exposed I could see where they were almost translucent with her arousal. She'd clearly enjoyed my little show earlier. Taking hold of the waistband I gently started to pull them down as she shifted her position and allowed them to be pulled away from her bottom. I fancied that I could smell her arousal as I slid them off her feet, then she opened her legs wide allowing me access to kneel between them.

I gazed admiringly at her carefully trimmed pussy, wondering if this night was indeed reality and not just a dream that I was about to wake up from. I could feel my own arousal pushing

257

against the panties between my legs once more as I slowly, deliberately leaned in towards her most intimate of areas. As I drew close enough to inhale her feminine scent I paused for a moment. Running my finger along the length of her lips I could see her wetness oozing from her.

I leaned in further and replaced my finger with my tongue, running it along the length of her moist lips so as to taste her for the first time. I sensed a shiver run through her as I began to lap at her swollen cunny, delighting in her taste and feel.

'Mmmm...Louise!' She moaned from above. Hearing her refer to my female name seemed to increase my own arousal, a fact that didn't escape my own thoughts. I pushed myself deeper, parting her slick lips with my tongue and inserting myself into her warm, wet hole. She gasped and once again I felt a pair of hands upon the back of my head, pulling me in further. I began to drink from her greedily, coating my tongue in her juices and swallowing them down as she started to writhe against me. Her sex smell surrounded me as I delved ever deeper inside of her.

Coming up for air I once again ran my tongue along her pussy, finding her swollen clitty just waiting to be played with. As I rolled my tongue around it I knew she was experiencing waves of pleasure as she thrust her hips upwards, wanting more. My face was slick with her juices as I continued stimulating her, my own hand moving up underneath my dress and pressing between my legs, feeling the silky pantyhose with my fingers as I pressed my panties against my stiff trapped penis.

Glancing upwards for a brief moment I could see her head rolling from side to side, her eyes closed as she moved towards a fast growing climax.

'Oh god!' She called breathlessly, 'Lick me harder, Louise.'

I redoubled my efforts, slathering her juices across my face as I lapped furiously at her sopping wet pussy. I could hear her breaths becoming increasingly short and frantic as her body stiffened. Then her hands were pressing my mouth tightly against her as she let out a squeal of pleasure and bucked beneath me, her orgasm flooding forth and sending even more of her juices into my mouth. For a moment I couldn't breathe but I had no choice to stay as I was as her climax ran its course, emptying herself against my face. When eventually she sagged back onto the couch exhausted, I was able to lift my head enough to take a breath. I could feel her juices running down my face and onto my chin. I marvelled at the fact that I'd just brought Laura to an orgasm with my mouth for the very first time. Tonight definitely seemed to be a night of firsts for me.

When finally she relaxed enough to let go of my head I sat back. Once again wiping cum from my face and cleaning my fingers with my tongue, but this time it was girl's cum. I was painfully erect inside of my panties as I began to crave my own release.

'Wow!' She said. 'I see what Rick meant now.' I blushed yet again at the reminder of my earlier sex act with a boy. She slowly gathered herself together, pulling her panties back on and rearranging her dress. She glanced at the clock over the fireplace. 'Mom will be home soon, you'd better put your nightdress on.'

'What?' I asked incredulously. I desperately needed my own release at this point and was caught completely off guard by her instruction.

'I told Mom I'd make sure you were ready for bed when she got home.' She explained, clearly still drained from her orgasm. 'You'll find a nightdress and nighttime diaper on your bed.' I looked at her with a stunned expression. I was about to demand that she help me out when she seemed to notice my consternation. 'You'd better do as you're told or you'll be in trouble. Go on Louise. We can watch a little television before you go to bed once you're changed.'

I stood up a little shakily, feeling myself being demoted back to the position of her little sister in the space of just two minutes. I wanted to argue with her, to question why I was being treated as if I had no say in the matter, but yet again I became acutely aware of the fact that I was dressed in girl's clothing right now and that Laura and her mom were still holding all of the cards.

I sulkily left the room. Catching sight of a moody looking teenage girl in the hallway mirror as I passed it by only served to reinforce my position. Entering my own room I could see that Theresa had indeed left a girlish looking nightdress and a clean diaper on the bed ready for me. I took my time removing Laura's clothes, feeling a disappointment inside of me as I did so which I wasn't sure I really understood. Removing the panties last I could see a wet spot where I'd started to leak precum into them during the evening. I did briefly consider relieving myself before returning downstairs, but hearing Laura calling to me to hurry up I just stepped into the pull-up diaper. As I tugged it up my legs and into place my disappointment at taking off Laura's clothes seemed to lesson as I felt myself once again taking on a girl's persona, even if it were in nighttime diapers.

Once I'd slipped the nightdress over my head I examined the fairy motifs on the front before forcing myself to rejoin Laura downstairs. She was waiting patiently for me on the couch. Her expression seemed to change slightly as she saw my still sulky disposition.

'What's wrong, Louise?' She asked. As I slumped onto the couch next to her I wasn't really sure how to explain. Of course, one of the main problems I had at that precise moment was that I still craved my own release having been aroused for so much of the evening.

'It's just that you got to...you know...and I wanted to...' I realised as I was speaking that it all sounded a little confused and ridiculous, and so I stopped myself before I could make myself look even more childish. She looked me in the eyes for a moment before sliding up next to me and putting her arm around my shoulders.

'You do look ever so cute when you pout.' She said, giggling at my discomfort. 'Is it that you wanted to do a little spurt?' I peered at her face with a bemused expression, never having heard anyone refer to it like that. She clearly knew what the problem was and so I just nodded defiantly. 'Well, okay. We'd better hurry before Mom gets home.' She said.

I was about to hastily pull the diaper down when she batted my hands away. Rather than remove it she pulled it back up as high as it would go before resting her hand against the front of it. I was already partially erect as I felt the pressure of her fingers against me, causing me to quickly stiffen under her hand. This wasn't quite what I'd intended but my chronic arousal throughout the evening meant that I let out a moan of pleasure as soon as she did anything to stimulate me.

I saw her watching me with a smile upon her face as her hand pressed into me even more before starting to massage me through the diaper. I wanted to stop her, to tell her that I didn't want it this way but I was worried that she'd stop altogether and I'd miss out on having any relief whatsoever. I knew if that happened I'd probably end up masturbating myself in the diaper anyway, and so I let her continue.

I was soon fully erect as I began desperately moving my hips against her hand, my throbbing penis demanding to be allowed to cum. Then her lips were against mine as she kissed me deeply. I felt her tongue searching for a way in and I opened my mouth, allowing her to explore me as I did her. I raised one hand and found myself squeezing her breast between my fingers over her dress, increasing my rapidly growing arousal even more.

'Oh...oh...no!' I squeaked as I felt my climax rushing forward, impatient to be released into the diaper. I wanted to last longer, to give myself more time so that she may decide to pull the girlish diaper down and bring me to orgasm more directly, but there was no stopping it. 'I'm...I'm...cumming.' I moaned at her as if apologising for my speedy climax.

Then I was spurting into the absorbent diaper, squirming with delight as I was able to finally release my pent up arousal. Her hand squeezed and cupped me as I squirted my boy juice into my childish padded covering, feeling the warm cum running down my stiff cock and between my legs as it was soaked up by the diaper. She held her hand in place as I spasmed my way through an orgasm that seemed to last for an age, leaving me bereft of energy as the last few drops were pushed outwards and I drooped against Laura as she held me gently.

As my awareness slowly came back to me following my climax, I felt a little embarrassed by being made to cum into a diaper once again. My thoughts raced back through the evening as I recalled giving Rick a blowjob and then going down on Laura to get her off too. I felt a little used by all of this and a sense of humiliation seemed to hang there at the back of my mind, but I also felt more alive and gratified than I ever had before.

Theresa arrived home about half an hour after I'd made my diaper sticky under Laura's hand, finding us cuddled up together on the couch as if we'd spent the most innocent night of all together. She seemed happy that all was well and I was soon despatched to bed as the youngest in the household. I lay awake for a while mulling over my evening and how easily I'd fitted in as one of the girls. I was even getting used to being referred to as Louise instead of Louis. There was still a sense of confusion present in how my life had seemingly taken on such a perverse turn of events, but I had to admit that I was starting to get used to this strange new life of mine. It just remained to be seen for how long Laura and her mom would want to keep it up for.

Chapter 7

'Mom!' I called down to Theresa. It still occurred to me that three weeks ago I wouldn't have dreamed of referring to my girlfriend's mom as if she was my own, but things had certainly changed since then.

'Yes, Louise?' she replied.

'Can you help me with my hair please?' I still had difficulty with styling my hair at times, especially now that it was getting longer. We were heading off to the shops and she'd promised to buy me some new makeup. She still preferred to have me dressed as a younger girl when I wasn't with Laura, who now seemed to think of herself more as my older sister. Our relationship was certainly not one of siblings though, as she still liked us to indulge in intimacy on her terms. There was little doubt that she was the one in charge of our relationship.

The thing was that Theresa now also acted more like my mom in many ways and had also managed to persuade me to call her 'Mom', even though she also liked to initiate a level of physical intimacy between us. I still didn't know if they were both aware of each other's actions with me in that area, but it didn't seem necessary to say anything as they both seemed happy with the arrangement.

'You look nice. How about we put your hair into bunches today?' Theresa said as she arrived in my room. I was standing there wearing a floral sleeveless dress with a pink bow tied at the back and knee high white socks. I still made use of Nicole's old clothes when dressed in this way, as was quite the norm now, especially when staying at home. I was lucky that I seemed to pass easily for a girl regardless of what age range I was dressed in at the time.

I sat at the dressing table and watched in the mirror as she tied my hair into bunches with matching pink ribbons. I still questioned where this was all supposed to be leading when I gazed upon my feminine reflection. I'd not seen any trace of my boy clothes since that first day that they'd caught me dressed in Nicole's clothes, disgracing myself upon the couch. I strongly suspected that they'd actually thrown them out by now as they were always evasive when I tried to question them.

'All done!' She said, stepping back to admire her work. She'd actually confessed to me some time ago that she'd loved having young girl's to fuss over when her daughters were young and she was more than happy to do the same for me now. 'Come on then, hurry up.' She said, leaving the room.

As I slipped my Mary Janes onto my feet I wondered which shopping centre we'd be off to today. We normally went to an out of town one when I was dressed like this, presumably so that we didn't inadvertently bump into any of Laura's friends with me dressed in a younger mode. In all truth they had now become my friends too as I quite often accompanied Laura to one of their houses or on the odd shopping trip. I still had to borrow some of Laura's clothes for this but my own wardrobe of teenage girl's clothes had now started to grow.

As we made our way around the stores I found myself browsing some underwear in the girl's section. I picked up a particularly cute bra with small cups without thinking, feeling the soft material with my fingers.

'That's a training bra, Louise.' Theresa said, 'It's for when your breasts start growing.' I raised my eyebrows before putting it back. 'That's something we'll have to look into very soon.' She added.

'What? Growing breasts?' I asked, feeling I should remind

264

her that this wasn't going to happen. 'But...I can't.' I whispered.

'Well, we'll see about that. There are things we can do, Louise.'

'What?' I said again, looking at her as if she were quite mad.

'The word is 'Pardon', not 'What'.' She reminded me sternly. Then, taking my hand she began pulling me along the aisle. 'Now come along as we have other things to do.' Being tugged along behind her was yet another way of being put into my place. I wondered what people would think if they knew that not only was I a boy called Louis, but that I was also eighteen years old and had been attending college just three weeks earlier. Nobody seemed to bat an eyelid as they watched this woman pulling what appeared to be her young daughter through the store. In fact, I suspect their main thought would be why this girl wasn't in school just now.

She seemed in a hurry to purchase our items and return home and I suspected that I knew the reason why. I'd noticed her looking at some rather raunchy lingerie at one point, and knowing that she hadn't been on any dates for a while I could sense that she was feeling in need of some 'personal' time, as she liked to call it. I imagined that before the day was out I would find myself wearing some sexy underwear and engaging in some form of sexual act with her in order to satisfy her needs. I didn't mind too much though, as it certainly beat spending time in college.

That was something else that I'd also puzzled at earlier that day, as I'd seen a college application form lying upon the kitchen table that had been partially filled out. I hadn't had a chance to read it properly before I was being sent upstairs to get dressed, but I had noticed the gender was filled out to say female with my own date of birth underneath. I had a growing suspicion that she now intended to enrol me back into college as her daughter, but quite how she thought she'd get away with that I didn't know, and besides, surely she had to ask me first?

My thoughts drifted back to the present as we hurriedly made our purchases and headed back towards the car. I decided any such questions would have to wait as I wondered if she'd let me wear the white satin lingerie that she'd worn the last time we'd spent some 'personal' time together, it was very pretty and I was sure it would look just as good on me. I'd soon find out!

REBECCA STERNE -- TURNED INTO GIRLS!

Turned into a Sissy Sex Slave

One boy's confession of forced feminisation and sissy submission to a dominant woman

Rebecca Sterne

Chapter 1

Turning the street corner I approached the steps leading into my apartment building and stopped. I wondered if my landlady was at home, waiting for me to make an appearance. It was the third time I'd missed her deadline for paying the rent I owed on the small apartment at the top of the building, and I knew her patience was running thin. There were only so many excuses I could make, but the truth was I'd little chance of making up the payments with my working hours being cut back at the local coffee shop.

Not for the first time I feared that I'd find myself out on the street with little means of finding anywhere else. My college work would soon suffer and if I failed my course I'd be left with minimal prospects of a better job. Life was a bitch sometimes!

I glanced back down the street and considered simply turning about and heading in the other direction, but I'd have to come home sooner or later. I'd just be putting off the inevitable moment I'd step through that door and find her waiting for me.

It was of course perfectly possible that she was out somewhere. She went out a lot. Quite often I'd see her being picked up outside by a man and driven away. I didn't know much about her life, other than the fact that I paid her rent every month, at least, that was what I was supposed to do.

Taking a deep breath, I pulled myself up to my full height - which was a rather unimpressive five feet five inches, and steeled myself to enter her domain as a man, although I tended to feel quite unmanly in her presence most times. She was only a couple of inches taller than me, but her penchant for wearing high heeled shoes meant that she often towered above me. She was a curvy woman. I guessed they'd refer to her shape as an hourglass figure, like someone out of an old Hollywood film. Her build was still bigger than mine though. My slender frame and long blond hair were not exactly the epitome of classic masculinity, in contrast, her short dark hair gave her the look of a dominant figure, one that I struggled to place myself on an equal basis with.

A dog walker passed by me, giving me a suspicious look as I stood aimlessly watching the door at the top of the stairs. I half smiled at her, trying to appear casual but only achieving an awkwardness that made me want to be off the street and out of sight as soon as possible.

With a defeated sigh I headed up the steps, pulling my key from my pocket and letting myself inside. The door creaked slightly, making me flinch as I looked beyond the doorway expectantly. There was no sign of anyone, although it was never that likely that she was waiting behind the door to jump out on me.

Closing the door softly behind me, I turned toward the staircase and began the climb up to the relative safety of my apartment. By the time I reached the third floor I was starting to relax, relieved at not having had to endure yet another demand for the rent money - yet.

I hurried to let myself into my inner sanctuary, eager to be out of the hallway. As soon as I stepped inside, letting the door bang shut harder than I'd've liked, I knew something was wrong. It's a strange thing when you detect something out of place in your home environment - without ever seeing anything obvious, but I knew someone else was there nonetheless.

For a moment I wasn't sure what to do, and then with a spark of bravery and a sceptical voice inside of my head telling me that I was simply imagining things, I walked along the hallway, peering into the bathroom first, then my bedroom before finally walking into the open plan kitchen area only to find - much to my astonishment - my landlady standing there, hands on hips staring at the doorway as I entered.

'Miss Palmer!' I blurted out at the sight of her, my manly resolve to discover the source of my discomfort dissipating almost at once, 'What are you doing here, in my apartment?' I demanded.

'I'm here, Mr Tuck, because you owe me rent. And I'd remind you that you're in *my* apartment, young man. One that requires you to pay for its use.'

It seemed a little demeaning being referred to as "young man". I was twenty-one and I'd gauge that she was in her mid to late thirties at most. I could feel my legs weakening as I realised I was in a very precarious position.

'I-I'm sorry, Miss Palmer. I'm afraid I've not got the money just now, but I promise I'll have it soon.'

'You said that last time, Jesse.' She switched to using my first name, making me feel more like a child who was being told off by his teacher, 'I can't let you stay here for nothing, can I? You'll need to pay your way one way or another or you'll be out.'

'I ... but ... my hours have been cut and I'm trying to ...'

'Well, maybe you'll just have to find another way of compensating me.'

I stopped my stuttering attempt at an explanation as her words sank in. I looked at her curiously as I realised she was offering me a way out of my predicament. I didn't know what to suggest other than money. Then it struck me.

'I could help you out around the apartment block. Maybe I could work for my rent?' I suggested tentatively. I wasn't the handiest of males so I knew I'd only be capable of some fairly basic chores, such as cleaning and the like. 'I could clean for you?' I added.

She studied me appraisingly for a while as I stood there feeling increasingly awkward. I tried to force a little smile, to lighten the atmosphere but it probably came across more as a grimace.

'Yes, I'm sure you could.' She said finally, 'I think we'll start with my apartment downstairs. Follow me.'

As she strutted passed me in her stiletto heels I caught a whiff of her perfume. It was pleasant enough but hardly the floral feminine scent that I expected for some reason. I watched her firm and rather pert bottom as she stepped out into the hallway, her shiny skin tight trousers seemingly drawing me in as I followed her back out of the room. As with everything she wore, her top clung tightly to her shapely body. I was relieved on one hand to have been given another chance to keep a roof over my head, but something in the back of my mind was nagging at me, telling me that I wasn't yet safe from an uncertain future.

In my mind I began calculating how many hours I'd likely have to work for her before I was fully paid up once more. It was impossible to say as no mention was made of an equivalent rate of pay, but I hoped to clarify with her later, hopefully having proven myself a good enough worker to be worth her while employing.

As we reached her door on the ground floor I realised I'd never set foot inside before. She had this floor pretty much to herself which meant her apartment would be at least twice the size of mine, probably more. She unlocked the door and stepped inside, not waiting to check whether I was still behind her. Hesitating for a brief moment I followed, closing the door softly behind me.

I was correct in my assessment as it was immediately apparent that she had considerably more spacious accommodation than myself, although this wasn't at all surprising considering she managed the building.

'I think we'll start with the bathroom.' She said over her shoulder as she led me through the large living area, with an open plan kitchen on one side, 'I'm afraid I'm not the tidiest of people. You'll need to put my clothes in the laundry hamper, and you can clean all of the surfaces and the floor.'

I felt myself baulk a little at the prospect of being put to work so quickly and in such a dismissive manner, but I knew I needed to get her on side if I wanted to stay in my apartment. She pointed out the cleaning supplies and showed me to the bathroom. She was certainly telling the truth about not being the tidiest of people. There were several discarded items of clothing strewn across the floor in the general vicinity of the laundry hamper. I gazed around with a critical eye as I judged what needed to be done.

'I'm afraid since my maid moved on I've not had the time to get anyone else in, so it's quite fortunate that you're in need of such work.' She said, 'I'll leave you to it then, shall I?'

'Yes, Miss Palmer.' I said, frowning at the work that lay ahead of me, 'I'm sorry, I don't know your first name.'

'My name's Victoria, but I'd prefer it if you just called me Miss Palmer, or Miss, if that's a little too formal for your liking.'

I began to laugh in response before realising she wasn't making fun of me. She held my gaze for an uncomfortable amount of time before I had to look away. 'Yes, Miss Palmer.' I said, feeling as though I were being manoeuvred into my rightful place.

As soon as she left I let out a heavy sigh. The sooner I got on with it the sooner I'd be finished, and so I stepped across the room to begin picking up her clothes. It wasn't until I'd grasped a couple of items and straightened up that I realised I was actually handling her worn underwear. I stopped in my tracks and looked down at my hand where a pair of silk panties were dangling from my fingers. I glanced around at the open door, feeling anxious for some inexplicable reason before holding them up before me. There was a definite dampness to them, and as I looked closer I could detect her womanly scent. As with many boys of my age, I couldn't quite stop myself from inhaling her intimate aroma as I spread them out with my fingers. It felt naughty to be doing such a thing, but as it was her that had bade me to tidy her soiled clothing away, I excused my behaviour as inevitable under the circumstances.

Almost immediately I could feel myself becoming aroused by the sight, smell and touch of such a sensual item of hers. She was an attractive woman, there was no doubt about that. I looked around at the handful of other items still laying on the floor, spying a bra and a pair of stockings with wide lace tops, all matching in black. I picked them up too, running the stockings through my fingers before examining the bra. In my mind I imagined her dressed in nothing but her lingerie, and my arousal grew.

'I think you'll need this, Jesse,' I heard her voice as she rounded the corner of the doorway and immediately lowered the clothing that I was still holding. My cheeks began to heat up at the thought of what I was doing, 'we don't want you to get ... are you alright, young man? You look a little ... flushed.'

'I ... um ... yeah, sure. I was just tidying up.' I tried a nonchalant shrug but my awkwardness made it feel stiff and unnatural.

'So I see.' She peered down at where I was clutching a

handful of her underwear, making my ears burn as well as my cheeks, 'I was going to give you this.' She held up an apron, 'We don't want you getting your clothes all dirty, do we?'

Shifting the clothes into one hand, I took the apron from her with a mumbled "Thanks". She looked amused by my embarrassment. I looked down at my hand when she'd left, staring at the underwear as if it were to blame for my actions, although I doubted that she'd have known anything was amiss if I hadn't reacted so self-consciously. I turned my attention to the apron that she'd brought to me. It was white and very frilly, clearly a left over from when she'd had a proper maid in her employ. I huffed my annoyance at being offered such a thing.

Despite my growing discomfort at the entire situation I couldn't help but wonder what it'd be like to wear it. Taking several deep breaths as my face began to cool, I opened the laundry hamper and with an effort managed to ignore the rest of the clothing inside whilst throwing the lingerie on top. I was left with a bathroom to clean and an apron in my hand, which despite my misgivings I found myself tying behind my back before straightening it across my shoulders. A quick glimpse at my reflection was enough to confirm that I looked somewhat silly in it, although not as silly as I thought I should.

Chapter 2

The next hour or so was spent scrubbing and cleaning the bathtub, shower, basin and floor. It wasn't that it was terribly dirty, but more that I could justify an hourly rate for my efforts. By the time I was finished I was feeling quite pleased with my work. I left the room in search of Miss Palmer.

As I entered the main living room I saw her standing there with what looked like the remainder of a traditional looking maid's outfit in her hands. She was holding it out in front of her with a frown of concentration on her face.

'Miss Palmer, I've cleaned the bathroom.' I said, feeling my continued embarrassment at being caught with her worn lingerie in my hands nudging at the back of my mind.

'Oh, Jesse,' She said, looking away from the dress, 'I was just trying to work out whether this would fit my niece. It's too small for me so there's not much point in me trying it on.' She explained. I tried to look at least mildly interested, although I did wonder why her niece would want a maid's outfit. Her brow furrowed once more as she looked me up and down. 'In actual fact, she's about your size.'

'Oh, right. Is there anything else I can do today?' She

274

continued to look as though she were gauging my size as I tried to come up with a way of broaching the subject about my financial settlement.

'You know, you could do me a huge favour.' She said brightly as her eyes grew wider.

'Sure.' I said, a little too eagerly it would seem.

'If you could just try this on for me, I'd be so grateful.'

'Eh?'

'Try this on. I'm quite certain that you're the same size as my niece, so it's an obvious thing to do.'

'But ... that's a maid's dress!' I pointed out to her in my astonishment at being asked to put a dress on.

'Yes, Jesse, I know that,' she said in an overly patient manner as if speaking to a simpleton, 'and I'd like you to try it on for me, please?' She lowered the garment in front of her as I hesitated to respond, not quite knowing what to say to her, 'You're already wearing the apron, so I don't see why putting the dress on should make a difference,' I glanced down as I was reminded of what I was still wearing over my clothes, 'and we can discuss your rent afterwards, can't we?'

'I ... um ...' Her mention of my rent payments gave me reason to pause. I didn't know if there was an implied threat there or not, but I wasn't sure if I was brave enough to deny her what she simply described as a favour. 'I suppose.' I said in the end, swallowing hard at the thought of such a thing.

'Don't look so worried, Jesse. No one will see you, will they? Now, take off your things and we can try this on for size.'

I slowly unfastened the apron from behind my back and slipped it off my shoulders. Telling myself that I need only slip my shirt off to try this on I undid the buttons and slid that off my shoulders too, feeling a little "on show" as I revealed my naked torso to this woman. Her eyes never left me as I draped my shirt over a nearby chair alongside the frilly apron. I held out my hands for her to pass me the maid's dress.

'You can't try it on over your jeans, can you? And you may as well take off your socks as well. I need to see how it'll look on my niece.' She stared at me expectantly.

I stared back at her, shocked at the idea that she wanted me to strip down to my underwear. When her unwavering stare continued I felt my resistance crumbling away. In reality it only meant letting her see me in my undershorts. A small price to pay for keeping my apartment, I thought.

Feeling as self-conscious as ever I had in my life, I kicked off my shoes and pulled my socks from my feet, laying them carefully on top of my shirt. I had to force myself to carry on as I became acutely aware of undressing in front of my landlady. I unfastened my jeans and slid the zipper downward as she continued to watch me with some amusement. Taking a deep breath and determined to simply get this over with, I pushed them down my legs, stepping out of them awkwardly. I could feel my embarrassment rising once more as I folded them neatly onto the pile of clothes next to me.

'Now, let's find you something more appropriate to wear under the dress, shall we?' She said as she suddenly moved towards me. For some reason I took a step back, dropping my hands in front of my crotch as if to protect myself as she swiftly approached. I watched silently as she gathered up my clothes and walked away, leaving me too surprised by her unexpected act to question her.

As she disappeared from the room I found myself looking around in disbelief. I'd no idea what she was intending to bring me, but my supposed favour at modelling her maid's outfit was suddenly taking on an uncomfortable aspect. I waited dubiously where I was, not sure whether to follow her. As my discomfort increased and I found myself feeling more and more on edge, I heard her returning down the hallway. I must've looked quite the sight, standing there in just my underwear looking quite lost as to what was happening. She giggled at the sight of me.

'Here you are, these'll be far more appropriate with that dress.' She held up a bundle of what looked like female underwear.

As I took it from her I noticed the sheer black stockings hanging down. A closer look made me realise she'd retrieved the very lingerie that I'd recently thrown into the laundry hamper in the bathroom. My belly flipped over at the thought that she was presenting me with her worn underwear.

'But ... I ...' My throat seemed to tighten as I tried to voice my discomfort, strangling the words before I could force them out.

'Oh, don't be silly. It's just some panties, a bra and some stockings with a garter belt.' She waved her hand dismissively, 'I can't very well judge what the dress'll look like if you're wearing a pair of bulky boy shorts underneath, can I?' Placing her hands on her hips she stared at me as if exasperated by my obtuse behaviour.

'I ... It feels a bit ... weird!' I finally managed as I stood there, one hand holding a bunch of her underwear, my other held protectively in front of my crotch.

'Look, if you'd rather not come to an arrangement I'd be quite happy to give you another week to pack your things and leave.' She said, sounding almost helpful in her offer. 'Of course, you'll still owe me the money, but I'm sure we can ...'

'Um, no ... that's okay.' I interrupted her as I felt myself moving a step closer to being out on the street, 'I d-don't mind, really.'

'Very good,' She folded her arms with satisfaction, 'you'd better hurry up then.'

'Is there somewhere I can ... change clothes?' I asked tentatively, feeling too embarrassed to strip off entirely in front of her.

'Oh Jesse, you really are adorable.' She giggled, 'I'll just wait by the door. I promise I won't look.' She stepped passed me and made herself comfortable in the doorway, facing the other way.

It was immediately apparent to me that not only had I just agreed to put on her worn lingerie, but that she was also blocking the only way out should I have a change of heart. I felt somewhat trapped by my own weakness and distinctly precarious financial position, and so it seemed I had little choice but to complete my humiliation and dress up in her underwear, which I was beginning to suspect was purely for her amusement more than anything else.

Trying to steady my nerves, I placed the bundle of underwear onto the chair and gripped my undershorts. Taking a breath I pulled them down and stepped out of them before I could change my mind. Then, with a trembling hand I picked up her panties and shook them out in front of me. I couldn't deny the flutter of excitement that gripped me as I anticipated putting them on. In an effort to ignore such feelings and to suppress the additional embarrassment of being aroused by my coerced cross-dressing, I tried to think of other things as I stepped into them and began pulling them up my legs. My mind was soon preoccupied with the feelings that were now beginning to overwhelm me. I found myself full of nervous excitement as I felt

277

the soft lacy panties sliding up my legs that were surprisingly hair free for a boy, sending an electric thrill up through my body that seemed to jolt my member into life, making my little cock swell with interest. I couldn't quite get my mind off the fact that this sensual, sexy woman had been wearing these very panties not so long ago. As I tugged them all of the way up, cupping my balls in their soft embrace and trapping my partially erect cock against my belly I let out an involuntary whimper.

'Are you okay, Jesse? Do you need any help?' I heard her say from the doorway.

'N-No, I'm fine, thanks.' I said in a croaky voice.

I had to take a couple of steadying breaths before I picked up her bra and having examined it for a moment, wrapped it around my waist and fastened the clasp. I spun it around my body before pulling the straps over my shoulders, feeling myself being cosseted within her feminine undergarments. I hesitated for a while as I contemplated the sheer black stockings. My inner excitement grew as I ran the soft material through my fingers before rolling first one then the other up as I'd seen on so many films, before slowly, cautiously working them up my legs. Their sensual embrace was almost too much to bear as I felt my legs being encased in the very epitome of female attire. My breathing had become shallow, more rapid. My entire body felt as though it were trembling softly as I ran my fingers over my stockinged legs. The garter belt proved an altogether more difficult challenge, and I huffed and puffed my way through the process of attaching the straps to the stocking tops. I heard my landlady huff her impatience several times as I struggled with the rear straps before finally standing up, fully dressed in her black lingerie set.

Looking down at myself I could see my partial stiffness outlined in the front of the panties and groaned at the sight, knowing she'd see it as soon as she looked at me. It was as I was about to try tucking it back between my legs in a bid to hide any signs of arousal from her that she turned to face me.

'You look very sexy in my underwear, Jesse.' She said, 'Does it make you feel sexy?' She asked after a moments consideration.

Her question surprised me and I automatically looked down to the front of the panties.

'Yes, I can see you're enjoying wearing my panties.'

Naughty girl!' She said.

I froze where I was as she approached, bringing the black dress with her. I quailed under her gaze as she examined me closely. She straightened the bra straps upon my shoulders, causing me to gasp with surprise at her touch. Her hand lingered on my back before it slid downward, coming to rest on my panty covered bottom. I held my breath, feeling her pressing the panties into my flesh before giving my bottom a squeeze.

'Right, put this on.' She held out the dress, helping me slide into it before she fastened the buttons.

Next she wrapped the apron that I'd already been wearing back around my waist, pulling it onto my shoulders as I meekly let her dress me. All the time I could feel myself being immersed into a feminine form of submission. I felt my resistance to her will crumbling as I realised how I must now look, fully dressed as a traditional domestic maid. As I looked down I realised the dress only came to about mid-thigh, if that. It was certainly designed to show off the legs of the person wearing it. Seeing my stockinged thighs emerging from below the short hemline my cock twitched between my legs, betraying my growing arousal at being dressed in such a way.

'You look lovely, Jesse. I think you may as well wear this for the rest of the day, don't you?' I spun around to look at her, 'Just like a proper little maid.'

'What? I can't ... I mean ... I look silly dressed like this.'

'I think you look quite sexy, and besides, there's no one else here to see you.' Her hand shot out in front of her as she stepped toward me, her fingers probing beneath the short dress before finding my engorged cock through her silken panties. 'I think you like being dressed as a girl, don't you?'

I let out a surprised moan as I felt her wrapping her fingers around me, rubbing my cock as I continued to engorge. I was soon fully erect in her hand as I tried to decide what to do, but my mind was a muddle of conflicting thoughts as I felt myself being touched in such an intimate way. Every slight movement of my body reminded me of what I was wearing. The bra shifting against my flat chest, the straps on the garter belt tugging against the stocking tops, the panties being rubbed against me by her hand. She looked into my eyes, forcing me to look away in disgrace as I failed to put a stop to my shame. I could feel my belly fluttering madly. My legs turning to jelly as my balls tightened. I began to groan miserably as I felt myself being masturbated in such a humiliating way.

'Oh ... Oh, p-please ... M-Miss P-Palmer ...' I pleaded, wishing for her to stop this before she'd taken me too far, but at the same time desperately wanting such an erotically charged release.

My arousal was building swiftly. I closed my eyes and clenched my fists by my sides as she continued to molest me against my will, and yet I did nothing to stop her. I could feel my orgasm building, precum beginning to ooze out into her panties to mix with whatever emanations she'd previously left in her own underwear. My mind's eye was full of the sight of her soiled underwear, I could smell her once more, feel the heat from her body as she used her own panties to bring me toward a climax.

'Oh, M-Miss ... I'm going to ... I think I'm c-cumming!' I confessed breathlessly as my orgasm began to break and I could feel my cock spasming in her hand.

'That's a good girl,' I heard her say through my sex fogged mind, 'let your sissy juice come out. You feel nice wearing my panties don't you?' I nodded bashfully as I felt the first jet of cum being forced out into her underwear, 'You like being dressed as a girl, don't you? As a little sissy maid?' I nodded once more, only too pleased to agree as I came hard under her hand. 'Would you like to be my sexy little sissy maid, Jesse?' In my mind I hesitated as I tried to process what she was saying to me, 'Would you like that? To keep living here as my little sissy girl?' As I filled her panties with my warm cum I heard my chance to keep a roof over my head.

'Y-Yes, M-Miss.' I said, just as my orgasm began to wain and the flow of cum slowed.

I grunted as my whole body spasmed. The last of my seed being ejaculated as an overwhelming weakness came over me. I found myself leaning against this woman as she stood over me, reduced to a quivering mess dressed up in her lingerie and maid's outfit with her cum soaked panties clinging to my softening penis beneath. She slowly withdrew her hand as she finished milking me of any last vestiges of dignity or indeed masculinity.

'I always knew you was a natural sissy.' She said, stepping away from me and holding up her hand that now glistened with my cum, 'I think our new arrangement is going to prove quite satisfactory, for both of us.'

In my post orgasmic fog I wasn't quite sure what I'd just agreed to, but I had a pronounced sinking feeling that this wasn't going to be quite as satisfactory for me as for her.

Chapter 3

The rest of that day proved to be a most surreal experience. I could barely look my landlady in the eye having debased myself in such a way, and no end of embarrassed pleading was enough to get her to return my normal clothes. In fact, she managed to invent a number of other cleaning chores around her apartment that meant I was kept busy in my maid's outfit for some time, all the while having to suffer the ignominy of wearing a pair of cum soaked panties underneath the dress. Every time the stockings brushed together as I moved around, every time the garter straps tugged or the panties shifted against my cock I was reminded of my state of dress and how she'd had me humiliate myself at her hands.

When finally she said that I could go for the night it came as a relief, although I couldn't help but wonder what her next move would be. She had one final humiliation in store for me, one that would leave me with a strange mixture of feelings.

'You can go back to your apartment as you are. I'll expect you to wash my underwear and report back tomorrow evening.' She instructed me with a firm voice, 'You've a large debt to work off and the sooner you start the better.'

I attempted to argue as I had visions of being seen by one of the other residents before making it back to the safety of my apartment, but it was of no use. In the end I was forcibly nudged into the empty hallway as she watched me scurry up the stairs. My stockinged legs brushing furiously against each other as I prayed that no one would see me. I was lucky to get away with it, hearing another door opening on the floor below just as I let myself into my apartment. I leaned back against the door with relief before casting my eyes down at myself and wondering quite how I'd gotten into this.

One of the most confusing aspects was that I'd actually been turned on by being put into her underwear. Despite my feelings of embarrassment and humiliation at my ordeal, now that I was back in the privacy of my own apartment I surprised myself by spending the rest of the evening as I was. There was no need to pretend to myself that I wasn't secretly turned on by wearing this woman's underwear, and so I even wore it to bed that night, pleasuring myself as I lay back recalling the touch of her hand as she masturbated me through her own panties.

Of course, I later came to realise this was just as she'd intended. Knowing full well that someone of my nature would be unable to resist the sexual feelings being stirred up by the presence of such sensual lingerie upon their body. I was falling into her trap body and soul, and I didn't even realise it.

-o0o-

I spent the morning in college before returning to my apartment in the early afternoon. I didn't see my landlady on my arrival, much to my relief. I retrieved her lingerie from my bedroom, the panties still damp from my forced climax and decided to hand wash everything. I was sure that she'd find a way of making me pay if I were to take them back still soiled.

It came to the time she'd instructed me to return to her and I was stood anxiously inside of my apartment, trying to decide whether to follow her instructions or not. The unpaid rent loomed over my head, pushing me to do whatever was necessary to avoid losing my apartment. Steeling myself for what was to come I carried the maid's outfit and the clean lingerie downstairs, discreetly held in a plastic bag. I was glad I did as I passed my neighbour as soon as I stepped outside my door, mumbling a greeting as I self-consciously hurried away, feeling that she could see right into the bag. It was silly I know.

Knocking on Miss Palmer's door on the ground floor, I started to think she may not be at home as the seconds ticked by. I was about to head back upstairs, a sense of relief building inside when the door was opened.

'Jesse, you're late.' She said at once, immediately putting me on the back foot.

'I ... yes, I'm sorry, Miss Palmer. I ...'

'You may just refer to me as Miss. It sounds far too formal calling me Miss Palmer.' She said.

I was waved inside impatiently. Being anxious to prove that I'd dutifully washed her underwear I was quick to take it out of the bag and present it to her.

'I washed your underwear, Miss Palmer ... I mean, *Miss*.'

'So why aren't you already dressed?'

'Dressed?' I was nonplussed as to what she meant for a moment before realising she'd expected me to turn up in her maid's outfit again, no doubt wearing her lingerie underneath. 'I ... I didn't realise you wanted me to wear it again.' I said weakly.

'I can see I'll need to make myself very clear in future.' She said.

I looked at my feet.

'Hurry up then, you might as well get changed now.'

'What?'

'Oh for goodness sake, Jesse, you really are being an infuriating girl!'

'I'm ... a what?'

'Stop arguing, Jesse, and get changed immediately while I find you some footwear to match.' She scowled at me, 'Well? Hurry up then!'

I looked about myself in astonishment at how quickly everything had started to happen since walking into her apartment. I was standing next to the bathroom, and with little idea of how else to proceed I stepped inside and closed the door. I began to move as if in a dream. Robotically stripping my male clothes away as I tried to comprehend where all this was leading to and whether I wouldn't just be better off by giving up the apartment. A voice in my mind practically shouted back at me that this would be a very

284

bad choice indeed, and that she would soon tire of her games. Besides, as long as no one else ever saw me where was the real harm? And it *was* kind of exciting in a strange and unexpected way.

Stepping into her panties once more gave me just as much a thrill as the first time I'd done it, despite spending most of the previous evening wearing them. I was soon working her soft sheer stockings up my legs to attach to the garter belt, quickly followed by her bra. I couldn't help but pause to look at myself in the mirror, admiring how my slender almost feminine form was accentuated by the lingerie. I tried holding my long hair up, or pulling it back into a ponytail to see how it'd look in a more girly style. I was quite taken by surprise when the door was flung open and I saw my landlady's reflection staring back at me as I froze in mid pose.

'I see you're enjoying my underwear again, Jesse.' She grinned triumphantly, 'You can put these on with your dress, when you're quite finished posing in the mirror.' She dropped a pair of black high heeled shoes on the floor by the door.

I stared at them as she left, wondering how on earth she expected me to walk in something like that. Feeling embarrassed by being caught looking at myself in such a way, I quickly pulled on the dress and fastened the frilly apron about my waist.

I'd never even come close to wearing women's shoes before, and to try wearing high heels for the first time seemed a daunting prospect. I slipped them on whilst holding onto the door frame and took a moment to balance myself. They didn't feel as uncomfortable as I thought they would, and so I took a few tentative steps around the bathroom before deciding I could probably get used to them. I couldn't help but take another look at myself in the mirror before stepping outside to face my fate, admiring how my stockinged legs were even more shapely as a result of the heels.

My insides were flopping about madly as I left the bathroom and went in search of my landlady. I found her in her bedroom, laying back in nothing but a set of white lingerie. She was gazing over at an open drawer and as I was about to announce my presence she looked over and smiled.

'You look very nice, Jesse.' She said, taking a moment to look me up and down, 'You're an absolute natural. Now, I've some washing that needs to be taken care of by hand. You'll find it waiting for you in the utility room behind the kitchen.'

I gazed over at her, trying and failing to tear my eyes away from her lingerie clad body.

'You're not the only one that likes wearing my lingerie you know, Jesse.' She said, seeing my embarrassment as I felt a familiar burning in my cheeks, 'Hurry up and get to work, my panties won't clean themselves.'

'Y-Yes, Miss.' I said, turning about and tottering unsteadily along the hallway in my heels.

I was still wondering what she meant by being a "natural", thinking she couldn't mean being a maid, when I entered the utility room to find what was clearly a pile of underwear waiting for me. I felt my breath catch in my throat as I stepped forward, looking down at the mixture of colours and textures before picking up the topmost pair of pink lace panties. Her scent was everywhere and it was obvious she'd done more in some of her panties than simply wear them. I could feel myself becoming hard between my legs as I breathed in her musky aroma, touching that most intimate of places in her underwear where she'd soiled them sexually. Trying desperately to keep my mind on the task of washing this erotic mound of soiled clothing, I set about my task. There were panties a plenty in the pile. Bra's, garter belts, stockings and pantyhose. My mind was being overloaded with eroticism as I gently washed and rinsed everything in front of me.

At one point I realised I was subconsciously rubbing myself up and down against the front of the basin as I leaned over, my cock stiff inside of her panties. I groaned out of frustration as my arousal demanded an outlet but I knew I had to try and get through this without humiliating myself once again. It was proving to be a tortuous task.

For one moment of clarity I imagined what I must look like. Dressed in this woman's lingerie, wearing a maid's outfit and high heels, hand washing her most intimate of clothing whilst humping the sink in frustration. I let out an audible groan at the very idea.

'I see you're enjoying your work, Jesse.' Her voice startled me from behind and I turned my head to look at her.

Realising I was still pressing my crotch against the basin I moved back, hanging my head out of embarrassment as I continued to rinse the last few pairs of panties in front of me.

'Don't be embarrassed, Jesse, it's perfectly normal for a sissy girl like you to act like this.' I could feel her eyes upon me, 'I'm sure we can keep this just between us, especially whilst you're able to live here in my building. Don't you think?'

I could feel her silken trap wrapping itself around me as I sunk ever deeper into her world of femininity and sexuality. I forced myself to nod, not trusting my voice in that precise moment as I was more focused on my raging arousal beneath the dress. Had I been listening more clearly to her words I may have showed more interest in her repeated references to being not only a "sissy", but a "girl" too. As it was, my state of chronic sexual arousal was fogging my brain to the point of making rational thought a distant prospect.

'I think it's time you had a reward for being such a good girl.' I turned my head to look at her, wringing out the last of her panties as I did so. She was still dressed in her white lingerie, making my arousal even more pronounced as I gazed upon her beautiful womanly body, 'Come with me.'

She wagged her finger at me before turning away and leaving me to stare after her, wondering if my legs would even bear my weight at this point. I hung up the pair of panties I was holding and followed her out. Her plump bottom moved seductively in the lace backed panties, my cock twitched and I thought for one fearful moment that I would cum there and then in my panties, so chronically aroused was I. By the time she stopped and sat down in one of the modern dining chairs that surrounded the expansive table, I was feeling desperate for some relief.

'Kneel in front of your mistress, Jesse, there's a good girl.'

Ignoring her continued references to me as a girl I did as she said, glad that my legs no longer had to hold me upright. I watched mesmerised as she slowly opened her legs in front of me, showing off her panty covered pussy as I gaped openly at her crotch.

'Crawl in between my legs, Jesse, be a good girl. It's time you learnt to pleasure your mistress.' She said, running her fingers up and down the front of her panties, making my need even greater.

I did as she said, no longer in control of my own actions as I moved toward her hidden honey pot. My face was mere inches from her most intimate and secret of places when I settled onto the floor and glanced up at her, wanting to be certain that I was truly being invited in between her legs. She nodded, smiling down at me as I returned my gaze to her panties that were already showing signs of dampness.

I shuffled forward those last few inches and lowered my head, feeling her stockinged thighs pressing in on me from either side as I inhaled her sweet aroma, opening my mouth and pushing my tongue forwards. At first I began to trace her swollen pussy lips through her panties, feeling the heat of her sex as she allowed me to taste her through her underwear. Quite soon she took hold of them and pulled them aside, opening the way for me to taste her juicy quim.

She began to squirm against me as I lapped at her copious juices. Her fleshy lips were soft against my mouth, her scent surrounding me and her taste coating my tongue. I felt light headed as I sank my tongue between her folds, finding her wet hole. I pushed inside of her as far as I could, drinking her nectar as my face glistened with her juice and I heard her moaning from above me.

'That's a good sissy girl, pleasure your mistress.' She said, pulling my face into her crotch.

My cock was fully erect now, pushing against the panties that still held it teasingly in their grasp. I felt the straps on the garter belt tugging at my stockings as I began to move in and out, humping the fresh air between my legs as I rocked backward and forward. I became more desperate. My tongue found her clit and I rolled it around. Teasing it, licking it. I wanted to mount her, to have my arousal sated but I knew I dared not move without her direction. I was already her lap dog, although I didn't fully realise it at the time. Her copious juices filled my mouth and ran down my chin as I continued to pleasure her as instructed. Her moans increased as her hips began to thrust against me.

'Mmm, that's a good sissy. Drink your mistress's nectar. Be a good sissy girl.' She mewled as her breathing grew more rapid.

She started to pant, her body growing rigid as her first orgasm swept through her. She sagged back into the chair for several seconds as I continued to work on her pussy, pushing my tongue inside of her again as my hips began to move. Then she was cumming against my face again, her juices gushing forth and leaving me slick with her cum. I was immersed in her smell, her taste, her feel as I felt my own climax building inside. When finally her orgasm waned she pushed my head away, battling to return her breathing to normal. I whimpered desperately, needing my own release.

'P-Please, M-Miss?' I begged, looking up at her with pleading eyes, my hips still moving crudely back and forth as my cock jumped and pulsed inside of my panties. She looked down at me with that amused smile once more as I groaned softly.

Then it happened. I shamed myself right in front of her as my body took matters into its own hands and I suddenly felt my orgasm rushing forward. I barely had time to look down, as if I needed to confirm with my own eyes what I already knew was happening. I sat back onto my heels in a panic, thrusting my hands between my legs as if to hold it in but it was of no use. I started to cum in her panties again, grunting feebly as my body jerked about on the floor. I felt ashamed and humiliated, unable to control my own body. I could feel the panties growing wet with cum as I shot my load, releasing my pent up arousal in one embarrassing and demeaning act of shame.

When I finally began to gain some control over myself I sobbed with embarrassment as I hung my head. I still hadn't moved from between her legs. I didn't know if I even had the strength to do so.

'Well, it looks like my little sissy has wet her panties again, doesn't it?' She said, sitting up straight in the chair and closing her legs as she pulled her own panties back into place. 'Jesse? Doesn't it?'

'Y-Yes, Miss.' I answered, feeling as though I were losing my mind as well as my dignity to this woman.

Chapter 4

As she continued to study me I quickly wiped her juices from my face, smelling her sex scent all about me. I could feel my own cum escaping my panties and running slowly down between my legs. I sat stiffly in place, not sure what to do as I felt myself shrinking under her gaze.

'I suppose we'd better get you some clean clothes, hadn't we?' She said, standing up. As she crossed the room she cast a look over her shoulder, 'Don't just sit there in your wet panties, Jesse, follow me.'

I pushed myself from the floor and stood with shaky legs for a moment before following on behind, feeling like a lost puppy. My identity as a male seemed to be blurring around the edges, fading into the background as this woman had me crossing the line between boy and girl. As much as I tried to think straight at this point, the feel of my sodden cum filled panties and the brushing of my stockings as I tottered after my landlady was enough to make any rational thought impossible. Before I realised it, I'd arrived in the bathroom behind her as she went about gathering a few supplies.

'You'll need to take a shower,' She said quite matter-offactly, 'and you can rid yourself of any boy hair whilst you're there. I'll leave you some cream and shaving supplies. When you're finished I don't want to see any trace of body hair. Is that clear?' I glanced over to where she'd placed some depilatory cream alongside a pink razor and shaving gel. My mouth worked in protest at this latest assault on my manhood, but no words would escape. 'I said, is that clear, Jesse?' She asked once more.

'I ... um ... I'm not sure I ...'

'Not sure of what?' She demanded before I could finish my faltering sentence, 'That you like wearing my underwear? That you enjoyed servicing me between my legs? That you want to continue living in my apartment block?'

This last point brought me up sharply as I realised she was giving me little choice but to do as I was told. I swallowed nervously as I considered what she wanted me to do. *It wasn't a big deal.* I reasoned. *No one would know, and it was only body hair at the end of the day. It wouldn't be of any great loss.*

'Okay ... Miss.' I nodded, 'I'll do it if you like.'

'I do like,' she confirmed, 'and I suspect so will you, once you're all nice and smooth.'

She smiled at me for a moment before brushing passed, patting my pantied bottom as she went. It felt demeaning and thrilling at the same time to be treated in such a way. And so, just as she'd commanded, I found myself stripping off my maid's outfit and her lingerie before stepping into the shower. I'm still not sure why I submitted to her will so completely at that point, but it suddenly seemed important to make as good a job of it as possible, and so, I shaved and depilated myself to the point of being completely and utterly hair free - apart from my long blond hair of course. By the time I stepped out of the shower I could hardly keep from running my fingers over my legs and body, so smooth was my hair free flesh. It felt sensual and clean somehow ... and feminine.

It was as I was primping my hair in the mirror - quite naked still, that she entered the bathroom and admired my smooth hair free body. I tried covering my privates with my hands but she simply batted them aside impatiently before running her hands over my legs.

'Very good, Jesse.' She said, 'That's much nicer. Now, time to make you up properly.'

291

She took my hand and pulled me from the room. I felt perfectly vulnerable at this point, being led around this woman's apartment stark naked having just rendered myself as hairless as a newborn. When I found myself being forcefully led into her bedroom I began to tremble with anticipation of what she had in mind. It was only now that I realised she'd changed her own outfit, dressed as she was in a pair of tight-fitting leather look trousers and figure hugging top. The lingerie set she'd been wearing during my servicing of her was laid out upon the bed - waiting for me.

'You may put those on.' She said simply, indicating her discarded underwear. I could see immediately the soiled panties that were a result of her earlier arousal, placed seductively on top of the matching bra, garter belt and stockings. I felt my throat begin to close up at the prospect of once more donning her most intimate of clothing having already been worn to good effect by the woman. 'Hurry up, Jesse,' She prompted, hands on hips, 'We've got other things to do.'

With a heady mixture of sexual excitement, relief at being able to cover myself up (at least partially anyway) and an underlying sense of acute embarrassment at being forced to dress in such a way, I picked up her still moist panties and stepped into them. I wasn't quite prepared for the sensation of drawing them up my freshly depilated legs. The touch of the soft feminine material as they brushed against my smooth flesh sent a thrill through me of such force I felt the need to sit down before I fell. I finished pulling them up around my crotch as I desperately tried to hide my feelings, but my soft member was soon giving me away as it began to engorge in response to the dampness I now felt between my legs. I pulled on the bra and fastened the garter belt into place as swiftly as my trembling hands would allow, before my attention was turned to the pure sensuality of her sheer white stockings. As I rolled them up in my hands, pushing my toes carefully into them I could feel myself drowning in this woman's intense femininity. I rolled them up slowly, losing myself in the utter bliss of having my smooth legs encased by their gossamer touch. By the time I fastened the last of the garter straps into place I was in a blissful state of mind quite unsurpassed by anything I'd ever experienced before.

'Come and sit here, at my dressing table.' I heard her say. Her voice was softer, gentle almost as she waited for me take a deep breath before doing as she bid. My mind had become a complete blank at this point. I moved as though in a dream, feeling every slight brush of the stockings, every movement of her damp panties against my cock. I dropped slowly onto the stool in front of me and awaited my next torment without protest. 'You must watch what I do, Jesse,' She began, 'I'll expect you to apply your own makeup after this.'

It seemed to take an age for her words to truly penetrate my brain before I understood her meaning. I found myself meekly looking at my own reflection as she began to apply the makeup. A light covering of foundation (it was all I needed for my boyish hair growth), some contouring, eye shadow, mascara and eye liner. I watched in amazement as my face transformed into that of a young girl with very little effort. By the time she applied an ultra feminine shade of pink lipstick I was enthralled by my own reflection.

'We'll have to do something about your hair,' She said, contemplating my long yet unkempt blond locks, 'wait here.'

I sat where I was. Fascination with my own reflection was enough to keep me entranced. I moved my head from side to side, examining the effects of the makeup and recalling her techniques. It took a while before I realised I was actively trying to remember how to apply the makeup for myself. It was as if I'd forgotten I was a boy for a moment, so lost in my new girly persona had I become. Recoiling in mild surprise, I stood up, stepping away from the mirror and catching sight of my lingerie clad body, a damp patch still evident in the crotch of my panties. I gasped as the stockings brushed against each other and the garter straps tugged teasingly against them. I felt breathless, peering down at my slim figure and knowing that the only thing that truly gave me away was my growing erection.

Chapter 5

Hearing a sound in the hallway I tried to shake myself out of it. For a moment I wasn't sure what I'd heard but then I realised there were two sets of footsteps fast approaching. I spun around, looking desperately for something to better cover myself but it was too late. The door swung open as Miss Palmer walked in, closely followed by another young woman. To my horror I recognised her immediately as the woman who lived in the opposite apartment to me. She was in her mid twenties, attractive and only marginally taller than me. Her long blond hair was almost a match for my own, a fact that hadn't escaped my attention on the numerous occasions I'd passed her in the hallway or on the stairs. In truth I'd always had a crush on her ever since I'd moved in, but had never had the courage to do anything about it.

At first I didn't know what to do with myself. I spun around as if in search of an escape, but knowing there was none I was forced to face the two women once again. I felt my face and indeed my body beginning to flush with embarrassment as I realised I'd been exposed in such an unexpected and compromising state of dress, or undress, depending on your perspective.

'M-Miss P-Palmer ... I ... I ...'

'Stand still please, Jesse. Let Kirsty see you properly.' Said Miss Palmer, showing the young woman in.

'I almost didn't recognise you, Jesse.' Said Kirsty, a slightly shocked expression on her face as she stared open mouthed at my feminised appearance. 'I never knew you liked to dress as a girl.'

'I ... I don't!' I protested.

'Oh come now, Jesse. You don't need to hide yourself from Kirsty here. She's already agreed to restyle your hair into something a little more appropriate.' Said Miss Palmer, 'It's quite fortunate that we have a hair stylist in the building, don't you think?'

I could no longer speak at this point in time, so preoccupied was I with the fact that this attractive young woman who was probably only five or so years my senior, was now looking upon me dressed in nothing but our landlady's lingerie, with my face made up as that of a girl.

'You look very pretty in your lingerie.' Said Kirsty, a mischievous grin spreading across her face, 'Very sexy.'

'It's ... It's not mine, it's M-Miss Palmer's.' At first it felt important to make this distinction, as if denying that I owned any women's underwear would deflect any thoughts of me being a crossdresser, but as she giggled at my response I realised I'd probably only made matters worse.

'She's really rather sweet, isn't she?' Said my landlady.

'I wish I'd known, I'd've styled her hair for her long ago.' Said Kirsty, clearly starting to enjoy the situation, 'Sit down, Jesse. This won't take long and you'll have hair just like mine.'

I glanced from one to another before being guided back to the dressing table and pushed down onto the stool. I placed my hands in my lap, trying to hide my budding erection although it had diminished somewhat following my embarrassing exposure to my neighbour. Not wanting to see what she was doing, I just stared at the floor as Kirsty set to work. It wasn't until she was making some final adjustments to the front of my hair that I suddenly thought of what I'd look like to people at college, or even the coffee shop if I was now sporting an obviously feminine style. I turned as soon as she had finished, stepping away from me as she announced that it was ready. I could feel my insides sinking as I saw a girl looking back at me, with a very obvious fringe cut across the front. In fact, my hair was styled identically to Kirsty's.

'Do you like it, Jesse?' Asked Kirsty, 'I think you look cute.'

'I ... I can't go out like this!' I blurted out as I imagined being made fun of by just about everyone I knew. I started to wonder why I'd even let them do this to me. I could've refused. I could've walked out. I could also have found myself out on the street.

'Of course you can't, you silly girl!' Replied Miss Palmer, 'You'll need to put something on over your underwear.'

I wasn't sure if she had deliberately misunderstood my meaning but Kirsty was giggling furiously from behind me.

'I'd love to show her off to my friends,' Said Kirsty, taking me quite by surprise, 'I bet they wouldn't even realise she was a boy.'

'I'm sure they wouldn't,' agreed Miss Palmer, 'but Jesse here still needs to learn a thing or two before she can properly act as a girl outside. One thing we'll have to get under control is her sissy clit.'

'Her what?' Kirsty was as nonplussed by Miss Palmer's words as I.

'Her sissy clit, my dear.' Miss Palmer explained patiently, 'It does tend to swell up quite often, and we need to make sure she doesn't embarrass herself when she's outside.'

I couldn't believe these two women were standing there talking about me in such a way as I listened open mouthed. My world had taken a turn for the surreal, of that there was no doubt.

'Stand up, girl.' Ordered Miss Palmer.

It took a second to realise she was referring to me before I did so. I kept my hands in front, wary of letting them see that I was still partially aroused. Miss Palmer walked behind me. As I made to turn around and follow what she was doing she forced me to face Kirsty as before.

'Don't move please, Jesse.' She said as I heard her opening a drawer. 'A nice belt is needed, I think.'

I puzzled why she was looking for such a thing as I felt her approach from behind. I looked down as she wrapped a pink belt around my waist and fastened it in back. I was still confused as to what importance this had when I felt her tug my arm back and wrap something around it. I heard an ominous click and looked down, only to discover that my wrist was now bound to my side by the addition of a pink cuff that was chained to the belt. I began to say something, to ask what she was doing when she tugged my other arm back and before I could resist further had clamped this one in another similarly fixed cuff on the other side. Suddenly my crotch was exposed and I had too little movement in my arms to be able to cover myself.

'What ... What are you doing?' I challenged her too late, 'L-Let me go ... now!'

'Shush, Jesse.' She stepped back in front of me as I became aware of my pantied cock being on show to Kirsty, 'I have a little present for you.'

I only had time to see something pink and plastic looking in her hand before she was reaching between my legs. I thrust my bottom back on instinct, pulling away from her as I backed up in a panic. As I came up against the closet behind me she followed, her hands pulling the wet panties aside and groping for my privates. I began to squirm as I felt myself being molested, and then she had a hold of me and I froze, fearful that she would hurt me if I continued to struggle. I had no idea what she was doing at first as I felt myself being manipulated by her hands. I looked up at Kirsty with a pleading expression, looking for help, but was met with an amused expression as she giggled nervously at what was happening. Another click from between my legs signalled that she'd achieved her aim and she stood back slightly, her hand cupping my cock and balls that were now firmly locked inside of a pink chastity cage.

'There you are, Jesse. Do you like it?' Asked Miss Palmer, as if she'd just presented me with a piece of especially nice jewellery, 'It'll keep your sissy clit from getting all swollen, won't it? At least, for when we don't want it to get swollen.'

I looked down in horror as I realised I was now in chastity, my wrists manacled to my sides as I stood there in her lingerie.

'Oh, it looks so cute!' Cooed Kirsty as she stepped forward to take a closer look at my caged cock.

I knew I was bright red with embarrassment by now. I felt utterly powerless. Little more than a feminised toy for her to play with as she wanted.

'Can I touch it?' Asked Kirsty, causing me to groan desperately.

I could do nothing other than stand there. I watched through half closed eyes as this young beautiful woman stepped forward, her eyes transfixed upon my still exposed crotch. As Miss Palmer stepped to one side, she put out her hand slowly, painfully so in fact. The anticipation was unbearable as I waited for the inevitable moment this girl would touch me there, completing my humiliation by playing with my caged and useless little cock. Or at least I believed this would complete my humiliation at the time.

As I felt her warm hand encompass the plastic cage, squeezing me there, I let out a tortured breath. My throat was constricted, my belly fluttering wildly as my arousal began to insistently push outward against its confinement. The enforced restriction I now found myself under only seemed to arouse my body even more intently. I felt myself trembling all over as her soft slender fingers gently probed my most intimate of areas. With her other hand she began stroking the top of my stockinged leg and I was once more acutely aware of my hairless body. Even my crotch was entirely hair free, which I now questioned in my mind as to whether this had been completely necessary or whether I'd taken things a step too far in following my instructions.

'She's getting very excited, Miss Palmer.' Said Kirsty, giggling delightedly at my tortured arousal.

'Please, call me Victoria.' Said Miss Palmer, 'Don't worry, her clitty can't escape her pretty pink cage, although its still possible she could squirt given just how excited the poor little sissy has become. It's quite adorable seeing how they get so much enjoyment from being treated this way, and this one's particularly sweet, don't you think?'

'Oh, yes, Victoria.' I thought by the look on Kirsty's face that she was a little bewildered by Miss Palmer's treatment of me still, but she continued to caress my caged cock all the same, her other hand running freely across my lingerie clad body which only served to make my arousal even more pronounced.

At some point I think I entered such a state of sexual excitement - despite my best attempts to resist, that my mind was no longer able to focus on anything except my overwhelming physical and mental stimulation. I felt myself beginning to thrust my hips back and forth against her hand as though I no longer had any control over my body. As I glanced to the side I caught sight of myself in the mirror. It was a shock to see that apart from my flat chest, there was little evidence of my manhood anywhere to be seen. In fact, the only sight that greeted me was one of a young girl dressed in nothing but her sexy underwear, her hands locked to her sides, with another girl's hand between her legs teasing her toward a forced orgasm.

I could feel my climax building but was confused as to how I could orgasm with my cock unable to fully engorge inside of its cage. Regardless of its situation, my climax continued to build in such an explosive manner that I could do nothing other than submit myself to a most tortuous, humiliating and shockingly powerful orgasm as I felt my balls tightening and my cock spasming. I almost collapsed onto the floor as my knees buckled at the point I started to ooze cum out through the cage and into Kirsty's hand.

'She's ... She's cumming in my hand!' Shrieked Kirsty as she realised just that.

'She really is a dirty little sissy girl, isn't she?' Said Miss Palmer, grinning widely.

I squeaked with embarrassment and total and utter humiliation as my entire body trembled. My cum continued to pump out of my partially erect cock from inside the cage as I moaned with frustration and relief at my desperate release.

'Oh ... Oh, I'm s-sorry, K-Kirsty.' I felt obliged to apologise at filling her hand with my cum, yet she held it there still, allowing my orgasm to run its course as I continued to ooze cum into her cupped palm.

As I drained myself into my neighbours hand my eyes refocused on her face. She watched with an amused fascination as I debased myself in front of her. When eventually I sagged back against the closet door, breathing hard and quivering with shame, she took her hand away and held it up.

'Arghh!' She laughed as she stared at her cum filled hand.

'I think our little sissy girl should clean up her sissy mess, don't you, Kirsty?' Asked Miss Palmer with a decidedly evil glint in her eye.

I baulked at her words. Not really understanding her intentions but knowing nonetheless that they were not at all innocent. Kirsty was clearly as bemused as myself, but she had the look of someone who'd become curious enough with the events at hand to play them out in their entirety.

'You may clean Kirsty's hand for her, Jesse.' Said Miss Palmer, as if I should know exactly what she was getting at.

I groaned at my frustration and displayed my cuffed wrists as if it were necessary to show my inability to follow her instructions.

'You silly girl.' She shook her head as if talking to an uncomprehending child, 'You may lick her hand clean of your sissy juice.'

I looked at Kirsty's upraised hand, a pool of my own cum laying in her palm. I have to admit, the first thought that crossed my mind was that I'd often wondered what my own cum would taste like, although I'd never quite managed to bring myself to try it. I felt my shame deepening as I contemplated what she was suggesting. Glancing at the other woman's face I saw a brief moment of disbelief in her eyes before she grinned at me.

'It's okay, Jesse, it's only a little cum. Look, I'll show you.' Said Kirsty, and then she was holding her hand up to her mouth and flicking her tongue out. She lapped at my cum, taking it into her mouth and seemingly savouring it for a moment before swallowing. 'There, now your turn, Jesse.'

She held her hand up in front of my face, close enough that I could smell my own sex juice. With nowhere to go, my hands held fast at my sides and little in the way of dignity left, I bowed my head and pushed my tongue out. As I forced myself to follow her lead and lap my own cum from her hand I shivered at the thought of what I was doing.

It's taste wasn't as unpleasant as I'd imagined it might be, but it was a strange sensation to be tasting my own juices. It was still warm as I forced myself to swallow. She moved her hand to indicate I should clean the rest up, and so I licked my cum from her palm, feeling belittled and emasculated by my own act. My tongue was soon coated in the thick cum as I continued to lick her hand clean. She giggled as my tongue ran over her fingers before finally pulling it away from me.

'Good girl.' Said Miss Palmer, in much the same way as you'd praise your pet dog for obeying your commands.

REBECCA STERNE -- TURNED INTO GIRLS!

Chapter 6

Kirsty's gaze wandered down to between my legs, and then she was pulling the panties back across to cover my caged cock. In that one simple act it was as if my ignominy had been sealed. I looked to the floor as I continued to taste boy cum in my mouth.

'How long has she been your sissy, Victoria?' Asked Kirsty, stepping back so as to look me up and down more easily.

'Oh, not long.' Said Miss Palmer, 'She's really quite new to this, not that you'd know. Well, thank you for your help, Kirsty, I'm sure you'd like to get on now.'

My landlady showed the young woman out of the apartment, promising to let her visit again. At this point I was on the verge of sobbing, so confused and humiliated by my treatment that I could no longer understand whether this was all due to Miss Palmer, or whether I hadn't been complicit in my own treatment to some extent. The thought that on some deep seated level that I wasn't as adverse to being treated in this way as I thought I should be, was a shocking and rather disconcerting one.

I was left to my own thoughts for some time. Standing alone in this woman's bedroom whilst wearing her lingerie, in full makeup and sporting a new feminine hairstyle. Unable to use my hands properly and with my little cock locked securely away inside of a pink cage, I tried desperately to understand my situation and how I'd come to be here. I came up with very few answers other than the obvious. My financial debt to this woman had been enough to buy my initial obeisance, but something inside of me felt as though it was awakening. Something I'd had no awareness of until now. Despite feeling entirely humiliated and shamed by this woman, I was also experiencing an intensity of arousal that I'd never known existed before.

When finally she reappeared in the room I looked up at her cautiously, unsure of what this woman had planned for me. She smiled back at me, hands on hips as her eyes roamed up and down my feminised body.

'Well, I think we'd best get you something else to wear over my underwear, don't you?'

I nodded gratefully, wanting nothing more at that point than to experience some sense of normality after what could only be described as a surreal series of acts. She flung open her closet and began to look through the array of clothing hanging up before pulling out a tight fitting and rather short looking pink dress.

'Perfect!' She said, holding it up in front of me. 'I'm going to release your hands. I expect you to behave as a proper young sissy girl, Jesse, as I won't tolerate any nonsense. That is, if you want to be dressed in more than just my underwear?' She looked at me intently. I could feel myself quailing under her stare as I dropped my gaze, unable to feel anything other than subservient to her in my current state.

'Yes, M-Miss Palmer.' I quietly agreed.

'Yes what, Jesse? Yes, you'd like to be allowed to wear my dress?'

'Y-Yes, Miss Palmer.' I said a little louder, annoyed that she was making me ask to be able to put clothes on over my lingerie.

She studied me for a while before unlocking the wrist restraints and removing the belt. Her eyes never left me as she seemed to watch for any sign of me rebelling against her will. I know I should have then; as soon as my hands were free once more, but I didn't. It was as if my strength had failed. Withered away as she'd exposed me to such intense humiliations and emasculating treatment that my manhood no longer dared to show itself to her.

As I stepped into the bright pink dress I felt a little relieved to be dressed in a more dignified way. At least, I did until she'd pushed some rolled up pantyhose into my bra and presented me to the mirror so that I could see the full effects of her transformation.

'There, such a pretty girl.' She said from over my shoulder as she held me firmly in place. 'It's a wonder you've been dressing as a boy all of this time.'

I groaned at that, gazing reluctantly at my reflection and seeing just how much of a girl I'd become in such a short time. I was still wondering how I might disguise my obviously female hairstyle once dressed in my normal clothes again as she had me step into a pair of matching high heeled shoes.

'Right, all ready to go. Come on, Jesse.' As she pulled me along the hallway toward her apartment door I feared the idea of being made to climb the stairs back to my apartment dressed as I was, but knowing my immediate neighbour had already seen me in a lesser state of dress - not to mention a most compromising sexual act, I pushed this aside. The fact that I wasn't wearing a maid's outfit made me appear all the more normal to anyone outside. I did however feel anything but normal.

It wasn't until she kept going passed the stairs, pulling me firmly along behind her as I concentrated on not toppling over in my heels that I realised she intended for us to leave the building entirely.

'N-No! M-Miss P-Palmer ... I Can't ...' I shrieked a little more girlishly than I would've liked as she pulled the main door opened and continued to take me with her.

'Don't be silly, Jesse, you look fine.'

I tried to pull back against her insistent tugging, but as I came close to overbalancing I was forced to take another step forward and then another. Before I knew it I'd half stepped, half tripped across the threshold and was now standing at the top of the stairs leading down to the busy street outside. I looked about in blind panic, feeling that everyone in that street knew immediately that I was a boy underneath the pink dress and makeup.

'Don't make a scene, Jesse, you'll only embarrass yourself.' She said sternly before forcing me down the steps and onto the street itself.

The first time someone looked at me I wanted to

disappear into the background. I felt myself blushing furiously within moments, but then they were gone, paying far less attention to me than I did them. At one point I almost fell over my own feet, stumbling in my heels and bringing several amused looks from passersby, yet they soon turned away as I righted myself. It was soon apparent that no one was taking any real notice of the two women walking together; no one apart from the occasional man who'd gawk wantonly at the pair of us, their eyes lingering upon me that extra few seconds. I tried not to take any notice but I knew exactly what they were thinking. I wondered quite how they'd react if they knew the truth, that this attractive young girl in the tight pink dress was in fact a boy - I tried not to ponder this too closely.

I was blissfully unaware of where we were heading as I was guided along the street by Miss Palmer. Had I realised quite what she had in mind I'm sure I'd've resisted this latest assault on my dwindling masculinity, yet I was perfectly blind to what was about to happen to me.

At some point in time I became aware of where we were. I looked up at the coffee shop just a few more yards in front and came to a stand still, suddenly conscious of just how easily I could be seen by someone I worked with, albeit in a shrinking hourly capacity.

'M-Miss Palmer,' I whispered urgently as she turned toward me, 'Someone will see me. Can we go another way?' I asked, hoping she'd divert our course away from the shop.

'Of course not, Jesse,' She said, looking at me as if I were being quite silly, 'that's where we're going.'

'What? B-But ... I can't ...' I was trembling at the very thought of being exposed in front of people I knew. Some of the waitresses even went to the same college as me.

'You can and you will!' She told me, 'No one will recognise you if we don't tell them. Unless you want to draw attention to yourself by making a scene, I suggest you come with me.'

I looked passed her to the coffee shop that now seemed quite daunting to me, even though I'd worked there a good while. She took hold of my hand and pulled, making me stagger toward her as I tried to keep my balance. Once my momentum was flowing once again she continued on, leaving me with little choice but to accompany her as she grasped my hand tightly in hers.

'Why are we going in here?' I hissed at her as I tried to

look as normal as possible.

'Because I have a friend in here who'd be most interested in making your acquaintance.' She explained enigmatically.

Stepping through that door felt as though I were being led to my doom. It sounds awfully dramatic I know, but having never dressed as a girl before - let alone ventured into the street as one, I felt incredibly vulnerable and exposed. I tried to hide behind Miss Palmer as she took us toward the counter. The man serving was the manager and owner, someone I'd always had the impression wasn't particularly struck on me. He was a good six feet four inches tall and his powerful physique and manly presence was in perfect contrast to my own, even when I was dressed normally as a boy. It seemed even more pronounced now than ever before, as I cowered beyond my landlady's shapely frame.

'Martin,' Miss Palmer addressed him with familiarity, 'I'd like you to meet Jesse, one of my new ... *girls.*'

The way she emphasised the word "girls" clearly meant something to them both. I saw him smile as he looked in my direction. I did my best to look away, to not meet his gaze, but I couldn't help it. Like a rabbit caught in headlights, I struggled to tear my eyes away from him as I detected a predatory look in his eye.

'Funny,' he said, 'I've got a lad named Jesse who works here.' He frowned as he studied me a little closer, 'He's got blond hair too.' By the puzzled expression on his face I could tell he was close to realising the truth.

'Yes, Martin,' Miss Palmer smiled at me proudly, 'but as you can see, she'd very much like to work here in her new ... *role,* shall we say?'

As realisation dawned upon him, his expression changed from puzzlement to shock, to outright amusement. Then he began to look at me in an entirely different way.

'You mean, she'd like to work as one of *our* girls?' He asked, raising his eyebrows.

'Oh yes. You see, she owes me quite a substantial amount of unpaid rent, and this is probably the only way she could ever hope to pay me off and keep a roof over her poor little head. Isn't that right, Jesse?'

'I ... I ...' My head was spinning. I couldn't understand why my landlady would want me to work in the coffee shop as a girl instead of a boy, but if that was all it would take to pay my debts, then I was reluctant to say no, especially as she'd already exposed me to the manager. 'Y-Yes, I suppose, Miss Palmer.'

'We'd have to try her out first; make sure she was up to the job.' He said.

'Of course, any time you'd like, Martin.' She said.

I was perplexed. They both knew I was experienced at working there already, so it seemed a little pointless putting me onto some kind of a trial first. I supposed it may be to ensure that I was able to convincingly work as a girl without embarrassing myself first. As it turned out I was correct on one level, but thoroughly mistaken on another.

'No time like the present,' Said Martin, as he untied his apron and slung it onto the counter behind him, 'I'll have Paula take over, she's out back.'

He shouted through to the back room before walking out from around the counter. I looked up at him sheepishly, curious as to what he thought of his male employee showing up as a girl. I was soon to find out.

Chapter 7

I'd always known that my employer ran another enterprise apart from the coffee shop, but I'd little idea of what it entailed. I'd seen him in the company of young women on many occasions. My assumption being that he was simply a ladies man. Given his physical presence and good looks it was hardly surprising to me. As I was led through the back of the shop and up some stairs toward his own private apartment, I began to wonder just how many of them had in fact been "girls" more akin to myself.

I was beginning to feel like a lamb being led to an uncertain fate as Martin led the way and Miss Palmer guided me from behind. It took considerable concentration on my part to negotiate the steep staircase in my heels without incident and I was flushed with relief at having not toppled over as I tottered behind him into a large open plan apartment.

As my landlady closed the door behind us I felt my anxiety levels rising. I still had no idea what awaited me, but I was now clearly at the mercy of these two people. I glanced behind me nervously, receiving a reassuring smile from Miss Palmer.

'Don't look so worried, Jesse. I'm sure you'll do fine.' She said, giving my arm a little squeeze. Looking back to Martin I saw him peering at me with an appraising look.

'I guess you'd better take that dress off, so I can see what's underneath.' He said.

I just stared at him, taken aback by his request. Miss Palmer was looking at me steadily, as if she'd been expecting this.

'Well, Jesse? Do as Martin says.' She prompted with a firm nod of her head, 'You do want to get the job, don't you? After all, how else are you going to pay your rent?'

'I ... um ...' The thought of exposing myself in nothing but her lingerie, with the additional embarrassment of having my cock locked away in a little pink cage was almost too much to contemplate. I gasped as I realised they were both quite serious.

'You do want a job, don't you?' Asked Martin, looking a little put out by my hesitant reaction.

'Y-Yes, Martin, but ...'

'You'll address Martin as Mr Bates or simply, *Sir.*' Said Miss Palmer, 'Is that clear, Jesse?'

'I ... er ... yes. Sorry, Mr Bates ... Sir.'

They both found my flustered apology amusing as they shared a look between them. I found myself shifting my weight from one leg to another as I felt their eyes upon me. As much as I was determined not to admit it, being looked upon as an attractive young woman was creating an inner excitement in me which I wished fervently was not there. It was as if my own body and mind was betraying me by secretly enjoying the attention I was now receiving, which was certainly unlike anything I'd ever received before.

Almost without coming to a decision my hands moved up to my shoulders and began to slip the dress off. I still didn't know if I wanted to do this, but my body was already obeying this man's wishes regardless. I felt like an observer as I watched myself sliding the figure hugging pink dress down my body and stepping out of it. As I kicked it away I looked up for a second, and as my eyes met his I looked away, blushing intensely under his unwavering gaze.

'Very nice, Victoria. Very nice indeed.' He said, his mouth curling up into an appreciative smile as he casually looked me over.

Thrusting my hands downward I quickly covered my caged cock, unwilling to let him see my latest ignominy at Miss Palmer's hands, even though it lay hidden beneath her white panties. As I caught sight of my stockinged legs I felt myself begin to shake slightly. Whether it was from nervousness, shame or excitement I did not know. At least, I refused to examine my own thoughts too closely for fear of what I would discover.

I was acutely aware of my own vulnerability as I stood there, dressed in nothing but Miss Palmer's underwear and looking for all the world like a perfectly natural young lady. There was something else though. A feeling that I wasn't entirely powerless somehow, at least not when it came to the man standing in front of me. I thought I saw him lick his lips briefly. The look in his eye was one of unbridled lust as he stepped closer. I breathed in sharply as I felt his masculinity towering over me.

'Let's see how you handle a real man, shall we?' He said, moving his hands in front and beginning to unfasten his jeans.

My mouth dropped open slightly as I followed his every movement. I could see what he intended, but my body was frozen. My throat began to tighten up as I watched with a mixture of horror and nervous anticipation as he dropped his jeans in front of me and kicked them off. Then his hands lingered for several excruciating seconds about the waistband of his underwear before pulling his shorts down, revealing a very swollen cock as it sprang outward.

I let out a little yelp as he straightened. His manhood far more impressive than my own and staring straight at me in its rigid state of arousal. It was an effort to force my gaze from him as I began to note how thick and veined his member was, looking to my landlady for some kind of guidance as to what to do. She herself was looking at him too, yet her face bore a look of delight as she met my eyes and grinned.

'On your knees, Jesse. Show Mr Bates what you can do, there's a good girl.'

I turned back to where my boss was still standing there, his bottom half fully exposed. His phallus rampant with desire. I should've refused. I should've grabbed my dress and ran away from there, but something stopped me. Afterwards I told myself that I had little choice in the matter, but I knew this wasn't strictly true. There was always a choice, and I'd made it without realising.

As I slowly lowered myself to my knees I could feel my breaths becoming shorter, more rapid. My entire body was shaking softly. I forced myself to breathe as I raised my hand in front of me, moving my trembling fingers toward the source of my fears and the focus of my excitement. I held my breath as I wrapped my fingers around his already throbbing cock. Feeling the power surging through the man's member as he let out a heavy sigh. It was a strange feeling indeed, touching another man in that way, but in many ways I felt far less of a man myself at this point which helped to ease my mind to a fashion.

Something happened to me then. As I began to move my hand up and down his sturdy shaft I could almost feel myself transforming inside. I spared a brief look at his face as he loomed above me, seeing him peering down at where I was slowly masturbating him with my slender fingers, with an evident look of pleasure in his eyes. With my other hand I automatically cupped his heavy balls. I felt their weight as I gently squeezed them, bringing a sharp gasp from the man. I continued to watch my own hand as I pumped this man's cock mere inches from my own face. Watching as my fingers rolled over the bulbous, shiny head before letting it pop back out as I jerked him off with a steady rhythm.

'Oh yeah!' He mumbled from above, 'You've done this before, Sweetheart.'

I was about to argue this. To tell him that I had never even thought of doing such a thing to another man in my life, but it seemed a pointless gesture under the circumstances, and so I closed my mouth and continued to pleasure him with my hands.

'P-Put it in your mouth, Jesse,' I heard him say, 'show me how much you want it.'

I slowed my hand as his words penetrated my brain. A wave of fear washed over me as I wondered whether I could bring myself to do such a thing. In some distant part of my mind I also questioned what it was that I was supposed to *want*, exactly. My job? My apartment? *His* cock? I licked my lips anxiously, seeing his cock head beginning to ooze precum in my hand. It felt wet and a little sticky as I tried to process the idea that it was my hand that was bringing him to this.

'Go on, Jesse,' added Miss Palmer as I felt her hand unexpectedly stroking my hair, 'put it in your mouth like a good sissy girl.'

Her intervention surprised me enough that all thoughts of resisting his desire were forgotten as I automatically leaned forward. I opened my mouth wide and took my first cock in between my lips, tasting his precum on my tongue as I sucked on his glistening glans. It was a surreal experience that first time, one that blew my mind from the first moment I felt this man's manhood enter my sissy mouth. He pushed into me, thrusting his cock further in and forcing me to start sucking on him in earnest. I was still pumping his shaft with one hand and squeezing his balls with the other as my head began dipping in and out of his crotch. I could hear his breathing change as he put his hands on the back of my head, holding me there as he worked his hard cock in and out of my mouth with increasing speed.

I felt like a complete slut at this point. Like one of those girl's I'd seen in porn films, and it was turning me on. I could feel my own cock swelling inside of its cage, despite having my balls emptied twice already that day. The sexual excitement of performing oral sex on such a man, dressed in borrowed white lingerie with full makeup was an experience like none other. In that moment as I felt him moving toward his climax I was as much a girl as I could ever be. No longer a man and not truly female but something in between. A sexual beast that was the focus and source of an intense sexual arousal in another that made me feel both subjugated and powerful in the same moment.

A change in his breathing and a powerful spasm in his cock told me this man was about to cum. My first thought - which I still wonder about now - was to feel a thrill of excitement at the idea that I'd brought this man to a climax so easily, the second was that if I didn't take him out of my mouth and pull away swiftly, I'd have another man cumming into my mouth. The realisation of what was about to happen brought me back to reality with a bump as I began to quiver with fear.

Any attempt to pull away before the unthinkable happened was left too late on my part, as I felt the man's body grow stiff and his cock pulse in between my lips. There was a moment of intense clarity as he teetered on the brink of his orgasm and I surrendered myself to the idea that I was about to receive a mouthful of his seed. I saw a glimpse of my future in that moment, one I couldn't bring myself to fully believe but I'm sure I saw the truth in it all the same. Then his cock spasmed and a stream of hot cum was ejaculated into my waiting mouth. It coated my tongue and began to slide to the back of my throat as another and another were ejaculated into me. I was forced to swallow hard as my mouth was filled with man seed. I whimpered pathetically as I found myself wriggling like a fish on a hook as my own arousal pushed painfully against it's pink prison.

As the flow of cum into my mouth slowed and he emptied himself into me, I felt a sense of shame and embarrassment overcome me as I wondered how I could so easily be manipulated into such a position. My cock was twitching between my legs so that my own arousal at what I'd just done only served to further humiliate me.

I'm not sure why, but I even took my time to lick my boss's slowly softening cock of any remaining cum as if it were my fault that he'd ejaculated, which I suppose it was. By the time I gently let go of his member and sat back on my heels I was feeling like a perfect slut. I suspect if I hadn't so recently been drained by my neighbour, I would've squirted inside of my panties regardless of having a chastity cage confining my full arousal. Such realisations did little to decrease my overall feelings of debasement and shame.

Chapter 8

I could taste the man in my mouth for a long time after that. They had me stand up and parade myself around the room in my underwear. It felt humiliating to be looked upon as little more than a sex object, but regardless of how outraged I thought I should feel about the entire episode, I couldn't quite shake that nagging feeling that I was secretly enjoying my treatment at their hands.

After a while it almost felt normal to be walking around as a girl in lingerie. By the time they'd finished having their fun I'd been assigned another shift in the coffee shop that day. Mr Bates agreed to walk me home afterwards given my anxiety at being out alone as a girl. One of the most harrowing parts of the day was when I was reintroduced to my two work colleagues as female. Much to my annoyance Mr Bates announced that I would be working there as a girl from now on. I blushed furiously as the two girl's looked at me in amazement having not recognised me to start with.

'I think it's really brave of you, Jesse.' Said one girl, hugging me to her in a display of affection that I'd rarely experienced as a boy.

'You look much better as a girl.' Said the other, looking me up and down as I balanced on my heels in front of her, tugging the short hemline of the pink dress downward as I caught her staring at my stockinged legs.

By the time my shift had finished and I was ready to head back to my apartment my feet were aching. Having never worn high heels before it'd been an ordeal to wear them for so long that first day. Mr Bates escorted me out of the door as he locked up, smirking incessantly as he watched my continuing discomfort. Not only as a result of the shoes, but because he knew I was entirely within his power at that precise moment.

'Let's get you home shall we, Jesse. I'm sure you can't wait to slip into something more comfortable.' He laughed as he slipped his arm around my shoulders and led me away.

It simply never occurred to me that Miss Palmer might have an ulterior motive to having me spend several hours working before returning back to my apartment. As with many things, in hindsight I feel I should've picked up on something at the time, but as it happens I was caught completely by surprise at what I found waiting for me back at the apartments.

-o0o-

Mr Bates accompanied me up the steps and into my apartment building. I needed to retrieve my keys from Miss Palmer before heading upstairs so I quietly knocked on her door whilst the man continued to eye me up. I looked at him coyly for a moment before returning my gaze to the door in front of me. It was opened after an uncomfortable wait.

'Ah Jesse, good, you're back.' Said Miss Palmer as she swung the door inward, 'Has she been good, Martin?'

'Indeed, Victoria. She'll fit in much better now that she's been ... transformed.' He laughed as he made a point of glancing down at my bottom.

'Um ... can I have my keys please, Miss Palmer.' I said quickly before the conversation could take another sexual turn, 'I need to get into my apartment.'

'*Your* apartment, Jesse?' She said, looking a little confused, 'I'm sorry, Jesse, but in view of how much rent you owe me I've had to take it away from you, but don't worry, you can rent a room

314

inside my apartment for now.'

'What? What do you mean?' I blurted out, 'What about my things? You can't do that!' I protested, stamping my foot like a petulant teenager before getting myself under control.

'Oh, I'm afraid I can, young lady. Now, stop acting so ungrateful and come inside. I've already moved your things out and you have everything you need in your new room.'

'But ... I ... you can't ...' I saw no sympathy in Mr Bates expression as I looked around in astonishment, not sure what to do. I was on the verge of crying as I realised my entire world was being turned on its head.

'Come on, let's take a look at your new room, shall we?' He said, once more putting his arm around me as he firmly guided me through the door.

I could feel my legs turning to jelly as I considered the prospect of living alongside Miss Palmer. It was a firm bet that she'd intend to continue her little games with me, now that I was so utterly under her control. I couldn't think straight as the door was closed behind me and I was taken through the apartment, passed Miss Palmer's bedroom and on to a room at the end of the hall that I'd never been inside before. I shuffled along obediently as the woman led the way.

At first I couldn't believe my eyes. I had to blink in order to assure myself that the room was indeed as pink and girly as I first thought. In some ways it had the look of a young teenage girl's room, with fairy motifs on the walls and a pink and white theme throughout, but at the same time it had the feel of an ultra feminine boudoir, with a fully stocked dressing table, complete with a wide selection of lipsticks, eye shadows and the like. The bed itself had an intricately fashioned metal bedstead that looked like something a "working girl" would own.

As I continued to take it all in, I started to spy various objects of my own that had clearly been brought down from my apartment. Certain knick knacks of sentimental value, although as it was a fully furnished apartment, I had in fact collected very little clutter apart from my clothes since living there. The thought of my clothes sprang to mind and I hurried across the room, expecting to find some male attire to change into in a bid to reassert a semblance of normality to my day.

Flinging the closet doors open I stepped back in shock as

I was presented with a selection of dresses, skirts and girly tops. Numerous high heeled shoes and boots were arranged below. In a panic and thinking this was simply some of my landlady's clothes still hanging there, I crossed to the nearby set of drawers and begun to open them with growing despair. What I saw were drawers full of panties, bra's, garter belts, stockings, pantyhose, nightdresses; just about everything except a single piece of male clothing.

'What's this?' I demanded, rechecking the drawers I'd already opened and rummaging through the closet in case I'd missed something, 'Where're all my clothes? You said you'd brought everything down from my apartment.'

'Oh, Jesse, you are a silly girl!' Miss Palmer scoffed as if I were being insufferably obtuse, 'You don't need *boy* clothes any more, I've disposed of all those. You have everything you need right here.' She said proudly. 'Isn't it lovely? Perfect for a little sissy girl like you.'

For a moment I thought I would pass out. I sat down heavily on the bed before I fell.

'You ... *disposed* of them? *All* of them?' I asked, feeling utterly defeated.

'Oh yes, these are all the clothes you'll be wearing from now on, Jesse. Aren't you lucky?' She said.

I couldn't speak at this point. My mind wanted to shut down. My body wanted to curl up into a little ball on the bed, and it was a nice soft bed, I had to admit that. There were a few too many pink fluffy pillows strewn across it, but I guessed I'd get used to them over time.

'We'll leave you to settle in and I'll expect you to be ready for bed in a while. You've already found your nightdresses so I'll let you pick one out for tonight.' I barely heard Miss Palmer's words as I continued to stare forlornly around at the ultra feminine room, 'I'll see you in a while, Jesse.'

As they left I heard a soft click from behind before realising that I'd actually been locked inside. It only served to reinforce my overwhelming defeat. At first it all seemed quite unreal to me, but after a while I managed to force myself up from the soft welcoming bed in order to examine the contents of the room more closely. I had to admit, there was nothing I was missing from my apartment that was of any value to me, apart from every single item of male clothing and paraphernalia that I had previously possessed. It was as if Jesse the boy had suddenly ceased to exist almost overnight. This thought caused a sudden wave of panic to wash over me as I thought of my college course and how I could possibly turn up dressed as a girl. I had to sit down again to think this through. Forcing myself to think rationally for a moment it did at least seem likely that I'd be allowed to attend that part of my life as Jesse the boy. I made a mental note to raise this with Miss Palmer.

I'm not entirely sure at which point I began to accept my subjugation to this woman and her rather outlandish plan to feminise and control me, but at some point I had clearly done just that, as I no longer considered the idea of returning to my former life, rather, I began to consider ways of at least holding on to certain aspects of it - with Miss Palmer's agreement of course.

If at this point you think that my life could not possibly take a turn for the worse, or at least the more absurd then read on, as it was soon apparent that Miss Palmer's and Mr Bate's plans for me were only just coming to fruition.

At this point I decided I'd had enough of fighting with my emotions over my fate and began to sort through the impressive selection of nightwear that I'd been provided. Most of the nightdress's were quite short and clearly of a sexual nature. I wondered how many of them were passed on from Miss Palmer herself, if in fact they hadn't all been. Finding nothing particularly modest in the drawer I finally pulled out a thigh length sheer pink nightdress with matching ruffled panties. Not wanting to attract Miss Palmer's ire any further on that day I stripped off the dress and her lingerie before taking a look at myself in the mirror. It was a strange sight, seeing my face and hair made up as a girl, with my diminutive cock encased in its pink plastic cage between my smooth hairless legs. Even for me it was difficult to say whether I looked more girl or boy, even without clothes. I tested the cage for a while, attempting to free myself from its grip but it was quite secure, the only person having the key to my release being Miss Palmer.

In some ways I'd like to be able to say that I was reluctant or resentful of pulling on the pair of pink ruffled panties, or slipping the sheer pink nightdress over my head, but in truth it felt nice to be wearing something so soft and sensual. By the time Miss

Palmer returned to my room I was all prepared for the evening, although she still had one added form of subjugation up her sleeve for that night.

My heart skipped a beat as I heard the door being unlocked. I moved to the bed before she could see me admiring my girly reflection in the full length mirror, feeling flustered as she entered.

'All ready for bed, Jesse?' She said, looking upon me with some satisfaction, 'Good girl. I have another little surprise for you for tonight. Something that little sissy girls like you learn to love over time.' I looked up at her suspiciously, 'It's not that I don't trust you, Jesse, it's more a way of making you feel more at home in your new role.'

With a flourish she produced a pair of pink fluffy handcuffs from behind her back. At first I wasn't sure what they were, but as I recognised the deceivingly feminine looking device for what it was I pushed myself up the bed away from them in fear.

'Oh don't look so worried, Jesse. Just think of them as your new bracelets. Pink ones for a pink girl!' She laughed softly as she continued to move toward me.

I looked passed her to the open door, and for one fleeting moment I seriously considered bolting from the room. I took too long to think about it though as whilst I was darting furtive glances beyond this woman she grasped my wrist and clamped one of the handcuffs over it. I squealed in surprise and confusion as to what she was going to do, and in a flash she'd pulled my wrist toward the metal bedstead behind me and fastened the other end around it. I was trapped! Locked onto the bed by a stout pair of pink fur covered manacles.

'P-Please, Miss P-Palmer ... I ...' I wanted to plead with her to let me go, but I couldn't quite get the idea out of my head that I had nowhere else to go. I had no boy clothes to wear and I was locked to a bed in my sheer baby doll nightdress and ruffled panties. My voice trailed off as the hopelessness of my situation bore down on me.

I think one of the worst parts was when she gently and caringly ensured I had everything I needed for the night within reach before kissing my forehead and saying goodnight. It felt comforting in a strange way to feel as though I were being looked after. Controlled - yes, but looked after all the same.

Chapter 9

It took me some time to find a comfortable position in which to fall asleep that night. Thoughts of what had happened to me over the past couple of days kept running around my head as I shifted position, feeling the shoulder straps of the baby doll nightdress digging into my flesh as I wriggled around. When finally I did sleep it was with dreams of crawling up between the legs of Miss Palmer or Mr Bates to service them both as if it were the most normal thing in the world.

The following morning I had to wait for Miss Palmer to unlock the door and free me from my overnight restraints. It was strange indeed to be waking up in such a mode of dress, in a pink room with little that was familiar to me. It was as if I'd fallen through a hole in space and time and woken up to a new and rather surreal life.

It being the weekend I had no need to attend college - fortunately for me, and Miss Palmer had me dress in the maid's outfit with black lingerie underneath once more. On numerous occasions as I tottered about the apartment carrying out the chores that she'd assigned me did I wonder why I was still going along with all of this, but frequent reminders from her about my financial debt and lack of resources to pay any back without her and Mr Bates's patronage was enough to keep me subdued.

She instructed me often on how I should walk and talk as one of her "girls". She taught me how to walk with my hips so as to wiggle my bottom seductively as I went. How to bend over and show off my pantied bottom to best effect. I even found myself quite enjoying the almost constant attention as she praised me for being a "good girl", although if I did something wrong or failed to pay attention to her instruction she quickly became stern with me, even threatening to punish me on more than one occasion. I think my submission and rather meek obeisance saved me from anything more than a smack on the bottom, but I did begin to wonder what would happen if I were blatantly resistant to her will.

It wasn't until that afternoon that I plucked up the courage to ask her what her intentions were with my ongoing college attendance and how often I could return to being a boy. I found her in her bedroom having just gotten off the phone. I coughed politely and waited for her to turn toward me as I stood self-consciously in the doorway.

'Miss Palmer?' I caught myself about to curtsy to her, mentally kicking myself for being so easily subjugated, 'I know I'm now working at the coffee shop as a ... *girl*,' The words stuck in my throat as the absurdity of what I was saying struck me all of a sudden, 'but, I'll need to wear my boy clothes for college, won't I?'

'Oh Jesse, you are a silly girl!' She laughed, 'You're not going anywhere as a boy any more. You're a sissy girl now, and you'll just have to get used to it.'

'But ... I can't turn up like ... like this!' I gestured to my maid's outfit as I looked at her in surprise.

'Of course not, Jesse, and you won't.' I breathed a sigh of relief at that as I tried to control my breathing, 'You'll dress just like any other college girl, which reminds me, tonight will be your coming out party so I'll need you nicely smooth and made up. I'll pick out your clothes in a while.'

'What? I *can't* go as a girl!' The rest of her words sank in then, stalling my horror at the idea of attending college as a girl, 'Coming out? Wh-What do you mean?'

I was still suffering from a surge of panic at the thought of being exposed to everyone at college as she quickly marched across the room and took my hand. Without saying a word she pulled me over to the bed and sat down, dragging me across her lap as I tried desperately to keep my feet in her high heeled shoes. I think I was so shocked by where I now found myself, sprawled across my landlady's lap that I couldn't force any words of protest out of my mouth. I felt my dress being pulled up my back, exposing my black lacy panties. Then she was pulling them down, leaving me bare bottomed as I tried to squirm away from her. With one hand clamping down on my back she picked up a hairbrush that was laying next to me and brought it down firmly on my defenceless bottom cheeks.

THWACK!

'You will not talk back to me like that again.' She said before bringing the implement down upon me again and again.

THWACK! THWACK! THWACK!

The stinging took my breath away as my body tensed under the blows. Eventually I let out a squeal of anguish and pain as I found myself being paddled like an insolent child.

'P-Please, M-Miss ...'

THWACK! THWACK! THWACK!

I sobbed my apologies as I ground my crotch into her leg, trying to move my bottom out of the line of fire.

THWACK! THWACK! THWACK!

'Are you going to be a good girl, Jesse, or do we need to continue?' She demanded, the hairbrush held threateningly in mid air.

'I'll ... I'll be good, Miss. I-I Promise, Miss.' I cried as I felt my bottom cheeks continuing to burn.

'Good girl.' She said, pulling my panties back up before pushing me to my feet.

I felt ashamed of how easily I'd been overpowered and subdued by this woman. I carefully rubbed my reddened bottom as I gathered myself together, unsure of what to do or say next.

'Now, you may finish your chores and then we'll get you ready for your little presentation.' She approached me once more, this time stroking a stray hair from my face with a tenderness that made me want to please her once more, 'Are you excited, Jesse? It'll be fun for everyone, I'm sure.'

'Y-Yes, Miss Palmer.' I said, not entirely sure why I should feel excited by the prospect of being exposed as a sissy to yet more people.

If I had any thoughts that this was to be anything approaching a regular kind of a party, they were thrown into disarray once she showed me just what I'd be wearing. I was about to find out just what it truly meant to be one of their "girls", and my life was never to be the same again.

-o0o-

'I've already picked some things for you to wear, Jesse.' Said Miss Palmer as she entered the utility room where I was once again busy with her soiled underwear. I stopped rubbing my caged cock against the basin as I heard her walk in. 'Follow me please, as we need to get you properly fitted out for tonight.'

I hung up the panties I'd just finished rinsing and followed her through the apartment to my new room. Every time I entered my bedroom it seemed to reinforce my new girly persona. Grinding down any remnants of masculinity as I surveyed its ultra feminine decor and assorted clothing and accessories. There was nothing even remotely masculine here, even I was no longer convinced I was a true male.

Peering down at the bed I saw that she'd laid some clothing out for me. I say clothing, but in actual fact it was no more than a very erotic looking set of bright pink lingerie. A matching bra, garter belt and stockings with wide lace tops were of no great surprise, but what I did find disconcerting was the obviously crotchless panties that were included. I just hoped that whatever I was wearing over the top was enough to hide my pink chastity cage from view, not to mention my bottom hole that would clearly be exposed.

'I'm going to help you with your makeup once you've made yourself nice and smooth. You may use the floral soaps and perfume that I've left out for you.' She sent me scampering to the bathroom to begin my nighttime transformation.

I probably took longer than I should have as I showered and shaved my body. A suspicion that what was planned for me that evening may not be altogether to my liking played across my mind as I tried to predict who would be invited and quite what was meant by "coming out". As I finished drying my long blond hair, conscious of the girly cut across the front, I used the feminine scented perfume before taking a deep breath and heading back to

323

my room, wondering of she'd still be waiting for me. She wasn't there as I entered, and in a bid to at least cover myself to some extent, I quickly fastened the bra and garter belt in place before rolling the sheer pink stockings up my legs. I experienced no less of a thrill at this point than the first time I'd encased my smooth, hair free legs within a pair of nylon stockings. The sensations seemed to wash over me, leaving me light headed with the beginnings of a sexual awakening between my legs. This time however it had nowhere to go, still imprisoned in its cage that now matched the colour of my lingerie.

Picking up the panties, I held them in front of my face as I examined them closely. There'd be little coverage afforded by these, that was for sure. Knowing I'd be given little choice I stepped into them, trying to ignore my arousal as I pulled them up over the soft stockings and tugged them into place. As suspected my caged cock was left perfectly uncovered by the open crotch, with my bottom hole just as exposed. Fluffing my hair out I stepped in front of the full length mirror and sighed disconsolately as I saw just how on show my pink chastity cage was.

'Oh good, you're already dressed.' Said Miss Palmer from the doorway as she returned to check on me. 'Let's get your makeup on and then we can finish with your accessories.'

I'd heard many a time women talking about accessorizing, but what was to follow was quite different in nature to the every day meaning of such words, at least as far as I was concerned.

I watched in the mirror as she went about feminising my face. Her choice of pink eye shadows and lipstick with the addition of pink ribbons holding my hair in bunches turned me into a picture in pink. I didn't think I could look any more girly if she'd tried.

'Now, let's put your accessories on, shall we?' She said, having stood me up and examined me from every angle, including checking that my little cock was already suitably swollen in its confinement, 'I don't want any fuss now, Jesse. Be a good girl and we won't need to punish you again, okay?'

'Y-Yes, Miss.' I said, recalling the pain in my bottom as she'd brought the wooden hairbrush down upon it.

I must have entered a sort of daydream at this point as I was primped and prodded, as I barely noticed as she wrapped a dainty pink collar around my neck before locking it into place with a small padlock. I only began to realise how far she was going as I felt her fasten a familiar looking pink belt around my waist and proceed to fasten its attached cuffs to my wrists. I flinched for a moment, trying to pull my one remaining free arm away from my side with a half-hearted gesture before she roughly pulled it back and locked it into place.

'I said I don't want any fuss, Jesse,' She berated me in a firm voice, 'now behave.'

I obediently stepped into the matching pink high heeled shoes before I looked down and saw her manacling my ankles together with similar pink restraints. I could feel myself shrinking away inside, feeling like I'd already lost all control over my own fate. I was now shackled hand and foot. Only able to take small mincing steps in my heels and with little use of my hands, strapped to my sides as they were. As she clipped a thin pink lead to my collar I thought my humiliating form of dress was complete. That there could be nothing else added to make the indignity of my complete and total emasculation any worse, but as usual I was mistaken.

'There's just one more thing to add, Jesse, and it's going to look so pretty in you.' She said happily.

I thought for one moment that she'd be referring to some kind of outer garment. Something that would at least provide some level of dignity to my sissy outfit, but as I pondered her use of the words "in you", deciding that she'd simply misspoken, she retrieved something from one of the drawers that I was entirely unprepared for.

'A nice pink jewel for your sissy hole.' She said.

What she was holding up was a large pink jewel attached to what was clearly a metal butt plug. I gasped with surprise as I realised she intended to insert this into my virgin bottom. My mouth formed the word "no", but no sound came out as I stared fearfully at the plug that she was showing me.

'It's okay, Jesse. A little gel and you'll hardly feel it going in,' She said reassuringly, 'and it'll help prepare you for later. Now, bend over, there's a good girl.'

I tried to take a step away but I was only reminded of how my ankles were chained together. I couldn't bring my hands up to protect myself. I was at her mercy as she took hold of my pink lead and tugged on it, dragging my head down so that I was suitably bent over in front of her. I whimpered with fear, sobbed with embarrassment and cried out with humiliation but none of it did any good as she busied herself with preparing the plug. Glancing behind me I saw her coating the intimidating device with a clear gel lubricant before moving closer and spreading my bottom cheeks apart with one hand.

'Stay still, Jesse, I don't want to hurt you.' She said as I felt the cold gel covered metallic tip nudging up against my tight rosebud.

I tensed my body. My bottom tried to resist this foreign object as it was being pushed into me. I'd never been penetrated like this before and I began to tremble as I felt the insistent pressure building, trying to prize me open.

'Oh ... Oh ... N-No ... Miss P-Palmer ...' I squeaked through gritted teeth as I tried to decide what to do, and then it happened.

I felt myself being opened as the butt plug began to enter me. My bottom burned as the pressure continued and I could feel the wide tapered object forcing my anal sphincter apart as it pushed ever deeper inside of me. I held my breath as I felt her manipulating it against me, easing the pressure before once again starting to progress it ever further inside of me. My bottom hole was being stretched beyond anything it'd experienced before. I gasped and yelped as I felt it push all resistance aside and penetrate my bottom, and then I seemed to close around it as the bulbous end cleared my hole and I was left with only a large pink jewel on show. I could feel its presence inside of me, its shaft holding me apart although I realised it was now far more comfortable than to begin with.

'Stand up, Jesse. You can have a look if you like.' She said, drawing me back toward the mirror. 'You do look very sweet. A very pretty little sissy slave.'

She helpfully spread my bottom cheeks so I could see the sparkling pink jewel now fixed in place as I felt every movement of the plug within. I couldn't stop the look of despair that crossed my face as I viewed my ultra feminine and submissive sissy persona now on show. There was nothing left of the boy I'd grown up knowing.

'There, you're all ready for tonight!' She proclaimed as we both continued to gaze upon my submissive sissy self.

REBECCA STERNE -- TURNED INTO GIRLS!

Chapter 10

Teetering on my heels I was forced to mince after Miss Palmer as she led me around the apartment by my lead. I'd somehow managed to completely relinquish all say over my own body and any force of my own will as this woman took control of my very existence. I felt no more than a toy to her now. Little more than a doll to play with. To dress up and be made to perform in any way that pleased her. It felt as though all hope of recovering any sense of self determination had gone, along with my masculinity, dignity and pride.

When finally she seemed to grow tired of playing with me it was only because her guests were due to arrive, and I was apparently to be on show to them from the moment they entered the apartment. She had me stand just inside the doorway that led into the main living area. My hands strapped to my sides, my ankles chained together and a butt plug inserted inside of me.

The first person to arrive was Mr Bates. He seemed pleased to see me again, no doubt wondering when next he could partake of my oral pleasuring as he eyed me up lustfully.

'She looks perfect, Victoria.' He commented as he looked me over, 'Did she object to having her jewel inserted?'

REBECCA STERNE -- TURNED INTO GIRLS!

'No, Martin, she was most compliant,' Said Miss Palmer, talking as though I weren't there to hear them, 'I do believe she's quite enjoying her new role in life.'

I was left to wait where I was, feeling like an interesting decorative addition to the room that would no doubt provide a talking point for the guests. In my mind I kept wondering just who else to expect. Fervently hoping that no one else I knew would appear in order to witness my most ignominious of downfalls.

It wasn't long before the first set of unknown guests arrived. Two women and two men who I didn't know walked in, clearly amused by what they found waiting for them inside.

'Curtsy to our guests, Jesse.' Ordered Miss Palmer, and so I did, not wanting to cause myself any further embarrassments in front of these strangers.

They helped themselves to drinks before returning to take a closer look at me as I stood forlornly in place. Every time my bottom clenched I could feel the plug inside of me. My caged cock felt incredibly exposed between my legs as I tried to avoid eye contact with anyone. The next to arrive was Kirsty, my neighbour, who seemed perfectly amused by my predicament and couldn't wait to observe the pretty addition hidden between my bottom cheeks.

'Feel free to take a look, Kirsty.' Said Miss Palmer, 'I'm sure she won't mind, after all, she's already squirted for you.'

Kirsty stepped around behind me and suddenly I felt her hands on my bottom. She seemed to pause for a moment before pulling them gently apart and giggling as she set eyes on my bejewelled bottom hole.

'It's so cute!' She exclaimed, 'It suits her so well.'

The biggest shock of the night was when one woman turned up with someone I at first took for her daughter. It wasn't until she had the girl take off her long coat that I saw that she was in fact a boy just like me, her cock caged between her legs, dressed in black underwear and sporting her own bright red jewel. She began to serve the guests as the last few people arrived. Another of whom turned out to be a sissy boy, this time dressed all in white.

'So, Victoria, when will your sissy debutante introduce herself?' Asked one woman, a lustful glint in her eye as she stared at me from across the room.

'Well, Nina, now's as good a time as any, I believe.' Said Miss Palmer, agreeably. 'Jesse, come over here please?'

I had to swallow hard in order to shift the large lump that had appeared in my dry throat. As I began mincing toward her with all eyes upon me I felt my face growing hot.

'Oh how sweet, she's shy.' Commented another woman as I passed her, my eyes firmly fixed upon the floor in front of me.

'This is Jesse, everyone. She's twenty-one and is an absolute natural. She will now introduce herself to you all before we indulge in a roast in her honour.'

I was still naive enough at this point to think that they were going to have a meal in my honour. I wouldn't've felt quite so flattered had I known what kind of a "roast" was really planned for me, especially as I was the intended main course.

'Kneel down in front of this stool, Jesse.' Miss Palmer directed me to a stool that'd been placed to one side of the room. As I knelt unwittingly in front of it I looked around nervously, wondering what was to come next. 'I'll go first I believe, and then she can introduce herself to everyone else.' She said, sitting down in front of me. I watched with trepidation as she pulled her short skirt up and out of the way in order to expose her own crotchless panties beneath. 'You know what to do, Jesse. It's time to serve your mistress and her friends.'

At first I couldn't believe that she intended for me to pleasure her in front of her guests, but from the eager looks on their faces and the way she stared down at me expectantly it was clear that this was exactly what she wanted me to do.

'M-Miss ... I ...' Feeling the need to clarify all the same, I started to ask her if that was what she really wanted. She didn't wait for me to form the question as she leaned forward and took hold of my lead, pulling me down between her legs.

I could do nothing to resist her. My hands were useless. My mouth was instantly pulled against her pussy, a dampness within its folds giving away her sexual anticipation. With no choice left to me I pushed my tongue out and began to lap at her, finding some small amount of comfort in the idea that I was now partially hidden from the view of her guests; between her legs as I was. It was a childish thought I know. Much like the infantile belief that if you can't see someone, then they in turn can't see you. It wasn't much, but it at least enabled me to continue in my duties.

She quickly became wet as I licked along her sweet pussy and pushed my tongue into her moist hole. Her womanly scent and heavenly taste quickly had me aroused in turn, and I felt instantly frustrated as my growing erection was thwarted by its pink cage. I let out a muffled groan as I found her swollen clit and rolled my tongue around it, causing her to grind her mound into my face as her stimulation grew.

I threw myself into it, determined to lose myself in the act of pleasuring her as I tried to forget the other guests. The sexual frustration that was building inside of me at my inability to touch myself or even achieve a fully engorged cock, drove me on in search of my own fulfilment as much as anything else.

She came quicker than I'd expected, as if the situation itself was arousing her. As her hips bucked against me I continued to tongue her, causing her to peak a second time before she finally called a halt to my ministrations by pushing my head away from her. I daren't look up for fear of seeing all those present watching me. My mouth and chin were slathered with her sex juice. Unable to clean myself up I stared down at the floor in front of me in embarrassment.

'She does look pretty with her sissy jewel on show like that, Victoria. Is it my turn now?' Asked one of the female guests from behind.

I tensed as I heard the eagerness in this woman's voice to have me perform orally upon her too. I couldn't help but take a brief look at my lingerie clad body, seeing just how feminine I looked and knowing that I must have presented quite the perfect sissy girl to the assembled audience. In my mind I think I already knew that there was more to this occasion than my simple "outing" as a subjugated sissy.

Miss Palmer closed her legs in front of me before leaning forward to speak.

'Now you be a good girl for my friends, Jesse. Your new life awaits you, either as my perfect little serving girl who has an assured life as a pampered and primped sissy, or as a hopeless young man who can't even afford to pay his rent.' As she paused to let her softly spoken words sink in, it seemed that there was a clear choice to be made. 'It's up to you, Jesse, but I hope you choose wisely as there'll be no turning back afterwards.'

I looked up at her as she stroked my cheek fondly. I could

still taste her in my mouth and my arousal was an uncomfortable reminder of how, despite my reluctance to admit to such a thing, her humiliating treatment of me as I was used as a feminised sex object was awakening feelings that I'd never knew could exist. I could feel the other's eyes upon me as the weight of my coerced decision bore down. It was difficult to think straight through the fog of my arousal as I tried to comprehend the choices laid out for me. I detected a frown forming upon her face as she waited for some sign of a decision. In the end I think it was more of a desire to not appear rude or to spoil her party in front of her guests that made me nod back at her. I don't recall voicing a decision either way, but that one act of naive contrition seemed to seal my fate.

With a kiss on my forehead she got to her feet and gave up her position so that the other woman could take her place. I was still trying to work out whether I'd agreed to continue being used in such a way when she opened her legs to present me with her immaculately trimmed pussy. There was no more than a thin strip of neatly trimmed pubic hair there that pointed the way to her waiting sex. I could see she was already wet, no doubt having been turned on by seeing me going down on my landlady.

'And now, it's time for Jesse's sissy roast to begin!' I heard Miss Palmer announce as she moved behind me. 'I believe it's Martin's turn to open our new girl's flower.'

I felt her hands upon my bottom as she spread my cheeks before taking hold of the pink bejewelled butt plug that was sitting surprisingly comfortably inside of me. I gasped as I felt her withdrawing it, twisting and pulling it gently but firmly from my greased bottom hole. It stretched me further and further apart as it's bulbous end was pulled out of my tight hole, causing it to burn momentarily until I felt its widest part clear my sphincter and my bottom slowly close back up as its tapered end was removed. It felt as though I was still open, as if my hole had been stretched so that it was reluctant to tighten up fully once more.

As I turned my head away from this unknown woman's crotch to look behind, I saw my landlady brandishing the butt plug triumphantly as she nodded to Mr Bates. My jaw dropped open as I saw that he'd already removed his jeans and that there was a clear bulge in between his legs. He winked at me as he approached.

'I'm sure we're both going to enjoy this, aren't we Jesse?' He said.

332

Not waiting for a reply he stepped up behind me and dropped to his knees. With a swift movement he freed his erection from his shorts, allowing it to drop in front of him, pointing its way toward my bottom. I could hardly breathe as I saw what he intended to do.

'Give our guest a nice sissy kiss, Jesse. It's rude to leave her waiting.' Said Miss Palmer, slapping my bottom cheek as Mr Bates forced me to open my legs further and allow him access to my now empty and very exposed bottom hole.

The woman in front of me took hold of my head and pulled me around to face her, before forcing me to bury myself into her crotch. Once again I had a mouthful of wet pussy as I tried to focus on pleasuring her as I continued to sense my boss nearing his target. It was as if my mind had frozen at this point, unable to accept that I was about to be penetrated from behind by a man as I lapped at another woman's pussy on all fours. I didn't know what to expect, nor did I know how to react. I was scared it was going to hurt. I was ashamed that I was going to allow such a thing to happen to me. I was terrified that I was going to gain some form of pleasure from it.

As I felt the man's rigid cock nudge up against my rosebud I began to tremble. I found the woman's swollen clitty with my tongue and concentrated on that instead. He pushed against me and I felt a man's glans pressing into me for the first time. I should've been outraged by being treated in such a way, by being used by another man, but I could no longer think of myself as entirely male. I was somewhere in between male and female. As such, it didn't really feel as emasculating as it should've done at this point, as I'd already lost the majority of my male identity along the way.

His cock started to open my bottom hole under its unrelenting pressure and I began to breathe rapidly. I could feel myself being stretched open once again, but this time it was easier. The butt plug had done its job I guess, as my body was no longer fighting to stop itself from being penetrated in such a way. I squealed girlishly as I felt my rosebud suddenly give way, allowing his hard cock to push inside of me. Suddenly I was filled with man meat and my mind had become a blank. My every thought, feeling and physical sensation was centred around having another man's erect phallus inside of me, pushing ever deeper before pulling away again. He began to slowly pump in and out of me, making me squirm and sob with humiliation and pleasure in almost equal measure.

The woman pulled me tighter into her warm wet pussy as my mouth was filled with her juices. I was drowning in her sexual embrace as she moved against me. My tongue was inside her just as Mr Bates's cock was deep inside of me. As he pushed into me, I in turn was forced to press myself into this woman's hole. I'd become a living sex doll. Being used by both men and women at the same time for their pleasure, but what shocked me the most in all of this, was that I'd become so heavily aroused by being used in such a way that my own sissy cock was now pressing painfully against the pink plastic chastity cage between my legs. I could see in my minds eye how I must've looked to all those in that room. A perfect sissy in pink makeup and pink lingerie, with a pink cage between her legs jiggling back and forth as she was pumped from behind by a perfect example of manhood as she lapped obediently between the legs of another dominant woman.

I could feel my embarrassment washing through me, competing with a powerful sense of arousal and shame. I think I lost myself at this point, so immersed in the sexual pleasuring of others as I was. My bottom was stinging but it was no longer an unpleasant sensation. I could feel a climax building inside of me as I was fucked mercilessly from behind and my mouth filled with pussy juice.

I'd no sense of time or space after a while, and when I felt Mr Bates tensing in between my legs. Thrusting into me with one final urgency as he came inside of me, I felt something break deep within. The woman I was pleasuring came then too, her pussy pulsing and grinding against me, her juices flowing out copiously as I tried to swallow them down. I was no more than a receptacle for their climactic juices as they came both on me and into me. My own climax was still lurking beneath the surface, struggling to achieve its release as my cock twitched and pulsed against its relentless imprisonment.

I was confused by my feelings as Mr Bates withdrew his cock from me. Feeling an emptiness inside as some of his cum escaped down my leg to my stocking tops. The woman left me also, leaving my mouth and tongue with nothing to do as I savoured her taste that still lingered, licking my lips greedily. I was so overwhelmingly submerged in a kind of sexual stupor that I was only vaguely aware when another woman I didn't know took the others place, closely followed by a man I didn't know pressing himself up against me from behind, another stiff cock forcing itself between my bottom cheeks. My only reaction to this was to welcome the opportunity to taste the third pussy in a row that I'd been presented with, and to invite a second hard cock inside of myself to replace the first. I became a writhing, squirming sex befuddled sissy sex slave being used time and again, with my own frustrated climax constantly competing for attention as I sought my own release between these dominant women's legs and on the end of the men's cocks.

When I'd serviced all of Miss Palmer's guests, leaving them obviously satisfied with my sexual obeisance and servicing, I was pulled to my feet and made to stand where I was. I could feel thick rivulets of cum oozing from my bottom, trickling slowly down my legs as it soaked into my pink stockings below. This was now made worse by my own precum that'd been leaking for some time, my own desperately needed orgasm still tantalisingly close, yet painfully far away. My lips, chin and cheeks were glistening with pussy juices. This too was left to run down my face and neck, tickling as it ran down to my pink bra. I was breathing heavily. My mind was fogged with a most tortuous level of arousal.

'As Jesse's been such a good little sissy for us,' Miss Palmer's words sounded far off, even though she was standing right next to me, 'I think we should allow her a release for her "coming out" party. Lindy? Would you do the honours please? One sissy girl to another.'

I had to blink several times to focus my eyes. The sissy boy that I'd seen serving drinks earlier approached me, wearing black lingerie much like my own. She couldn't've been any older than me I guessed and looked perfectly subservient to these people. Miss Palmer bent down and I felt her unlocking my cage before pulling it away, leaving my partially erect cock exposed. It felt strange at first to be free of the cage, but my underlying arousal soon caused it to engorge further. I felt it twitch several times as if testing its own freedom.

The next thing I knew, Lindy was kneeling down in front of me and taking hold of my cock. She began to gently stroke it as it grew to its full yet unimpressive slender size. I sobbed with embarrassment and frustration that it was another sissy that was now handling me. On principle I refused to allow myself to become aroused at her touch, but it was of no use. I was soon fully erect in her hand as she gently stroked my shaft back and forth. I heard myself making a strange mewling sound as my hips began to move back and forth, putting on a most humiliatingly vulgar performance of frenzied sexual pleasuring at another's hands. I didn't last long before I felt my orgasm rushing forward. I squealed once, twice and then I was spurting into her hand as I finally achieved the release that I'd been so desperate for. I knew even as I was cumming in front of everyone in such a pathetic manner that I'd thoroughly debased myself, but it didn't matter at that point. I just needed to be sated.

Chapter 11

Waking up the following morning, I knew something fundamental had changed. Something inside of me. I was no longer Jesse, the college boy. I was now Jesse, the sissy sex slave. I'd never suffered a broken bone before, but I imagined this was somehow the psychological equivalent of having a piece of yourself breaking apart, only instead of knitting back together as it was, it'd now grown back quite differently.

I no longer felt like the old Jesse. I no longer felt like a boy. I no longer felt as though I were adrift in life, because now I had a purpose and a place.

I opened my eyes and gazed upon the pink sissy decor around me. Running my hand down into my crotchless panties that I still wore from the night before, I touched the pink plastic cage that'd been replaced once I'd been given the luxury of a full blown sissy orgasm. It was reassuring in a way, in another it was quite unnerving. I felt incredibly sexual and alive. I was desired and controlled in a way that was both exciting and scary.

In two days time I was due back at college and I knew I had to broach the subject with Miss Palmer. Before that there'd be work to do as I was certain I'd be expected to clean the apartment

337

following my "coming out" party the previous night. As a special treat I'd been tasked with going around the female guests before they left and collecting their worn panties, soiled by their aroused bodies as they'd watched me perform my sissy duties. They'd have to be hand washed by me as a little reminder of my sordid acts of sexual servitude.

My bottom was sore, but not unpleasantly so. I'd been allowed to leave my sissy jewel out for the rest of the night following my deflowering at the hands of the male guests, my sissy hole leaking cum for the rest of the evening - much to my ongoing embarrassment.

As I stretched out in the bed it felt good to have my arms and legs free of the restraints, but I knew they'd be something else to get used to in my new life. It was all so overwhelming to come to terms with such a drastic change in my fortunes, and in such a short space of time. I could never have imagined becoming what I am now. A sissy sex slave.

I would offer a warning to any males finding themselves in a similar position to me. To be wary of such dominant women in case you find yourself losing your manhood to them, but I can't quite convince myself - let alone anyone else, that this wasn't a blessing in disguise. There's an inner contentment in me that is growing day by day that I've never experienced before. I no longer have to prove to the world who I am, because now I've been made to face my true nature - and I'm told I'm a sissy girl at heart.

College may be a different challenge altogether, especially if my mistress decides I must attend as a girl, but I'll face up to that when I have to. For now I'll just lie here a while and think of all that's happened to me in recent days, whilst I touch my little sissy cock through my pink cage and anticipate all the moist panties that I'll be washing in just a short while. I can sense my chronic arousal growing already. It's going to be another one of those days where I can barely see through my own sexual torment to think straight, but it's going to be delectable just the same. I just hope Miss Palmer will take pity on me and allow me a release, after all, I am still quite new to being a sissy.

REBECCA STERNE -- TURNED INTO GIRLS!

About the Author

Rebecca Sterne is a bestselling author of erotic fiction. Her books regularly occupy the Top 100 Transgender Erotica list on Amazon with most of her books becoming number one bestsellers.

She lives in the UK and is passionate about being an author. Now a full time writer she enjoys nothing more than exploring the world of transgender fiction and erotica, bringing her own unique brand to both the Transgender and ABDL worlds.

For the latest news and updates, visit Rebecca's website at:

https://rebeccasterne.wordpress.com

Or follow her on Twitter:

@rebecca_sterne

Other books by this Author

The following titles are also available by Rebecca Sterne:

Collections / Anthologies

The Taboo Feminisation Collection
The Taboo Feminisation Collection 2
The Schoolgirl Feminisation Collection
The Sissy Baby Erotica Collection

Diaper Stories

From Bad Girl to Baby Girl
My Husband is now my Sissy Baby Girl
My Husband is now my Sissy Baby Girl 2
My Husband is now my Sissy Baby Girl 3

Feminisation Stories

A Husband Maid to Serve
Aunty's Little Sissy
Becoming Mommy's Girl
Becoming Mommy's Girl 2
Femboy Finishing School
From Stepmom to Stepdom
From Stepmom to Stepdom 2
How I Was Turned Into My Girlfriend's Little Sister
Turned into a Female Nurse
Turned into a Girl at the Office
Turned into a Sexy Hotel Maid
Turned into a Sexy Santa Girl
Turned into a Sissy Sex Slave

Female Transformation Stories

Bitten by a Werewoman

The Taboo Feminisation Collection

Becoming Daddy's Girl
Becoming Daddy's Girl 2
Caught in Mommy's Panties
Feminised by Mommy
Feminised by Mommy 2
In Mommy's Shoes
In My Sister's Panties
In My Sister's Panties 2
In My Sister's Shoes
Our Feminised Brother
Punished in Mommy's Panties
Turned into the Girl of the House

The Schoolgirl Feminisation Collection

Feminised by Schoolgirls
From College Boy to Schoolgirl
My Sister Turned Me Into A Schoolgirl
The Making of a Schoolgirl

Sinful Shorts Collection

College Slut for a Day
Feminised by the MILF Next Door
Feminised for Halloween
Mommy's Little Panty Boy
Playing in my Sister's Clothes
Sister's Dressing Up Girl
So You Want to be a Baby Girl?

Schoolgirl Stories

Taming Jessica

Transgender Fiction

Ten Years a Woman

Printed in Great Britain
by Amazon

68751892R00200